GOLD DRAGON

HERITAGE OF POWER BOOK 5

LINDSAY BUROKER

Gold Dragon

Heritage of Power, Book 5
by Lindsay Buroker
Copyright © 2018 Lindsay Buroker

No part of this book may be reproduced, scanned, or distributed in any printed or electronic form without permission. Please do not participate in or encourage piracy of copyrighted materials in violation of the author's rights. Thank you for respecting the hard work of this author.

This is a work of fiction. Names, characters, places, and incidents either are the product of the author's imagination or are used fictitiously, and any resemblance to locales, events, business establishments, or actual persons—living or dead—is entirely coincidental.

CHAPTER 1

LIEUTENANT RYSHA RAVENWOOD FLUNG HERSELF to the ground, ducked her head low, and wriggled under the latticework of ropes. Mud spattered her face, sticking to her spectacles and her tongue, but she barely noticed. She dragged herself by her elbows and shoved with her knees, and finally burst out on the far side of the mud pit.

The last obstacle came into view. Nerves and fear tangled in her belly like drunken vipers in a barrel, but she sprinted toward the burly sergeant as if her life depended on it. Her dreams did.

She ran down the sawdust-coated path toward him, raising her fists as she approached.

This time, she would make it, and without chicanery or any words spoken. She would get past him as the instructors demanded, by physically knocking him aside.

The grizzled sergeant lifted his fists. Rysha expected a contemptuous sneer, a bored yawn, or simply professional readiness. Instead, he kept glancing over her shoulder, toward the wall she had climbed at the beginning of the course. Toward—

Do you wish me to assist you at this crucial juncture, Storyteller? Shulina Arya, the gold dragon who had decided Rysha would become her rider, and who was perched atop the obstacle-course wall, asked telepathically.

The interruption startled Rysha, and she almost tripped. *No, thank you.*

As much as she appreciated having a dragon cheerleader, she was struggling to convey to Shulina Arya that she had to do this without help. In addition to the sergeant she had to fight, a timekeeper watched the course, and nearby Major Kaika and Colonel Therrik oversaw everything. Therrik, his brows drawn into a V and his muscled arms crossed over his chest, appeared to be watching intently for dragon shenanigans.

The sergeant shifted his attention back to Rysha and lowered into a crouch as she approached. She exhaled a quick puff of air. This was it. Her partner was still struggling to get over the wall—perhaps due to the dragon distraction atop it—so she didn't have anyone to help her pass this final obstacle.

Unlike the last time she'd attempted the course, the sergeant didn't wait for her to attack first.

He lunged forward, jabbing with his left fist, then throwing a punch with his right. It came straight toward her face—toward the spectacles perched on her nose. Rysha dodged the jab and swung her arm up to block the punch, deflecting it despite the strength behind the blow.

The sergeant recovered instantly and threw a backhand punch. She danced away, and it swished harmlessly past her face.

Rysha was pleased to evade the attacks, but she had to enact her strategy if she wanted to get past him. She planned to use her six feet of height and long legs to keep him out of punching range by throwing a barrage of kicks.

As he sprang after her, she lifted her knee and drove the ball of her foot toward his groin. He seemed surprised by the speed of her attack and couldn't quite get out of the way in time. He twisted and took the brunt of the kick on his meaty outer thigh. At least she'd made contact.

That didn't faze him. He came in, assailing her faster this time, launching a chain of jabs, straight punches, and uppercuts.

Rysha stuck to her plan, blocking the first couple but then springing back, light on her feet as she did her best to stay out of his range. She also shifted to the left as she skittered away from him, subtly navigating around him and toward the path on the opposite side.

She launched her boot at him again, this time feinting toward his face to startle him into throwing his defenses up high. As soon as he did, she twisted and slammed a side kick toward his chest. He drew his arm down to block, but the power of her blow sent him back a step. Once again, he recovered quickly and raised his fists for another attack, but Rysha, knowing the timekeeper's clock was ticking, turned and sprinted away. She didn't have to defeat him; she only had to get by him, and she'd made sure her maneuvers were shifting her in that direction.

He spat and gave chase, but only until he reached a white line painted in the mud and sawdust, marking the end of that segment. She made it across it, and he pulled up. Grinning, Rysha sprinted the rest of the way down the path toward the timekeeper, who stood blandly watching, his clipboard and watch in hand.

She couldn't be positive she had made it, not until he yelled out her time, but she had climbed over the wall far more quickly today than in the past, and she didn't think that fight had gone on overly long.

She lunged across the finish line and spun toward the timekeeper, tempted to tear the watch out of his hands so she could check for herself.

A sublime performance, Shulina Arya spoke into her mind. *But you did leave your enemy standing. Shall I fly down and smite him?*

No, he's in my unit. He's only pretending to be an enemy right now. Rysha leaned over the timekeeper's shoulder. "Well, Sergeant? Did I make it?"

Are you certain? the dragon asked. *He is having predatory thoughts about your hindquarters.*

What? Startled, Rysha stared back at the sergeant she'd faced.

His smile did not seem predatory to Rysha, though his gaze was toward her butt. He caught her looking and lifted his eyes, then gave her an approving salute. She saluted back, hoping that meant he was pleased she'd fought well enough to pass him. *She* was. She had worried about this test for the last three weeks, especially since she had missed so many of her practice runs of the obstacle course, along with the daily combat drills and gymnasium exercises, when she'd been off on her mission with Trip and Kaika.

Those aren't predatory thoughts, Rysha explained to the dragon. *I believe they're lecherous ones. You may have noticed Captain Trip having similar ones about my, uh, hindquarters.*

Are they welcome or unwelcome?

From the sergeant? So long as he doesn't try to act on them, they're fine.

For a moment, Rysha forgot all about the course and the training, and flashed back to that freighter in Lagresh, where a bronze dragon in human form had tried to sexually force himself on her. Fortunately, it hadn't gone further than kissing and groping, but the memory still angered and shamed her. She felt the fool for not having sussed out what the dragon was sooner. She still hadn't told Trip about the incident, and she hoped she could get away with never doing so. He wouldn't blame her, she was certain, but he might think... Oh, she didn't even know. It was more her own shame that she didn't want to face or share with him.

"Four minutes and eight seconds," the timekeeper announced, lifting a pencil to his clipboard. "You made it with twenty-two seconds to spare. Impressive." He looked toward Colonel Therrik and Major Kaika, who were walking up. "I believe that's a little faster than Major Kaika ran the course when she first passed twenty years ago."

"*Sixteen* years ago, Sarge," Kaika drawled. "Don't make me sound older than I am."

"My apologies, ma'am." He saluted both officers.

Rysha did the same, doing her best to look professional and not at all giddy as she did so. That wasn't that hard since Colonel Therrik's dour face did not inspire giddiness. And the dark frown he directed at Shulina Arya made Rysha uneasy.

"How do we know the dragon didn't help her?" Therrik growled.

A shot of fear went through Rysha. He outranked Kaika and everyone on the field, so if he decided she had cheated somehow, he had the power to nullify her test results. King Angulus had said Rysha could become Shulina Arya's rider, making it an official military position, but only if she passed the elite troops training. Specifically, *this* test.

"She didn't help me, sir. She only came to lend moral support."

"A morally supportive dragon?" Kaika asked. "I didn't know there was such a thing."

"You got over the wall easily for a woman," Therrik said, his eyes still narrow.

"Are you being sexist, Colonel?" Kaika arched an eyebrow, looking as calm and relaxed as ever, but there was a dangerous glint in her eye.

Since Therrik outranked her, Rysha couldn't imagine Kaika challenging the colonel in any serious way, but she was glad to have Kaika standing up for her.

"Just stating facts," Therrik growled. "Women can't pull themselves up as easily as men."

"I have no problem gripping things and pulling myself up. I can climb anything or anyone."

Therrik grunted. "So the barracks rumors say. You know I don't have a problem with you being here, Major, but this young… *officer*—" he waved at Rysha, specifically her spectacles, and she was certain that wasn't the first word that had come to his mind, "—isn't you."

"No," Kaika agreed. "We're clearly different people. I don't *have* a morally supportive dragon." Her gaze lifted to the sky, warning Rysha that Shulina Arya had left her perch.

As the soldier Rysha had been partnered with trotted up, his lip bloody from his own encounter with the sergeant, the dragon flew down and landed behind them. The soldier squealed in alarm and sprinted toward the barracks.

"Fail that kid," Therrik growled to the timekeeper, as he eyed the dragon warily. He looked like he was trying not to step back and appear intimidated.

Rysha tamped down a smug smile. Even though she hadn't asked Shulina Arya to claim her as her rider, nor had she truly dreamed of that as a possible career path, Rysha had to admit it was delightful having a dragon standing at her back.

"I've already noted that he didn't finish the course in sufficient time," the timekeeper said.

"Also note that he wet himself when he saw a dragon," Therrik said.

The sergeant hesitated. "There's not a place for that on the form."

"Make one."

"Er, yes, sir."

Kaika clucked and shook her head.

"What?" Therrik asked.

"We were all hoping Lilah would mellow you, but you're still hard and crusty."

"Don't tell me you want that kid defending our country when dragons show up." Therrik pointed to the retreating back of the fleeing soldier.

"Perhaps not, but I do want Lieutenant Ravenwood defending our country."

Therrik squinted at Rysha and at the dragon. He looked like he was going to voice a protest again, but Shulina Arya lowered her massive head so that it hung over Rysha's shoulder. She felt like a doll in comparison.

The dragon's violet eyes gazed into Therrik's. *Is there a problem here? Has the Storyteller not sufficiently proven her skill and ability in your warrior course?*

Seconds passed as Therrik stared back at Shulina Arya, his body not moving, his eyes transfixed on hers. Even though Rysha wasn't the recipient of the dragon's stare and had no aptitude for sensing magic, she could feel the power radiating from Shulina Arya. Kaika, too, gazed at the dragon with that slightly blank and transfixed look.

Can you ratchet your aura down a few notches? Rysha asked silently, trusting the dragon would be monitoring her thoughts. *These are my superior officers, not our enemies. We're not supposed to manipulate them.*

The male suspects you of cheating, Storyteller. His mind is most surly.

It'll be surlier if he later realizes he was manipulated. And he might be even more suspicious of me then.

"Who the hells is the Storyteller?" Therrik shook his head, as if to shake away the dragon's influence.

"That's her name for me, sir. Whenever there's time, I share my knowledge of history with her. About Iskandia's past, the advancement of human science and technology over the centuries, and the political climates in the various countries around the world, past and present."

"And she *likes* that?"

"I try to make it entertaining. The other night, I made sock puppets and acted out our troops repelling the Second Cofah Invasion on the beach at Durogonia."

Therrik's expression screwed up into one of disbelief. Maybe she shouldn't have admitted that.

Kaika thumped him on the arm. "When is Lilah plopping your little one out? You may want to ask her for tips. Babies probably like socks."

He stared at her. "You're a weird woman."

"No arguments here, Colonel." Kaika took the clipboard from the timekeeper who'd been watching the exchange neutrally, other than throwing a few concerned glances at Shulina Arya. "Sign off, will you, sir? I have a date tonight. I want time to wash off the mud spatters. And Rysha will want to celebrate with her strapping young gentleman after she lets him know she's passed the exam."

"Strapping..." Therrik's brow furrowed.

Rysha couldn't tell if he was confused or repulsed. Either way, her cheeks warmed.

"Technically, Captain Trip isn't all that strapping," Kaika said, "but I understand he can do amazing things with his magic. It's like a tongue, but better."

Rysha's cheeks went from warm to molten lava. "*Ma'am*. I didn't *say* that."

"No, but Jaxi is a little gossip. Of course, I could have guessed from the way you've stuck to his side since we left the dragon's lair. His personality isn't that engaging unless he's got his dragon scy-thing—aura turned on."

"*Scylori*," Rysha murmured.

"I assumed right away that interesting things were happening under the blankets."

Rysha had no idea what to say.

Therrik, his mouth drooping open, appeared to share the feeling.

"You're lucky," Kaika went on. "My own experience sheet wrestling with a dragon left something to be desired. The magic was all for *him*. If a half-human dragonling is a more assiduous and thoughtful lover, then he's a keeper."

"Seven *gods*, Kaika. This is a workplace." Therrik snatched the clipboard from her, scribbled his name on the bottom, and stalked away.

Kaika tucked the clipboard against her hip, nudged Rysha, and said, "You're welcome."

"For embarrassing me?"

"For distracting him. *I* know you didn't cheat, but some men have a hard time accepting that women can pass the same tests they can. And it actually *did* look a little suspicious with your dragon watching you from atop the wall."

"She's not *my* dragon, ma'am," Rysha said, aware of Shulina Arya still standing behind her. "She's her own being. She's simply being kind and watching out for my welfare."

"So long as you two are ready to go into the sky and battle enemies at a moment's notice." Kaika looked toward the gray cloudy sky over the sea, making Rysha wonder if she'd heard intel that enemy dragons were on the way.

It had been quiet in the capital during the three weeks since Rysha, Kaika, and Trip had returned from Rakgorath, but reports kept coming in from other cities and small villages throughout Iskandia. Dozens of dragons were about, consuming livestock, burning buildings, and killing people who were caught out—or who risked running out to shoot at the invaders. Wolf Squadron had been sent off several times in pursuit, and Rysha had barely seen Trip since they'd returned. With so much chaos in the country, she couldn't be upset that they still hadn't found time for a romantic walk along the harbor beach, but she did lament it. They also hadn't had a chance to try having sex in an actual bed.

We are most certainly ready to fly valiantly into battle and defeat our enemies. Shulina Arya stretched her wings, making an imposing figure in the muddy field.

"Not by regaling them with sock puppets, I hope." Kaika signed the second instructor's spot on the bottom of the form.

Not all dragons are as enthused by stories and entertainment as I am, Shulina Arya said. *Many of them are stuffy, pretentious, and old. I'm young and vibrant and wish to enjoy life when I'm not engaged in ferocious battle to defend my new homeland.*

"Glad to hear it."

Rysha's stomach flipped as she watched Kaika finalizing the form, and as the realization that she had done it crept into her. She grinned, forgetting her earlier embarrassment over tongues and magic. She envisioned striding through the army fort, wearing an elite troops pin on her fatigue jacket, and being assigned to special missions. Granted, she'd already gone on special missions, but that had been because of her academic knowledge, not her position in the elite troops, as only the second woman ever to pass the tests and officially be welcomed into the unit.

"Congratulations, Lieutenant." Kaika switched the clipboard to her left hand and lifted her right for a sincere salute. "I knew you could make it, but I'm glad to see that proved true."

Rysha bit her lip and returned the salute, touched by the words. "Thank you, ma'am."

"The induction ceremony will be the day after tomorrow."

"Are there any *missions* planned?" Rysha asked, more interested in that than in ceremonies.

She already knew her parents wouldn't ride up for the presentation or to help her celebrate this. More likely, they would spend the night she shared the news drinking, lamenting that she had passed and would continue to put her life at risk instead of returning to the world of academia. If her grandmother had still been alive, *she* would have come up, even if it meant riding miles along the highway on horseback by herself. Rysha felt a twinge of sadness at the memory of her pointless loss.

"As it so happens," Kaika said, "I was told to report to the castle early tomorrow morning. You better come to."

"Uhm, am I expected?" Rysha worried that King Angulus, or whoever had called this meeting wouldn't be pleased if she invited herself. Or if Major Kaika presumed to invite her.

"Your dragon is."

Rysha blinked and turned toward Shulina Arya.

Indeed, yes. At the castle in the morning. My parents told me to come.

"Your parents are in the city?" Rysha asked.

In the past, Shulina Arya had mentioned being raised by two male bronze dragons who'd rescued her from her birth mother, a cranky female who'd considered her scrawny and who had wanted to sacrifice her. But Rysha had never met them. She hadn't even been certain they were alive or had come through the portal into Linora.

They just arrived today. It will be good for you to meet them. I once told them I wanted to find a noble warrior of a rider to fly into battle with one day. They always said I could do anything I wished if I merely focused on it. Now, I will show you to them.

Rysha made herself smile, but the idea of her being introduced to Shulina Arya's family as the culmination of some dragonly goal made her feel... She couldn't even describe it. She hoped she wouldn't disappoint these dragons.

"Meeting the family, huh?" Kaika asked, having apparently heard the telepathic conversation. "Do you think they'll be impressed with sock puppets?"

CHAPTER 2

CAPTAIN TELRYN "TRIP" YERT ROLLED his flier into the hangar, trailing after Major Blazer and Captain Ahn, and gave the dashboard a little pat as he navigated W-38 into its parking area. The sleek one-man flier was brand new, fresh from the factory and of the latest design. He'd been tickled to take it up into the air, though he admitted to being a touch lonely without Rysha in the seat behind him. He might have even settled for the dour Dreyak.

Thinking of the dead Cofah warrior made him grimace. He owed Dreyak's mother a favor, and he owed Prince Varlok, current ruler of the Cofah empire, an explanation. Technically, he only needed to deliver a magical dagger to the prince, and *it* would do the explaining. In its own ancient, arcane way. Trip had briefly explained his obligations to King Angulus when he, Rysha, and Major Kaika had returned from Rakgorath, but Trip hadn't heard anything about it, or seen the king, in the weeks that followed.

He hated to be a nag—was nagging royalty *allowed*?—and Iskandia had its own problems to deal with, but he had made a promise.

"She must fly real good," a voice drifted up from the hangar deck. Captain Duck. "You're already caressing her, and we didn't even find any dragons to fight this time."

Cheeks warming, Trip withdrew his hand. It had been more of a daydreaming, absent-minded touch than a caress, but he doubted he could say anything that would keep him from being mocked.

"She handled nicely as we went past a couple of belligerent seagulls." Trip pushed his goggles up on his forehead and unfastened his harness. "I'm positive she'll knock the scales off any dragons we encounter and leave them bald."

He grabbed Azarwrath's scabbard from the holder he'd made next to his seat and stood to climb down from the flier, but paused, realizing Duck wasn't alone down there.

"Bald dragons?" General Zirkander asked. "Sounds moderately appalling."

"I imagine so, sir."

"I *have* seen a dragon react with distress to acid eating through its scales, courtesy of one of Tolemek's early goos. I understand he's been ensconced in his lab and is making more since your team brought blood samples back from the portal mission."

"That's good, sir." Realizing Zirkander wasn't going to mock him for caressing his dashboard, Trip slid down, accidentally clunking Azarwrath's hilt on the side of the flier. There were days he did not feel like a powerful sorcerer. Or even a powerful sorcerer-in-training. "Will I get to meet Dr. Targoson? I asked Captain Ahn if he was nice, and she shrugged and grunted at me."

"A shrug *and* a grunt?" Duck asked. "You must have caught her on a loquacious day."

"Loquacious, Duck?" Zirkander asked. "Have you been reading dictionaries?"

"I've been reading plenty of things, sir. Big, thick books from ye olden days when they used lots of fancy words. Cradarkin, Grundier, Lady Marchthicket. Classics."

"Those are classic romance novelists, aren't they?"

"Well, some might call them that, but there's a lot of swashbuckling in the stories, and there are wars and politics and intrigues. And tips for how to be a gentleman and win a lady. Did you know it's considered impolite to discuss medical conditions, people's age, gossip, scatology, and animal mating habits in the presence of ladies?"

"I wouldn't have guessed."

"I *know*. I've been doing it all wrong, sir. I can't help it that it's hard to make a good tracking metaphor without mentioning scat."

"What's left to talk about?" Trip asked, bemused by the direction the conversation had gone, but relieved he wasn't the one being teased anymore.

"Food and fashion and music are what the book suggests," Duck said. "I'm writing down some conversation starters about army rations that I can use the next time I'm at the tavern and sit down by a pretty lady."

"I'm sure that will do the trick." Zirkander patted him on the shoulder, then turned a more serious expression toward Trip. "Believe it or not, this wasn't what I came over to talk about."

"Shocking, sir," Trip said.

"You, Duck, Blazer, Colonel Tranq, and Captain Ahn are cordially invited to the castle in the morning to discuss the dragon problem with the king. Some of the elite troops sword wielders will also be there."

"I'm invited, sir?" Duck sounded surprised.

"It was more of a requirement than a request, I confess," Zirkander said. "Because you have more prior experience with dragons than most of our pilots. Maybe you can chat with Angulus about army rations if you're not sure what else to discuss."

"I was planning to use those opening lines on a *lady*, sir."

"Maybe you can trot them by Blazer and Ahn. I expect Kaika will be there too."

Duck's mouth twisted, and Trip suspected he was trying to think of a polite way to suggest Kaika wasn't the kind of *lady* he had in mind.

Trip wondered if Rysha would be there. She should have had her elite troops final test by now. Had she passed? He'd been out of town for several days and had no way to know. He'd used his magic to look for her on the training field as the squadron had flown in, but it had already been empty, the testing complete. If she'd passed, she ought to officially be a dragon rider now. As the only one Iskandia had—unless one counted Tylie, Phelistoth's rider, who was of Cofah origins and hadn't volunteered to hunt down Iskandian enemies on a regular basis—she ought to be invited to any important meetings.

"Be there early. I'm sure the king will want everyone's input." Zirkander scratched his jaw and looked at Trip. "Have you met Shulina Arya's parents?"

"No, sir."

"Apparently, they're the reason for the meeting."

"A couple of bronze dragons? Did they say what they wanted?"

"No, but I gather Angulus is pleased that they requested an audience rather than simply flying into the country, ravaging the landscape, and eating people's cows and sheep, as has been the norm for most of the dragon visitors we've had."

Any idea what to expect, Azarwrath? Trip asked. He'd given Jaxi back to Sardelle, so he only had one soulblade riding on his hip these days. Azarwrath was on the quieter side.

No, but I dread hearing more about army rations, Telryn. When will you take me to a restaurant with fine china, chefs in the kitchen, and a sommelier waiting tableside to tell us about the best vintages in his cellar?

Quieter, but not less eccentric, Trip decided. *A somme-what?*

The soulblade sighed into his mind. *A wine steward, Telryn. Now that you are realizing your powers and becoming respected among your people, it's time for your tastes to mature.*

Maybe I can borrow some of Duck's books. The swashbuckling sounded promising. Though I'd rather read metalworking and engineering periodicals to see what new processes are being invented. The classics are a tad dry.

The soulblade sighed again. Trip wondered if Azarwrath ever regretted his decision to accept a lowly Iskandian with lowly tastes as his wielder.

"Oh, and Trip?" Zirkander had started away, but he turned back around. "Are you coming for tutoring tonight?"

"Yes, sir."

"Good. Sardelle invited the surrogate mothers to come for a checkup and to see if she could do anything for them. I assume most of them will bring the babies with them, in case you want to see them."

"Yes, sir. I do."

A night spent with squalling babies, Azarwrath said. *So different from a night of fine dining.*

Maybe there will be cookies.

You have simple tastes, Telryn.

Last time we were there, General Zirkander's mother brought those cookies with the butterscotch chips. Trip had only had butterscotch a few times in his life and had considered them exotic. *Didn't you think those were good?*

Azarwrath issued another mournful sigh.

Young Marinka raced around the oversized couch made from flier parts singing, "Company, company!" while kittens scampered about. The sleek black-and-white mother cat ignored her offspring while keeping an eye on a foot-long lizard that scuttled about but mostly hid under the end tables. Even if Trip hadn't recognized the lizard—it had grown since being released from its stasis chamber—he would have sensed the dragon blood in its leathery green body. The rest of the animal menagerie was being housed in the bunkhouse out back, alternately tended by Sardelle's two younger students and Tylie. Apparently, the monkey was being trained to do chores.

Marinka finished her dead sprint around the house by twirling on the rug in front of the couch, throwing her arms up, and giving a final cheerful, "Company!"

The two surrogate mothers who had already arrived and sat down in plush chairs shifted their babies in their laps and clapped politely. Marinka bowed deeply, her ponytail almost brushing the floor.

Sardelle, who stood with her baby boy, Olek, cradled in her arms, watched this display with some bemusement.

"I was a quiet, introverted child," she explained to Trip.

They had wrapped up his sorcery lesson when the first of the mothers arrived, and now waited for the rest.

"My guess is that General Zirkander wasn't, ma'am."

Sardelle nodded. "His mother has confirmed this for me. She told me about how she struggled to keep him under control when his father was gone—and also when he was home—and that he drove her to drink a few times. I may have to take up a beverage stiffer than tea once mine are both ambulatory." She tilted her chin toward the baby.

"How long until babies learn to walk?" Trip figured Sardelle's had a ways to go, but one of his siblings was almost a year old, or so his surrogate mother suspected. Nobody knew their exact ages for certain since that hadn't been included on the plaques. Only a couple had been labeled with names.

Trip hadn't seen enough of the eldest boy to know if he could walk yet. He'd spent most of his time interacting with little Zherie. Sardelle had volunteered to take care of her alongside her own two, so she was always here at the house. Trip sensed Tylie out back with her now, perhaps showing her the monkey.

"Usually by the time they're a year or so. But crawling commences before then." Judging by Sardelle's face, that was when the trouble began.

Trip wondered how trying his mother had found him. Maybe she had expected him to be unusual, given his origins, and had been prepared for it. Or maybe she had spent a lot of time asking Trip's grandparents for help.

He'd finally found time to send them a letter a couple of weeks earlier to update them on the mission, the parts he was at liberty to discuss, and he'd decided to tell them about the babies too. He wasn't sure the army wanted the word getting out about them, but they were *his* siblings. He figured he had the right to tell his family members about them.

Out on the rug, Marinka flopped down next to a toy box and began extracting blocks to play with. One of the surrogate mothers placed her squirming charge on the rug, and the little boy demonstrated crawling. Marinka, probably uninterested in all the babies invading her house, ignored him. She did pat the cat when she sashayed past on the way into the kitchen, ignoring four wrestling kittens along the way.

Trip spotted the fish puzzle he'd made and was inordinately pleased when Marinka selected it. Had she tried the puzzle yet? Was she old enough for puzzles?

A knock sounded at the door, and Sardelle waved it open with a nudge of power. One of the mothers, a curly-haired woman in her twenties who had two boys but had lost her last baby in childbirth, walked in carrying a four-month-old girl.

"Hello, Mladine," Trip said. "Are you all right?"

Her eyes were tight, and he sensed distress from her. He checked the baby, and she seemed fine.

"Yes, Telryn. Thank you, but…" Mladine looked to Sardelle. "I took the children to visit my parents at their little dairy in the countryside up north. A silver dragon flew over the area yesterday and destroyed the neighbor's silos. He ran out with a shotgun. I don't know what he was thinking it would do, but he was determined to protect his property and fired at the dragon. It swooped back down and..." She glanced around the room. The children weren't paying attention, but the two other mothers had turned to listen. "He didn't make it," Mladine said.

"We've been hearing the reports of trouble," Sardelle said grimly, "especially in the rural areas. They largely seem to be stealing livestock, but when people object... it gets ugly. And sometimes even when people don't object, from what I've heard."

"Were you—is your family all right?" Trip asked, hesitating to come forward and peer at the baby. He didn't want it to seem that his little sister was his only concern and he didn't care about Mladine and the rest of her family.

"Yes, we stayed out of it, but it was terrifying. My husband stayed behind to help." Mladine must have noticed him checking on his little sister, because she stepped forward. "Do you want to see her, Telryn?"

He nodded and peered into the blanket wrapped around her, finding the baby alert and curious. Her small hand made gripping motions in the air, and Trip stuck his finger into her grasp. She seemed to find this delightful. He found it sweet and shuddered to think about what would have happened if that dragon had taken offense to Mladine's family's dairy rather than the neighbor's silos.

"She's been grabbing her own feet a lot lately," Mladine said. "Newly discovered body parts."

"Does she need a fun toy to grab?"

"Careful, Trip," Sardelle murmured before he could grow too excited at the prospect of designing an interesting grasping toy. "They'll all be here tonight. You don't want to promise too many toys."

"I can make them quickly. It's not a problem."

He smiled at Mladine, and she smiled back. If the surrogate mothers thought him odd for being half-dragon, or having an overly developed interest in building things, they had been too well schooled to show it.

"Have a seat, Mladine," Sardelle said. "My students should have some snacks for us soon."

"Should I be relieved you don't make me prepare snacks as part of my training?" Trip had seen Ylisa and Ferrin cracking eggs and manipulating stirring spoons with their minds.

"I wasn't sure if you would consider it beneath you. Though knowing how to make cookies and tarts *is* a good skill to have. Even if I didn't acknowledge that until I was a mother myself, and someone with frequent winged houseguests who enjoy sweets."

When Mladine sat down, the other two mothers quizzed her on the dragon. Trip listened as the story was relayed in more detail and grew troubled.

Something needed to be done. Nobody would be safe as long as dragons were marauding in Iskandia. His *siblings* wouldn't be safe.

He vowed to change that.

CHAPTER 3

TRIP SMOOTHED HIS UNIFORM, TUCKED his cap under his arm, and scraped his fingers through his short hair, aware of the guards at the solarium door eyeing him surreptitiously. He wasn't sure if it was because he looked too young to have been invited to this important meeting at the castle or if it was because there were rumors going around the capital that he was a powerful sorcerer. He decided to hope for the former, since the latter had resulted in a write-up in a newspaper and a couple of old ladies on the street making superstitious gestures at him for warding off evil spirits.

When he'd envisioned journalists writing about his exploits, it had involved heroic flier battles in which he saved the country from certain doom. Not articles that speculated about his heritage and suggested that dragons had sent him to live among humans as a spy.

He hadn't received much better treatment from the guards at the front gate, who had patted him down before letting him enter the castle, and told him he would have to leave his sword with them. Trip had been mortified when the guards abruptly changed their minds, saying he could go right in and that he and his sword should have a nice day.

Azarwrath hadn't confessed to the mind manipulation. He hadn't needed to.

"You can go in, sir," one of these guards said, no doubt wondering why Trip had been standing in front of the double granite doors leading into the king's solarium for a minute without knocking or saying anything. "Most of the others are already inside."

Yes, his senses told him that King Angulus, Sardelle, Zirkander, Blazer, Duck, and Kaika, along with a dozen people Trip didn't know, waited within. Finding them all in there added to his nerves—was he considered late?—but maybe he would be able to slink into a back corner, unnoticed.

As he lifted his hand toward the handle, a faint clacking noise sounded from around the corner of the wide corridor leading back to the castle's main entrance. He didn't have to reach out with his power to sense a dragon in that direction—Shulina Arya—though the noise was somewhat perplexing. She had shape-shifted and had a significantly diminished aura. Otherwise, he would have been aware of her approach much earlier. Was she in human form? Interesting. So far, he'd only seen her as herself or as a golden ferret.

Ah, he sensed Rysha walking behind her. He smiled and stood tall, feeling much better about heading in to see the king with her at his side. From what he had observed before, she wasn't intimidated by Angulus at all. Probably because she was noble-born and her family rubbed elbows with other noble people, kings included.

"What is that?" one of the guards asked, picking up the rifle that had been at his side, its butt against the floor by his boots.

"Wheeee!" came a young woman's voice from around the corner.

"You can't do that in here!" someone shouted.

As Trip was trying to sense exactly what the shape-shifted dragon was doing, she came around the corner, and he got his first view.

Shulina Arya, in human form, rode some kind of wheeled board with a crate attached to the front half of it. Handlebars stuck out of the top of the crate, and she bent low, grinning as she gripped them and steered around the corner.

A golden blonde ponytail set high atop her head flowed behind her, and her violet eyes gleamed with pleasure. Freckles splashed her cheeks and nose, and if Trip had to guess her age—her human age—he would have estimated sixteen or seventeen. She'd told them she was a few hundred years old, but that was young from the dragon perspective.

"Stop," one of the door guards cried, striding forward and lifting his rifle, as if someone on a crate scooter in the castle represented a great threat to king and country.

The other one also sprang forward with his rifle.

Trip, fearing for their safety if they tried to shoot a dragon, reacted on instinct. He used his mental power to jerk the weapons out of their hands. They flew back and landed in his grip before he could consider if he'd made a mistake—was there a rule against magically confiscating the rifles of castle guards?

Shulina Arya barely seemed to notice the exchange. Still grinning, she waved and rolled past the double doors at top speed, continuing past the solarium and toward the courtyard garden, her wheels hitting the cracks between the floor tiles and sounding like trains riding the rails.

One guard sprinted after her, his hand dropping toward a truncheon at his belt. The other whirled on Trip, eyes bulging as he spotted his rifle in Trip's hand.

"That's a dragon," Trip said, hoping that would explain everything.

"You took my rifle, you witch." The guard snarled and leaped for him.

Azarwrath reacted before Trip did, raising an invisible barrier. The guard struck it chest-first and stumbled backward.

"I'm just protecting you," Trip rushed to say.

Another "Wheee!" sounded farther down the corridor. Shulina Arya had found another corner to go around. The guard, boots pounding the marble tiles, could be heard running after her and ordering her to "cease and desist, right this instant."

"If you were to shoot a dragon," Trip added to the glowering guard still in front of him, who had also pulled a truncheon from his belt, "the bullet would ricochet off its—her—defenses, and might come back to hit you. Or one of the priceless vases on those stands all along the hall. I'm trying to help you."

"Trip," Rysha blurted, running into view. When she wore her uniform, as she did today, she usually looked professional and dignified, but right now, a frazzled expression stamped her face as she ran toward him. "She got away. Did you see—"

"Stop!" the distant guard yelled as Shulina Arya came back into sight, her scooter somehow zipping along at top speed even though she wasn't using her foot to push off the floor.

She rounded the corner too quickly and brushed one of the stands holding one of the priceless vases Trip had referenced. It wobbled alarmingly before settling back to a stop.

Rysha reached Trip's side, and Azarwrath lowered the barrier so she could step close and grip Trip's arm. He wasn't sure if it was to push him to safety or because she needed emotional support.

Shulina Arya rolled past them, looking like she was having far too much fun to stop caroming around the castle for a meeting.

The double doors opened silently behind Trip. He might not have noticed except he sensed a familiar presence.

Sardelle leaned her head into the hallway. "Is there a problem out here?"

The guard that had been chasing Shulina Arya since the beginning raced past, his face red, his arms pumping and his truncheon clenched in his white-knuckled fist.

"Uhm." Trip groped for something more articulate to say, but he hadn't started reading Duck's vocabulary-laden classics yet, so fancy words eluded him.

Sardelle watched, her face impressively serene. Or maybe she was just good at masking her thoughts.

"Ma'am." Rysha turned hopefully toward Sardelle. "Are Shulina Arya's parents in there?"

Sardelle's serene expression shifted into one bordering on bemusement. "They are."

"Maybe they could convince her to—"

Shulina Arya rolled back into view again, this time returning from the king's vast audience chamber. "Coming through, human friends!" she called.

Trip tugged Rysha out of the way as Sardelle pressed her back to one of the open doors to make way. The guard looked like he wanted to lunge forward and tackle Shulina Arya as she approached, but she wrinkled her nose, and he froze in tableau.

She zipped past Trip, the breeze ruffling his hair, then weaved around some large potted plants as she disappeared into the solarium.

Trip didn't stretch his senses out toward the people inside—he wasn't sure he wanted to know what they thought of the intruder, nor did he want to witness it if a legion of the king's bodyguards tried to tackle her—but he still felt the ripples of alarm and surprise.

"And to think," Rysha said, her hand to her cheek as she looked through the open doors into the solarium, "meeting Shulina Arya's parents was what I was nervous about today."

"Maybe you shouldn't have agreed to bond with such a young dragon," Trip observed mildly, still keeping an eye on the guards. They were both back in front of the door now, their glowers turning toward him. He offered them their rifles, hoping there wouldn't be repercussions and also hoping they would forget he had used magic to confiscate them.

There's nothing wrong with a young and perky individual, Jaxi spoke into Trip's mind—into all of their minds, he imagined.

The soulblade was sheathed in her usual spot on Sardelle's hip.

Good morning, Jaxi, Trip thought. *I've missed your commentary.*

He couldn't say he'd missed listening in as Jaxi and Azarwrath argued, however, and was glad they were usually separated now. Sometimes, they made up for lost time when Trip reported to Sardelle's house for his lessons. It was hard to concentrate on magic with arguing voices in his head.

Of course you've missed me. I'm not sure how you keep from falling asleep every time Azzy opens his mouth to drone on.

His... mouth?

His mental mouth. It certainly puts me *to sleep. You must have excellent stamina.*

Azarwrath issued a long-suffering sigh into Trip's mind.

Trip looked at Rysha and smiled, thinking of suggesting that Jaxi could ask *her* about his stamina, but that seemed uncouth, so he refrained.

Please, I doubt she remembers what your stamina is like, Jaxi said, apparently reading his thoughts. He must still be, as she'd observed previously, leaving his bank vault door open when he thought of Rysha. *You two haven't rutted since that disgusting alley in Lagresh.*

It wasn't a disgusting alley. It was one of the less fragrant ones.

You're lucky she still wants to rut with you. Though she may not if you don't remember to congratulate her on passing her test.

Oh! Trip turned to Rysha, though she wasn't looking toward him anymore. She and Sardelle had turned toward another newcomer striding up the corridor, this one with more dignity than Shulina Arya and a haughty upward tilt to his nose. Phelistoth. His silver hair was pulled back in a tie, and layered robes hung to his feet, straight and unwrinkled. He walked past them without a word.

"It's true that young and perky dragons *are* a pleasant change," Sardelle murmured, then inclined her head toward the solarium. She gave the still-fuming guards a warm smile before leading the way inside.

Trip didn't sense her employing any manipulation, but they did seem to cool down a few degrees. Maybe they liked having pretty women smile at them.

Rysha looked at Trip as they walked in together, and he sensed her excitement, that she wanted to share the news of her success.

Congratulations, he whispered into her mind and touched her hand.

Maybe he should have waited for her to say something, but he felt like a heel because he'd been distracted and hadn't congratulated her already. He'd heard the news from General Zirkander the night before when he'd come home to the large mother-gathering in his living room.

Thank you. I'm so excited. Rysha seemed comfortable with telepathic contact these days, which warmed Trip's heart. She was growing comfortable with him. All of him and all of his eccentricities. *I'll get invited to go on dangerous missions now!* she added.

More dangerous than the ones we've already been on?

She grinned, elbowed him, and nodded ahead of them. *I guess we'll find out soon. But, uhm, it would be nice to celebrate before we're sent off on whatever the next mission is.* She raised her eyebrows toward him. *I haven't seen you very much since we got back.*

Her tone seemed hesitant. Uncertain. Did she think he'd been avoiding her? Definitely not.

You've been off training every time I've come by your barracks room to look for you.

Oh? I hadn't realized you'd stopped by. It's true—I have been training a lot. I was terrified I wouldn't pass the tests, and that I'd lose Shulina Arya and my chance to make it into the unit.

I know. That's why I didn't hunt you down. I didn't want to interrupt. And I've been training too. Not in the way of one-armed pull-ups but in the way of altering images on a printed page and redrawing them on another page.

Her lips quirked. *I'm glad you mastered the fish workbook.*

Just the first exercise.

Do you want to come by tonight? Rysha asked. *We could go to dinner and for a walk if it's not raining.*

I would love to. A zing went through his body as he imagined partaking in the romantic beach walk with her that he'd envisioned for so long.

They reached a large wrought-iron table in the center of the solarium and found all of the seats were filled. Rysha stopped behind someone in uniform, someone large, hulking, and hard to see around. The man, a few specks of gray in his short, dark hair, turned and glowered at Trip, though Trip didn't think they had met before. Had *everyone* read that ludicrous newspaper article?

Rysha saluted the glowering man. "Good morning, Colonel Therrik."

Trip also snapped up a salute. He recognized the name, if not the face, and suspected the officer ate those who didn't salute him quickly enough.

The colonel growled, returned the salute brusquely, and turned back around.

I don't think he likes having people behind him, Rysha thought. *Some of the elite troops can be a touch paranoid.*

Trip was close enough, with his mind open to her, that he heard her silent words. *Why? I promise I'm not going to squeeze his butt.*

I suspect he's more concerned about getting daggers in the back than butt squeezes.

Given what I've heard about him, I suppose that makes sense.

A throat cleared near the head of the table. "Is that our powerful sorcerer?"

Hells, was that the king?

Someone else large and looming stood next to Therrik, and a cluster of officious-looking men with pads of paper and pens blocked the route to the table on his other side, so Trip couldn't easily make himself seen. He chewed on his lip, debated on using his power to nudge people out of the way—or maybe he could levitate himself over all their heads for a dramatic entrance—but he decided to step up onto a sturdy-looking cement planter.

Belatedly, as his boot slid into the loamy soil underneath a fig tree, he decided that might not have been the most dignified choice. Especially when Therrik stepped to the side, obviating the need for an elevated perch.

King Angulus was indeed gazing in Trip's direction, his broad face difficult to read. Trip decided not to pry into his thoughts. If his monarch was irked with him, annoyed with him, or simply unimpressed by him, he didn't want to know.

"Good morning, Sire," Trip said, gripping the trunk of the fig tree so he could salute with the proper hand without falling off the planter. Belatedly, he realized he could step down from the planter, since Therrik had moved.

Trip jumped down, but landed on a puddle leaking from the bottom of the planter and slipped. He pitched against Therrik, their shoulders bumping. Trip had encountered marble statues with more give.

Therrik glowered at him again. Trip would *definitely* not be squeezing his butt.

"My apologies for the tightness, Captain," Angulus said, glancing at the shivering branches of the fig tree. "I wasn't expecting someone to bring a vehicle to the meeting." He looked to the side—somehow Shulina Arya had made it to the head of the table and stood near him, her hand resting on the handlebars of the crate scooter.

"A vehicle?" Shulina Arya asked. "This small human toy?"

"Perhaps I could make her a more compact version," Trip said, feeling the urge to be helpful, especially since a lot of people sitting at the table, some he recognized and others he didn't, were frowning in his direction. "Or a folding one."

"How does one make a crate fold?" General Zirkander asked dryly from one side of the table, shoulder to shoulder with Sardelle. She'd found her seat quickly. Maybe she had levitated.

"It wouldn't be that difficult, sir." Trip eyed the contraption, ideas already percolating in his mind.

"Don't ask her how she got it," Rysha whispered to him. "Or about the forlorn youth wondering if he'll ever get it back."

"She *stole* it?" Trip's mind boggled at the idea of a dragon mugging some teenager in a back alley.

"She landed a couple of blocks away from the castle—I suggested we not come down in the courtyard and alarm any trigger-happy guards on the grounds—and startled some boys racing each other in the street. They fled, leaving their toys behind. She thought their racing game looked like great fun, so she took one of the scooters..."

"I will most certainly return it," Shulina Arya said, her human voice sounding every bit as perky out loud as it did when it resonated in Trip's mind. "I simply wanted to try it. I—"

An older man with copper hair stepped forward to draw Shulina Arya away from the table. He wore spectacles and a blue suit a size or two too large for him. An unlit pipe stuck out of one pocket. When he pulled her back, it was to join another copper-haired man with similar fashion tastes, though the second fellow wore quirky inventor's goggles with the lenses lifted up.

It belatedly occurred to Trip that those two were dragons. Between Phelistoth's and Shulina Arya's presences, he hadn't noticed the pair in the back.

"Are those... her parents?" Rysha whispered.

"They are dragons shape-shifted into human form."

It seemed strange to refer to the two men—two male dragons—as a set of parents, but Shulina Arya apparently considered them to be that.

"I see that everyone who was invited to this meeting is here," King Angulus said, nodding around the table, and also toward those standing in the back.

Trip was surprised he wasn't holding this meeting in his big audience chamber, but perhaps he considered the table and the plant-filled setting more intimate than addressing people from the throne atop his dais. There was still room for servants to move around the solarium, filling drink glasses. If Trip hadn't been wedged between Therrik, Rysha, and the fig tree, he wouldn't have found the space that crowded.

"A couple of dragons who inform me that they are scientists have come to speak with us," Angulus went on, extending a hand toward the professorial types. "They're not trying to solve Iskandia's dragon problem, but from what I've heard already, it's possible some of what they tell us will spark some ideas among our brighter minds."

Angulus looked at Sardelle and then at a bronze-skinned Cofah man with shaggy black hair who sat near the end of the table by Captain Ahn. Tolemek Targoson. Trip had met him the night his siblings had been removed from the stasis chambers.

"Should I be offended that he didn't look at me when he said that?" Zirkander whispered to Sardelle, not that softly.

"Your people are here to provide aerial transport to those with bright minds who come up with worthy plans to try," Angulus told him, his eyes narrowing.

"Still the flying rickshaw service, I see," Zirkander murmured.

Sardelle stuck an elbow in his ribs. They looked at each other, and Trip suspected a telepathic conversation.

He asked why she did that, and she said because General Ort retired and isn't here to kick him under the table, Jaxi explained.

Are you supposed to be sharing their private conversations with me? Trip asked.

If I didn't, who would?

Trip wondered if Jaxi had been missing him since he'd returned her to Sardelle's care. It was a strange thought since she had spent so much of their adventure remarking on his failings.

The dragon professors—dragon scientists?—stepped up to one corner of the table, leaving Shulina Arya to sit on the lip of a long rectangular hedge planter. Trip was sure it was only his imagination that she was sulking after some parental reprimand.

"Greetings, humans," the dragon in the blue suit and spectacles said. "I am Wyleenesh, and this is my colleague, Bhajera Liv."

The other dragon tipped his head, and his goggle lenses fell forward, the dark shades covering his eyes. He pushed them back up.

I'm beginning to see why Shulina Arya was drawn to Rysha, Jaxi spoke dryly into Trip's mind.

Because she likes smart intellectual types?

Or beings with spectacles.

"We are bronze dragons and scientists among our kind. We enjoyed studying our world of *Serankil* before we left, and we enjoyed studying the great volcanoes of the new world we entered through the Portal of *Avintnaresi,* and now we are studying here again. We are researching the populations of dragons, humans, and various herbivores—our preferred dietary staple—on the continents here."

Is it me, Azarwrath said, *or is it not clear from the way he created that list that humans aren't part of the preferred diet?*

Don't worry, Azzy, Jaxi said. *Nobody likes to eat swords. Especially grumpy ones.*

"We estimate there are four hundred to five hundred dragons that have returned." Wyleenesh looked at Angulus.

The king nodded and looked at Trip. "That's what we've heard."

"Didn't we kill some of them?" Zirkander grumbled.

"Not enough to put a dent in the estimate," Sardelle said.

"Indeed," Wyleenesh said. "And there have been a few new births already. Very encouraging for our kind."

Nobody at the table looked encouraged.

"But there is a problem." Wyleenesh removed his spectacles and used his shirt to wipe them. He frowned at a resistant piece of gunk on one lens. Trip felt a tiny bit of power being called upon, and a flame appeared on the glass, burning off the gunk. The dragon wiped the lens again, then replaced the spectacles on his nose. "The human population has increased drastically since we lived in this world last."

"*Drastically*," his colleague agreed, his goggles rattling as he nodded.

"There are fewer wild lands where dragons can hunt, especially on this continent and on the large one across the ocean."

"Cofahre," Angulus said.

"I suspect this is part of your problem, human king. We dragons see animals grazing on open land, and we are hungry, so we pluck them up and consume them. They seem little different to us than wild prey, except that they're usually easy to grasp because they're in the open. It's quite pesky to fly around trees in jungles and forests to find sufficiently sized prey to consume."

Trip looked at Rysha, wondering if she knew where this meeting was going. Were the dragons only here to justify why they were eating people's sheep?

"Are you saying," Zirkander said, "that our farmers' sheep are too enticing a target to resist?"

"Indeed. They are delicious. And, as I stated, easier to acquire than wild animals. But dragons do not mind a challenge. If there were more wild animals, we would happily chase them and enjoy the glory of the hunt before sinking our teeth into fresh flesh."

Ew, Jaxi said into Trip's mind.

Azarwrath did not comment, though he was perhaps thinking that dragons were unlikely to employ sommeliers at their dinner gatherings.

"This is what is happening on *Yveranoar*, your jungle continent."

"Dakrovia?" Angulus asked.

"I believe this is what you call it, yes. Human settlements are much smaller, with less land cleared for your farms and livestock. There is a great deal of wild hunting land, and many dragons have gravitated there."

"Lucky Dakrovians," Zirkander said.

"But many dragons in one area leads to many battles for territory. The most powerful dragons claim what they wish and are able to defend it. The less powerful are either killed or, more often, driven off to squabble over inferior hunting grounds." He gestured toward one of the glass walls of the solarium. Indicating Iskandia as a whole? "As you may be aware, more and more dragons have been coming to your land. Many are indifferent to your presence on it and simply wish to hunt. Others believe humans are evil, that they're the reason there are fewer prime hunting grounds now—which is undoubtedly true to some extent—and will attack without provocation, simply because they are irritated with the situation."

"Is there anything you can suggest we do?" Angulus asked.

"I have a possible solution," Bhajera Liv said, stepping forward.

"It will not work for them," Wyleenesh told him.

"It is a possibility they may wish to consider, nonetheless."

"I highly doubt it."

Phelistoth, who had found a seat on one side of the table and gripped what appeared to be a steaming mug of coffee, sighed noisily and muttered, "Bronzes."

The two speakers ignored him.

"My suggestion," Bhajera Liv said, holding a hand up with curled fingers toward his colleague, "is for you humans to get rid of your farmlands and plant trees all over the continent, so it will return to wilderness such as it once was, and thus improve the habitat for dragons."

Rysha snorted softly.

I don't think the king is going to go for that, Trip told her silently.

Not when seventy percent of the nation's food comes from farmlands, no.

"That would not improve the habitat for humans," Angulus said. "We need the farmlands to feed our people."

"Yes," Bhajera Liv said, "but if there were fewer farmlands, your species would have less food and perhaps be less fecund. In future generations, there would be fewer humans in the country, thus creating more balance in the world."

"Balance," Angulus said darkly.

"I told you they would not be amenable," Wyleenesh said, elbowing Bhajera Liv aside. "My colleague is overly blunt, but he is correct that right now, the population of dragons and humans is not in balance. We estimate there are one *billion* humans worldwide."

Are there truly that many people? Trip silently asked Rysha, the number sounding incredibly huge to him.

Possibly. We only have estimates, but there are hundreds of millions in the Cofah Empire.

"A thousand years ago, before dragons were tricked into leaving this, our homeland—" Wyleenesh frowned around the table, as if to suggest someone there was to blame, "—there were approximately three-hundred-and-fifty million humans worldwide and two thousand dragons. Even though there were still battles over resources, that was closer to a sustainable number. Now..." Wyleenesh spread a hand.

"It wasn't a problem before dragons came back," someone Trip didn't know muttered, one of the people with clipboards and pens.

"This is *our* homeland too," Wyleenesh said. "Our absence from it was involuntary. And our species did not thrive in the other world. Birthrates were abnormally low." He looked back at Shulina Arya. "There were only about a thousand of us left there at the time the portal was reopened. It is unfortunate that more of our kin did not make it through before it was prematurely closed." This time, he looked toward Trip, and Trip fought the urge to squirm. Yes, he had been a part of the mission to close the portal... "But," Wyleenesh went on, "perhaps it is for the best, since, as I said, we have a problem."

"Any ideas on how to solve it?" Angulus asked. "Besides by cutting the global human population in half?"

"Seven gods, please tell me none of the dragons are planning on making that a reality," a colonel in uniform murmured from one of the seats. He wore one of the sheathed *chapaharii* blades on his belt.

The two bronze dragons looked at each other, holding each other's gaze for several long seconds.

I don't find that silence encouraging, Azarwrath said.

Nor do I, Jaxi said. *I don't have many human friends. I wouldn't care for their numbers to be halved.*

Perhaps if your words were less lippy, you would have more friends, Azarwrath replied.

Perhaps if so many humans weren't afraid of magic and sentient swords, I would have more. I don't see you and your un-lippy tongue being invited to cocktail parties.

"There have been rumors of some discussions on that topic," Wyleenesh finally answered the king. "You must understand that we, as bronze dragons, are on the bottom of the power and social order when it comes to our kind, so we are rarely invited to meetings with golds or even silvers. I believe that those dragons who have claimed jungles and islands sufficiently large to have enough prey to suit their needs are unlikely to bother your country."

Trip thought of the bronze dragon that had claimed the Pirate Isles. Maybe he'd been smarter than he had seemed.

"Those who haven't been able to find a territory of their own are hungry and restless. It is very possible there are plans in place to remove the, ah, human infestation as some have called it, on some of the continents with territory in favorable climate zones."

"I suppose that's us," Zirkander said.

"The southern half of your continent is most warm and appealing, outside of those chilly mountains," Wyleenesh said.

"That settles it," Zirkander said. "We'll just move all of humanity into the Ice Blades."

"Your species would very likely survive if you did so," Bhajera Liv put in helpfully.

Trip looked upward, sensing another dragon flying over the castle. Bhrava Saruth. Had he been invited to the meeting too?

"Good to know," Zirkander said. "I'm sure we'll do very well if we shove the whole country into the Magroth Crystal Mines."

Angulus sighed and rubbed his forehead. Major Kaika, who sat in the closest seat on his right, sent him a worried look.

"Thank you for your presentation," Angulus finally told the dragons. "If you don't have any other suggestions—"

A gust of wind ruffled people's hair, and Trip sensed Bhrava Saruth landing on the perch of one of the huge glass windows overlooking the outdoor gardens. He shifted into human form before he walked into view, his sandy hair shaggy on all sides and tumbling into his green eyes.

"Greetings, worshippers," he announced, his voice booming into their minds as well as their ears. "Am I late for the meeting?"

Wyleenesh sniffed and adjusted his spectacles. "We've completed our presentation."

"Ah, then I've missed the boring part and have arrived at the perfect time. Are those pastries?" He pointed at one of several trays of baked goods on the table.

Angulus rubbed his forehead again, more vigorously. A number of murmured conversations started up as one of the pastry trays floated into the air toward Bhrava Saruth.

I think this meeting will be adjourning soon, Trip guessed, looking at Rysha. *Without much having been resolved.*

He thought of his visit with the surrogate mothers last night, and of Mladine's close encounter with a dragon, and he resolved that he would figure out something that could be done, even if nobody else around the table had ideas.

That's my fear as well. I am going to brainstorm some ideas so that I can share them with my superiors.

Tonight? I thought we might celebrate tonight. Trip clasped her hand.

I'm amenable to that. She rubbed the back of his hand with her thumb. *I've missed you these last three weeks.*

Me too. I mean, I've missed you. A lot.

A throat cleared.

"Trip?" Zirkander asked, tilting his head toward the king.

He dropped Rysha's hand. Angulus was looking expectantly at him. Nobody had spoken to him, had they? Maybe he'd missed a discussion *about* him?

Therrik exhaled heavily. Or maybe that was a disapproving growl.

"I understand you're studying with Sardelle," Angulus said. "Is there any chance you'll one day be powerful enough to convince the dragons terrorizing our country to stay away from here?"

"Me? I don't see how, Sire. I wouldn't even be able to convince that dragon to leave your pastries alone." Trip looked at Bhrava Saruth—he now held the tray and was taking alarmingly large bites of frosted cloud buns. Perhaps he should have shape-shifted into a form with a bigger mouth.

Would your king not find it alarming if I arrived at his meeting in alligator form? Bhrava Saruth asked, smirking over at Trip and proving Trip still needed to work on masking his thoughts, at least from such powerful beings as dragons.

"I thought not," Angulus said, "but I had to ask."

The disappointment emanating from him stung Trip. It wasn't as if it was his fault he was a *half*-dragon instead of a whole one, and an ill-trained one at that. But he would find a way to help, one way or another. Helping his country and his king—and now his little siblings—was all he'd ever wanted to do. He'd always imagined doing that by being a pilot and shooting down enemies, but perhaps he should expand his expectations of himself. Iskandia didn't need a pilot; it needed a dragon solution. He liked to find solutions and fix things. He just wasn't sure how to fix this one. Maybe he could brainstorm with Rysha later.

"We'll talk again later," Angulus said, looking around the table, and Trip sensed that he wasn't comfortable plotting ways to defeat dragons with actual dragons in the room. "If you have ideas on how to protect our shores, please give them to your unit commanders. Dismissed."

CHAPTER 4

RYSHA COMBED HER HAIR AND looked in the mirror for the fifth time, engaging in the hair-up-or-hair-down debate for the twentieth time. Currently, her strawberry-blonde locks fell about her shoulders, which she thought Trip might like—since they'd both been in uniform practically since they'd met, he hadn't seen her without it in a bun very often. But it was on the flat side with an odd kink from being in a bun earlier, and she glowered distastefully at it. Maybe a braid would be better.

If they were going to walk along the beach, it could be breezy, and a braid might make sense. Even though she liked the way her hair looked when down, it was a pain to constantly have to claw it away from her face. And when it grew tangled in the frames of her spectacles, and she couldn't get them off? Not a sexy look.

"Seven gods, when did you turn into a teenage girl?" Rysha grumbled, forcing herself away from the mirror.

Trip had seen her injured, bloody, and dying, and he'd seen her soaking wet and draped with seaweed. Not only that, but being in that state had led to cuddling and sex. Clearly, he didn't mind a woman who wasn't perfectly made up.

Oh, but she should put on a little lip paint. Just a touch. The raspberry rouge. That would draw his eyes to her lips and away from that kink in her hair. Or maybe his gaze would be drawn lower.

She'd chosen a silky blue blouse that hugged her breasts and flared at the waist. If she'd had a dress up here in the capital, she might have opted for one tonight, but she hadn't been thinking of evening wear when she'd packed to leave her family's manor for the army. And at her height, it wasn't as if she could run out to buy one. She always had to have clothing tailor-made, something that had been easier before her parents stopped giving her an allowance. Not that she cared about that. It had been their way of punishing her for enlisting, but she was glad to be independent of the family now and living on her lieutenant's pay. Besides, she'd spent the majority of her allowance on books, and she had limited space in her barracks room to accumulate a new collection.

A knock sounded at the door. Even though she had expected it—expected *him*—she jumped. She dropped the lip brush back into the tin.

"Coming," she called, though she doubted it was necessary. In the compact room, it was only two steps to the door, and Trip would magically sense her location.

Rysha opened the door, revealing Trip standing in the hallway and holding a wood, glass, and metal display case that looked like it could hang on the wall like a picture frame. A couple of female officers in fatigues strolled past behind him, giving it a curious look.

One of them paused, her gaze slipping to Trip's butt, and Rysha realized it wasn't the *case* that had drawn their attention. Trip wasn't wearing anything fancy, but his civilian clothing fit better than fatigues tended to do, making it easy to see his lean, powerful form. The sleeves of his button-down cream-colored shirt were rolled up, leaving his muscular forearms on display. He was fit for a pilot, and she wondered if having dragon blood helped one keep an appealing physique. She also wondered if he had intentionally left that top button unbuttoned, as if to invite someone to come along and unbutton the rest of them.

Realizing she hadn't said hello or done anything but stare at him, she smiled at him. And caught his dark green eyes tilted toward her chest. He jerked them up immediately.

"I'm not looking," he blurted, his cheeks reddening impressively given his darker-than-typical Iskandian skin.

Rysha grinned, amused that he'd been checking her out even as she'd been doing the same to him. She was also pleased he didn't seem to have been aware of the other women in the hallway.

"You can look all you want." Rysha touched her chest, took his arm, and led him into her room. "I'm glad you want to."

"I do. But I don't want to be rude. My grandmother always told me to look women in the eyes."

"My aunt always told me to slap men if they looked at my breasts or my butt. The older generation gives interesting advice, doesn't it?" She shut the door firmly behind Trip, so no other women wandering past would be able to ogle him.

He tilted his head. "Does that mean you're going to slap me?"

"Probably not until later." She patted his butt and grinned again.

"Hm, do I get to slap you if you look at *my* butt?"

"Probably not until later."

He chuckled and leaned against her. He looked like he might have given her a hug, but he was still holding the frame.

"Oh." He lifted it and turned it for display. "This is for you. This round slot is where the elite-troops badge goes. Actually, Major Kaika said it's more of a big bronze coin. You probably don't have it yet, right? I think you get it at the awards ceremony. That's tomorrow, isn't it?"

Rysha nodded and would have said more—she wanted to ask if he could get away from the hangar to come—but he continued on, almost burbling as he described the case.

"And here's how you hang it. I made it self-fastening, so you don't have to attach anything to the walls. See, here? And then these slots are for your medals. The first four go here, and then this folds out. You can alternate which ones you want to display, and if you get tired of the color of the velvet background, I made it easy to remove and replace."

"I don't have any medals," Rysha said.

Unless he wanted to count the various ones she'd been awarded for sports competitions as a girl. They were all back in her bedroom at the manor.

"You will," Trip said firmly, then seemed to run out of words. He bit his lip and thrust the case out, his eyes hopeful.

Was he afraid she wouldn't like it? She was positive he'd made it by hand. In what free time, she couldn't imagine, since between his training and his work and checking in on those eight babies, he couldn't possibly have any.

"It's beautiful, Trip. Thank you." Rysha accepted it and ran her hand along the mahogany frame, touched that he had taken the time to craft it. And that he believed she would be awarded medals.

"We should have gotten one already, really," he said quietly, perhaps reading her thoughts.

Funny how the idea of having him in her head had bothered her once, but now, it just seemed natural. A part of him. She wondered if General Zirkander and Sardelle spoke telepathically to each other. Probably. She was positive Jaxi, at least, butted into the general's mind.

"For destroying the portal?" she asked. "Or for finding all those *chapaharii* swords? Or for finding eight half-dragon-half-human babies?"

"I don't think you get medals for finding long-lost siblings—and don't forget all the half-dragon animal babies too—but portal-destroying is definitely medal-worthy."

"Are the animals being properly cared for?" She realized that they would grow to maturity a lot faster than the human children would. How fast did lizards and lions and whatever else had been in there grow up? She would have to check, but she suspected the other houses on Sardelle's street were about to become even *less* likely to attract renters.

"By Tylie, Ylisa, and Ferrin," he said. "Sardelle's students. Mostly by Tylie. She's studying to be a veterinarian."

"A sorceress veterinarian? I wonder if King Angulus is distressed that she won't become a great mage-warrior who will hurl fireballs at enemies."

"I don't think fireballs are an interest for her. The last time I was there, she was trimming a raccoon's broken toenail."

"With magic or toenail clippers?"

"Magical toenail clippers."

"Is there such a thing?" Rysha asked.

"There is now." He smirked.

"*You* didn't make them, did you?"

"They grind as well as clip nails."

"That was a yes, wasn't it?"

Trip shrugged sheepishly. "Sardelle won't let me pay her for her lessons. I feel I should give her *something*. Besides, my grandmother also says you should never arrive at someone's house without a gift. Usually, she gives baked goods, but I don't bake."

"Does General Zirkander think it's odd that you're giving his wife gifts?"

"Not since I brought them a new combination coffee grinder and brewing machine, one made extra durable in case dragons lacking mechanical aptitude get cranky with it."

Rysha set down the display case and rested her hands on either side of Trip's face. "You're a good man."

She kissed him, only intending it as a thank-you for the gift and a sign of approval for his solicitude, but he returned it warmly, resting his hands on her hips, and her thoughts soon strayed back to the unbuttoning of buttons. She supposed that should wait, since they had planned to take that walk and have dinner at a restaurant before engaging in less clothed activities, but when Trip broke the kiss, she inadvertently made a protesting noise.

But he also eased closer, slipping his arms fully around her as he looked toward the bed, speculation in his gaze.

"I expected it to be bigger," he said.

"My bed?"

Admittedly, it wasn't large—certainly not designed for two—but after the cave and alley they'd had sex in, Rysha thought it would prove quite luxurious. It had a firm mattress with just enough spring…

"Your room and your bed both, I guess," Trip said. "Everything is the same size as mine."

"You're a captain. If anything, you should have a larger room." She was lucky she didn't have a roommate. She'd had one at the officer academy.

"But you're a woman."

"I'm glad you noticed." She leaned her chest against his, remembering him noticing at the door.

He must have liked that because he turned his gaze toward her again, lifting a hand to stroke the side of her head. A shiver went through her as some magical heat radiated from his fingers and trickled through her body, stirring all her senses to life.

"I like your hair down," he said.

"I'm glad." Rysha decided not to mention that she'd obsessed over it. Fortunately, he didn't seem to mind the kink. Or maybe he liked kinks.

The corners of his mouth quirked.

"You're not reading my thoughts, are you?" Rysha leaned her head against his hand, wanting more of his strong fingers touching her scalp.

"Who, me?"

He smiled and kissed her again, more tendrils of tingling warmth curling through her body, making her want to kiss him back—hard. And remove all his clothing.

Don't let me stop you, he whispered into her mind as his fingers slid up under the back of her shirt.

I won't. I'm a tenacious woman.

Excellent.

They worked their way over to the bed, undressing each other as they went. Rysha made short work of his buttons, and her shirt joined his on the floor before they tumbled onto the bed together. And promptly smacked their shoulders against the wall. As Trip had observed, it wasn't the largest bed, but they didn't let that slow them down for long.

All thoughts of dinners and walks fled from Rysha's mind as she tugged off every last shred of his clothing so she could run her hands all over his body. He shifted atop her, his own hands doing exploring of their own. His kisses sent molten fire through her, and she shifted her legs apart, inviting him in. By the gods, they needed to figure out a way to be together every night. Not just when—

The door opened with a cheerful, "Good evening, Rysha!"

She dropped her head back, pulling her mouth from Trip's, and gaping as the two people she had least expected to see that day strolled into her room. Her mother and Aunt Tadelay.

Trip, who had been poised to satisfy all her womanly desires, issued a distinctly unmanly squawk and pitched sideways, falling off the bed and onto the floor. He scrambled to his feet, reaching for the bedspread. He tugged, but Rysha was still on top of it, staring in startled horror at her family members who were staring back in equal horror at her, their mouths dangling to their feet.

Trip settled for a pillow, snatching it from the bed and placing it in front of his groin. Utterly naked aside from the pillow—and, by the gods, why was he still wearing one sock?—he turned to face the doorway.

"Uhm, hi, Mom." Rysha shifted to sit on the side of the bed, not sure if she should grab clothes and start dressing or merely be mortified in place. "Aunt Tadelay."

"Rysha Erilyn *Ravenwood*," her mother said when she found her voice.

"This is completely unacceptable," Aunt Tadelay said, her tone even shriller than Mother's. "Wantonly improper carnal copulation with a strange stark-naked man in the middle of the week. It's not even *dark* yet."

Would this be better if I wasn't naked? And if it was dark? Trip asked into Rysha's mind.

Rysha couldn't tell if he was joking or serious. With his cheeks that cardinal-bird shade of red, he appeared far too distressed to joke.

"He's not strange, Aunt Tadelay. He's a colleague and a good friend and…" Rysha gestured toward Trip, not quite able to spit out "my lover" even though that was obvious.

"Naked!" Aunt Tadelay cried, lifting a hand to shield her eyes from seeing Trip's chest. And pillow. "In a woman's room in a—is this not a female-only barracks? Doesn't the army have any propriety? Do not tell me that men are allowed to assail innocent women in this iniquitous place."

"He wasn't assailing anyone, Aunt Tadelay." Rysha sighed, pulling the bedspread up to somewhat cover herself as she shifted toward her mother, hoping for a more reasonable response. Mother was older than Aunt Tadelay, but the more progressive, or at least more reasonable, of the two. "He's my boyfriend."

There, that conveyed the notion of lover without suggesting so much… naked vigor.

"You never brought him to the manor," her mother said sternly, "or introduced him to the family. And he's certainly never come to your father to ask our permission to see you."

"*See?*" Aunt Tadelay demanded. "It's clear he's doing much more than *seeing* your little girl. She's been manhandled."

"Yes, precisely," Rysha said, losing some of her embarrassment and growing irked. She was a twenty-seven-year-old woman, not some fifteen-year-old girl caught kissing a boy behind the trees in the orchard. "And I enjoyed his handling very much."

"Er," Trip said. His first word since the door had opened.

"I'm—I'm—too flabbergasted to speak." Aunt Tadelay whirled, her long skirt flapping impressively, and stalked out into the hall.

Mother puckered her lips at Trip.

"Sorry, ma'am," Trip said, though it wasn't clear if he meant for sexing up her daughter or for his clothing-challenged state. "I'm Captain Trip—Telryn Yert."

He shifted his right hand off his pillow, careful to keep it plastered in place with his left, and stuck it out toward her.

Bow, Rysha thought, hoping he was monitoring her thoughts. *I mean, you don't have to, but that's what noblemen do toward noblewomen. Sometimes, they kiss the woman's hand, too, but she might not appreciate that, given your state of undress.*

As Mom was looking distastefully down at his hand, as if it was contaminated with all manner of sex germs, Trip jerked it back, placing it on his chest, and said, "It's an honor to meet you, ma'am."

My lady, Rysha thought.

"My lady," Trip said.

He bowed.

Mother lifted her eyes toward the ceiling. "Well, at least he's an officer and not some kitchen scrub boy."

"That is *not* the name of a noble family," Aunt Tadelay called from the hallway. Rysha wasn't surprised that she was still out there spying.

"No," Trip agreed. "My family is less noble and more… unique." He started plucking his clothing up from the floor, one-handedly of course, since the other was keeping the pillow firmly in place. He stood and squatted in such a way to keep his butt from showing to Mother. Too bad. It was a nice butt. She might appreciate his young firmness.

Rysha, Trip spoke into her mind, sounding horrified.

"I'll leave you two to speak privately, ma'am. My lady." Trip looked down at the clothes he'd managed to grab and scooted toward the door, making a wide berth around Mother.

His underwear was lying across one of the pillows still on the bed. Rysha thought about tossing it to him, but he was already moving past Mother and into the hall.

"Are you *stealing* that pillow?" Aunt Tadelay called, her voice loud enough that everyone in the barracks had to be aware of this entire conversation.

As Rysha dropped her face into her hand, Tadelay shrieked in horror.

Your aunt saw my beets, Trip told her apologetically.

She'll get over it.

I'm sorry I didn't sense… I mean, I wasn't trying to sense people in the hallway. I was focused on—

Me, I know. I like you focused on me when we're in bed, Trip. Don't worry about this. I'll smooth things over.

Should I have gone to ask your father if—

No. This is not the pre-industrial age, and I'm not a child. I'll let them know.

All right.

Come back later. Or do you want me to come to your room later? I intend to have wild and vigorous sex with you tonight. One way or another. Rysha smiled as her mother stopped sighing at the ceiling and looked over at her.

"Please put some clothes on, love," Mom said.

Uh, you could come to my room. It's doubtful any family members are on their way to visit.

Are you sure? Rysha picked up her shirt and tugged it on, lamenting that she had to redo the buttons far too soon. *What if your grandfather walked in?*

I think he'd pat me on the shoulder and say, "Good going, boy."

Men are much different from women.

Indeed.

"What brings you here, Mother?" Rysha asked. "I wasn't expecting you."

"*Clearly*," Aunt Tadelay said from the hall.

Rysha wondered if she would come back in or if she was too busy being mortally aggrieved by viewing… beets.

"We heard you graduated your military training school," Mom said.

"You came for the ceremony?" Rysha asked, stunned.

"We came to talk you out of the insanity of becoming a soldier in such a dangerous unit," Aunt Tadelay said, striding back into the room. "Putting aside the fact that it's completely improper for young women to fling themselves over walls and through mud puddles before shooting people, have you *seen* the newspapers lately?" She produced a recent issue of the *Pinoth Gazette* that Rysha hadn't read yet—she had been too busy. "Dragons are killing people all over the country. By the *hundreds*. And right at home, we had to suffer an attack. You were there for your grandmother's funeral. I can't think of a more appalling way to die."

Rysha thought of how she'd almost died from giant tarantula venom. That had been moderately appalling.

"You must give up this army nonsense immediately—if you enter that dreadful combat unit, they're sure to send you out to die. On a daily basis. And what is this in the newspapers about you cavorting with *dragons*? Even *flying* on one?"

She slapped the page on which Rysha could just make out a photograph of a dragon. It didn't look like Bhrava Saruth or Shulina Arya, but the dragon had posed for long enough for a photographer to capture it on film, so it had to be one of Iskandia's allies.

"That's completely unacceptable," Aunt Tadelay went on, shaking the newspaper for emphasis. "It's suicidal. You'll fall off. Or be eaten. Dragons *eat* people."

"Shulina Arya is more interested in eating tarts."

Aunt Tadelay sputtered.

"Calm down, Tadelay," Mom said, patting her sister's arm. "We're here to be reasonable, remember? She's not going to come home with us if we yell at her."

"I was reasonable until I saw my niece in bed with some mongrel from the stables."

"Trip is a pilot," Rysha said, trying to tamp down the irritation rising inside of her. It was hard. Somehow, their rejection of Trip wasn't as bad as the notion that they hadn't come here to congratulate her; they'd come to try to get her to quit. Again. "He works in the *sky*."

Her mother took a deep breath and waved her hand, as if to dismiss this lesser issue. "Honey, it's too dangerous to remain in the military right now. If you're not sent to battle dragons, you'll be sent out into the countryside to deal with our own people. Angry and fearful people. The Iskandian populace is afraid and acting like it. People are hoarding goods. Others are openly stealing from their neighbors to ensure they have enough to survive if trade lines are cut, and there isn't enough food to supply the hungry of the country. Why, someone even broke into the manor and attempted to steal our silver just last week."

Rysha blinked, some of her irritation fading. "Is everyone all right?"

"Yes, your father and uncle and Butler Tohomas were there and drove the would-be thieves off. They dropped their stolen goods in the courtyard—our silverware and candlesticks all stuffed into a bag, if you can imagine. Nobody was hurt, but honey, this is only the beginning. There's unrest in the countryside, and I'm sure it will grow even more problematic in the city. You'll be as likely to be sent to fight our own people rioting as you will dragons." Mother waved to the crinkled newspaper Aunt Tadelay still held. "If it's a fight you want, you can help your family strengthen its own defenses and stand ready to drive dragons and miscreants off the land."

"Assuming we *keep* the land," Aunt Tadelay muttered.

"What do you mean?" Rysha asked.

"Nothing." Mother waved her sister to silence. "My husband isn't going to sell his ancestral land. There's no need to worry her about that."

"He looked speculative, if you ask me," Aunt Tadelay said, oozing disapproval anew.

A knot of anxiety formed in Rysha's stomach. What had she missed going on back at home when she'd been off on missions and busy training for her test?

"We're going to shop for a few necessities for the manor while we're here in the capital," Mom said, "but then we're heading back tomorrow afternoon. We invite you to join us. Take a leave of absence from the army if you won't quit completely. Just until the unrest settles and these dragons go back to where they came from."

Rysha sighed. "They can't go back."

With the portal destroyed, that wasn't an option, even if there had been some way to trick the dragons into leaving again. Which seemed unlikely. Every dragon willing to speak to humans had been quick to point out that the world they had been stuck in hadn't been a pleasant one.

"And my ceremony is tomorrow. Mother, Aunt Tadelay, I'm only the second woman in the history of the Iskandian army to qualify for the elite troops. Won't you come to see me awarded and officially initiated into the unit?"

They pursed their lips, the expressions very similar as their eyes met.

"I told you she wouldn't come," Mother said.

"We need her at home, not throwing her life away here. Your other daughter saw our logic and is leaving her teaching position to come home. I can't understand why Rysha can't see the necessity."

"Because she's stubborn. Like her mother." Mother smiled faintly at Rysha.

"A dreadful disease."

"At least let us take you to dinner," Mother told Rysha. "I understand the New Merchants' Quarter is still relatively safe and unaffected by disgruntled subjects."

"Do insist that she finish dressing first." Aunt Tadelay pursed her lips again. "Really, Rysha, it's inconsiderate of you to stand there in your brazen nakedness while we have this discussion."

Rysha realized she had let the bedspread slip. She sighed again and picked up the rest of her clothing. She wanted to go to dinner with *Trip*, not her family, but her mother and aunt had her worried now in regard to what was going on at home. She had better find out as much as possible. Hopefully, there would be time to see Trip later.

CHAPTER 5

TRIP KNELT BACK FROM THE parachute he was carefully folding to place into a pack and checked his pocket watch. Fifteen minutes before he needed to leave the hangar so he could trot across the fort and arrive in time to see Rysha's initiation ceremony. He'd already gotten permission from Colonel Tranq to do so, though he'd had to promise to come back after final formation and finish packing parachutes. Seventy-five of the approved models, guaranteed to not get pilots killed if they used them, had arrived in crates that morning. He, some of the ground crew, and several others from Wolf Squadron had the honor of inspecting them and storing them for use.

"You're paying attention to what you're doing, right?" Colonel Tranq asked, walking up behind him.

"Yes, ma'am." Trip slipped the watch into his pocket.

"Because not all of us can flap our arms and levitate ourselves to safety if our fliers are shot down." She stopped at Trip's side to look down at his work.

A stout woman barely over five feet, Colonel Tranq rolled along like a tank when she was on the ground but had the grace and agility of a ballerina when in her flier. She kept her graying hair cut as short as most of the men's, and had a weathered face that made her appear closer to fifty than the forty she was.

"Trip doesn't flap his arms, ma'am," Leftie said from his side. "He just walks across the air real casual, like the hot air from his farts is pushing him aloft."

"Thanks so much for correcting her," Trip murmured.

"Any time, buddy." Leftie, who also knelt in front of a parachute, made a circle with his thumb and fingers in the typical pilot's ready or all-good sign.

"I'm sure something of his flaps," Tranq muttered and walked off to inspect other people's work.

"Yes, ma'am, but he keeps that buttoned in his trousers."

Trip shook his head, not particularly mortified, as penis and fart humor was an hourly occurrence in the hangar. It certainly didn't seem to bother Colonel Tranq.

"What's taking so long, Ahn?" Tranq asked, stopping behind the captain. "You knitting that parachute from scratch?"

"No, ma'am," the slender Captain Ahn said, her fingers sliding along the line of the parachute. "I'm carefully inspecting the seams before folding it for the pack. When I was a young lieutenant, I was among those who tested the early models of parachutes. I was along when one of our people didn't make it."

"Ah, carry on, then."

"And I also do not have anything to flap to get myself to safety." Ahn, freckled, fine-featured, and also short of hair and height, cocked a single eyebrow in Trip's direction.

It had been three weeks since Trip had gotten back from his mission and truly joined Wolf Squadron, and he'd flown on a few short missions with the pilots, but they hadn't seen much true danger together yet, and he wasn't sure how his new squadron mates felt about him. He was doing his best not to sense the emotions and thoughts of his fellow soldiers, mostly because the first few times he'd done it, he'd found them wary and mistrustful of going up with someone who had magic. As if he might do something unprecedented and dangerous that would put the squadron at risk. Apparently, they didn't mind flying into battle with ally dragons, but having an ally who was half-dragon… That was just weird.

"Nothing extra in the trousers, eh, ma'am?" Leftie asked Ahn. "I bet that Deathmaker of yours is tickled."

"He prefers to go by Tolemek. Or Dr. Targoson now that he's earned an Iskandian medical degree."

"Does he? He sounds kind of stuffy."

"Perhaps you shouldn't irk Captain Ahn," Trip suggested to Leftie, "given her reputation for marksmanship."

"What did I say that could irk her? Now, I could see Dr. Deathmaker being irked, but…"

"You called her boyfriend stuffy."

"Some girls like that in a man."

Ahn had turned to have a quiet conversation with Colonel Tranq and was ignoring Leftie's further comments. That was likely good for Leftie.

There is trouble afoot, Telryn, Azarwrath spoke into his mind from his spot in Trip's flier. *Folding clothing is not the best use of your time today.*

What trouble? And it's not clothing.

Folding anything is beneath you. Dragons are coming.

Trip stretched out with his mind and immediately sensed a dragon flying over the harbor. He stood up, turning toward the open hangar bay.

Outside, rain fell from heavy gray clouds. Trip recognized Shulina Arya's familiar aura and was relieved, since it didn't look like a fun day to fly into battle. Then he sensed Rysha on her back and frowned—why was she flying in the rain instead of standing ready for her ceremony?

Shulina Arya flew toward the hangar, and Trip sensed a second dragon heading in their direction from farther up along the coast. Bhrava Saruth, perhaps flying south from his temple.

Rysha? Trip sent the question out toward her.

Trouble, she replied promptly. *I was getting ready for my ceremony when Shulina Arya arrived to let me know. A bunch of dragons just converged on Portsnell, and they've proclaimed it's now theirs.*

I have been there before, Bhrava Saruth announced, thrusting himself into their telepathic conversation. *My high priestess's mate's mother's sister lives there.*

General Zirkander's… aunt? Trip asked, working through all the relations.

Yes, I believe that is the human term. She makes lovely cinnamon dragon-horn cookies. Also, I have sixteen worshippers in the town. It is imperative that we protect them. I would have already gone, but the odds of surviving a battle with all my scales intact against six dragons are poor. Against three, I am certain I would be victorious.

Uh huh.

"Now, I'm certain you're not paying attention," Colonel Tranq said, walking up to frown at Trip, then out the open hangar door at the empty gray sky, then back at Trip.

The dragons hadn't yet come into sight.

"Trouble is coming." Trip looked down at the parachute and willed it to fold itself so it would deploy properly when needed. Given the size of the item, this wasn't a subtle display of magic. Usually, he wouldn't have shown off his powers in front of the others, but if the squadron was sent north to fight those dragons, someone might need that parachute soon.

Tranq stared as the folded parachute slid into its pack, seemingly by itself, and the straps tightened, buckling themselves. "That's…"

"Major Kaika calls it creepy," Trip said.

"Does she? That seems callous."

"I wouldn't mind it if someone called my powers delightful."

"Doesn't Ravenwood do that while you two are writhing like snakes under the sheets?" Leftie stood, also turning to face the open hangar door.

"We're nothing like snakes. We're like two meshed gears rotating together to create the perfect amount of torque."

"Seven gods, Trip, you don't say things like that to women, do you?"

"It's not any worse than the lewd things you say."

"Trust me, it is. And torque? That's rotation, isn't it?"

"Sometimes." Trip gave him a cryptic smile, even though his off-the-cuff simile perhaps hadn't been entirely accurate. What he'd *meant* to say was that they fit together perfectly to create something greater than the whole. Was it too late to amend the statement? Or maybe he shouldn't. Leftie was now wearing a speculative expression.

"Which dragon is that?" Tranq asked, ignoring them and touching the pistol at her belt, as if that would do anything against a dragon.

"Shulina Arya, and Bhrava Saruth is on the way too," Trip said, as Shulina Arya flew above the level of the bluff and into view, her golden scales gleaming with moisture. Rysha rode astride her back in her full-dress uniform. She had definitely been getting ready for the ceremony. But she had Dorfindral, her *chapaharii* sword, belted at her waist, so the dragon must have found her while she was still in her room. "To warn us of trouble in Portsnell," Trip added.

The small door in the side of the hangar opened, and General Zirkander jogged in. None of his usual affable mien showed on his face, so maybe Bhrava Saruth had already told him the news.

A thrum of anticipation coursed through Trip's veins as he realized a battle was imminent. He should have been nervous and filled with dread rather than excited, especially at the prospect of *six* dragons, but he couldn't help it. The part of him that craved taking to the sky like a deadly predator and pitting himself against foes hadn't seen the light of day for weeks.

As Shulina Arya dropped onto the runway outside the hangar and Bhrava Saruth flew into sight, Trip waved his hand to duplicate the magical folding of the rest of the parachutes. His fellow soldiers jumped back, some cursing, some merely issuing startled squawks. The last parachute tucked itself neatly into a bag as General Zirkander reached Tranq.

He had been eyeing the self-packing parachutes as he jogged up and said, "That's a little…"

"Trip prefers it when you call it delightful rather than creepy, sir," Leftie said.

"Uh, right."

"Maybe later, he'll offer to torque something of yours," Leftie added.

Zirkander frowned at him. Trip elbowed Leftie.

Even though Trip knew Zirkander much better than he had a couple of months ago, he still wouldn't presume to quip and make jokes with him. He was the commander in charge of all the flier squadrons throughout the country, after all.

"If I need anything torqued, I'm sure I can find an appropriate tool without Captain Trip's help," Zirkander said. "Report, Tranq."

"I don't know anything yet, sir. They just got here." Tranq pointed at the dragons.

Trip eased back a few steps, both so he wouldn't intrude on their conversation and because he felt embarrassed after Leftie's dumb joke. But Zirkander lifted his eyebrows and waved him forward again.

"You were just going to pack all the parachutes and flee, Captain?" he asked as Rysha dismounted and ran toward them.

"I didn't want to get in the way."

"Powerful sorcerers are allowed to be in the way. Or so Sardelle tells me."

Trip thought about pointing out that his powers, such as they were, weren't well-trained yet, so he hardly deserved special status, but the senior officers had turned their attention to the new arrivals.

Bhrava Saruth flew over Shulina Arya's head, his talons almost flicking her scales, then tightened his wings to his body and arrowed through the open hangar door. He landed in front of Tranq and Zirkander as Rysha reached them. She'd been in the middle of snapping up her salute and jumped at the dragon suddenly looming over her shoulders.

Trip nodded at her when their eyes caught, but he didn't run over and hug her like he wanted to. Her dress uniform was soaking, and her bun hung limply at the base of her cap, with a few strands of wet hair plastering her cheeks.

Human followers, Bhrava Saruth announced, *dragons are invading your northern town where sixteen of my worshippers live and create offerings for me.*

Shulina Arya, who perhaps hadn't been inside the hangar before, entered more carefully, walking instead of flying. It seemed strange that the wide doorway, perfectly adequate for a two-seater flier, was cramped for a dragon with wings fully outstretched.

"Portsnell?" Zirkander asked.

"You know the name of the city based on how many followers he has in it?" Tranq asked.

"It's my gift," Zirkander said, though he didn't crack a smile. "Are they attacking the city now?"

He glanced around the hangar, as if planning to order everyone to make ready, but everyone was doing exactly that, pilots running to their fliers and the ground crew topping off everybody's oil supply.

They are not attacking, Bhrava Saruth said. *Yet. They have ordered all humans to exit the town except for those who can provide food. They demand a tribute of one hundred cattle, sheep, and horses, or they will raze the city.*

"Sheep and cattle?" Zirkander asked. "Portsnell is a fishing and tourism town. It's a good fifty miles before you get to any farms or ranches."

Perhaps the citizens could offer baked goods as a delaying tactic, Bhrava Saruth suggested.

That would only delay a dragon like you, Shulina Arya said.

"Ahn." Zirkander waved the captain toward their group. "Are they all gold dragons, Bhrava Saruth?"

There is only one gold, in fact. But four are silvers, and they are still able combatants, though they lack fire. There is a bronze dragon also, a female. Bronze dragons are notoriously shifty. It is possible she is the ringleader. Dragons rarely work together unless they are mated. This is a disconcerting development.

Rysha grimaced, and Trip thought of the bronze dragon that had tricked them in Lagresh, making them believe he was an old friend of hers rather than a dragon after a journal. He wasn't trying to read Rysha's thoughts, but something flashed near the surface, and for an instant, he saw the bronze dragon in his copper-haired human form pushing her up against the wall.

He almost asked her right there what had happened, but Ahn reached them first, and Zirkander spoke again.

"Did Tolemek's new bullets arrive yet?"

"Yes, sir. There's a case in the office. Guaranteed to pierce dragon scales—if their magical shields are down."

"Trip has brought them down before." Zirkander's gaze shifted to Trip. "Can you do that again? I know you've had more practice with dragons since we last flew into battle together."

Trip had been looking at Rysha—*worrying* about Rysha—but he would have to ask her about that moment later. "I may be able to, sir. I have had some luck reading their thoughts even with their defenses up."

"I don't want you to read the dragons, Trip. I want you to utterly destroy them. Or at least lower their defenses so we can utterly destroy them."

"Yes, sir. I'm not sure about my odds of doing that against *six* dragons, but I'll do my best."

That answer didn't seem to reassure Zirkander, and Trip wished he could be more positive. He'd had practice battling the bronze dragon Xandyrothol, and had forced his defenses down once during that fight, but he still felt it was more a matter of rage than calculation that let him do that. Unfortunately, rage was hard to harness. He dearly preferred calculation, complete with equations featuring more constants than variables, to emotion.

"Grab Leftie, Duck, and some of the ground crew," Zirkander told Ahn. "Get bullets in every flier that's going out." He raised his voice toward the hangar. "Everyone in Wolf Squadron, mount up. As soon as our elite troops with the magic-hating swords show up, we're going to fight some dragons."

A whoop went through the hangar as the activity level increased further.

"Does that mean you're coming out with us, sir?" Tranq asked.

"You don't think I ran all the way up here in the rain just to pat your butts and send you off, do you?" Zirkander asked.

"I don't know, sir," Tranq said. "Some people here like your butt pats."

"Like who? I know it's not Blazer, and your husband would be alarmed to hear it's you."

Tranq snorted. "I mean the young men who idolize you."

She looked at Trip. It was probably only because he was the last "young man" standing there.

When Zirkander's eyebrows rose in his direction, Trip blurted, "I only like Rysha's butt pats."

Maybe that hadn't been the most professional thing to say…

Rysha made an odd face—or was that an embarrassed face? "Thanks, Trip."

Sorry, he whispered silently. He almost added more, but she turned toward Shulina Arya, and he sensed them communicating.

"Wolf Squadron is yours, sir," Tranq said, nodding, "as always."

"Thanks, Colonel." He thumped her on the shoulder and ran toward his flier to prepare it for battle.

Trip followed, veering toward his and trying not to worry about how to lower the defenses of six dragons.

CHAPTER 6

RAIN SPATTERED RYSHA'S SPECTACLES AND pounded her back as she flew north along the coast on Shulina Arya's back. When she'd imagined riding into battle with the dragon, she hadn't envisioned rain. But she couldn't complain when Trip and fifteen Wolf Squadron pilots flew behind them, their cockpits just as open to the elements.

This is marvelous! Shulina Arya announced into her mind. *Finally, we get to fly into another battle together. Against six foes this time, not just one puny half-defeated dragon. Can you not wait?*

Shulina Arya twirled in the air, and Rysha clutched at her smooth scales for purchase, even though she knew the dragon's magic would keep her from falling off. Her stomach gurgled, a queasy feeling emanating from it as the ocean's choppy waves appeared above her head, then under her feet, then over her head again.

Do you not mind the rain? Rysha asked while she groped for a polite way to ask the dragon not to twirl so enthusiastically.

I prefer warm rain, but it does not interfere with my flying. I see with my mind, not my eyes, so visibility is not a problem.

Visibility wasn't Rysha's problem. Well, technically it was, but not in the same sense as the dragon meant. She fumbled in her pocket for her handkerchief, which was as wet as the rest of the clothing, so she could wipe her spectacles.

You do not enjoy being wet? Shulina Arya asked, sounding surprised.

Not in my clothing. Fearing the dragon might make her uniform disappear, Rysha hastily added, *And not from the rain. A warm bath is pleasant.*

Ah, like flying into a temperate ocean. Yes, most appealing.

I was thinking of a tub full of bubbles.

I will use my magic to shelter you from the rain while we fly. Once we engage in battle, I may be too distracted to focus on small comforts.

Rysha was about to say that Shulina Arya didn't need to waste the energy doing that, but a wave of warmth coursed through her body, and her clothing instantly dried. Even the water droplets spattered on her lenses disappeared. She almost melted all over the dragon in gratitude.

What's going on over there? Trip spoke into her mind.

His flier had outdistanced the others and flew between Shulina Arya and Bhrava Saruth. A faint red glow came from his cockpit—Azarwrath? Maybe the soulblade was also eager to enter into battle.

Rysha couldn't tell if the man in Trip's back seat was as eager. Colonel Grady, armed with one of the *chapaharii* swords, a rifle, a truncheon, and two pistols, sat behind him. Rysha had seen the officer in the hangar and thought he looked like a walking armory, but Major Kaika and Colonel Therrik, the two other elite troops soldiers along on the mission, were similarly armed. Knowing Kaika, she had a bag full of explosives with her too. Rysha was surprised Grady—and his *chapaharii* blade—was flying with Trip instead of with a pilot that didn't have dragon blood.

We're discussing warmth, she replied.

Ah. I was checking on you, felt your discomfort, and was pondering what I could do about it. But then you abruptly seemed extremely comfortable.

Rysha smiled, delighted that he was keeping an eye on her and wanted her to be comfortable. *Flying dragon-back is a luxury experience, Trip.*

I'll stick to my flier.

Are you sure? Nobody is riding Bhrava Saruth. Perhaps if you brought him an offering, he'd allow you aboard.

My understanding is that Sardelle rides him into battle if anyone does. She is his high priestess, after all.

I'm glad Shulina Arya doesn't seem to believe humans should worship her.

Just feed her tarts?

That seems an equitable tradeoff for the assistance she's offering.

I won't disagree. You can't hear our chatter over the communication crystals, right?

No.

We're over here strategizing. Now I wish I'd thought to dig one out of an unused flier for you. Or maybe I could figure out how to make extras myself.

Is there something you wish Shulina Arya and me to do? Rysha realized he wasn't in command and that the question should be for General Zirkander. Though Trip was out in front, as if he led the squadron. Maybe he had been put in command.

No, Trip said dryly. *I've been sent ahead to take the brunt of the first wave of the attacks.*

Oh, you're cannon fodder.

Since I have Azarwrath to help shield the flier, it makes sense. And with Colonel Grady behind me with one of the chapaharii *blades, that should be further protection. Assuming he doesn't brain me. He seems affable in general, but I've caught him fondling his hilt and glowering at me a couple of times.*

You know the command words on the original blades if he—or it—gets uppity.

True. As to what you should do, I just asked the general. He asked if your dragon would accept commands from him or do what she wants.

Uh. Rysha remembered the shape-shifted Shulina Arya sailing around the castle corridors on that crate scooter, completely ignoring the guards' orders for her to stop.

A sensation of amusement came from Trip. *Got it. I'll let him know.*

The city is almost in sight, Shulina Arya announced, flapping her wings harder. *We shall lead the way into battle. With our combined powers, we're much deadlier than Bhrava Saruth.*

Rysha rested her hand on Dorfindral's hilt, but didn't point out that *her* power was borrowed.

The sword thrummed at her touch, as if to let her know that it was also eager to go into battle. Interestingly, the *chapaharii* blade had stopped sending such intense urges through her to attack whenever Shulina Arya showed up. It was as if the sword understood that this dragon was their ally. Rysha wished she could get the blade to accept that about Trip.

I assume from watching you pull into the lead that you're definitely not amenable to following orders, Trip observed.

I am, but you're right about Shulina Arya. She seems to have her own ideas about how this battle should go.

I'll tell the general that you'll work independently. Our plan is to lure the dragons away from the city so we can fight them over the ocean, where we won't likely hurt people or do damage to buildings or ships in the harbor. Right now, three of the six are holed up in Lord-governor Arrowwood's headquarters. The other three are at the outskirts of the city, standing guard, it looks like. A gold and two silvers. Those would be good ones for you, Shulina Arya, and Bhrava Saruth to go after. Hells, what now?

Trip? Rysha saw him craning his neck in his flier, looking toward the dark clouds over the sea. Lightning flashed out there, but she couldn't make out anything in the water or the sky.

I sense another dragon out there. I'm not sure if he's an ally to these six or not, but he's a big powerful gold.

We'll keep an eye on him—and these three—while your team goes in to get the others.

Good. Be careful.

Rysha could make out the spires and towers of the city ahead. Even though Portsnell's population was smaller than the capital's, it still housed more than fifty thousand people. Fifty thousand people who were in danger of having their city razed.

A gold dragon perched atop a lighthouse on the rocky shore south of the city sprang into the air. It flapped its wings and flew toward them. Rysha's stomach clenched with nerves, but she gritted her teeth and drew Dorfindral.

Trip attempted to wall off his mind as he piloted Colonel Grady and the other fliers toward Portsnell. His brain crawled with the discomfort of having so many dragons in close proximity to each other.

The gold and one of the two silvers had left the city and were flying toward the formation now as lightning flashed over the ocean. Trip sensed the second silver lingering near the harbor. The two other silvers and the female bronze were still in the government headquarters building. Their auras were diminished, and Trip suspected they were shape-shifted. So they would be less likely to be noticed? Or so they could fit into the building?

Trip had never seen dragons hide inside a building to avoid a battle. What did they think was in there that would be of value to them? Not livestock, surely.

"I want half the squadron to help our ally dragons with these three dragons outside," Zirkander said. "If Bhrava Saruth or Shulina Arya can knock down their barriers, you'll be able to hit them with your bullets. I'm concerned about the dragons in the headquarters, so every pilot with a sword wielder, head over there to check on them. They could have hostages. Even though the gold is with the ones outside, it's possible these dragons are diversions."

"Awfully large and shiny diversions, sir," Captain Duck drawled.

Since Trip was still leading, he took the initiative and dipped toward the shoreline and the city first. He had never been to Portsnell, but his senses told him where that government building was.

The gold and one silver dragon continued to fly high, toward Bhrava Saruth and Shulina Arya. The second silver remained in the harbor, lurking.

Though Trip worried about being separated from Rysha, he had to trust that she had the tools—and dragon—she needed to take care of herself.

As he flew along the harbor, Trip glimpsed the silver there on a cannery rooftop. It looked balefully at him but did not move from its perch. He didn't know why it wasn't leaping into the air to join the battle, but the fewer enemies for his allies, the better. So long as it wasn't harassing the locals.

A few fishing boats and sailing ships were tied up at the docks around the dragon, but not nearly as many as Trip would have expected given the stormy weather. Maybe crews of other boats had seen the dragons coming and had sailed out toward other ports, hoping they wouldn't be noticed.

A large crabbing boat floating in the harbor was the only vessel with people out on deck. They carried rifles and clubs, as if they meant to fight off any dragons that came for their ship. Trip lifted a hand toward them, admiring their spirit, even if it would do little good.

"My sword wants me to attack that silver dragon," Colonel Grady called over Trip's shoulder.

"Does it still want you to attack me, sir?"

"Yes, but I sense that the full-blooded dragon is more of a draw."

Trip was glad to hear that. "Don't worry about passing the silver. Three full-blooded dragons are waiting for us in that building. They're just less noticeable to the sword because they're shape-shifted into humans right now."

"Three dragons are better to battle than one."

"You elite troops officers have interesting notions, sir."

"We're a special bunch."

Trip passed the harbor and spotted the flat roof of the two-story government headquarters. The three dragons were still inside. He felt a twinge of disappointment, realizing he would have to land his flier and go in after them. An air battle would have been much more enjoyable.

"The enemy dragons have engaged our dragons," Zirkander stated.

Trip fought the urge to twist in his seat and look back into the rainy afternoon sky. His battle waited for him below.

Now that he was closer, he realized that only one of the dragons was in human form. The other two had turned into… bears? Trip sensed actual humans in the building, too, all down in the basement. Being held there as hostages? As Zirkander had guessed? If so, to what end? This behavior was not typical for dragons.

Trip veered for the rooftop, deciding to land there instead of in the yard below, though he doubted it would matter. It wasn't as if they could take the dragons by surprise.

"We sure going in is the best idea?" someone asked.

"No," Zirkander said, "but we can't blow bullets through the windows of one of our own buildings. If you can force them to come out, we'll happily shoot at them from the air."

"Are the pilots going in, too, sir?" someone else asked—Trip recognized Captain Pimples' voice. "Or just the sword-slinging combat studs? My flier's machine guns got all the good ammo. My pistol doesn't have any dragon-slaying bullets."

"Don't worry, Pimples," Zirkander said. "Nobody's making you lead the charge."

"That's our job," someone else growled, his voice not coming through as clearly since he was in a back seat.

Trip was fairly certain it was Therrik. After their brief meeting in the solarium, Trip wasn't that eager to go into battle with him, but he didn't think he would get a choice. Pimples might be permitted to stay outside in his flier, but as a sorcerer and soulblade-wielder, Trip would be expected to help infiltrate the dragon-filled building.

"Major Kaika wishes me to inform you all," Captain Duck drawled, as Trip's wheels touched down on the rooftop, "that she is indeed a sword-slinging combat expert but that she is not a stud. And I bet Angulus is right happy about that. Ow."

Trip snorted. He didn't have to see Kaika smack Duck on the back of the head to know she had.

Colonel Grady unbuckled his harness and jumped onto the rooftop as soon as Trip powered down the thrusters. Captain Ahn, who'd been flying Therrik, and Duck, who had Kaika, also landed on the rooftop.

"You want any more of us with you, Trip?" Zirkander asked.

"No, sir." While Trip wouldn't have minded as much help as he could get entering a building with three dragons waiting inside—three dragons up to something shifty—he agreed that the other pilots would be like Pimples, armed with modest personal weapons and not trained to fight dragons from anywhere but their cockpits. "But maybe there should be another pilot down here to keep an eye on the fliers while we go in."

"Will do. Sending Leftie down."

"What're you asking him for, Zirkander?" Therrik growled, leaning over Ahn's shoulder to speak into the crystal.

She narrowed her eyes at his hulking form, but as a captain, she couldn't object to a colonel looming over her.

"*I'm* the ranking officer on this incursion team," Therrik added.

"Lucky for the incursion team, and that's *General* Zirkander." Judging by Zirkander's tone, he'd corrected Therrik on the title numerous times over the years. "A rank you'll possibly be given one day if you become more personable and easy to work with."

"You were only given that rank because the king likes the way you twirl around dragons in the sky."

"We've had this discussion before. I twirl around the dragons *and* shoot them. Trip, I know you can speak telepathically with all of us, but take one of the communication crystals with you and keep in touch that way."

"Zirkander," Therrik growled. Intending to object that Trip was getting special orders again?

Trip silently obeyed the order, twisting the crystal to extract it from the dashboard.

"You're the commander, Therrik," Zirkander said, "but Trip is the dragon expert. Pay attention to him, so I don't have to tell Lilah a dragon ate you."

Trip expected another surly objection from Therrik and was careful to jump down several paces away from his flier. Duck and Kaika were already on the rooftop. But Therrik only grimaced and said, "I'm not getting eaten."

"I should hope not," Kaika said, her sword already drawn and ready. "You've got to be tougher and stringier than year-old dried meat left to harden in the sun."

Therrik hopped down to the rooftop and glared at her, but then his focus shifted to Trip. He drew his *chapaharii* blade, the original one, Kasandral. It flared a sickly green, and Trip grimaced, realizing he was going on a strike team with three people with swords that wanted to kill him. That might have been somewhat acceptable if Rysha had been one of those people, but she was two miles away, already engaged in her own battle.

Trip gazed toward the southern end of the city where the dragons fought over the breaking waves. He couldn't see Rysha, but he could sense her, sense the dragons twisting and writhing in the sky, clawing at each other and throwing power and fire. Shulina Arya was battling the gold while Bhrava Saruth stalked the silver. She tried to come in and turn, giving Rysha opportunities to strike with her *chapaharii* blade.

"You ready, Dragon Boy?" Therrik pointed his sword at Trip, and it flared a more intense green. He frowned at it, muttered something under his breath—the control words?—and jerked it toward a door. The only door on the rooftop. It led into a stairwell offering access down into the building. "That our best option?"

Telryn, Azarwrath said. *Do not allow this man to speak to you in an insulting manner.*

He's my superior officer. That means he can insult me whenever he wants.
"They'll know we're coming, sir," Trip said aloud. "May as well be direct."

This is not how mages were treated in the Cofah army in my time. No matter what their rank, they were respected by mundane officers. Only a mage more powerful than you and higher ranking than you would have the right to treat you poorly, but quality officers did not lower themselves by doing so.

I'll be sure to mention that at the next meeting with the king that I'm invited to.

Do so. It's clear this man has no idea that you could fry the hair off his balls or stop his heart with your mind if you wished.

I'm not sure which of those notions is more horrifying.

"I'd rather have a plan about how we're *not* going to be direct," Therrik said. "Can't you wriggle your fingers and make it so they don't see us?"

"Not with dragons. I can make it so the humans inside don't see us, if you think that would help."

"You're not going to be as mouthy as Zirkander, are you?" Therrik squinted at him. "You remind me of him."

"I... don't think so." Normally, Trip would be delighted to be compared to the general, but it clearly wasn't a compliment coming from Therrik.

"I suggest we go, sir." Captain Ahn wore a Mark 500 sniper rifle on a strap—the weapon was almost as tall as she was—and cradled it in her arms. "Time may be of the essence."

"It always is," Duck said.

"I'll lead," Therrik said. "Ahn, you and your rifle take up the rear. Keep your buddy back there with you and out of trouble. Seven gods, pilot, is that little pellet gun all you brought?"

"It's a standard issue AB-7, sir," Duck said.

"Dragons aren't standard issue. Ahn, keep him alive and watch our backs. Grady, Kaika, you come in the middle. Watch my ass."

"We have Lilah's permission to do that, sir?" Kaika asked.

Therrik growled.

"Just checking," Kaika said.

"Was that a yes or a no?" Grady whispered to her. Trip assumed Therrik had more years in rank than he did, since Grady hadn't objected to Therrik being in charge.

"I believe what he said was that his wife requests we not let a dragon sink fangs into his ass," Kaika said.

"That much in one growl? Impressive."

"Dragon Boy, you're with me." Therrik looked at Trip, jerked his head toward the door, and started walking. "Let me know when we're getting close to one." His hand flexed on Kasandral's hilt.

Telryn, Azarwrath said, *if you do not correct him, I will.*

You can't do anything to him as long as he's carrying one of those swords.

We shall see about that. If nothing else, I can flash nightmarish images into his mind.

I doubt anything gives that man nightmares. Trip followed Therrik.

Apparently not quickly enough. Therrik gripped the latch on the door, saw that Trip hadn't caught up yet, and said, "What's the hold up?"

"My sword would prefer it if you call me by rank or name, sir. Not Dragon Boy."

"Yeah? Your sword can talk to my sword." Therrik held Kasandral aloft and looked down at Azarwrath's scabbard.

To that ignorant heap of ore? Please.

"Are you really married, sir?" Trip didn't bother to hide the puzzlement in his tone.

"He is," Kaika said, stopping behind them. "To General Zirkander's cousin. I understand family gatherings are full of warmth, cheer, and booze."

"A *lot* of booze," Therrik said.

The door was locked. Before Trip could use his power to thwart the mechanism, Therrik heaved and ripped the door open, metal squealing.

"Subtle, sir," Kaika said.

Therrik must have had enough banter. He strode into a dim hallway, the pale glow of his sword washing the beige walls and wood office doors.

The *chapaharii* blades were all glowing strongly. They would lead their wielders to the dragons without Trip's help, but he would do his best to advise.

"All three of them have moved down to the basement floor, near… I read about thirty people down there with them."

"Hostages?" Therrik asked, turning down the first stairwell they reached.

Trip paused, and Kaika and Grady almost bumped into him.

"I'm not sure," Trip said. "Maybe just prisoners that are being guarded because…" He didn't know.

GOLD DRAGON

As he followed Therrik down the stairs, he reached out with his mind, not trying to sense the dragons this time, but trying to connect to the humans. It was hard to single them out for contact with the dragons so close. Even though their auras weren't as pronounced as when they were in their normal forms, they radiated power that drowned out the essences of the mundane creatures—and people—around them.

Hello? Trip asked, trying someone in the center of the group. They were all in one basement room lined with shelves and filing cabinets.

The person he sought to contact, a man, mentally recoiled and did not answer. He clawed at the air in front of him as if he could drive Trip's presence away.

Doubting he had time to convince him that he was a friend, Trip shifted to one of the other people in the room, an older woman with a hint of dragon blood. Maybe she would more easily accept telepathic contact.

Hello, I'm Captain Trip with Wolf Squadron, he said, figuring he should make it clear he wasn't a dragon.

The recipient paused, and Trip sensed alarm and wariness.

Are the dragons holding you hostage? We're trying to reach you.

Yes. I am Lady Skymoor, the governor's wife. My husband and many prominent citizens are here too. And an odd number of bakers. They want to trade us for the region. They—

Do you think we cannot intercept your communication? a voice boomed into Trip's head. *That we do not know a puny little mage is accompanying those sneaking into our new lair? You cannot harm us. You must come and take our demands to your king. Send forth your greatest leader.*

"Dragon Boy." Therrik snapped his fingers in front of Trip's face. "I said which way."

"I do think you should find a more flattering name for him, Therrik," Colonel Grady said, gripping Trip's shoulder from behind. "Even though my sword here believes I should skewer him."

"He hasn't done anything yet to prove he deserves flattery. Falling off a pot and running into me doesn't count."

"At the least, choose something that's more easily rhymed than boy. I'm scribbling down notes, should I need to immortalize our mission today in a ballad. There *are* options—soy, bok choy, corduroy—but *man* would make everything much simpler.

Therrik growled at him. "You're even less deserving of flattery, so far, Grady."

"That's hardly fair. We haven't yet done anything."

"A dragon is speaking to me," Trip said. "They know exactly where we are and want us to send our greatest leader forward to negotiate. They're prepared to free the hostages if we give them this region."

"*Region?*"

"The city isn't enough?" Grady asked. "The greed of dragons knows no bounds."

Tell your leader to tell your king. We have decided that our earlier demands were too modest. If we do not have a treaty granting this region to our band of dragons by morning, we shall slay these humans and destroy the city.

If you're trying to take over the city, why would you destroy it? Trip asked.

Human dwellings mean nothing to us. It is the land and the sea and all the life teeming upon and within it that will be ours. You humans stole the world from us. You owe us this. The voice grew so booming in Trip's mind that he had to grip the wall for support. *Tell your leader.*

Trip reached out to General Zirkander, not because the dragon told him so—at least he hoped he wasn't being so easily influenced—but because Zirkander needed this information.

Sir?

What is it, Captain? Zirkander promptly responded, though Trip sensed him piloting his flier upside down as he arrowed toward a silver dragon, leading the squadron against the creature during a moment when Bhrava Saruth and Shulina Arya weren't close enough to be in danger of being hit.

I have a message, Trip told him and relayed it.

I see.

Do we keep going? Try to defeat them?

Yes. Angulus isn't giving up any of the country to blackmailing dragons.

Understood, sir.

Trip had been doing his best to keep his telepathic communication pinpoint so it wouldn't be easily overheard by the dragons, but there was no way to shield Zirkander's thoughts, as far as he knew, and a deep growl sounded in his mind, like that of some irritated predator.

At the rear of their group, Captain Ahn abruptly turned, facing backward and pointing her rifle toward the stairs they'd come down.

"I heard something," she said quietly.

"I don't sense anyone back there," Trip said, double-checking as he spoke.

"Something is there. I—"

A faint clatter came from the level above them. Or maybe the roof? Imagining the dragons using their power to annihilate the fliers, Trip hurried to check, already half-constructing a barrier that he could wrap around them. But he detected Leftie sitting in his cockpit with his rifle and his lucky ball, twirling it on its chain as he watched the aerial battle with the dragons and felt disgruntled that he hadn't been included—the rest of the fliers had gone to join in. He didn't appear worried by any immediate threat to the rooftop.

Another clatter sounded in their passage, followed by a scraping from the ceiling—or perhaps the floor above—directly overhead.

The shadows stirred in the hallway behind them, and Ahn, already with her rifle butt pressed into the hollow of her shoulder, shifted her aim. But she didn't fire. As far as Trip could tell, there was nothing to fire *at* but shadows.

I believe the dragons may be attempting to scare you, Azarwrath said.

"Why would they bother with little tricks?" Therrik asked, and Trip realized the soulblade had spoken to everyone in the group. "Every dragon I've met before just tried to kill me."

"Imagine," Kaika murmured.

"I don't know, but the general said to take care of them. They're down one more level from here." Trip pointed to a dark stairwell at the end of the hallway. The door leading to it stood open, and a faint moan emanated from it.

An intense feeling of dread came over Trip, along with the urge to flee. He sensed the power behind it, the manipulation, and he also sensed the being, the dragon, responsible for it. A silver in the form of a bear. It had left the room with the prisoners and waited at the bottom of the stairs with one of its allies, a silver also in bear form. Only the bronze remained back with the humans, but Trip didn't see another way down into the basement.

"Shit." Duck whirled and stepped toward the exit.

Kaika caught his arm. "Stay where you are."

"But death is coming for us." Duck's eyes were wide with terror.

Captain Ahn's face had grown pale, and her gaze darted to either end of the hallway, but she didn't look like she meant to bolt.

"Actually, it's a bear." Trip noted the *chapaharii* wielders were less affected than the pilots, but they also appeared to have felt the gust of fear. "Two of them."

"Kaika, Grady, get my back." Therrik strode for the stairs with Kasandral held aloft.

The other two sword wielders pushed past Trip, leaving him with Duck and Ahn, neither of whom looked to be in a hurry to go down those stairs. Though he didn't know if it would work, Trip tried to bolster them with courage and to extend his mental defenses around them—hadn't one of the soulblades once said he could learn to do that?—so they wouldn't be affected by the intangible waves of fear rolling up the stairs.

He also formed a barrier around them because he sensed the dragons would attack soon. The message had been delivered. They would want to get rid of the threat in the headquarters building. He only wished he could protect the sword wielders with his power, too, that the magic-hating blades would allow it.

As Therrik stepped over to the landing at the top, a snarl floated up the stairwell. Then the floor quaked, stone cracked, and metal squealed. Mortar crumbled, and tiles snapped.

Azarwrath reacted before Trip, and he suddenly found himself floating in the air, hovering inches above the floor. A floor that fell away underneath him as snaps and groans erupted all around them. Stone and wood rained down from above, pelting his barrier. He fed power into it, strengthening it as he looked back, fearing Ahn and Duck would have fallen.

But they also floated, looking angry and alarmed now rather than simply afraid.

A shout of pain came from the stairwell. Trip turned back as the entrance to it collapsed, and rubble fell from above, burying the three elite troops—and the *chapaharii* blades.

CHAPTER 7

YOU THINK TO CHALLENGE ME, puny humans? the gold dragon snarled. *This land belonged to us long before your people left their rude mountain caves, and it will be ours again.*

Wind rushed past Rysha's face as Shulina Arya dove and twisted, turning her back toward her foe so Rysha could reach the gold dragon with Dorfindral. The blade glowed fiercely as rain spattered it. Rysha stood atop Shulina Arya's back, magic holding her in position, and she lunged, slashing with the blade. It flared even brighter as it bit into scale and flesh.

A screech of pain sounded in her mind, and the dragon contorted in the air, its tail whipping straight toward her.

Not sure if Shulina Arya's defenses would protect her when she carried Dorfindral, Rysha dropped down, flattening to her belly. The thick gold tail whipped past over her head.

Die, vile enemy! Shulina Arya cried, and some invisible power slammed into their foe, sending the other dragon hurling talons over head and tail.

As soon as the gold tumbled away, machine gun fire opened up. General Zirkander and four of the Wolf Squadron pilots strafed the dragon, flying over it and raining bullets.

Rysha watched, worried the bullets would bounce off a magical barrier—that was what had happened earlier. But between her attack and Shulina Arya's, the dragon's defenses were down. The bullets bit into its scales, and more pained screeches sounded in Rysha's mind.

In everyone's minds, she realized, as the wings wobbled on some of the fliers, the pilots wincing inside their cockpits.

Zirkander finished his run and swooped into a loop to come back for another one. If the mental screams bothered him, he didn't show it.

Rysha was glad for the help, but with so many fliers up here in the sky with them, who was handling the three dragons in the city? Surely, not just Trip.

Our enemy's strength is flagging, Shulina Arya announced when the gold didn't turn back to engage them again, as it had numerous times before. *When we drive it away, we will help Bhrava Saruth, since it is clear he is challenged without a rider on his back.*

Bhrava Saruth flew over the harbor, hurling flames at two silver dragons that danced and dove away, weaving between the tall masts of the sailing ships, attempting to elude pursuit rather than engage. Several more fliers were over there, taking shots when they could, but they were understandably hesitant to rain bullets down on the docks. There had to be people hiding in some of those ships.

Bhrava Saruth, thankfully, wasn't wanton in his chase and avoided using his power and fire right around the sea vessels and the docks. That was the only reason, as far as Rysha could tell, that he hadn't defeated his opponents yet. Unlike the silver dragons, he didn't wish to damage property.

Rysha suspected those dragons were buying time rather than outright trying to defeat Bhrava Saruth, and that worried her. What was this cohort of dragons up to?

Bhrava Saruth doesn't seem to be injured, Rysha thought, trusting Shulina Arya to read her thoughts. *Maybe it would be better to finish this one off and then help Trip and the others. I'm concerned the dragons have set a trap down in that headquarters building.*

Hm, yes, that is possible. Not all bronze dragons are thinkers, but many are like my parents. They would definitely use guile rather than facing gold dragons, and if this one has convinced a gold and four silvers to work with her, she must be well-spoken and clever. She has convinced others to come out and face your dragon-hating sword.

I'm not the only one here with a chapaharii *blade. I think Kaika and Therrik went in with Trip. What if the dragons anticipated that and that is why they set a trap? To capture the weapons so we would have fewer resources that are effective against them?* Rysha grimaced, worrying anew about Trip and the others, as Shulina Arya took her in the opposite direction, chasing the wounded gold along the cliffs to the south of the city.

I will interrogate this one as you rain a thousand cuts on him, Storyteller!

With Shulina Arya diving toward the gold, the dragon having already been wounded with at least a dozen cuts, Rysha didn't have time to form an answer. Shulina Arya caught up with their foe, hurling fire at the gold's broad head.

Though their enemy was injured, it still raised a concave barrier, deflecting the flames.

In a maneuver Rysha was growing accustomed to and ready for, Shulina Arya banked at the last second, turning her back toward the dragon—and the barrier. Rysha leaped to her feet again so she could extend her reach, then swept Dorfindral overhead.

Though the barrier was invisible, Rysha felt it pop, a jolt of energy running up her arm. She attempted to slash again, now that the dragon's defenses were down, but she couldn't reach its scales.

Their foe roared, twisting in the air, and retaliated. A shower of fire sprayed from its maw. Rysha recoiled instinctively and crouched low on Shulina Arya's back.

Some of the flames made it to her scales before she got her own barrier up, and Rysha felt their heat as the brilliant light stung her eyes. Even though the fire was warm and far too close for comfort, Dorfindral flared an intense green, and the flames did not burn her. The sword's hilt felt cool in her hand.

The fire halted abruptly as Shulina Arya got her own barrier up and angled so Rysha was protected, even though her blade would not allow a bubble of magic to fully encapsulate her.

Forgive my slowness, Storyteller, Shulina Arya said as she wheeled to get away from the gold—or to ready herself for another attack. *I was attempting to drill into his mind and extract the information you need.*

It's fine, Rysha thought. *The sword protected me.*

It is good that those foul dragon-loathing blades have a use. I may be able to forgive that one for constantly telling you to slay me. Do not think I do not witness the influence it tries to use on you. Foul magic. But good for poking enemy dragons with.

Very true. Rysha wanted to ask if Shulina Arya had learned anything, but their enemy must have thought it had gained an advantage, for it flapped its powerful wings and arrowed after them. Or maybe Shulina Arya had managed to extract some information and it was desperate to keep her from sharing it?

The dragon threw all its speed into a chase. Rysha believed Shulina Arya had meant to turn back into the battle—she didn't seem to have the word *retreat* in her vocabulary—but she let out an indignant snarl as the other dragon lunged close, jaws snapping.

He thinks to bite me in the butt? Shulina Arya cried, whirling to snap back. *This is not the mating season, and I am not in heat.*

She hurled a gout of fire right into the dragon's eyes.

Even on her back, Rysha felt the heat from her inferno, and she had to squint against the light. Despite the roiling orange flames, she saw that the other dragon had its defenses back up, and the stream of fire parted and flowed around him.

Since Shulina Arya seemed too irritated to do their traditional maneuver—the two dragons were hovering in midair, facing each other, she hurling flames and the other perhaps throwing a mental attack back—Rysha adopted a less traditional one. She stood and ran up Shulina Arya's neck so she could see over the top of her head, then hurled Dorfindral point-first like a spear.

Though she feared the sword would end up in the ocean far below, she knew from past experience that she and Shulina Arya could retrieve it from the bottom if necessary. And she had the satisfaction of seeing that barrier disappear. The flames spewing toward it struck the gold dragon full in the face.

It roared as its scales charred black, then wheeled and spun away. But Shulina Arya did the aerial equivalent of a lunge, coming in close and snapping her jaws down on her foe's long neck. Her sword-like fangs bit deep, the gold's scales crunching loudly under the assault, and she shook her head like a dog finishing off a rat.

Rysha grimaced as louder crunches sounded. Bone breaking?

Shulina Arya's body shook beneath her in response to the violent movements she was making, and Rysha dropped astride her, holding on in case the dragon forgot about using magic to keep her there.

But Shulina Arya soon let go, startling Rysha with how abruptly she released the dragon, and dove.

They arrowed toward the ocean far below, wind whistling in Rysha's ears. She realized they weren't arrowing toward the ocean but toward her sword. It must have been hung up on the dragon for a few seconds, because gravity hadn't yet swept it below the surface of the water.

Shulina Arya streaked downward at hundreds of miles an hour, her wings flattened to her sides, her tail stretched out like a spear behind her. Rysha worried about her ability to snatch the blade out of the middle of its thousand-foot fall without cutting her own hand off.

Telling herself that it had likely already reached terminal velocity and the rate of its fall would be a constant did *not* help. All it did was make her wonder how the dragon was falling faster than that—she imagined some magical version of a flier's propeller adding thrust from behind Shulina Arya. Then she told herself this wasn't the time for mathematical speculations.

Shulina Arya turned so that her back would be toward the sword as they caught up with it. Doing her best to ignore the blue water below them, water growing closer and closer by the second, Rysha reached out. With the wind slipping behind her spectacles and tearing her eyes, she could barely see.

"One... two... three." She snatched outward, wrapping her fingers around the sword.

Thank the gods, she caught it by the hilt and not the blade.

An instant after her fingers wrapped around it, Shulina Arya pulled up. Even with her magic holding Rysha on her back, Rysha felt the tug of the force pulling at her, and she marveled that she wasn't hurled from the dragon's back—or torn into dozens of pieces. She also marveled that she managed to keep hold of Dorfindral's hilt. It hummed in her hand, and she imagined she felt reproach in that hum.

A giant splat sounded, water droplets spraying the side of Rysha's face. The other gold dragon had struck down into the ocean, less than a dozen feet away. It wasn't moving. Its wings and tail splayed outward, and it started to sink.

Shulina Arya issued the mental equivalent of an indignant—or smug?—sniff. *That dragon will not nip at my hindquarters again.*

I'm glad, Rysha thought as they flew upward again, turning north toward the city. *Did you learn anything from questioning him?*

Yes. It is as you feared. The dragons here are enacting two plans. First, they wish to force your king to sign a document giving them part of your country. They believe that humans put much worth in such papers and will abide by them. Second, they wish to rid your country of all the deplorable dragon-slaying swords it has recently acquired.

Rysha didn't point out that one of those swords had just helped Shulina Arya defeat another gold dragon. She was too worried about the rest of the statement.

Some of our people are heading in to deal with those other dragons right now, Rysha said.

Yes, they are walking into a trap.

We need to go help.

I am flying that way, Storyteller, but there is another threat which we must be concerned with.

The silver dragons Bhrava Saruth and the pilots are fighting? Rysha leaned out to peer past Shulina Arya's head as they flew toward the city and its harbor. She saw some of the fliers they had outpaced when they'd been chasing after the gold, but she couldn't yet see the other dragons.

No, the pilots are harrying one silver, and Bhrava Saruth is dunking another one in the water repeatedly and telling him to yield, that his life is empty and meaningless because he does not know the joy of being loved and worshipped. He is a very *quirky dragon.*

I've noticed.

My parents have forbidden him to court me.

Er, has he asked them?

Not in such a polite and honorable way. He suggested to Wyleenesh that there would be room for a carving of me in his temple and that we might rule over his human worshippers together.

Dozens of questions jumped into Rysha's mind, but she forced them down. She had more pressing concerns right now than whether or not that was how dragons attempted to establish relationships.

If not the silver dragons, what's the new threat?

Remember how your mate and I sensed another dragon far out to sea?

Yes.

He is a very old and powerful dragon, a contemporary of your mate's sire. Bhrava Saruth recognized him and said his name is Drysaleskar and that he was one of the elders back when dragons ruled this world before.

Rysha thought about pointing out that dragons hadn't technically ruled the world, at least not from the human point of view, but that wasn't important. *Please don't tell me he's coming this way.*

He is.

You better tell Trip. Do you think we can beat this new dragon in battle?

Rysha had mostly heard youthful bravado from Shulina Arya so far, so she didn't expect the answer she got.

No.

Trip and Azarwrath, still levitating over the empty space where the floor had been, used their power to push aside the rubble that had buried the entrance to the stairwell. Trip worked as quickly as he could, knowing that brick and timbers filled most of the space inside, with Grady, Kaika, and Therrik buried underneath.

He could still sense their auras and knew they lived, but he also sensed their fear and their pain. Worse, he sensed the two bear-shaped dragons at the bottom of the stairs, clambering over the top of the rubble, trying to reach the trapped officers.

A muffled ursine roar emanated from the stairwell.

We shall bury those foul blades forever, came a telepathic cry from one of the shape-shifted dragons.

"Hurry, Trip," Ahn whispered, right behind him.

Worried and irritated with the slowness of his progress, Trip wrestled with the rubble. He had cleared the doorway on their side, but large blocks were wedged inside and he couldn't get them out. In a fit of frustration, he growled and envisioned the roof being torn open and tons of rubble flying up and out.

Duck cursed, and Ahn sucked in a startled breath as his vision came true. Rubble flew upward and disappeared through a gaping hole in the roof. Rain spattered down through the opening.

Without stopping to marvel at his work, Trip scrambled onto the warped landing, heavy debris still scattered on it and more piled on the stairs leading down—the stairs leading to the two silver bears.

One was already halfway up, a paw raised as it stood over a bloody arm sticking out of the rubble. The creature paused and looked at Trip.

Azarwrath hurled lightning at it, but the bear attacked them at the same time. A pulse of mental power slammed into Trip so hard he stumbled back, shoulder blades hammering into the wall. Daggers seemed to plunge into his brain, and he gasped at the pain.

Azarwrath stopped attacking and threw a shield around Trip. It did nothing to stop the mental attack, but an instant later, a wave of palpable power rolled up the stairs at him, and though the soulblade's barrier shuddered, it held. The rock in the wall behind Trip was pulverized, and dust flooded the air.

He glimpsed Ahn in the doorway, her rifle ready, trying to get past his barrier so she could join the battle. Still fighting the mental attack from the first bear—it was the second creature that had hurled the physical attack—Trip waved for her to stay back. She and that rifle wouldn't be of any use against the dragons.

For that matter, *he* couldn't do anything against two dragons, either. He had to free the sword wielders.

Distract them, he told Azarwrath, snarling and attempting to wall off his mind as that bear stared at him, silver reptilian eyes out of place in its ursine face.

I must keep the barrier up to protect you.

As Azarwrath spoke, the bear farther down the stairs sent another blast that hammered his barrier. More rock crumbled behind Trip, and more snaps and groans came from within the building.

The closer bear, seeming to believe Trip wasn't a threat, went back to attacking the man—Therrik?—buried in the rubble.

Just attack them for a second, Trip thought. *I'm going to try something.*

Trip sensed Azarwrath's reluctance, but the barrier dropped and the soulblade hurled waves of his own power at the bears.

Trip gathered his mental energy and focused on the rubble again. As he'd done before, he willed a blast of air to rush under the rocks and force them up into the air, through the hole in the roof and out. To his surprise, the closest bear flew up along with the rubble.

With the rocks and beams gone, Kaika, Therrik, and Grady lay exposed on the stairs, battered and bloody. Therrik lifted his head and looked straight at Trip, but only for a second. He mustered some energy and sprang to his feet, wobbled, then found his balance. With the *chapaharii* sword still in his grip, he leaped down the stairs toward the bear at the bottom.

It hurled an attack at him, one Trip hurried to raise a barrier to defend against. The gust of power breezed past Therrik, Grady, and Kaika to batter at Trip's defenses. He hardly cared. Therrik reached the bear and thrust his sword at it.

The silver-furred creature reared up and slashed with its claws, but not before the *chapaharii* blade popped its defensive barrier and sank into flesh.

Kaika and Grady clambered to their feet, both shaken and wounded—Grady gripped his ribs with one hand and drew in wheezing breaths. They had both retained their blades, however, and started down the stairs, looking for openings to get around Therrik's broad back to help with the fight.

Gunshots came from the rooftop. Trip sensed Leftie firing at the second bear. It had landed unharmed amid the rubble. It raced back to the opening in the rooftop, ignoring the bullets bouncing off its shielding.

The bear appeared on the ragged ledge and roared as Kaika and Grady looked up, raising their swords. It jumped down, straight toward them.

Trip wanted to knock the bear aside with a gust of power, but feared its shields would protect it. Instead, he launched an attack at its mind, forming a mental dagger to stab into its brain. It twisted in the air, batting its paws at its head. Kaika and Grady jumped to either side as it came down on the stairs, then leaped back in, plunging their swords into its flanks.

The bear roared and shifted in front of their eyes, trying to turn back into a dragon. Trip read its thoughts, its plans to fly away.

He gritted his teeth and focused on the creature's mind, redoubling his attack and hoping to buy the others time to stab it repeatedly with those blades. And they did. They hewed at the creature like loggers racing to cut down the most trees in a competition. The *chapaharii* swords sank in again and again, and their foe couldn't complete shifting to dragon form. Half roaring, half screeching, the creature lashed out weakly at them.

Kaika leaped onto its misshapen back, drew her sword up like a spear, and plunged it into the dragon's head. The fight left it, and its body slumped down motionless on the stairs.

Relieved, Trip leaned a hand against the wall for support, his legs weak after the mental effort he had expended. But he feared he couldn't relax for long. Scratches and grunts came from the bottom of the stairs as Therrik continued to battle the other dragon, still in bear form, by himself.

Kaika and Grady jumped off the dead silver and raced down to help. The bear's shields were down, and it was battling Therrik without magic, muscle and claw versus muscle and sword.

Trip summoned his dwindling strength to blast the creature with a mental attack. The bear had strong defenses around its mind, and Trip didn't think he'd done much, but it jerked its head back and snarled, distracted if nothing else. That gave Therrik a few seconds to leap forward and sink his sword into its chest.

"Back off," Therrik growled at his fellow officers. "This one's mine."

He yanked his sword out and plunged it in again and again. Kaika and Grady stepped back and lowered their blades.

Trip leaned his shoulder against the wall and stretched out with his senses, worried about what the bronze might be doing to her human captives while this battle went on. But he didn't detect the other dragon, not in human form or any other. The people remained where they had been earlier, all still alive, thank the gods.

Did you see where the bronze went? Trip asked Azarwrath.

She fled a couple of minutes ago.

Because she knew we would win?

Because that elder gold dragon you sensed earlier started flying this way. Azarwrath did the soulblade equivalent of pointing a finger toward the sea.

Trip sensed Bhrava Saruth, along with Zirkander, Tranq, and many of the other pilots, wearing down a pair of silver dragons fighting just south of the harbor. Shulina Arya and Rysha were flying toward the headquarters building; they were less than a minute away. Lastly, he spotted the old powerful gold that had been far out to sea when the team first arrived. It was in the harbor, attacking that crabbing ship.

Rysha! Trip reached out to her.

Are you all right? she replied immediately. *We thought you were going into a trap.*

We were, but we've taken care of it. Someone needs to stop that new gold.

Rysha hesitated. *Shulina Arya says we can't, not alone. Can you and the other blade wielders help?*

Trip looked down the stairwell to make sure the silvers were indeed dead. Kaika, Grady, and Therrik stood near the fallen foes, all hunched over, gripping their ribs or leaning on their swords and panting. After being buried under all that rock, they were covered with blood and bruises and would need a healer's attention, but none of them looked to be in danger of dying or needing immediate help.

I can help. Trip wished he could shape-shift and fly up there to join her.

"The bronze is gone," he told the team down below. "Get the people out of the basement. I'm going to help with the battle at the harbor."

Shulina Arya sailed past the gaping opening he had torn in the roof and landed near Leftie and the fliers.

Therrik looked up at Trip, and Trip expected him to object to *Dragon Boy* giving orders. But all he did was wave and say, "Go get them. We'll join as soon as we can." His dark eyebrows twitched. "Dragon Man."

Grady smiled slightly.

Trip sprang upward, using a gust of wind to propel him to the roof. He ran toward his flier—Leftie stood in the cockpit of his, the rifle he'd fired at the silver dragon still in hand.

Wait, Shulina Arya said from the edge of the rooftop. *He has stolen all of the crabs in the hold, and now he is leaving.*

Trip spotted the massive gold dragon flying up from the harbor, heading out to sea. He thought Bhrava Saruth and the others might give chase, but he sensed them far down the coast now. The two silver dragons had fled, and he and the pilots were pursuing them.

As Trip reached his flier, he realized there was little point in jumping into the cockpit. The elder dragon had picked up speed as it flew out to sea, and already, it disappeared over the horizon.

He didn't actually kill anyone, Azarwrath observed, drawing Trip's attention to two of the crabbing crew swimming toward the docks. Other men stared at their destroyed hold, the inside empty save for a few forlorn crabs left behind.

Just damaged their ship and stole their cargo?

Many dragons have done far worse. Also, his presence seems to be what caused the bronze and those silvers to flee.

Are you sure they weren't afraid of Shulina Arya's approach?

They all grew noticeably agitated at the elder's arrival. The bronze broke a hole in a wall, shape-shifted, and flew out, abandoning her plans.

You are the one who can more easily read dragons' thoughts, but I believe she would have attempted to use the hostages to negotiate with us.

Hm. Trip gazed thoughtfully out to sea.

"Trip?" Rysha dismounted and ran over to him. "Are you all right?"

"Yes. Are you?" He lifted an arm and looked her up and down. He needed to go heal the others, but he would gladly take a moment to help her if she needed it. Or simply to hug her.

"Yes." She wrapped her arms around him. "We think they were trying to get the swords."

"Or at least ensure *we* couldn't get to them anymore, yes."

"I think they'll try again."

He sighed and rested his cheek against her hair. "That does seem likely." He gazed off toward the horizon again. What had that elder dragon's name been? Drysaleskar?

Trip stretched out his senses and located Zirkander and the others. They had given up on chasing the silvers and were heading back to the city.

Sir? Trip telepathically contacted Zirkander. *I have an idea.*

CHAPTER 8

THREE MORNINGS AFTER THE BATTLE, Rysha waited outside the army's stables for Trip. While the higher-ups debated what to do with the dragon problem, lowly lieutenants and captains had a day off. Trip had invited her to come out to see his little siblings with him, and she was glad to do so, though she wouldn't have minded spending the day in her barracks room with him. They had *finally* been able to enjoy an uninterrupted night together and had found that her bed, though not spacious, was indeed more comfortable than a cave floor. Albeit somewhat noisier than a cave floor, with the old wood creaking and groaning under the admittedly robust use.

Rysha grinned, remembering Trip pausing to peer at the frame underneath the mattress and make suggestions regarding the support brackets and a cracked board. Naturally, she had tugged him back into her arms and informed him that repairs could wait. It hadn't been hard to divert his attention back to her, but she had woken at dawn to find him using his magic to improve the bed. He hadn't yet added cup holders, but it was just a matter of time.

"Good morning," Trip said, strolling out of the stable leading a mare. He must have caught her smiling—or grinning in remembrance—for he offered a return smile.

"Good morning."

"Shall I saddle you a mount or do you want to ride together? It's not far to Sardelle and General Zirkander's house, so I'm sure the mare could carry two." He wiggled his fingers toward her waist. "Holding would be involved."

"Sedate holding or vigorous holding?"

"Well, the mare might object to the latter."

"You think so? She seems placid."

Greetings, Storyteller! Shulina Arya announced into Rysha's mind from wherever she was this morning. *You're not going to ride somewhere on that inferior beast, are you?*

We're going out to visit Sardelle and the babies. Do you wish to come?

Naturally. It is most enjoyable for me to spend time among magical beings. Also, I have not had any tarts in almost three days.

That is an eternity.

It is. I was especially depleted after the battle and would have relished sweets. There should have been tarts waiting for us when we returned.

I'll suggest it to my superior officers.

I've already informed your king of this necessity.

Rysha grimaced, hoping the dragon hadn't been wheeling around the castle on a scooter as she'd made the request.

Trip, gazing skyward, didn't seem to notice Rysha's long silence.

"Your dragon is coming," he informed her, though Shulina Arya wasn't visible in the sky yet.

"I know. We're chatting. She thinks it would be beneath me to ride a horse."

Trip's eyebrows drifted toward his hairline. "I knew when I started dating a noblewoman with her own castle that she would be accustomed to the finer things in life, but I didn't know a horse wouldn't qualify. Especially elite army horses from quality lines."

"It's a manor, not a castle," Rysha said, smiling at the old joke, though it prompted her to remember her mother's visit.

When she'd gone out to dinner with her and Aunt Tadelay, she hadn't been able to extract any more information from them about the troubles at home. And they'd said no more about that hint that her father might be considering selling the family land. Rysha found that inconceivable, but the mere suggestion made her want to go home to dig further. Perhaps, if Shulina Arya was willing to fly her around today, she could make it down there later and talk to everyone at dinner. Of course, she might be met with silence on the matter of her concerns, and she couldn't imagine asking Shulina Arya to telepathically poke into her parents' thoughts. Someone subtler would be ideal for that. Someone she needed to officially introduce to her parents anyway, even if that would be more awkward after the barracks room incident. Maybe they wouldn't recognize him in clothes.

"Do you want to go to dinner with me tonight?" Rysha asked.

Trip appeared puzzled at the topic change, but promptly said, "Yes."

"At my family's home?"

"Er."

"You're not going to change your answer, are you?"

"No. I just… Are you sure it's allowed? That I'll be invited? After…"

"It's my home. I can bring anyone to dinner that I wish." Rysha was on the verge of adding that she could use his help in sussing out information, but the mare squealed, her brown eyes growing large.

She reared up on her hind legs, almost pulling the reins from Trip's hands.

Rysha scurried out of the way. Trip made soothing sounds and tried to catch the mare's gaze.

Suspecting what was coming, Rysha didn't think he would be successful in calming her. More alarmed whinnies came from the stables, and a shadow blotted out the sun.

Surprisingly, as Trip gazed into the mare's eyes, she settled down. Her nostrils continued to flare—she surely knew a great predator was drawing close—but she didn't rear up or try to jerk away again.

"Am I correct in assuming Shulina Arya has offered to fly you to Sardelle's house?" Trip asked.

"I believe that was implied."

"If she's willing to take me, too, I'll put the mare away."

"Yes, I think the mare would like that."

As Trip led the horse into the stables, Shulina Arya landed in the yard in her full golden majesty with her wings spread wide. The alarmed whinnying—or was that screeching?—from inside escalated. Rysha winced, imagining Trip being struck in the head by hooves as horses reared in their stalls. But the whinnies grew quieter, and much of the noise subsided.

"Are you doing that?" Rysha asked Shulina Arya.

No, it is difficult for a mighty predator such as myself to calm prey animals. I could, but your mate is doing a sufficient job. He has admirable power for a human, and he is conscientious and appealing.

The compliments startled Rysha. She hadn't realized Shulina Arya had noticed anything about Trip. *I hope I can get my parents to think so.*

If you decide you no longer desire him as a mate one day, I may take him as mine.

Rysha almost fell over.

Trip walked out at that moment, lifting a hand as if to catch her. She steadied herself on a hitching post. He looked at the ground in puzzlement, no doubt wondering what had tripped her.

Rysha, cheeks flaming red, hoped he hadn't heard the telepathic conversation.

"Is it all right to climb onto her?" Trip asked, waving at Shulina Arya.

Rysha couldn't keep from making a choking noise. "Yeah, more than all right, I gather."

Trip tilted his head in further puzzlement, seemingly unaware that the dragon's violet eyes were regarding him. Not with sexual consideration, Rysha hoped.

Fear not, Storyteller. I would never take a mate from my rider. That would be a most despicable practice. And I do not feel sexual attraction for humans when I am in dragon form. I only note that some human males are more appealing than others. That Captain Duck has very noble thoughts regarding me too.

"Are you all right?" Trip touched Rysha's sleeve. "You look dazed. Did something happen?" He frowned around the stables yard, no doubt ready to leap to her defense if someone had passed by and slighted her.

"Sorry, I'm fine. I was just having a conversation with Shulina Arya that I didn't realize she was old enough to have."

Really, Storyteller! I am a fully mature and fertile female.

Rysha thought of Shulina Arya racing around the castle on her scooter, her ponytail streaming behind her, but only replied with, *I apologize. I hadn't realized you were, uh, fertile.*

I've had two mating cycles now. I have not let any male dragons breed with me, however. I do not desire young at this time. And so many males are so ridiculously full of themselves.

Like Bhrava Saruth?

Indeed!

"Yes," Rysha said out loud, realizing Trip was gazing at her, waiting for an explanation. She decided not to offer it, instead waving to Shulina Arya's back. "I believe we can climb on."

The dragon settled onto her belly to allow easy access, but Trip waved a finger, and Rysha, who wasn't carrying around Dorfindral on her day off, floated into the air. They settled atop Shulina Arya's back together.

See, conscientious, Shulina Arya observed.

Yes, I've noticed.

Fortunately, the dragon hopped into the air and flapped her wings without remarking further on Trip's attributes.

From behind her, he slipped his arms around Rysha's waist and rested his chin on her shoulder. She leaned back into his warm grip, though it was hard not to forget Shulina Arya's words and comments on being fertile.

Perhaps a dragon might be less likely than a mare to object to vigorous holding, he murmured into her mind, kissing the side of her neck.

Uh, I think we'd be far more likely to get commentary.

But not objections?

No, I think Shulina Arya might like seeing your vigor.

What?

Never mind. As they soared over the walls of the army fort and toward the city walls, Rysha decided it was time for a subject change. *I confess to having an ulterior motive for asking you to dinner.*

Oh? You want to lure me off to a higher-quality bed that doesn't creak so much? I believe I fixed that this morning, but a little grease would—

That's not the reason. Rysha knew he was joking, but she was mortified at the idea of having sex in her parents' manor. In the bedroom she'd grown up in. That was just down the hall from her parents' bedroom. And Aunt Tadelay's bedroom.

Trip squeezed her shoulder. *Go ahead. I'll be serious.*

Rysha wished she had responded with a joke instead of horror. He was *always* serious. And so often grim. Hadn't she been the one to tell him to have fun more often?

She reached back and patted his thigh. *When my aunt and mother came to visit, after you absconded with my pillow, they said they were worried about riots in the countryside and trouble among*

Iskandia's subjects, due to worry about the future. The potentially dragon-filled future.

I've heard similar stories and read about a rise in crime in the newspapers.

I think there's trouble in my own home. They alluded to something, but wouldn't go into details. I was hoping that a telepathic sorcerer might be able to sneak into my father's thoughts in particular and try to get information.

You want me to intrude upon your father's privacy?

To help me help them. If they need help.

Don't you think I've, ah, caused affront enough to your family already? By being naked in my bed?

That was the affront I was thinking of, yes.

If it makes you feel better, you could have Azarwrath do the spying. How's the food at your castle?

Rysha glanced back, startled by the question. *We have a chef. It's always good.*

Azarwrath may be distracted then. Especially if there's a sommelier too.

We don't have a sommelier, Rysha said, surprised he knew of the occupation. She'd never heard him mention enjoying alcohol of any kind. *We're not that rich.*

Right, only a chef, a butler, and a maid. Quite impoverished.

Keep teasing me, and you're never going to get vigorous holding.

You would withhold holding? Even after I fixed your bed?

It wasn't broken. It was old and had character.

If it's like everything else on the army installation, it was built by the lowest bidder.

Shulina Arya, who had set a leisurely pace flying them to Sardelle's house, tilted her wings and soared toward the rooftop. For some reason, she liked to land on it, rather than in the yard.

I'll lift you down, Trip told her. *Even though you're potentially withholding holding and also officially an elite troops officer now, and I know hopping off a rooftop is a simple matter for you, perhaps preferable to using stairs or ladders.*

You're very kind.

I'll also go with you to dinner and spy on your father.

Extremely kind. I withdraw my objection to vigorous holding.

Excellent.

So long as it's not done in front of my father. Or my mother. Or my aunt. Or my sister.

Are we allowed to touch at all in your castle?

We'll see.

Trip held his chin up as he walked along the lakefront road toward the sprawling stone manor. He did his best to look stately and acceptable. Since he kept nervously smoothing the jacket of his dress uniform, he wasn't positive he managed the look. Also, mud spattered his boots and his shins, since the gravel road featured a lot of potholes brimming with rainwater. Even though the calendar promised summer was only a few weeks away, the frequent precipitation in this part of Iskandia made it hard to tell.

"Can you de-mud us before we get up to the front door?" Rysha glanced down at the slacks she wore, they, too, being adorned with damp spots. The sandals she'd chosen, perhaps dressing according to the current pleasant and calm weather rather than the rain that had dominated previous days, left her skin exposed to the elements.

Though Shulina Arya had offered to land on the rooftop of Rysha's manor, she had adamantly told the dragon that it wasn't necessary, asking her instead to drop them off on the opposite side of the lake. A wise choice. The charred remains of her grandmother's house remained near the shoreline there, and Trip doubted her family would appreciate the appearance of a dragon, even a friendly one.

"De-mud?" he asked.

"With your powerful magics."

"Hm." Trip eyed the mud spatters. "I've never turned my power to de-mudding."

"Surely, cleaning clothing must be within a mage's repertoire. It's at *least* as important as incinerating enemies."

"If Jaxi were here, she would recommend incinerating the mud."

Rysha touched her shoulder where she'd been shot the month before. "I remember her tendency to consider that a solution to *all* problems."

With enough precision, you could incinerate mud, Azarwrath chimed in.

"Oh dear," Trip said.

"What?"

"Jaxi may have rubbed off on Azarwrath."

Hardly that. Azarwrath sniffed loudly into his mind. *I'll ensure you look fabulous by the time you reach the door. Later, I'll give you grooming tips.*

That sounds like something to look forward to.

If your lady wishes her attire cleaned, a good sorcerer should be able to assist her. Ah, but what is that I detect? Do you smell it?

Probably. Trip sniffed and turned his nose in the direction of smoke rising from one of the twelve—no, fourteen—chimneys poking above the rooftop of the sprawling manor. *I assume you're sensing things through my nostrils.*

I am, indeed. Meat is being smoked. Pork, I believe. And is that the hint of a sweet barbecue sauce simmering in a pot over an open flame? Barbecue was invented in Cofahre, you know. It was originally considered a peasants' dish, but a couple of centuries back, it grew trendy for culinary experts to refine the sauces and the smoking methods. A good chef today can ensure the meat falls off the bones and melts in your mouth. Telryn, is your mouth watering now?

Trip could smell the meat smoking, but he had no idea about the barbecue sauce. And he was growing more concerned that he and Rysha approached the front doors and were still bedewed with mud.

Worried that Azarwrath was unduly distracted, he focused on his trousers as he and Rysha climbed the three wide flagstone steps. Avoiding thoughts of incineration, he tried to envision every speck of mud that stuck to them, willing them to fly away from their clothing, leaving it pristine.

One of the doors opened as his magic was in the middle of working. All at once, the mud flew from their legs and feet toward the man who stepped onto the threshold. Countless brown droplets spattered against his legs.

Trip cursed to himself, checking the man's face, hoping he hadn't felt anything, and also hoping this was the butler or some servant who wouldn't be horrified by a few dirt smudges. Or make that a few dozen. He certainly had *concentrated* the grime, hadn't he?

"Father," Rysha said at the same time as Trip recognized the man from their previous meeting.

Her father's lips started to curve upward at Rysha, but he noticed Trip right away, and those lips shifted into a frown. Not one of recognition, Trip decided, sensing the man's surface thoughts. Maybe because Trip was clad in his dress uniform instead of the fatigues he'd worn when he flew Rysha down to see her family a couple of months earlier? Or maybe because on that day, the man had dismissed Trip as someone worth forgetting.

"Rysha," her father said—Trip groped for his name, but didn't think she'd ever given it. Lord Ravenwood would have to do. "It's good to see you." He stepped forward and gripped her wrists, but then decided a hug was preferable and gathered her into his arms.

Trip sensed surprise from Rysha—apparently, her father wasn't one to show affection through physical means, especially in front of others. From Lord Ravenwood, Trip sensed a mixture of relief and sincere happiness at seeing Rysha.

Feeling uncomfortable witnessing the man's emotions, Trip almost walled off his mind so he wouldn't sense them, but he remembered this was the reason he was here. To spy.

"Your mother didn't lead me to believe you were coming down," Lord Ravenwood said.

"Just for tonight." Rysha returned the hug. "For dinner. I've missed you all and wanted to make sure everyone is all right."

Trip sensed her discomfort at the partial truth.

"Only for dinner?" Lord Ravenwood released her and stepped back to look her up and down.

She had chosen not to wear her military uniform or the newly awarded badge that proclaimed her a member of the elite troops. Only her civilian clothes. Trip knew she was proud and would have loved to come in the military attire, but also that she knew her family wouldn't appreciate it. It stung her that they couldn't accept her choice and that her parents wanted her to leave the military, that they had no interest in celebrating her achievements within it.

Trip looked away. He hadn't meant to spy on *her* thoughts.

"Yes, sir," Rysha said. "I have work tomorrow."

"Ah."

"This is Captain Telryn Yert. He goes by Trip. I invited him to dinner."

Trip sensed Rysha bracing herself and wondering if her father had heard the story of the barracks-room nudity.

"I see." Lord Ravenwood didn't scowl at Trip, not exactly, but his expression wasn't welcoming as they made eye contact. He didn't hold the gaze for long, instead looking back to Rysha. "It's unfortunate that you didn't let us know you were coming. I know your mother and aunt have a list of appropriate young men that they would love to invite over to meet you."

Rysha gritted her teeth, and her cheeks grew pink. "Because that's what's important now, I'm sure. Dragons are invading Iskandia, and there's civil unrest all over the countryside, but let's make sure to find Rysha an appropriate nobleman to make babies with."

Lord Ravenwood lifted his hands and stepped back, truly seeming apologetic. "Neither of us intends to pressure you to have children—" He glanced at Trip, appearing appalled at speaking so bluntly about such things in front of a stranger. "I just know they want you to have a reason to stay closer to home."

"To quit the military, you mean."

"Rysha—"

"Can we come in, please? It was a long ride down here."

"Ride?" Lord Ravenwood looked past them. "Did you already take your horses to the stable?"

"Our mount is cared for."

They had left Shulina Arya to hunt for some of the rabbits she'd spotted darting in and out of the hedgerow along the road. While rabbits were but a scant appetizer to dragons, the flavor was appealing, especially with the plump ones, or so Shulina Arya had informed them.

"*Mount?*" Lord Ravenwood asked, his thoughts hitching on the singular use of the word.

"Mm, does Chef need help preparing dinner?" Rysha asked. "She probably wasn't expecting extra mouths. We don't mind cutting vegetables."

Lord Ravenwood looked at Trip.

"I don't mind," Trip said, though he wasn't sure if that was the question in that look. "I'm amenable to anything."

"I'll bet," Lord Ravenwood muttered, but waved for them to follow him inside.

"Does Tohomas have the day off?" Rysha asked as they entered a grand foyer, the flagstone of the portico giving way to large marble floor tiles. "I was surprised when you answered the door yourself."

"Tohomas recently decided to pursue other work, and we haven't replaced him yet."

Rysha faltered, and Trip rested a supportive hand on her back as a feeling of loss radiated from her. "Tohomas left? But he's worked here my whole life."

"After the dragon attack, many of our workers left. They didn't feel safe."

Trip squinted at the back of Lord Ravenwood's head, sensing a half-truth there. Should he start spying now? Or wait until Rysha steered the conversation to the topics she wanted information on? He didn't want to pry only to discover something he didn't want to know and that she wouldn't want to know either.

Then she looked over at him. She didn't form any words in her mind, but maybe she sensed her father's evasion, simply using human intuition, and she wanted his opinion.

"Who else has left?" Rysha asked as they kept walking slowly down the long hallway, ignoring a piano room and guest wings opening up to the sides.

Trip let his awareness shift deeper into Lord Ravenwood's thoughts, trying to keep his touch gentle so he wouldn't be sensed and also trying to be tactful in what he pulled out.

As Lord Ravenwood answered Rysha's question with a list of names, images flashed through the man's mind of faces of workers—even friends—he'd known for years. In the beginning, after the first attack that had resulted in the death of Rysha's grandmother, the workers had banded together with determination to fight off invaders. Trip was surprised at how many people lived on the property, some in the manor but far more up and down the valley in small communities near the areas they tended, orchards, farms, grazing and timber lands, and even a cranberry bog.

A few weeks had passed without further dragon attacks, at least not in their valley, and business had returned to normal, but then a silver dragon had appeared, flying over the family's property every day, sometimes multiple times a day. For some reason, it had shown undue interest in them, and its frequent visits made everyone nervous.

Occasionally, it plucked up livestock, devouring the animal from some rooftop while in plain sight.

After a couple of weeks of this, nervous workers had arrived at the manor, singly or in small groups. They'd reluctantly turned in their resignations, almost all of them saying the same thing, that they were moving to the city to be closer to the army installation and the king's protection.

Lord Ravenwood had understood, but he'd also been surprised and stung at how many workers had deserted the estate over this, especially when no human deaths had been reported. Ravenwood believed the dragon was simply attracted to the fertile land and feeding off the wild animals and livestock here. Or at least, that was what he had believed until—

Trip bumped his shoulder against a coat rack he hadn't noticed, and he grunted, hurrying to catch it before it fell. It clacked against the wall, and the heavy stone base rattled noisily on the marble as he righted it. Lord Ravenwood and Rysha both stopped to stare at him.

"Sorry," Trip said. "I was distracted."

"Officers aren't what they were in my grandfather's day," Lord Ravenwood muttered, then gestured toward a sitting room. "Have a seat. I'll round up the rest of the family. I'm sure they'll enjoy having dinner company."

Even though the bump had broken his link with Lord Ravenwood, Trip still sensed the lie, that the man thought Trip's presence would ruin what otherwise would have been a nice family meal with Rysha. Having their daughter home—without a strange dinner guest with skin that was too dark and eyes that were an odd shade of green—would have been a welcome change from all the disruption the silver dragon's presence had caused.

Rysha took Trip's arm and guided him into a large sitting room with tall glass windows overlooking a garden. There were four different seating areas, some focused on the fireplace and others on gaming tables. She stopped at a trio of chairs and a sofa by the fireplace where wood crackled and flames danced, even though it wasn't cold this time of year. Trip sensed that she wanted to sit on the sofa with him but knew her parents would object to such blatant closeness, so she chose a plush leather chair for herself.

"Normally, I would be depressed that my father's first impression of you is that you're a klutz and a meager officer,"

Rysha murmured quietly, "but perhaps for tonight, it's for the best that he underestimates you."

"You can't tell me I'm the first young man to visit your castle who's bumped into the coat rack. It's practically in the middle of the hall. And why is it so far from the door?"

"That was the second coat rack, in case people change their minds and want to remove some layers before sitting down."

Trip paused, wondering what his grandparents would think of a house that required multiple coat racks, then shook his head. "Even so, I'm sure other people have bumped it."

"Other people haven't caused mud to go flying and spatter his trousers," Rysha said. "I assume that wasn't intentional."

"No, he opened the door with unexpected promptness. And he didn't notice that, so I know he's not judging me based on that. I don't think he knows I have any power at all."

Rysha shook her head and patted him on the leg. "I'm just teasing you."

"Good, because I only ran into something because I was concentrating on spying."

"Already?" Her eyebrows rose.

"I thought you wanted me to when you gave me that look in the hall."

"Oh. No, I was just thinking that you look dashing in your dress uniform. And then you bumped into the coat rack."

"That diminished your opinion of my dashingness?"

"Sorry. I'm a shallow girl." Rysha smirked at him.

"Yes, as shallow as the Zevian Trench."

Sensing a woman's approach, Trip looked toward the hallway.

Someone's coming, he warned Rysha. *In case you don't want to be seen fondling my thigh.*

Fondling it? I was simply attempting to make you feel less rejected.

I believe your aunt would object to that.

Rysha grimaced. Trip held back a similar expression as the familiar woman walked up, instead standing up and nodding formally toward her.

Aunt Tadelay's clothing was fitted, perfectly matched, and immaculate, with her brown hair swept back into an elegant bun pierced with ivory sticks. Unexpectedly, she carried a tray of drinks.

"Aunt Tadelay? You're, uhm…" Rysha waved to the tray. "Bringing us refreshments?"

"I do know how to carry a tray, dear." Tadelay smiled quickly if somewhat sardonically at Rysha, then looked at Trip and sighed. "Don't take this the wrong way, Captain, but I was hoping not to see you again."

Trip scratched his jaw, debating if he should stay silent and not ruffle feathers or stand up for himself. He had a feeling "standing up for oneself" was considered rude among the nobility. At least if one wasn't *of* the nobility.

"What would be the *right* way to take it?" Trip asked.

Tadelay set six drinks down on the table, ice cubes clinking in the pale pink liquid—it smelled slightly of cranberries—a testament to an icehouse somewhere on the property. Trip wasn't surprised. What was the point of living in a castle if one couldn't have ice cubes on demand?

"Trip is smart, brave, loyal, and one of the best men I've ever met," Rysha told her aunt firmly.

Tadelay made a clucking noise—was that disappointment?—and walked out with the empty tray.

Wondering who else would join them, Trip reached for a glass, making sure to choose one that wasn't close to him. "This isn't going to be poisoned, right?"

"My family isn't *that* dreadful." Rysha rubbed the back of her neck. "Maybe this was a bad idea. I should have waited until times were more settled before bringing you. Or at least until the memory of us together in bed had faded from my aunt's and my mother's minds."

"You don't think the image of my magnificent form will stick with them forever?"

She swatted him. "More likely, the image of your magnificent form falling on the floor. Then hiding itself behind a pillow."

I have detected a few things in your father's thoughts, Trip said, switching to telepathy. He was aware of several people in a nearby kitchen. *Give me another hour, and I may have a better idea of what's going on here. I've already learned that a silver dragon seems to be involved.*

Trip sensed Rysha's alarm, though she only reacted by dropping her hand on his forearm. *What?*

I don't sense another dragon in the area right now besides Shulina Arya, but perhaps, the next time she contacts you, you can ask her if she's aware of any silvers visiting your valley.

Rysha looked like she wanted to say more, but men's voices sounded in the hallway. Trip sensed three people about their age approaching. Her brothers?

She rose and faced in that direction. The three tall men who ambled in appeared to be in their twenties, all sturdy and athletic, one with spectacles similar to Rysha's. They all grinned and came forward to hug her and thump her on the back.

"Congratulations on passing your army thing," the one with spectacles said.

Trip sensed a little disgruntlement from Rysha at having the elite troops—and the intense training she'd gone through to get in—summed up as a *thing*, but she was also glad to receive a modicum of support. And she was pleased none of them had opened up with a suggestion that she promptly leave the army and return to the estate.

"This the one we heard about?" One of the brothers frowned as he looked at Trip.

Trip had sat back down after Tadelay left, but he stood again, since he felt towered over, especially as their collective attention turned to him. A little over six feet in height, he wasn't used to feeling short, but the men were all several inches taller than he. He could imagine what they had "heard about" if Rysha's mother and aunt had been the source.

"This is Captain Trip Yert," Rysha said. "Trip, these are my brothers, Krey, Severin, and Jhory."

Krey had a chipped tooth, and Trip remembered the story Rysha had told about wayward piggyback rides in her youth.

"Yert?" Severin asked. He was the tallest of the men, with a thick brown beard that took up most of his face despite being tidily trimmed.

"No, he's not noble," Rysha said, "and no, you're not going to tell me it matters."

"Oh? Glad we got that straightened out."

"This isn't the new Wolf Squadron pilot that they say is a witch, is he?" Jhory asked, lifting his spectacles and squinting at Trip.

Trip froze. Thanks to that newspaper article, he knew there were rumors about him in the city, but he wouldn't have guessed they had made their way out into the countryside. Or to Rysha's family.

He looked at Rysha before answering, not sure if sorcery was typically brought up the first time a noblewoman brought a boy home to dinner.

"Male mages are called sorcerers, not witches," Rysha said. "Even female magic-users prefer the term sorceress."

Jhory exchanged long looks with his brothers. They all oozed worry and two out of the three wondered if they had a brotherly obligation to protect Rysha by pounding Trip into the floor. Though Severin was now worried Trip would shoot fire out of his nostrils if they tried.

Telryn, Azarwrath said, turning the name into a long sigh. *Simply stop dampening down your aura, and let these people see the real you. If you wish, you can turn on your allure to charm them, though that's not necessary and admittedly not your strength—besides, you don't want your lady friend's mother and aunt drawn to you sexually.*

Trip made a choking noise. Fortunately, the brothers were too busy muttering darkly among themselves to notice. Rysha noticed, gave him a concerned look, and glanced at the cranberry beverage he'd tasted.

I believe if you let your aura show, Azarwrath continued, *the family will treat you with respect, not like some idiot delinquent who seduced their little girl.*

Respect or fear? Trip already did not care for the unease he sensed from the brothers.

Perhaps some of both, but either way, it will be an improvement over this shrinking into yourself that you're doing. It's unseemly. You're not thirteen. You are a half-dragon man and a sorcerer coming into your powers. A trickle of disappointment came from Azarwrath along with the words. Maybe even embarrassment, as if he didn't care for riding on the hip of someone who acted subservient.

Was Trip truly being that? He just didn't want to make trouble for Rysha. And the plan had been for him to be incognito so he could more easily spy on her father.

Are you all right? Rysha asked silently, touching his hand.

Yes, I just didn't expect to be recognized. Or have my power recognized, I should say. Azarwrath thinks I should try less hard to quash everything. What do you think? I came to help you. I'm not sure if it's better to be seen as my normal self or as a powerful sorcerer.

I'm not sure my family will be able to tell the difference. None of them are familiar with magic or those who use it.

Trip remembered the way people had looked at him in that restaurant in Lagresh when he'd let his aura out. Even Grekka, a sorceress in her own right, had been affected, even drawn to him. Drawn to do as he asked. He didn't want to have that effect on Rysha's family. It seemed to be cheating to use his power that way, even if it would have felt natural to let his aura leak out. He was so used to repressing it that it wasn't that hard to do so, but he did sometimes wonder what it would be like to simply let it out and walk around with it on full display all the time.

More voices came from the hallway, and Trip sensed Rysha's father again, this time walking with a man who put him ill-at-ease. When the pair came into view, Rysha frowned, not recognizing the person at her father's side. He was gray-haired and significantly shorter than her tall family members, only slightly over five and a half feet tall. He didn't carry any obvious weapons, nor did he have the mien of a soldier or anyone dangerous. Yet Lord Ravenwood was definitely uncomfortable.

"We'll be having a dinner guest," he said, looking toward the hallway where Aunt Tadelay was returning, along with Rysha's mother. "Another one. Lord Lockvale has come to discuss business with me after we eat." He forced a smile.

Trip let his senses trickle toward the newcomer. This Lord Lockvale did not have any dragon blood and was easy enough to read, especially since one prominent thought simmered right at the surface. He hoped to obtain the Ravenwood estate for himself.

CHAPTER 9

D INNER ROLLS, BAKED BEANS, AND platters of several kinds of meat were passed up and down the time-polished cedar dining table where Rysha had shared countless meals with her family, both as a child and also later on, when she'd been studying at the university and had come home on the weekends. Only recently had she started to feel like a guest, or even a stranger, at the manor, coming home only once every month or two. Sometimes less, thanks to her parents' tendency to harp on her military career.

Tonight, they were too busy asking polite but pointless questions to the gray-haired newcomer and stealing glances at Trip instead of mentioning the army. Rysha wasn't sure whether to be relieved or not. Trip was being quiet, speaking only if someone asked him a question. He looked... not exactly miserable, but certainly uncomfortable. Far from the powerful sorcerer she'd gradually seen coming out over the last couple of months. Did she want him to look like a sorcerer here? Projecting his *scylori?* She didn't know. It might cause even more trouble than if her parents believed him a simple commoner.

Jhory had heard or read something, but Rysha couldn't tell if anyone else knew—or believed—the rumors yet. Trip running into coat racks wasn't likely to make people believe he was a supremely powerful being directly descended from a dragon.

"What brings you to our home tonight, Lord Lockvale?" Aunt Tadelay asked. "I've run into you at social gatherings before, I believe. You do property surveys for the kingdom, isn't that right?"

"Yes, my lady. I'm visiting folks in the area, making sure everyone is doing well. There have been reports of dragons in this part of the country, as you may know."

"And that's part of your job as a surveyor?"

"As a concerned Iskandian subject and nobleman, certainly." The man had a gray mustache to match his gray hair, and a greasy smile that put Rysha on edge.

She couldn't remember having ever met him at social gatherings or otherwise, though the family name was familiar. She didn't like that Father had been even more tense since his arrival.

"It's remarkable that you have so much time to worry about others," Tadelay said. "I'd heard that your family was having some trouble, due to some debts your father failed to pay off before his passing."

"Oh no, nothing serious, my lady." Lockvale waved a dismissive hand. "It's true we sold some of our lands a few years ago, but only because it was a burden to maintain them, not because we were impoverished or anything of the sort. How ludicrous to contemplate."

"Hm."

"Tadelay," Rysha's mother whispered. "You of all people should know it's improper to discuss finances at the dinner table."

"Yes, I suppose it is. Forgive me. I've had a glass or two already." She waved to the red wine next to her plate, though it was full, and Rysha thought it had been for the whole night.

Trip? she asked, hoping he was monitoring her thoughts. She touched his thigh under the table to make sure.

He'd been watching the newcomer and her father, but he promptly responded, *Yes?*

Are you busy?

Being lectured for not sampling something from every dish and every wine bottle? Moderately so.

Er, is that Azarwrath?

Yes, he lives vicariously through me and my taste buds. What's your question?

I wondered if you have any idea what this Lockvale is up to and why my aunt was carrying out beverages earlier.

So she could personally poison me, I imagine.

You drank the cranberry ale, and you're still alive. Nothing was poisoned.

Are you sure? It had a funny taste.

That's the secret ingredient. Lemongrass. I know the recipe since I used to make it with my grandmother as a girl. Rysha glanced toward the spot at the table where her grandmother had once sat. Family meals had been much more enjoyable with her here, especially since Rysha had joined the army. She'd always stood up for Rysha's choice and had loved to bring up all news events and all gossip at the table, whether appropriate for dinner discussion or not.

Lemongrass? I don't even know what that is.

A culinary and medicinal herb from Iskandia's southern regions. The recipe calls for two stalks, bruised lightly, then cut into half inch pieces.

I think that's what your aunt wants to do to me. Though she's admittedly glowering at me less now that this Lord Lockvale has arrived. And yes, I have learned a few things. Do you want me to tell you here? Your mother is concerned that you're touching my thigh under the table and gazing lustfully at me.

Lustfully? I'm looking at your knuckles, not your naked chest. Rysha did turn away and make a point of chatting with her brother on her other side, asking him how the wine business was doing.

"I heard the Swanvales are thinking of selling their timberlands," Aunt Tadelay said, apropos of nothing, though the shrewd look she sent at Lockvale made Rysha suspect it was apropos of *something*.

Did she believe this man a part of some scheme? Something that could affect their family? What did Lockvale want to talk to her father about?

"There have been a lot of bandits about," Lockvale said. "Perhaps they're joining those people who are selling their land and turning to the safety of the city."

"Timber bandits?" Aunt Tadelay asked, her voice dripping sarcasm. "Are they traipsing through forests and leaving with logs in their pockets?"

"I understand steam wagons and saws are involved." Lockvale sipped from his glass, then looked up and down the table, as if seeking a less prickly conversation companion than Rysha's aunt. His gaze settled on Trip. "Captain, you're in the flier battalion, is that right?" He waved at the flier-shaped pin on Trip's uniform.

"Yes, sir—my lord."

Lockvale smirked at the slip, looking down his nose at Trip.

Rysha gritted her teeth, recognizing that condescending I'm-a-noble-and-you're-not look. Maybe she should have told Trip to unleash his *scylori*, after all. Nobody lesser than a dragon would look down upon him then. Besides, it always seemed unfair to ask him to cloak his true nature, even if he hid it himself most of the time. She didn't think any of his Wolf Squadron comrades had seen him exuding his natural power.

"Seen any battles with dragons?" Lockvale asked.

"Several. As has Rysha."

"Oh yes. I'd heard one of your girls had become a soldier, Lord Ravenwood." Lockvale's gaze shifted to Rysha's father. "How pedestrian."

"We can't all be as noble as land surveyors," her father murmured.

Rysha caught Trip wincing, and she touched him under the table. She knew he'd meant to suggest she was doing the same kind of important and dangerous work that he was, not lead in to her or her family being insulted.

"Has the army come up with any idea about how to deal with these dragons yet, Captain?" Lockvale asked. "They are a tedious problem."

"We have a few ideas. It's true that we can't simply keep reacting to attacks on our land."

"That's a certainty. I suppose the army isn't the most imaginative institution though when it comes to solving problems, eh? You pilots just fly at things and shoot them, don't you?"

"That's my job, sir," Trip said coolly, and Rysha knew he hadn't made that slip, leaving off the *my lord,* accidentally.

"I'd prefer if you call me Lord Lockvale or my lord," Lockvale had the gall to say. What an ass.

"We don't always get what we prefer," Trip said.

Rysha's mother and father frowned at each other. They might not like Lockvale, but they would no doubt feel it their duty to ensure their class wasn't snubbed by some commoner. To Rysha's surprise, a faint smile tugged at the corners of Aunt Tadelay's mouth.

Trip, Rysha thought. *Can you tell if he's—*

Storyteller! Shulina Arya spoke into her mind, the word thunderous as it bounced around inside Rysha's skull.

Rysha gripped the table and managed not to fall off her chair. *Yes?*

There is a silver dragon snooping around your castle.

Rysha resisted the urge to correct the dragon about the house's more modest label, and asked, *What?*

Trip looked at her and nodded. To let her know he was being included in the conversation too?

He will not speak with me. Shall I chase him off?

Any chance you could question him and find out why he's here? Trip asked before Rysha could respond. He didn't sound surprised in the least about this dragon.

If I can catch him, I can most certainly question him. Storyteller, is this your wish?

Yes, Rysha said, bemused that Shulina Arya would ask her permission, or at least her opinion, before acting. *I'd like to know if my family is in danger. And I'd like for my family* not *to be in danger.*

I will valiantly battle him and slay him if he's a danger to them!

Questions first, please, Trip said, his gaze drifting back toward Lockvale, who'd found another dinner companion to chat with.

Rysha wanted to drag Trip off to a private corner to find out what he'd learned so far. As it was, she had to make an effort to speak with her brother again, lest her family find it odd that she and Trip were gazing silently at each other without talking.

Lockvale's head came up. "Lady Ravenwood, I thank you and your staff for the fine meal, but I don't believe I can eat any more. Lord Ravenwood, are you able to have that meeting with me now?"

Rysha's father had only finished half the food on his plate and didn't look like he wanted to leave the table, but he said, "Yes. Let's go to my study."

"Excellent. Have you any cigars to finish off the meal with? I do enjoy those imported Dakrovian ones of yours."

Father's jaw tightened, but he nodded and pointed toward the hall leading to his study.

Oh, he's flying away from me, Shulina Arya cried, the disappointment ringing in Rysha's mind. *The coward!*

Rysha tensed, feeling like she should be out there, on Shulina Arya's back to help her chase down an enemy.

Mother cleared her throat. "I assume you'll be spending the night, Rysha?" She looked at Rysha, tension tightening her eyes, then looked at Trip. "If so, I'll have the maid take your friend to the guest wing. I trust he'll stay there and that you'll stay in *your* room. This isn't a college dormitory—or an army barracks."

Jhory and Krey snickered while Severin's mouth dropped open and he glanced at Trip, looking appalled. Rysha's cheeks warmed.

"Thank you for your generous offer of a guest room for Trip, Mother," Rysha said, smiling through her teeth. "But we'll be returning to the city tonight."

Mother's eyebrows flew up. "It's after dark, and it's a long ride back to the capital. Even if it weren't, it's not safe to travel the highways at night anymore."

"We're trained soldiers, Mother." Rysha hesitated, debating if she should mention that they would ride Shulina Arya back, assuming she didn't get into trouble with that silver dragon, and could be back in the city in less than an hour.

"That doesn't mean you should court trouble."

"...think she's sleeping with a witch—mage?" Jhory whispered to Severin.

"If she is, what if he's controlling her?"

"He doesn't look like he could control his own prick."

Rysha dropped her face into her hand. What had ever made her think that bringing Trip to a family dinner would be a good idea? For that matter, what had made her think bringing *herself* would be wise?

Rysha gazed toward the cloudy sky, glad it wasn't raining, but feeling silly standing on the gravel drive a half mile from the house. Perhaps it had been premature to leave, but when her brothers had started speculating about whether Trip had used magic to make her fall for him, she hadn't been able to take it any longer.

"She *is* coming back, right?" Trip asked dryly, his voice sounding over the chirps of crickets and hoots of owls in the trees around the lake.

"I'm sure she is. Can you still sense her?" Rysha remembered that his range was supposed to be forty or fifty miles when it came to detecting dragons and their prominent auras.

"I can. She's about twenty miles that way." He pointed east, toward the mountains.

"Still over our property then. Our valley continues up into the foothills. Or it will as long as my father doesn't sell it. Were you able to learn anything about that?"

Trip stuck his hands in his pockets. "I didn't catch your father thinking about selling the property—actually, there was one thought about him *not* wanting to do it—but here's what I got: ever since this silver dragon started hanging around, the workers have been quitting left and right. The dragon hasn't hurt anyone, but they've all said they're too worried to continue living here where it's lurking. Your father has had trouble attracting new workers, and he's concerned he'll have to close down some of the family businesses."

Rysha frowned. "We're in the growing season now. He'll need more people, not fewer. Especially by the end of the summer and early fall when everything needs to be harvested."

"I could possibly make some interesting magic-powered machinery that could help with harvesting."

"Trip." She leaned on him and wrapped her hands around one of his arms. "I appreciate you wanting to help, but you should help people who are nice to you, not snobby elitists. Or silly stoat-heads." The latter, she applied to her brothers. She loved them, but they still acted like teenagers when they were together.

"I'd never help anyone if I made that rule," he said, his tone dry again.

Her frown deepened. "You *do* have friends."

"I know. It was a joke. Mostly. I'm aware that I… something about me rubs people the wrong way at times. A lot of times. I don't know how to change that unfortunately. I try to hide my otherness—you know that—but I think it oozes out anyway."

"It does, but people shouldn't be so quick to judge otherness. How infuriating."

He wrapped an arm around her back. "Something else you should know about the dinner," he said, not sounding particularly infuriated—maybe he was used to being judged as quirky, "is that I caught this Lord Lockvale thinking a lot about your family's land. It's clear he wants it. He intended to make your father an offer on it tonight, a *second* offer. He was here a couple of weeks ago and met with your father then too."

"I wouldn't think his family would have enough money to make such an offer. We own so much land that's fertile or has ore and timber on it that it's worth a lot even if we're not necessarily swimming in money.

We would be if we sold it. Well, maybe not right now." Rysha leaned back to look up at his face, though she couldn't make out his features in the dark. They had moved away from the gas lamps around the house, so her parents wouldn't know they didn't have typical mounts waiting out in the stable. "With all the uncertainty and unrest, this would be a horrible time to sell land. Especially if there's a dragon hanging right around here." Rysha imagined prospective buyers coming out to see the manor as a silver dragon sailed overhead.

"A horrible time to sell," Trip agreed. "An excellent time to buy if someone were forced to sell."

Rysha mulled that over. Would her father feel *forced* if he couldn't find enough workers to run the family businesses and help in the fields and orchards? Or would her mother and aunt and everyone else grow tired of worrying about that silver dragon lurking around? Was there a price at which they might feel tempted to sell the entire estate?

The thought horrified her, both because she'd grown up here and loved the valley and the lake and everything beyond, and because if her parents didn't have the businesses, they wouldn't be making an income. If they didn't get what the property was worth—or even if they did—would it be enough for them to live on? And Aunt Tadelay too? And her brothers, for that matter. Rysha and her sister were the only ones who didn't have incomes that depended on the family businesses.

"My understanding from my telepathic spying was that Lockvale's offer was disgustingly low and also that the offer he intended to make tonight was the same one, with the promise that he wouldn't offer as much in the future if your father didn't accept this week."

"You don't know the amount, do you?"

"No."

"If Father did feel he had to sell, I'm sure he could find another buyer, one willing to offer fair market value or close."

"How sure are you? Because that's not what Lockvale thought."

"Do you think he's just trying to take advantage of the situation?" Rysha asked. "Maybe making low offers to a lot of the nobles with land in this area? Or is he targeting my father in particular? He couldn't be working with this dragon, could he? How would that even work? It's not like bribing a dragon with money would do anything. I assume."

"What about bribing a dragon with tarts? Or stories?"

"I don't bribe Shulina Arya with stories. She just likes them, and I feel it's wise to accommodate dragons."

"Likely so."

Trip's arm felt good around her back, and she leaned in closer. Even though there weren't typically big swings between daytime and nighttime temperatures here, it was getting late, and Rysha noticed the chill in the air.

"I didn't catch him thinking about the dragon," Trip said, wrapping his other arm around her, "but I didn't pry deeper into his less-than-surface thoughts." He hesitated and shifted his weight. "When I've done that before, I've hurt the person. Inadvertently. I was angry at the time—it was that cultist leader—and it's possible I could be more careful about extracting information in the future, but seeing blood coming out of someone's nose as he grabbed his head in pain made me... a little afraid of myself."

"I'm sure it's scary to have power like that, especially if you can't always control it."

"Yes. I'm never sure whether I should use it or not. Would it even be legal to use it on an imperial subject—a nobleman? Were there rules against mind reading back in the old days when mages were commonplace?"

"I think you'd have to ask Sardelle. My expertise ends at dragons. They had very few rules about anything. The fittest survived and ruled and did whatever they wanted."

"I don't think I can do what I want just because I'm fitter than Lord Lockvale. Though Azarwrath would have been pleased if I did."

"I think my aunt would have been too. She didn't like him." Rysha leaned back in Trip's arms as a new thought occurred to her. A thought that chilled her and brought memories of Xandyrothol to mind, Xandyrothol imitating Horus Silverdale. "There's no possibility Lockvale is a dragon masquerading as a human to get what he wants, is there?"

Trip grew still. She wished she could tell what he was thinking.

"I didn't sense anything unusual about him, but I also didn't sense anything unusual about the would-be Horus. He did a good job dampening his aura and fooling us all. Though I don't know if he could have fooled an actual dragon. We can ask Shulina Arya whenever she gets here, as long as Lockvale is still in the house."

"Can you tell where she is now?"

"Ten miles farther away."

Rysha snorted. She almost asked Trip to speak telepathically to the dragon, if he had the range, and request a pickup. But if Shulina Arya was pursuing a silver dragon harassing the estate, Rysha didn't want to get in the way of that. If they had to, they could spend the night at the manor. In separate beds in separate wings of the house if Mother had her way.

Rysha? Trip asked gently, switching to mental communication.

Yes? she responded the same way.

Did something happen on the freighter before I got back? Did Xandyrothol... do something to you?

Oh hells, she hadn't wanted him to find out. He must have glimpsed her thoughts when the dragon had come to mind. They were standing so close that she supposed he couldn't have missed it.

Nothing happened. That wasn't quite true, and she didn't want to lie to Trip; she doubted she even *could* lie to him. *I mean, I let myself get caught alone below decks, because I wasn't as aware of my surroundings as I should have been, and he did push me against the wall with his magic. He kissed me and, uh, groped me.* She couldn't say the words—even mentally—without feeling shame and embarrassment. Kaika had warned her the dragon-man had a sexual interest in her, but Rysha had refused to see it and hadn't been wary when she should have been. *That's as far as it went. I got lucky. Kaika had her sword—mine was at the bottom of the harbor then, remember—and saw what was going on and drove him away.*

She was glad it was dark so Trip couldn't see her face or the shame scorching her cheeks. Not that vision mattered for him. He surely sensed her every emotion, if not her every thought.

I'm sorry that happened.

She shrugged. *Like I said, it was my fault for not being aware of the situation. I'm lucky it wasn't worse than it was.*

It was not *your fault. You didn't know he was anything other than human or that he had the power to push you around against your will. Most men don't.*

She shook her head, staring at his shoulder instead of looking into his eyes. She didn't think he was right, but she didn't want to argue about it.

Trip lifted his hand to the back of her head and stroked her hair.

Does it bother you? she asked silently. She ought to have dropped it and stopped dwelling on it, but she imagined Trip believing her sullied or indelibly marked by Xandyrothol's stupid kiss. Even as she had the thought, she knew it was silly. Trip would only care that she'd been hurt.

That someone mauled you? Of course it bothers me. I'd kill him if your attack dragon hadn't already handled that.

She smiled, having gotten exactly the answer she expected. *I understand you did quite a bit of damage before she got to him. She was disappointed you'd already put him through the wringer, and I think even a little impressed by your power.* She met his eyes and rubbed his chest through his shirt while deciding not to mention that Shulina Arya would consider him as a mate if Rysha ever gave him up. She had no intention of giving him up.

She would be less impressed if she knew I'd sat there and let your brothers gossip about me loudly enough for everyone to hear.

Well, I would have objected if you'd beaten them up.

I wasn't thinking of doing that, but Azarwrath... well, maybe he's right. Maybe I should let a little of my scylori, as you all call it, out when people are being disrespectful. But I don't want to be an ass or a bully. Maybe it's good for my humility to be disrespected now and then.

Rysha felt bad that her family had made him feel picked on. Even if he hadn't said those exact words, it was true. She should have stood up for him more. She was just so used to keeping her mouth shut, to not wanting to create a confrontation and drama within her own household. As a girl, she'd always run and hidden in her room and read a book if things hadn't gone her way. Maybe she needed to get some *scylori* too. Or a backbone. Why was it so much easier to deal with mortal enemies than one's own family?

I don't know about that, she replied. *If you let people walk on you because you're afraid to use your power on them, then you'll be frustrated and resentful, and it might build up inside of you until you end up lashing out, and then regretting it.*

True. That used to happen a lot in school, me getting frustrated and resentful. I only lashed out a couple of times because I was terrified people would realize I had dragon blood, and my life would be over. Instead, I'd go back into my grandfather's workshop and cut a bunch of wood and build something until I calmed down.

We're not dissimilar people, you know, Trip.
I've noticed that. But you're much prettier than I am.
It's my spectacles. I've been told they add to my sex appeal.
Have you?
Actually, no, but I always wished someone would say that.

Hm. He shifted from stroking his hand through her hair to holding the back of her head and massaging his fingers into her scalp.

When she leaned back into his hand, relishing his strong touch, he lowered his mouth to hers for a kiss. She returned it enthusiastically, suddenly not caring if Shulina Arya ever came back.

Much too soon, he broke the kiss and drew back, but only a few inches. He gazed into her eyes.

"What?" she whispered.

"I was considering your spectacles."

"And agreeing that they do add to my sex appeal?"

"Naturally. Should I get some for myself?"

"Would they still let you fly if you were half-blind?"

"Hm, perhaps not." He lifted a finger and touched the corner of her frames, seeming thoughtful.

"You're envying me my sexy accoutrements right now, aren't you?"

He chuckled, but didn't answer. She wondered what he *was* thinking about.

After a quiet moment, she said, "To answer your earlier musings, I think you could let a little of your heritage show without being a bully or seeming arrogant, if that's what you're worrying about. Remember when we first walked into Lagresh with the wagon? You were radiating a presence that made people not want to disturb you or get in your way. Maybe it was a little too much for using around friends, but is there a halfway version? You don't have to ooze magic for my sake, just so you know, but it's not like it would be disingenuous for you to let your hair down. Or let your scales show."

Trip snorted. "If I ever get scaly, I'm going to be concerned. I'll have to see Dr. Targoson. I hear he makes medicinal creams as well as bullets and acids for slaying dragons."

"He sounds like a handy man."

"Can I—this will sound silly, but can I practice on you?"

"Your aura?"

"Yeah. A low to medium level of it."

She patted him on the chest. "You make it sound like a phonograph."

"You're welcome to sing along if you want."

Rysha gazed at him, curious as to if she would notice a change when they were standing here in the dark. It wasn't as if she had magical senses to detect auras. Before, when she'd noticed him radiating power, it had been something she'd seen with her eyes, or so she'd believed. He'd projected a presence that anyone would have noticed, but it could simply have been a matter of confidence and body language.

Still, as they stood there, looking at each other, little visible in the dark, she started to feel drawn toward him. It seemed silly, since they were already standing chest to chest, his arms around her, but she had the urge to bury her face in his chest and rub her cheek against him, to breathe in his scent and press herself as tightly to him as possible.

Maybe this wasn't a good idea, he murmured into her mind.

Even though the words came as a whisper, they seemed to resonate more than usual. They didn't thunder painfully in her head the way Shulina Arya's did sometimes when she spoke, but there was a sense of power to them, something appealing.

I can feel you getting, uhm.

I can feel you too. She smirked.

Some of the draw lessened as he did something to adjust his *scylori*. Rysha was surprised how noticeable those adjustments were to someone like her.

I don't know how to do it without making it sexual, he told her.

I think that's typical. Almost like letting the power out also releases pheromones. I wonder if it's anything that would be measurable with modern instrumentation. We could do some experiments on it in a laboratory.

You want to experiment on me?

He sounded amused, so she didn't think she had offended him.

Just on your scylori.

It's attached to me.

That's not quite the right word. It's something you can hide or project to different degrees, isn't it? Consciously? What's it like if you don't try to hide it, but also don't try to exude it?

Trip hesitated, then she sensed the return of his allure, the increasing of her attraction, but something more as well. She could almost make out his face even though the light level hadn't increased. She reached up to touch his cheek, feeling something similar to what she felt when

Shulina Arya was close, a knowledge that she was in the presence of power, and also that she was safe here in its shadow. In *his* shadow. She felt a particular pleasure in knowing he had his arms around her, claiming her as his. She *wanted* to be his.

All the nearby insects and animals fell silent. The mournful howl of a wolf came from the distance. A coincidence, or did the animal sense him even from afar? Maybe that was a protest from the wolf, a complaint that a greater predator was here in the valley.

It seemed strange to think of Trip that way and yet that was what his heritage deemed him to be.

"Are you more comfortable like this?" she asked. "Not hiding anything?"

Another hesitation, and from it, she guessed the answer to be yes.

"I'm not comfortable with the way people react, but yes, it's a relief to just, as you said, let my hair down. It's like tearing off soggy clothes and being free to walk around naked."

She chuckled, but then made the mistake of imagining him naked. She realized she was rubbing his chest again—or maybe she had never stopped.

"Your colleagues in Wolf Squadron may not be ready for this, but if you want to walk around naked with me, you can. I'll get used to it. I'm getting used to Shulina Arya. Admittedly, her aura doesn't inspire me to have lurid fantasies, but I'll still get used to it. Or I'll constantly drag you to bed."

"Oh? If I'd known that would happen, I would have been stripping naked for you all the time." He returned to rubbing the back of her head, and she wondered if he was thinking about nudity and beds right now. Neither the gravel of the road, nor the wet grass alongside it seemed inspiring places for sex, but if he kept massaging her scalp like that, she would drag him off into the brambles if need be.

"I have to go for training with Sardelle tomorrow morning," he said, "but I'll help you figure out what's going on here with Lockvale. If your family is in jeopardy, I'll make sure they're protected."

A little shiver went through her, maybe because she knew he could protect them.

"They were all snotty to you tonight and don't deserve your help, but I do appreciate the offer."

"Good. I like it when you're appreciative." He brought his lips to hers for another kiss, and she sensed him grinning. He drew back. "Do you think your father would be appreciative if I made him an automated apple picker?"

Remembering their earlier conversation, she said, "You haven't been thinking about how to make one the whole time we've been talking have you?"

"Not the *whole* time."

Rysha returned his grin. As sexy as she found his powerful aura, it was the rest of him that she loved. She pushed her hands up under his shirt, letting them roam boldly as she kissed him. His hands also roamed, rubbing her hip and the back of her neck, and warm tendrils of his power embraced her, then seemed to be within her, lighting every nerve. The grass and the gravel started to sound more appealing.

Greetings, Storyteller! an overly perky voice spoke into her mind.

Your dragon is back, Trip informed her, though his lips didn't leave hers.

He squeezed her butt, pulling her tight against him, and she got the feeling that he didn't care if Shulina Arya sat on the road and watched. Rysha might not have either if not for the dragon's comments earlier in the day.

She'll take us to my room in the barracks, Rysha said. *It'll be better than the gravel.*

I was not able to catch the silver, I am ashamed to admit. The flap of wings sounded over the gentle lapping of the lake, and the great gold dragon landed in the gravel with a light crunch. *He must have entered races in his hatchling days. I wouldn't have believed a mere silver could move so quickly. I was unable to interrogate him, alas, so I do not know why he was lurking above your home, Storyteller. Your castle! This place is so much more appealing than your tiny stall at the soldier fort. Why do you not live here all the time?*

Rysha didn't want to stop kissing Trip and might not have, but he drew back—he must have heard all that burble too. It was something of a mood-killer, though if he'd kept kissing her and rubbing her neck, she might have been able to block it out. She took satisfaction in the quickness of Trip's breaths, of knowing he would have happily rolled around in the wet grass with her if they hadn't been interrupted. Either that, or he was excited thinking about mechanical apple pickers.

He rubbed his nose against hers. *What excites me is that you* like *it when I fantasize about apple pickers.*

She couldn't truly object. She *did* like his quirky engineer side.

Storyteller?

Yes, Shulina Arya. Reluctantly, Rysha lowered her arms and stepped away, though he hadn't dampened down his aura, and she found it difficult to walk away from him instead of toward him. *Thank you for trying to catch the silver. Maybe next time, we can set a trap. It's my understanding that this dragon has been harassing my family.*

A trap? Trip mused.

Goodness, did I give you something besides apple pickers to fantasize about?

Maybe.

She patted him on the arm, found his hand, and led him toward the dragon.

Your mate looks much healthier, Storyteller.

Rysha felt a moment of confusion before she realized Shulina Arya must mean Trip's aura. Of course, she would have the ability to sense it too.

You think he should let his scylori *out all the time?*

Of course. This is natural.

Rysha looked at Trip, suspecting he'd heard that. Would he change? She didn't know.

CHAPTER 10

TRIP WALKED INTO GENERAL ZIRKANDER'S office, his guts twisting with the usual nerves. He'd been called up here numerous times now, but he still didn't find anything ordinary or blasé about it. So far, Zirkander had always had a mission for him. Would he this time too? Trip would happily go on a mission, but for once, he wouldn't have minded staying home. He was worried that Rysha's family was in trouble, and he wanted time to find out what was going on. And maybe build a dragon trap.

"Morning, Trip." Zirkander stood behind his desk with a mug of coffee in hand and a folder open. "We're waiting for a couple more, and then we'll start."

Trip looked toward the other person—being—in the office, having sensed his presence long before he entered the citadel. Bhrava Saruth was in his golden ferret form, lying in an early morning sunbeam slashing through the window and onto the sofa. All four of his legs were in the air.

"Bhrava Saruth is not a morning dragon," Zirkander said.

"I'm surprised he doesn't have you rubbing his belly, sir."

"Generals have lieutenants around to pet the dragons if needed."

He was rubbing it earlier, Bhrava Saruth said sleepily into Trip's mind. *My high priestess's mate is a most agreeable worshipper. He helped with the construction of my temple, you know.*

I hear generals have to be versatile and have many skills. Maybe one day, Trip would find the courage to ask Zirkander if he truly considered himself one of Bhrava Saruth's worshippers, but not today.

Indeed. And amenable hands.

Zirkander tilted his head. "Did you get your hair cut, Trip? You look different."

"No, sir." After his talk the night before with Rysha, Trip had decided to very subtly let some of his aura show to see if it changed anything. Maybe people like Colonel Therrik would treat him slightly better if they sensed he had some magical competency. But Zirkander hadn't ever treated him disrespectfully so Trip didn't know if anything would change with him. "I did comb it."

"That must be it. Regulations do encourage that."

Bhrava Saruth opened a green eye and looked over at Trip, but didn't make further comments.

Trip sensed more people walking down the hallway to the office and stepped aside, happy to ride in the back seat for whatever mission assignment was coming.

Captain Ahn strode in, her sniper rifle strapped on her back, and she was followed by Dr. Targoson, who carried a satchel. Trip hadn't spoken much to the man outside of their meeting at Sardelle's house the night of the uncorking, as it were.

"Morning, Ahn," Zirkander said. "Tee, you have my acid for me?"

"I'm still not a pharmacy, Zirkander," Targoson growled.

"Are you sure? I have a memo here that says to keep copies of purchase orders sent to Deathmaker Pharmaceutical." Zirkander held up a paper.

Frowning, Targoson walked to the desk to look at it. "This says Daybreak Medicinal. That's the name of the business I formed to facilitate deliveries of my healing formulas to parties willing to pay."

"Unfortunate initials, don't you think?"

"Not to those who can read. Perhaps you need a vision correction."

"Oh? Do you have a cream for that?"

Trip stirred, remembering his thoughts the night before when he'd been with Rysha. Mostly, he'd been contemplating how to get more information from Lord Lockvale, but he'd also been wondering, not for the first time, if he could learn to heal her vision so she wouldn't need spectacles.

Targoson opened his satchel and pulled out a number of devices that looked like fragile grenades.

"Designed to break open on impact," he said. "But Cas tells me the sword makes her averse to touching my dragon-blood-using formulas and devices, when she's using it, so you may need someone else along who can throw them."

Targoson extended a hand toward her—Ahn had moved over to the couch, or perhaps been *drawn* over to it, and was rubbing Bhrava Saruth's belly.

"If Therrik wields Kasandral and Captain Ahn flies," Zirkander said, "she can throw them."

Targoson's lips thinned in disapproval, though Trip didn't know if it was at the idea of Ahn flying and throwing things at the same time or if it was for Therrik. Trip admitted he would be content not to go on any more missions with the man. Therrik hadn't thanked him for helping in that stairwell or for healing him afterward. His concession to calling Trip *Dragon Man* instead of *Dragon Boy* had been the only change. And Trip suspected that had been more of a concession to Colonel Grady and his rhyming preferences.

"Perhaps Colonel Grady and his sword would be appropriate for this mission, sir," Trip caught himself saying, even though he had no idea what the mission was yet. Well, not *no* idea. He'd caught Zirkander thinking of dropping the grenades onto a gold dragon's head as Tolemek had been laying out the devices.

As soon as Zirkander looked at him, eyebrows arching, Trip blushed. Captains weren't supposed to give their opinions when generals were assigning missions.

"Did you have a problem with Therrik in Portsnell?" Zirkander asked.

"He was just brusque. And called me Dragon Boy." Trip's cheeks warmed further. Surely, those were not legitimate reasons to object to a fellow officer's presence on a mission.

"Be happy he didn't run you through with Kasandral," Ahn said, eyeing Trip. "You're noticeably… dragony."

Her eyeing turned into a squint, and Trip wondered if she would also ask if he'd gotten a haircut.

Dragony? Bhrava Saruth asked, still stretched out in the sun on his back, one leg twitching as Ahn stroked his belly. *This is a marvelous thing to be. You humans should all learn to appreciate the wonderfulness of dragons. In particular, dragon gods. Under the armpit, yes?*

Zirkander blinked. "I'm hoping that last suggestion was for you, Ahn."

"I believe so, sir."

As Ahn shifted her fingers to scratch the ferret's armpit, Zirkander turned his gaze back to Trip. After a brief moment of contemplation, he said, "Very well. Colonel Grady will go with you. From what his commander tells me, he's a perfectly capable officer, if newer to the dragon-slaying swords."

"Thank you, sir," Trip said, though it occurred to him that he might be getting his way because he was letting some of his *scylori* show today. He didn't want to manipulate people, and worried he might have inadvertently done so.

No, they will simply sense your power and your right to lead and be heard, Azarwrath informed him, sounding pleased. *This is not bad, Telryn. Your blood gives you those rights.*

I'd rather earn rights through my deeds than because of my blood.

You will find you're given more opportunities to earn them as people regard you with the respect you deserve. It is not as if your blood is causing you to trick them. This is who you are.

Trip sensed someone else coming into the citadel, the aura strong even though she was in human form. Shulina Arya.

His heart warmed as Trip sensed Rysha walking at her side. Actually, she walked several paces behind. The dragon seemed to be running. Or was that skipping? Did dragons skip? Trip looked over at Bhrava Saruth.

Bhrava Saruth sat up on his haunches, chittered, then hopped into the air. When he landed, he was in his human form, shaggy blond bangs hanging in his eyes, and his clothing more appropriate for a day at the beach than a military mission. He patted down his loose terry vest, straightened his long beaded necklaces, then licked a finger and slid it over his eyebrows.

"Guess that means the female is here," Zirkander said.

"Greetings, humans!" Shulina Arya cried in her exuberant voice as she skipped into the room. "Captain Trip," she blurted, coming over to him. "My rider said you might be able to make me something called roller-skates."

"Would that facilitate the capture of a pesky silver dragon?" Trip asked.

"No, but they sound like so much *fun*."

Rysha walked in, immediately spotting Trip and smiling shyly at him. His body hummed at the memory of their night together. As much as Shulina Arya's appearance had seemed untimely the night before, it was better that they had ended up back in Rysha's barracks room rather than rolling around on her parents' gravel driveway.

"Silver dragon?" Zirkander asked.

"One has been flying over my family's property and scaring away workers, sir," Rysha said, coming to attention and saluting him. "But we'll handle it. Trip is going to build a dragon trap."

"A trap *and* roller-skates, Captain?" Zirkander quirked an eyebrow at him. "Shall we set up a metalworking shop in your cockpit?"

"I thought you were going to say in the hangar, sir," Trip said. "And I started to get excited. The cockpit would be crowded with shop presses and lathes inside."

"There's one in the fort I'm sure you could use."

"Oh?" Trip felt inordinately pleased at the notion of being invited to use the army's shop. He wagered they had the latest tools, far superior equipment to what his grandfather had in his woodworking area out back. "Thank you, sir."

"You sound more enthused about that than you would be about a promotion," Rysha said, stepping close enough to nudge him with her elbow.

"Tools are fun. Promotions mean an increase in responsibilities."

"And often a desk," Zirkander muttered. He raised his voice, "Since we're all here, let's begin. Assuming Bhrava Saruth is done playing with his eyebrows."

"Really, mate of my high priestess," the now-human-dragon said. He'd managed to ooze over to stand close to Shulina Arya, though she hadn't so much as looked at him. "I merely wish to ensure they appear well-groomed."

"I don't think it matters when your hair is covering them." Zirkander shifted to face all of them. "This is a small team as you can see. Captains Trip and Ahn, and Lieutenant Ravenwood, along with our dragon allies if they're willing to go." He extended a hand toward Shulina Arya and Bhrava Saruth. "I'll inform Colonel Grady that he and his sword will be joining the team. Ideally, you won't be picking a fight with anyone. Trip, you were the one to suggest this mission, so even though the colonel will be in charge, you'll be leading. I'm sure you and the dragons are the ones who'll be able to find him."

"Him?" Ahn scratched her head.

Trip was getting just enough of Zirkander's surface thoughts to understand who he was talking about. "Drysaleskar, the elder gold, sir?"

After the battle in Portsnell, Trip had mentioned the idea of making an alliance with the dragon, since all the other dragons had been terrified of him, but from the way Zirkander had neutrally said he'd think about the idea, Trip hadn't expected to hear about it again.

Zirkander pushed aside folders to reveal a newspaper on his desk.

"The king brought this to me personally last night and said to do something about it." He held up the paper to show the front page.

Above the columns of text, a dragon had been drawn sinking its talons into a large fishing vessel and thrusting its head into the hold, presumably to devour the crew's fresh catch.

"Is that supposed to be Drysaleskar?" Shulina Arya asked. "It's not an accurate rendition."

"I understand he doesn't stay around and pose for the cameras. He steals weeks' worth of fish, then flaps back out to sea. But as Trip noted, his presence may be what drove all those scheming dragons to flee Portsnell."

"Not *all* of them," Shulina Arya said. "My rider and I had already slain the big gold."

"Of course, excuse me."

"And naturally, I would have slain those silvers before they could escape," Bhrava Saruth said, "but I did not wish to do damage to the human structures along the water."

"We appreciate your thoughtfulness," Zirkander said.

"One of my worshippers in that town is a fisherwoman."

"The mission, sir?" Ahn prompted, glancing at the grenades lined up on the desk and then at Targoson, who merely shrugged in response.

"After some discussion with the king, he's agreed that Trip's idea has merit, especially since dragons seem to prefer warmer climates. Our Tlongan Steppes in the south aren't overly populated, so we could turn an area there into a private dragon park and invite this elder gold to live there. *With* the understanding that he would let other dragons know this is more or less his country, and that he'll chase off any of his kind that pester it."

"If he wanted the Steppes, wouldn't he have already claimed them?" Targoson asked.

"Maybe he hasn't been down to see the property yet and note all its fine merits."

"The ground is so dry that it cracks."

"For a dragon, that could be a merit. Plus, some of the area is adjacent to the ocean, and this dragon is fond of seafood. Angulus said we could pay a tribute of sorts to it for its help. Weekly deliveries of crab, lobster, fish, etcetera. It's not an ideal solution, but it would cost us a lot less than the crown is shelling out for repairs of buildings and infrastructure in cities and rural areas that have been attacked. Many insurance providers are refusing to cover destruction by dragon, and the king is getting dozens of petitions a week. He feels obligated to help his subjects, of course, but my understanding is that the coffers are running low. And then there are the human losses." Zirkander grimaced.

"While I can imagine a dragon wanting to lounge around and be fed—" Targoson looked at Bhrava Saruth, even though he was now standing and sneaking glances at Shulina Arya's chest rather than lounging on the sofa, "—would he truly agree to defend all of Iskandia from other dragons in exchange for a few lobsters tossed in his gullet?"

"He might not have to *do* anything," Trip said. "The other dragons fled at his approach. I don't know what discussion they had, but those dragons didn't come back. And it didn't even seem like Drysaleskar was angling for the city. Just the seafood."

"*We* might have been part of the reason they didn't come back." Rysha touched the hilt of her sword.

Trip spread his hand. "It would be nice to think so, especially since our teams did kill three of them, but I believe it was Drysaleskar's arrival that ended their ploy prematurely."

"Which is why the king wants you to locate him and offer him the Steppes," Zirkander said.

"Which one of us gets the job of negotiating with him, sir?" Ahn looked dubiously at Bhrava Saruth and Shulina Arya. The pair looked like teenagers ready to head to a music festival in the park.

"Captain Trip." Zirkander met Trip's gaze. "You'll be in charge of talking with the dragon."

"Yes, sir." Trip found the idea daunting, but he also agreed he was best qualified. Though their two dragon allies seemed to like Iskandia and humans well enough, he couldn't imagine entrusting negotiations to them.

"If it doesn't go well," Zirkander said, "you'll have two trained warriors with dragon-slaying swords along." Grady wasn't there, but he gestured at Rysha.

She looked pleased at this designation and lifted her chin.

"And acid grenades," Zirkander added. "Are those as fragile as they look, Tee?"

Trip imagined the devices rattling around on the floor of his cockpit as he flew into battle.

"No," Targoson said. "You'll have to make an effort to break them when you throw them. I trust it goes without saying that a dragon's magical barrier would need to be down so they can make contact with its scales."

Trip nodded, knowing that getting the dragon's defenses down would be his job. What he didn't know was if he had a chance at accomplishing that. Not only was a gold more powerful than the silvers and bronzes he'd battled, but this one sounded a lot stronger than a typical gold.

"Pack what supplies you need for the two fliers you'll be taking, and prepare to depart first thing tomorrow," Zirkander said.

"Only two fliers, sir?" Ahn asked. "Is that a big enough team if there's trouble?"

"Two fliers and two dragons. Bhrava Saruth and Shulina Arya have agreed to go with you to help convince Drysaleskar that Iskandia is a lovely country, worth defending and worth not ravaging."

"It will be even more lovely after I can zip through the streets of your city on roller-skates," Shulina Arya announced, looking squarely at Trip.

Did she expect them before they left? Those violet eyes certainly seemed hopeful, and Trip sensed the pull of her *scylori*, the desire to do whatever the dragon wished.

He snorted, somewhat amused that it worked both ways. He could affect people, but if he wasn't careful, he, too, could be affected.

"I suppose I can work on a pair this evening while I'm being tutored," Trip said, not certain the idea was entirely his.

"Excellent." Shulina Arya twirled.

Targoson blinked a few times, and Captain Ahn's eyebrows climbed. Zirkander didn't react—maybe he was so accustomed to the quirks of his dragon houseguests that one wanting skates didn't seem at all odd to him.

Did you know your dragon twirls, Rysha? Trip silently asked, noticing her faint smile.

Yes, she does it in the air too. I've been thinking of asking Dr. Targoson for something for my stomach, but I'm a little worried Shulina Arya would be disappointed if I had to take drugs to ride her. Do you think the dragon riders of old dealt with motion sickness? I don't remember it being mentioned in any of the texts from the First Dragon Era.

I believe we've established that those texts were woefully incomplete in some areas.

This is true, Rysha thought as Shulina Arya twirled again, then flounced out the door.

Bhrava Saruth trailed after her, admiring her backside.

Trip tried to decide if Bhrava Saruth was too old for Shulina Arya. In his human form, he only appeared to be about twenty, but he claimed to be thousands of years old. Shulina Arya was only hundreds of years old. Did that difference matter to dragons, or were females considered mature as soon as they started having breeding cycles? Whenever that was. Trip decided his brain couldn't handle speculation on dragon relationships.

"I think you'll be fine with your small group," Zirkander said. "We don't want Drysaleskar to feel ganged up on. This is a negotiation, not an assault. Besides, we've got Wolf and Tiger Squadrons going out in the morning to handle reports of recent dragon activity elsewhere on the coast." He nodded, somehow including them all in the gesture. "Dismissed."

"Yes, sir," Rysha, Trip, and Ahn said together.

Targoson waved a dismissive hand at Zirkander and said, "I'll invoice you for those grenades."

"I can't wait."

Targoson and Ahn walked together bumping shoulders and murmuring quietly as they headed out. Trip let them go ahead, then followed with Rysha at his side.

"I'm sorry this will delay my plans to make a dragon trap," he said, "but I'll get started as soon as we get back."

"Maybe if Drysaleskar comes to claim the continent and all of the king's complimentary lobster for himself, that silver dragon will disappear on his own. Or the countryside will calm down, and my father won't feel pressured to sell."

"That wouldn't be as fun as creating a snare for a dragon."

"You have roller-skates to make before you can start designing traps."

"Yes, and I understand I have you to thank for that request."

Rysha grinned impishly at him.

"You can *buy* roller-skates in a city this big, you know," Trip said.

"Yes, but whatever you make will be better."

He matched her grin, sensing it was a statement of truth for her, and not simple flattery. He appreciated that she believed that.

Rysha brushed the back of her hand against his. Since they were both in uniform, hugs, hand-holding, and butt-touching were out.

"Do you think it will take long to find this dragon?" she asked.

"I don't know. If he's staying near our coastline, I'll be able to sense him from fifty miles away, and our dragon allies may be able to track him down from even farther away. The question is whether he'll *want* to be found by us."

"Maybe we should take along some sample lobsters."

Trip imagined tossing seafood into a dragon's maw from his cockpit. He also imagined having to smell decomposing lobster sitting in his flier until they found this Drysaleskar.

"Would tarts be better?" he asked. "I can see if Sardelle has any extras on hand when I have my lesson this evening."

"I don't know if Angulus is prepared to add tarts to his tribute."

"So far, all the dragons seem to have a sweet tooth. Or sweet fang."

"I can't deny that."

CHAPTER 11

RYSHA SQUINTED AS THE TEAM flew southward over the ocean, the rising sun slanting into her eyes from the east. It shone above the fog still hugging the coast, obscuring the terrain, and she wondered if they had passed her family's valley yet. She hoped it wouldn't take too long to find this elder dragon and that she and Trip could return to hunt down that silver soon.

"Veering to the southwest for an hour or two," Trip said, his voice sounding tinny as it came from the communication crystal tucked into Rysha's buttoned pocket.

That morning, an officer with the dubious moniker of Captain Pimples had removed it from a flier for her and asked where on her dragon she would like it installed. Rysha was fairly certain it had been a joke, but he had seemed earnest, as if he could hunt down some glue that worked on scales if need be.

"For the random enjoyment of it?" Captain Ahn asked from her flier. "Or because you sense something?"

She was soaring parallel to Trip with Colonel Grady in her back seat while Trip flew with the human-form Bhrava Saruth behind him. The dragon had said he wished to experience human flying contraptions, but judging by the way his leg was thrown over one side, and his head leaned out the other, golden hair flapping against the hull, he wanted to nap rather than fly. Rysha suspected there was a reason Shulina Arya didn't find his romantic entreaties appealing.

So many reasons, Storyteller.

"While I do believe the southwest looks enjoyable," Trip said, "Bhrava Saruth has informed me that he senses a gold dragon in that direction."

"Bhrava Saruth doesn't look like he could currently sense his own butt."

"His naps are only intermittent."

"Uh huh," Ahn said. "Is it the dragon we want?"

"He's not sure yet. He said it's about a hundred miles away. I can't sense anything that far out."

"Why do I envision spending the next week zigzagging across the ocean, Captain?" Ahn asked.

"At least we packed plenty of supplies."

"Of all sorts, yes. I'm still trying to figure out why I, who have a year in rank seniority over you, ended up with smelly fish in my storage compartment, and you're carrying bags of baked goods."

"You can't smell the fish from the cockpit, can you?"

"I most certainly can. And so can Colonel Grady. Doesn't it seem like the powerful sorcerer who can probably make odors disappear should have the stinky things in his flier?"

"Well, I *do* have a dragon's bare foot dangling over the side beside my ear."

"That can't rival the smell of dead fish."

"Don't be too sure. I don't think dragons bathe."

What? Shulina Arya cried, and Rysha worried she was truly offended. *Dragons bathe frequently. Observe.*

That was all the warning Rysha got before Shulina Arya folded her wings to her body and dove toward the ocean like an eagle swooping down to pluck up a fish. Only she didn't want a fish. She plummeted a thousand feet and plunged into the water.

Reflexively, Rysha flattened her chest to the dragon's back, pressed her spectacles to her face, and squeezed with her legs. Fortunately, magic kept her astride as they dove beneath the surface. It even kept her dry.

Rysha glimpsed startled schools of fish taking off in all directions, and then they came up again, as if they had bounced off a trampoline. Shulina Arya flapped her wings and radiated a sense of pleasure and enjoyment as water sloughed off her scales.

"My apologies," Trip said. "I should have said that *some* dragons don't bathe."

Correct, Shulina Arya said. *I will forgive you since you made those glorious wheeled foot devices. I—Hm.*

"Trouble?" Rysha asked.

I now sense the dragons that Bhrava Saruth must have sensed. To the southeast.

"Dragons?" Ahn asked. "Multiple?"

Two golds, I believe, and a bronze, Shulina Arya said.

"Then that's not the dragon we're looking for," Ahn said. "I suggest we zigzag in another direction, so they don't notice us and decide to come pester us."

"We do have two dragons and two *chapaharii* swords with us," Trip said. "Spontaneous pestering seems unlikely."

"Better not to risk it," Ahn said. "They may smell the fish in my storage hold and be unable to resist the pull."

Rysha tried to decide if that was a joke. If so, Ahn had a deadpan delivery.

There is more, Shulina Arya told them as she returned to the same elevation as the fliers and stopped flapping her wings as vigorously—she could outpace the machines easily, so she had to glide often.

"More dragons?" Ahn asked.

No, humans in one of your flying boats.

"An airship?"

Yes, it is a large vessel and there are many aboard. Perhaps fifty humans. Another flying boat is closing on it. Also, the dragons are flying toward it too.

"It could be a merchant airship under attack," Trip said. "If so, it sounds like it's going to need help."

"We don't know if it's Iskandian," Ahn said. "And this isn't the mission we were sent on."

Colonel Grady leaned forward, tapped her on the shoulder, and said something that didn't quite come through Rysha's communication crystal.

Ahn turned her head and said, "Iskandian merchants were told not to fly or sail without an escort, sir."

"…don't always listen," Grady said, followed by something else Rysha didn't hear.

"The colonel wants us to check it out," Ahn said. "And if there are airship pirates harassing someone, to help out. Also, he's already composing lyrics to a ballad that features us nobly saving the lives of innocent merchants."

"I don't think dragons would be working with airship pirates," Rysha said. "Unless there's something on board the ship that they want." Rysha still couldn't imagine dragons teaming up with pirates. Though she supposed some dragons openly allied with nations—just as Shulina Arya and Bhrava Saruth were allied with Iskandia—so maybe it was a possibility.

"I guess we'll find out." Ahn looked over at Trip.

He gave the thumb-to-fingers ready sign.

Bhrava Saruth sat straighter in his seat, then leaped into the air, startling Rysha. He almost struck the tail of the flier, but missed it, and as he started to fall, he turned into his dragon form. He flapped his wings to stop his fall, then quickly caught up with Trip's flier, his sleek golden form dwarfing it.

How was your nap? Shulina Arya asked, the words ringing in Rysha's mind.

Not as enjoyable as I'd hoped, Bhrava Saruth replied. *Flier seats are most uncomfortable. Captain Trip, why are there not proper cushions and pillows?*

"Pillows?" Trip asked. "These are military aircraft."

Which precludes that their occupants be comfortable?

"I think that's in the rules, yes. We—hold on."

Rysha looked over at Trip, the wind whistling against her face, but he was staring straight forward.

"I sense the dragons now too," he said. "And I recognize one of them."

"Drysaleskar the elder?" Rysha realized as soon as she asked that it couldn't be, or their dragon allies would have recognized him.

"No, Telmandaroo." Trip glanced at Ahn's flier and added, "He's a bronze dragon we encountered on the Pirate Isles. We helped him dispose of the self-proclaimed pirate king who was ruling over the islands with the help of a sorceress and a *chapaharii* sword."

"I saw the mission report," Ahn said. "What's he doing out here if he has his own islands now?"

"A good question," Trip said. "I guess this doesn't change anything, right? We're still going to assist these people?"

"We are," Colonel Grady said, leaning over Ahn's shoulder to yell the words at the communication crystal. "But keep us apprised if you're able to learn any more information. Such as if we're on our way to help an Iskandian airship or one from another nation."

"Will we stop if we figure out they're not Iskandians?" Trip sounded disapproving.

Rysha smiled at his noble streak.

"Not necessarily," Grady called, "but we'll have to assess the risk to ourselves and the mission. We cannot fail the king, so picking a fight may be unwise in some circumstances. Also, I have to think of different rhyming words if it's a Cofah ship instead of an Iskandian one. It's a more formidable nation name to work into lyrics."

"Your life is difficult, isn't it, sir?" Ahn asked.

"Inspiringly challenging."

I have an update to report, Shulina Arya said, her voice as perky and enthused as ever, as if this was all new and exciting to her. Rysha supposed it was. Before these last few months, she'd only heard stories about humans and riders and missions where they worked together. *The two flying boats appear to have engaged in battle. They are shooting large metal balls at each other. Also, one of the gold dragons and the bronze dragon have broken away from the others. They are coming toward us.*

"I don't think we're going to get a choice about picking a fight," Trip said.

Feeling grim at the announcement, Rysha rested her hand on Dorfindral's hilt. It hummed eagerly, and images of slashing at dragons and driving the sword between their scales filled her mind. Dorfindral was never grim.

Who comes to interfere with our plunder? the voice of an unfamiliar female dragon boomed in Trip's mind.

He sensed the large gold dragon was about twenty miles away now, with the more familiar bronze dragon—Telmandaroo—flying at her side. It wouldn't take them long to close the distance.

As Trip had noted before, his team had two gold dragons on its side, along with the *chapaharii* swords, but he couldn't assume they would be victorious in a battle. He sensed great power from that female—her aura diminished and obscured Telmandaroo's, making him seem meek and puny in comparison—and suspected she was old, strong, and experienced in battle.

"I think that question is for you, Trip," Ahn said.

He snorted, but didn't disagree. Zirkander had implied this was his mission, even if Grady was in charge. Maybe he could come up with something clever to say in response to obviate the need to fight.

"On it," he said, then switched to telepathy to address the dragon. *Interfere? That is not our intent. We wish to join you.*

Join me? You've heard of the wise and powerful Drivortia?

Even though twenty miles separated them, Trip sensed great power scraping at his mind. He slammed his mental vault door shut, hoping the distance would steal some of the dragon's mind-reading efficacy.

Indeed. I have met your servant before. Trip took a guess that Telmandaroo wasn't an equal partner in whatever arrangement he'd found himself in. *He invited me to become one of his minions.*

A bronze dragon with minions? What a ludicrous thought. They are destined to be minions themselves.

Trip tried to sense Telmandaroo and what he was thinking, though if the bronze was protecting his mind, he wouldn't have a chance. To Trip's surprise, he felt the bronze's emotions easily, simmering indignation and loathing for the situation he found himself in.

I may accept you as a minion of mine, however, Drivortia said. *But do you not already belong to those two gold dragons?*

Belong to? I lead them.

Ringing laughter bubbled into Trip's mind. So that was what a truly amused dragon sounded like.

Admittedly, it had been a cocky thing to say, but he thought it might mean she would continue to communicate with him instead of switching to the dragons. Though she might not *want* to talk to them. She might only be coming out here to confront his team because she had sensed their presence. Had Trip, Ahn, and Rysha been in the fliers without a dragon escort, they might have escaped notice, or been noticed and ignored.

When the laughter finally stopped, Trip let loose all his restraints and attempted to project his aura outward. He knew it wouldn't impress a dragon, especially a gold dragon, but maybe he would at least look like a useful minion.

I lead them, he repeated. *They are allied with Iskandia, and I am an officer in the Iskandian military, the officer that leads this mission.*

A mission to plunder that which my mate and minions are already plundering? I assure you, you'll fail.

"They're fifteen miles out," Trip updated the others. "I think we're going to have to fight."

"I'm ready," Ahn said.

"Dorfindral has been excited for the last forty miles," Rysha said.

Trip decided to try one last tactic, something that might turn the tides in their favor, because if the other gold dragon, the one still back with the airships, decided to come out and help Drivortia, Trip's team would be outnumbered.

Telmandaroo, he thought, switching to the bronze and trying to make his focus very narrow in the hope that Drivortia would not overhear. A vain hope, perhaps, but even if she did overhear, maybe it wouldn't matter. *Do you remember me?*

I remember you. I see you still have those foul swords with you.

Of course. Someone must keep an eye on them. I took them from your islands, as I promised. What happened after that?

I claimed the fortress and had my minions rebuild it and bring me offerings. It was an excellent time, but then these two gold dragons came in and took over. They let me keep my life and live on the islands, but only if I agreed to serve them. Telmandaroo growled into Trip's mind.

Stay out of the battle, and you may join us if you wish. For our dragon allies, all of Iskandia is their playground. Trip imagined Angulus sputtering if he heard the offer. The king had probably already stomped around and cursed a lot at the idea of offering the Tlongan Steppes and a weekly tribute to Drysaleskar. *Providing you don't kill any humans.*

I do not kill my minions. Dead minions can't serve you.

You're a wise dragon.

You think to suborn my minion? Drivortia cried, her words thunderous and painful in Trip's mind.

"Ow," Ahn growled, apparently hearing them too. "What are you saying to that dragon?"

He is mine. And you shall soon be dead.

"Just starting a war, apparently," Trip said. "Focus on the gold. I didn't get confirmation, but I think the bronze will leave us alone."

As if we were worried about a puny bronze, Bhrava Saruth said.

The two dragons appeared on the horizon, and nobody responded to him. Trip focused on the female, hoping he could force her to lower her defenses long enough for the fliers to shoot.

"I'm going to try to get her barrier down as soon as we're within firing range." He touched the grips of his machine guns, guns loaded with a mix of regular bullets and Tolemek's acid-containing ceramic bullets. "Any dragons who want to help me with that are welcome to."

I will take in my rider so she can pierce the dragon's defenses with her sword, Shulina Arya said. *You won't have to lift a talon, Captain Trip.*

"That's good, since I don't have any talons."

Drivortia attacked first, before she and Telmandaroo were in firing range. Trip sensed the massive wave of power rolling toward him and threw up his defenses. The others had the *chapaharii* blades to dampen that power, but Trip had to concentrate if he wanted to survive this.

As the wave of magical energy slammed into his barrier, Azarwrath fed in power to reinforce it. Trip's flier wings didn't wobble, nor did the barrier falter. Not yet.

Trip kept the flight stick steady, driving straight for the gold female. Telmandaroo had put more distance between himself and Drivortia. It was possible that was part of a trick, that he would swoop in from their flank and attack, but Trip hadn't sensed any deception in his words. He believed the bronze dragon truly resented his current circumstances.

Another wave of power slammed into Trip's barrier, and he felt it through his defenses, like a jolt to his entire body that rattled his teeth and his joints. He couldn't yet see the female's eyes, but he could make out her maw opening. Readying to hurl fire at him?

She was within firing range, but her barrier remained up. Trip drew upon his power and tried to strengthen it with his rage—how dare the female target *him* over the dragons? Focusing on her mind, he hurled the mental attack, imagining her brain being crushed.

A roar sounded in his own mind, and pain erupted inside his skull as his head thumped back in his seat.

"Trip?" came Rysha's concerned voice as Shulina Arya picked up speed and sailed over his flier to take the lead.

"I do believe she's more powerful than I am," Trip rasped, struggling for nonchalance though his skull pounded, as if the dragon had left a spear embedded in it.

"Not for long," Rysha said with chilling determination.

Shulina Arya charged ahead and met Drivortia as she spewed fire.

Trip gasped, terrified for Rysha. Logically, he knew Dorfindral would protect her, and that Shulina Arya would, too, but that didn't keep the emotion from flooding him as flames engulfed her and her dragon. Longing to help her, he urged his flier to full speed.

Shulina Arya came through the flames, flew past the female, and banked, coming in hard toward Drivortia. She tilted in the air so Rysha could jump up on her back and slash Dorfindral over her head and toward their foe.

Trip sensed the blade popping the dragon's barrier like a soap bubble.

As Shulina Arya circled away to pick up speed for another attack, Trip soared in, machine guns pounding. Drivortia, distracted by Shulina Arya and Rysha, didn't see him. He strafed past, slamming bullets into her chest and flank. The ceramic projectiles shattered upon impact, and acid oozed onto her scales.

Halfway through his run, the dragon got her barrier back up. The rest of his bullets bounced off.

Drivortia hurled flames, not at him but at Shulina Arya again.

As the momentum of his flier carried him past his foe's tail, Trip imagined Rysha being bathed in flames, and that built far more rage in him than any affront to himself could. He launched that rage and all his mental energy into an attack, again targeting the dragon's mind.

Drivortia's barrier faltered, and he sensed pain from her. He didn't know if it was from his attack, from Shulina Arya's attack, or from the acid, but he was relieved to know they were doing damage.

Machine guns fired behind him, Ahn taking a run. Colonel Grady's roar came over the communication crystal, and as Trip took his flier in a loop so he could come back for another attack, he spotted Grady standing in his seat, one hand gripping his harness and the other slashing at the dragon.

Trip couldn't tell if they got close enough for him to strike her, but he trusted that some of Ahn's bullets had found their mark.

Help me, you coward! Drivortia cried.

Trip sensed not only anger but compulsion in that command.

Telmandaroo flew toward the battle, coming in behind Shulina Arya. *Look out!* Trip warned her, then piloted his flier toward Drivortia's back.

As Shulina Arya whipped around to face the threat of the bronze, Drivortia got her barrier up again. Trip had been about to fire, but he released the trigger. Red lightning streaked from Azarwrath's scabbard, snapping and flashing all around the dragon. Trip sensed her magical barrier flickering and could tell Drivortia was wounded, but she might recover if he didn't do something.

Shulina Arya hurled flames at the bronze dragon as Bhrava Saruth came in from behind Telmandaroo, battering him with a wave of power. The bronze was hurled to the side, head over tail as he tumbled through the air.

With the others temporarily busy, Drivortia spun away from Trip, her tail snapping toward his flier. He threw all his energy into strengthening his barrier and had the satisfaction of seeing the snake-like appendage bounce off. A jolt went through the dragon as Azarwrath hurled more lightning at her.

Trip met Drivortia's eyes, yellow reptilian eyes the color of her fire, and clenched his fist and launched another mental attack. Her head whipped back, much as his had earlier, and she screeched like a dying pig.

She'd finally had enough. She hurled one final desperate attack that Trip and Azarwrath deflected, then flew downward, toward the ocean. Drivortia spiraled out of control, and Trip's first thought was that she was already dead. But he sensed life from her, sensed the pain rolling off her. She struck the surface of the ocean and disappeared, plunging into the dark depths.

Her magic protected her as she sank quickly, reaching the bottom and crawling beneath a rock ledge. She must have tamped down her aura because she seemed to disappear from Trip's senses.

That dragon is playing possum, Shulina Arya said. *Shall we go down and finish her off, Storyteller?*

Rysha looked over at Trip. Ahn and Grady flew closer, also looking at him. Hells, maybe he *was* leading this mission.

"She's not a proven enemy of Iskandia," Trip said, "and she's clearly given up. I think we can leave her. As the colonel pointed out, this isn't truly our mission."

He looked around for Bhrava Saruth, expecting him to have an opinion.

Have no fear, Bhrava Saruth said. *I have removed the threat of the dastardly bronze.*

He was behind Trip's flier, flapping his wings enough to hover while he gripped the bronze dragon by the throat. Telmandaroo hung limp, his long neck trapped in Bhrava Saruth's jaws.

At first, Trip thought him dead, with his spine broken, but he sensed life from the dragon.

I did not wish to attack, he told them, his voice meek.

He is cowardly and easily manipulated, Bhrava Saruth said. *Shall I slay him?*

"You don't think he'd like to become one of your worshippers?" Ahn asked—apparently, the dragons were sharing their telepathic words with everybody.

Dragons make poor worshippers. They do not know how to be affectionate and appealing.

Let him go, Trip said. *He's no further threat.*

Hmmph.

Based on that dubious response, Trip wasn't sure Bhrava Saruth would actually listen. Trip met the dragon's green eyes, gazing steadily into them, and tried to convey that this was his mission and he'd been put in charge, at least when it came to dealing with other dragons.

To his surprise, Bhrava Saruth opened his maw. Telmandaroo tumbled out, falling dozens of feet before he recovered, flapping his wings and regaining his altitude. Blood dripped from the crushed scales of his neck, and Trip felt sorry for him, even if he'd been involved in pirating. He hadn't truly wished to attack this group.

Telmandaroo looked down toward the ocean, perhaps checking on the gold female, then over at Trip.

Human, you have saved my life. Telmandaroo sounded puzzled, either at the idea that his life had been in danger or at the idea that a human had bothered intervening on his behalf.

You're not going to offer to make me a high-level minion again, are you?

No. You are not a minion. I see this now.

Trip lifted his eyebrows. He wasn't sure what he had done to deserve such esteem, but he would not object.

We're going to stop the attack on the airship, Trip said. *Will you come?*

Telmandaroo hesitated. *You wish me to fight against Drivortia's mate? He is surly, grumpy, and has bad breath.*

I had no idea dragons were concerned about such things.

You are a strange human, Captain Trip, Shulina Arya said. *You believe dragons don't bathe, and you also believe we like our breath smelling foul?*

Well, I didn't know. Until a few weeks ago, I didn't know any dragons at all.

That is odd, given your heritage.

There's much odd about me. Trip caught Rysha's gaze and smirked wryly. He almost added his familiar statement, that he was glad Rysha liked odd men, but the dragons probably wouldn't understand.

I will accompany you, Telmandaroo said. *I do not wish to battle Drivortia's surly mate, but if you slay him, I can return to my islands and rule there again. I could become a great ally to your nation in the future.*

Telryn, Azarwrath said. *That bronze dragon wishes to use you.*

Yes, it's not the first time. So long as he doesn't attack us, I'm content.

Hm.

"Let's go," Trip said, speaking aloud as well as telepathically, so everyone would be sure to hear. "That airship could be in splinters by now."

Shulina Arya pumped her wings and took the lead. *It is a beautiful day to save lives,* she announced. *And also to valiantly slay enemies.*

Rysha patted her on the neck.

Bhrava Saruth picked up his pace so that he could fly beside Shulina Arya. Telmandaroo flew beside Trip's flier, with Ahn and Grady on the other side. They were an odd little squadron.

She is sleek, Telmandaroo spoke into his mind.

What? Trip glanced around, wondering if that comment had been sent directly to him or to everyone. Neither the other dragons nor Ahn, Rysha, or Grady reacted.

That female dragon. She is sleek and young. And supple. And she didn't call me an imbecile. Will you tell me her name?

Shulina Arya.

Is she the mate of Bhrava Saruth? I've heard of him.

I don't believe they're mates, no.

Excellent. Perhaps I will invite her to my islands when I get them back. I could have my minions rub her and polish her scales.

I'll wish you luck with that. So far, she hasn't appeared impressed by dragon wiles.

Bhrava Saruth spun in the air ahead of them as he flew. As far as Trip could tell, Shulina Arya didn't notice. Or noticed and didn't care.

That dragon is foolish. Even bronze dragons know him to be so.

It is possible that a different style of courtship would impress her more.

Telmandaroo fell silent after that, contemplating courtship styles perhaps. Trip was glad. He wanted to complete his mission and help his country, not help dragons get dates.

Trip stretched ahead with his senses, looking for the airships, but he needn't have bothered.

"Smoke ahead," Ahn said.

Trip nodded, spotting it. The airships were lower than their fliers, only a few hundred feet above the ocean, and one was losing altitude as the squadron approached. The faint booms of cannons reached Trip's ears, and a gold dragon swooped back and forth above the balloon of the damaged craft.

The smoking airship was painted in the blue and gold colors of Iskandia. Trip had been afraid of that. It wasn't a military craft, but it had clearly come from their shores.

"Colonel Grady says we're going in," Ahn added.

"I'm ready." Trip hoped they weren't too late.

CHAPTER 12

RYSHA SAT ASTRIDE SHULINA ARYA'S back, her sword resting on her thighs as the team flew closer to the smoking airship. After the first battle, she felt confident they could handle another dragon, but seeing the armored pirate ship harrying the ponderous Iskandian air freighter made her uneasy. Dozens of cannons and shell guns lined the pirate ship's deck, and Rysha could make out dozens and dozens of men with rifles, most of them near the railing and firing across the gap.

The Iskandian ship, its balloon torn and losing gas, wasn't putting up much of a fight, not anymore. Fires burned in numerous spots on the deck, and several ragged holes gaped on both sides of the hull. If the vessel was forced to land in the water, it wouldn't float, not for long. Even if Rysha and the others managed to drive away the dragon and the pirates, could Trip fix a mess like that to save the ship?

She glanced over her shoulder. Shulina Arya had outpaced the fliers, but Rysha could still see his flier—and the bronze dragon soaring beside it. She knew Trip had talked to that bronze back on the Pirate Isles and could understand why he'd wanted to spare his life, but she didn't trust Telmandaroo. She suspected he would say anything to save his life and would betray a new ally as quickly as befriend him.

The gold dragon has seen us, Bhrava Saruth announced. *And he called me a delusional and overstuffed gold turkey. I do not like him.*

"There are a lot of injured and hurting people in that airship," Trip said. "*Our* airship."

"Let's have our dragons focus on the gold dragon," Colonel Grady called from the back seat. "Ahn and Trip will take down the pirate vessel. We'll have to wait until after we've dealt with the threats to help the crew and see if we can save the ship."

"Yes, sir," Ahn and Trip said.

Rysha patted Shulina Arya's back. "It looks like we're fighting another dragon."

This is what I enjoy. To prove that my mother was wrong and that I am not a weakling. I am a strong dragon and am good at protecting those who are not strong.

Rysha smiled. She hadn't heard Shulina Arya explain why she liked helping humans before but could see why the dragon would feel prickly toward those who used their power to pick on the weak.

Shulina Arya headed straight toward the male gold—he was busy bathing the Iskandian airship's envelope in flames and did not look at the newcomers. That was surprising. Did he not yet know that his mate had been grievously injured? He had to.

I can sense a few of his thoughts, Trip spoke into her mind. *He's distracted. He knows his mate was injured, but he's focused on something else. He wants what's inside the Iskandian airship.*

Which is what?

I'm not sure. Food, I think. Pods? Beans? And some long sticks.

Sticks?

Canes? Maybe it's lemongrass.

Rysha snorted. *Catnip to dragons, I'm sure.*

Shulina Arya arrowed toward the male dragon and was almost close enough to breathe fire when he lifted his head and glared at them with icy green eyes. They weren't a deep emerald like Trip's but a chartreuse, more akin to the light flaring from Dorfindral's blade.

The male roared, and fire roiled from the depths of his pink throat. It shot a hundred yards, directly at Shulina Arya.

She didn't flinch. She erected a barrier and flew straight into the flames.

Be ready, Storyteller! You can drive your sword down his gullet.

I'm ready.

Rifles fired from below, startling Rysha. They were close to the airship battle now, and she'd almost forgotten about the pirates. Some continued firing across to the Iskandian freighter, but more men pointed their rifles upward, shooting at Rysha and Shulina Arya.

The bullets bounced off Shulina Arya's invisible shield, again manifested in a way that it protected Rysha even though she wielded Dorfindral. She gripped the hilt, smiling as they closed on the male gold, starting to feel that no single foe could stand against them.

Shulina Arya attempted to fly her close enough to strike, but the male must have sensed the *chapaharii* sword. He twisted in the air, flapping quickly away and lashing at them with his tail. Shulina Arya snapped her jaws to the side, catching the very tip of that tail and clamping down.

Rysha crouched, ready to join in the skirmish as soon as she was close enough. The male hurled a mental attack at them. Even protected by Dorfindral, Rysha winced, feeling something that felt like a hurricane gale knocking around inside her skull.

Shulina Arya cried out, letting go of the tail and shaking her head. She stopped flapping her wings, and they dropped. Rysha's heart sprang into her throat, and she dropped to her belly, afraid of falling off.

Shulina Arya recovered just short of landing on the Iskandian airship's smoldering envelope.

Machine guns fired behind them, Ahn and Trip taking a run at the pirate airship. Most of the crew ran for cover and to return fire as the fliers passed, but Rysha spotted a woman in black glaring in her direction. Next to her, a man in a pointed blue hat raised a bow.

Rysha almost laughed. What was a bow when everyone around that man was firing shell guns and rifles? Then she remembered that *she* was using a sword.

Bhrava Saruth flapped past after the fliers, breathing flames at the pirate ship and lighting its envelope on fire.

Brace yourself, Storyteller. Shulina Arya flapped her wings to take them back toward the battle, but there was a wobble to her flight that hadn't been there before. *The male is very powerful with mental attacks. I was not completely ready for that. Here he comes, aiming for us again.*

Rysha crouched again, hoping to get a chance to injure the gold so he would be less of a problem. But she kept an eye on that archer, suspecting he was more than he appeared. The man no longer faced her and Shulina Arya. Instead, he focused on one of the fliers. Trip's.

Trip flew his craft straight into the airship, between the deck and the envelope, its wings tipping left and right to avoid supports and cables. He fired all the while, driving the crew to dive for cover or run below decks.

The woman in black didn't flee. She lifted a hand toward him as the archer at her side fired.

Rysha was too far away to see if there was anything special about the bow, but she blurted a, "Look out, Trip!" just in case.

He tilted his wings so the arrow clunked into the underside of his flier instead of hitting him, but he let out a startled oath. Red lightning shot from his cockpit, from Azarwrath. It streaked toward the woman and the archer, but did not strike either. Trip yelled in surprise and pain as if something had struck him.

"Sorceress," Captain Ahn announced with surprising calm.

"Drop me off," Grady ordered.

Now, Storyteller, Shulina Arya ordered, and Rysha wrenched her attention from the other battle as the dragon took her straight into another gout of fire.

Rysha couldn't see anything but yellow and orange flames writhing around her, the heat palpable against her skin, even with her sword's magical protection.

"Ready," she said, raising Dorfindral.

They had to be closing on the male's head. Shulina Arya banked hard, and a pale green eye came into view, far too close for comfort. But close enough to strike?

Rysha lashed out and felt the popping of a magical barrier, but she couldn't quite reach that eye. Then the dragon's neck whipped toward her, and its maw opened wide, flames licking past its spear-like fangs.

Rysha almost shrieked in terror as those fangs lunged at her, and she realized she was the dragon's target. But she clamped her mouth shut, gritted her teeth, and jumped up as the jaws snapped at her. She drove her sword upward, the blade glancing off a front fang and sinking into the top of the dragon's mouth.

The gold jerked his head back, yanking the sword from her grip but not before pulling her from Shulina Arya's back.

This time, Rysha couldn't tamp down her alarmed cry. She tumbled through the sky as the male dragon shrieked, the noise battering her brain as well as her ears. Pain pulsed through her as she fell, but she twisted, trying to making sure her feet would hit the water first, though she feared she was so high that it wouldn't matter. The landing could break every bone in her body—or kill her.

She hit something far sooner than expected. The envelope of the Iskandian airship. It gave a little, and she bounced off. She glimpsed a fiery inferno on the deck of the pirate airship as she flew upward and then started dropping again, this time to the side of the freighter. She spotted the ocean, hundreds of feet below, as she picked up speed, plummeting like a boulder.

Then some invisible power grasped her, slowing her descent. She stopped altogether, hovering and looking up at the bottoms of the two airships. They were both smoking now, dark gray clouds hazing the air all around the battle.

Something huge fell past Rysha, startling her. A gold dragon. For a sickening second, she thought it was Shulina Arya. But it was the male, falling limply toward the ocean below.

I have you, Storyteller, Shulina Arya announced, flying into view, *but I was not able to extract your magic-hating sword, I regret.*

Extract? Rysha stared down as the male hit the water with enough force that he instantly plunged below the surface. She groaned as she realized Dorfindral must still be thrust into the roof of his mouth.

We will get it back. Shulina Arya sailed under Rysha, and they were reunited, dragon and rider.

Rysha was glad, but she also grimaced, realizing she had nothing to contribute to the battle until they could retrieve the *chapaharii* blade. She tried not to think about what would happen if the ocean was far, far deeper here than the Lagresh harbor had been.

Your officer has engaged the sorceress, Azarwrath said.
Good.

Trip was glad he didn't have to speak out loud, since he was panting with pain. He'd been shot in the arm, and agony blazed from the wound.

He made himself continue to manipulate the flight stick, taking them back around so he could help Grady.

The colonel was down on the pirate ship's deck, battling a sorceress and someone with a *chapaharii* bow, neither of which Trip had sensed. The aura of the gold dragon glowing so brightly dulled everything nearby. Besides, he admitted with chagrin, he hadn't expected mages and *chapaharii* weapons out in the middle of the ocean with pirates, so he hadn't thought to look for more than the dragon.

Nor did I, Azarwrath confessed. *Get us closer. I can finish off the sorceress. She is running from your colonel while the pirates get in the way—they are protecting her.*

Trip accelerated into a dive, the smoky deck of the enemy airship coming into view again. He saw Grady, whirling and slashing, deflecting bullets fired at him and cutting down pirates. He was a deadly force, but Azarwrath was right. The sorceress had run behind a lifeboat mounted near the railing.

Can we destroy this foul vessel? Bhrava Saruth asked, flying past on the opposite side of the airship and peering at the deck. *I can burn more than its little balloon.*

Not yet, Trip told him. *We have a man aboard it.*

Trip focused on the sorceress as she used her power to bring down a support beam that was over Grady's head. Trip shifted his attention to hurl it out of the way, though Grady must have heard it snap, because he sprang to the side before it would have struck. He glanced in Trip's direction and lifted a hand.

The sorceress also glanced in Trip's direction as he flew closer, her expression far less friendly.

Azarwrath sent lightning streaking toward her. Trip sensed her putting all her energy into her defenses. He squinted at her and imagined those defenses being ripped away. They fell instantly, and the lightning slammed into her, wrapping all around her and charring her flesh. She screamed and tumbled away from the lifeboat, slamming into the railing. Azarwrath hurled a blast of wind. The railing broke, and she fell over the side.

Trip winced, always more disturbed by killing human beings than dragons. He reminded himself that these people had been attacking an Iskandian freighter.

His flier's momentum had carried him past the pirate vessel, and he banked to come back in again. The crew ought to be ready to give up with their sorceress dead, but the man with the *chapaharii* bow might still be firing arrows. Earlier, one of those arrows had popped Trip's barrier right before a barrage of rifle fire came at him. He'd weaved and tilted his wings crazily, but the confines of the ship had limited his maneuverability, and that first bullet had taken him by surprise.

"The Iskandian airship is falling faster," Ahn said. "A *lot* faster."

Trip shifted his focus to it, hoping he had the power to levitate it or at least slow its fall enough that it wouldn't be destroyed when it landed in the water. Unfortunately, he had never attempted to affect something so large.

He'd barely started trying when he sensed someone else using power on it. The airship halted a few dozen yards above the ocean, its crew members on their knees, bracing for impact. They lifted their heads in surprise.

Ah, finally I have done some good, Bhrava Saruth announced. *Shulina Arya was hogging the battle with the male.*

It's not my fault you were so slow to attack, Shulina Arya said.

I could have attacked with great speed, but I did not wish my assaults to strike you as well as the male. You were so close to him that you could have licked his tail.

I bit his tail.

Trip looked around for Shulina Arya, wanting to see Rysha, to make sure she had come through unscathed. That archer had added an unexpected element.

She is fine, Azarwrath said. *Only you were shot.*

That's good then.

It would have been better if you hadn't been shot. Telryn, I know you are accustomed to shooting things with this flying contraption, but as a sorcerer, there is no need to get so close.

I'll keep that in mind.

Trip spotted the bronze dragon in the distance. Telmandaroo had stayed out of the way, never engaging. That was fine. Trip was happy he hadn't worked with the pirates against his team.

But where was Shulina Arya?

Look down, Azarwrath advised.

A dead gold dragon floated on the waves not far from where the Iskandian airship hovered. Shulina Arya was flying in circles around it.

"What's going on down there?" Trip asked curiously.

Rysha sighed, the noise just audible over her communication crystal. "I'm retrieving my sword."

"You threw it again?" Trip imagined them having to dive thousands of feet into the ocean to get it off the bottom. "I don't think you're supposed to do that with a sword."

"I didn't throw it. It got stuck."

Rysha slithered off Shulina Arya's back, surprising Trip. She landed in the water next to the dead dragon and swam toward his head.

"I'm landing on the pirate ship for long enough to pick up Colonel Grady," Ahn said. "He has singlehandedly cut down most of the crew."

"I'm sure your bullets took down plenty of them," Trip said—Ahn sounded a little envious.

"A few. The sorceress was protecting them. Was she a powerful one? She seemed strong."

Once Trip had known she existed and focused on her, it hadn't been difficult to defeat her. He thought that might sound like bragging, so he only said, "I believe she could have rivaled Sardelle in power, so she was strong for this era, yes."

"Got it," Rysha said, then grunted with effort. "Sort of."

Trip flew down closer in case she needed help. She planted her boots on the dragon's maw, one on a fang and one on a lip, and pulled backward, both hands on Dorfindral's hilt. The sword finally slid from the roof of the dragon's mouth. Rysha looked up at Shulina Arya, and Trip sensed her trying to figure out how to get back on her back.

He tried to lift her before remembering Dorfindral wouldn't allow it. He was surprised Shulina Arya could affect her as much as she could, since it was magic that kept a rider on a dragon's back.

Shulina Arya dove down into the water and came up beside Rysha so she could climb back on.

How long do I have to hold this hulking boat here? Bhrava Saruth asked, flying lazy circles around the hovering Iskandian freighter.

"If it's not seaworthy, it'll need a ride back to Iskandia," Ahn said.

You wish me to carry it all the way across the ocean?

Do you feel you won't be able to nap sufficiently if you have to do that? Shulina Arya asked, flying up from the water with Rysha aboard.

"Can you hold it there for a half hour or so?" Trip piloted his flier toward the airship. "I'll land on the deck and see if I can put out the fires and help the crew repair it."

A half hour? Bhrava Saruth sighed dramatically into their minds. *Very well.*

Bhrava Saruth is a very old dragon, Shulina Arya informed them. *It distresses him when he can't nap on an hourly basis.*

I am not old! I am magnificent and in the prime of my life. There is nothing wrong with enjoying a nap while the sun beats upon your scales—your skin—and someone else flies you. Though I do not believe I will sit in the back of one of those flying contraptions again until pillows are installed.

"We'll be sure to put in a work order for that," Ahn muttered.

What remained of the Iskandian crew scattered as Trip flew close, glad he had one of the two-seater fliers, since it had thrusters. He activated them and came down on a portion of the deck that appeared less charred than others. Flames still burned in numerous spots, though the crew seemed to have realized the battle was over and that they could come out and attempt to put them out.

People poked their heads out from behind supports and railings. Since Trip wore his Iskandian uniform and was in one of the iconic bronze dragon fliers, he didn't expect trouble, but he lifted his hand, the one on the uninjured side, and tried to look friendly. That was a challenge with the ache in his shoulder. At the least, he hoped he didn't appear dragonly or odd.

A ragged cheer went up. That was encouraging.

Ahn's flier also headed for the deck, Colonel Grady once again in her back seat.

"Can you handle talking to the crew, Captain?" Trip asked. "I'd like to focus on fixing their ship. Perhaps my shoulder, too, if there's time."

"What happened to your shoulder?" Ahn asked.

"I got shot."

"Ah. Yes, stay in your cockpit and do your magic. We'll have Colonel Grady talk to the civilian captain since he outranks us. And has half a ballad composed."

"Really, Captain," came Grady's voice from the back seat. "I've only composed a few lines in my head."

"You already titled it."

"Sometimes, titles come before the first words have been written. Captain Trip, I can't tell you how pleased I am about your nickname."

"Oh?" Trip wondered if he should feel wary.

"It rhymes with so *many* things." Grady sounded truly delighted.

The first words that popped into Trip's mind were drip, pip, and gyp, which left him less delighted.

How about airship, wing tip, and bullwhip? Azarwrath suggested.

Those sound like they could lead to slightly more promising lyrics, Trip allowed, noting that Azarwrath had come up with words with more syllables. Did that mean he was smarter than Trip, and if so, should he be concerned? *Can you heal my wound while I work on the ship?*

I shall endeavor to do so, though without Jaxi here to incinerate the bullet, I will be handicapped.

Was that sarcasm?

Of course not. That would be poor sportsmanship. Trip. Fan of the potato chip. Azarwrath grinned into his mind, apparently pleased by this new word game.

Trip closed his eyes and slumped back in the cockpit.

CHAPTER 13

BY THE TIME RYSHA SLID off Shulina Arya's back and onto the deck of the Iskandian airship, the pirate vessel had fallen out of the sky. It floated in the ocean below, its envelope half burned away, the tattered and charred remains whipping about in the breeze. The Iskandian ship remained aloft, thanks to Bhrava Saruth's magic. He continued to fly in slow circles around the vessel, waiting for Trip to repair it.

With her uniform dripping and her bun hanging wet and limp at the nape of her neck, Rysha walked toward the cluster of merchant sailors standing with Captain Ahn and Colonel Grady.

Several of the crew looked at her, and at Shulina Arya behind her, the dragon crouching with her wings folded in so she would fit on the deck under the envelope. They clapped and a few let out whoops of praise and thanks. Rysha felt embarrassed by the attention, even if it seemed more for Shulina Arya than her, but she was glad the crew was appreciative, especially given that there were a few dead being carried from the deck. Rysha wished her team had arrived earlier, so nobody would have been lost, but she reminded herself that only luck had brought them here in time to help at all.

"We're bound for the capital," a graying man was telling Colonel Grady and Ahn. "All of Iskandia will be glad that you were able to help us. It appears that, despite all the damage up here, the cargo and the hold are safe."

"All of Iskandia?" Grady asked. "What are you carrying that's so important? And why didn't you wait until a military escort was available to accompany you?"

"Military escorts are in short supply," the graying man said, the captain presumably. "We would have had to wait six weeks, and our cargo is perishable. We're carrying chocolate, coffee, and sugarcane."

"Ah, that *is* an important cargo."

"I know of several dragons who would have been distressed if the markets in the capital ran out of sugar." Rysha glanced back at Shulina Arya. "That being a primary ingredient in tarts."

The captain squinted at her, as if he was trying to figure out if she was joking or not. Then he looked past her, and his eyes grew rounder than silver nucros. He stumbled backward, almost tripping on his own feet.

Shulina Arya's head appeared over Rysha's shoulder, as large and intimidating as always. The crew must have found it easier to appreciate her from the other side of the ship. Up close, she was admittedly large.

The group took several more steps back when her mouth parted slightly, enough to reveal her long white fangs. Even Ahn and Grady appeared concerned.

Tarts? Shulina Arya asked. *Did someone say there are tarts here?*

"Sorry, no," Rysha said. "Merely one of the ingredients integral in making tarts."

That is disappointing. I find sweets delightful, especially after a strenuous battle. We did not have sweets in the other world.

"So *that's* why dragons came back," Colonel Grady said.

"I have a sack of jawbreakers in my cabin," the captain said, transfixed as he continued to stare at Shulina Arya.

Rysha didn't think the dragon was trying to manipulate the crew in any way, but they did appear influenced by her presence, her strong aura. Rysha tended to forget how powerful and compelling it was since she so often carried Dorfindral and was less affected by it.

Jawbreakers? Shulina Arya asked.

"I'll get them for you. You can try one." The captain ran for a hatchway leading below decks as if he worried someone would flog him if he didn't move quickly enough.

"Is he coming back?" Grady arched an eyebrow. "Or was that an excuse?"

"I think he's eager to please Shulina Arya," Rysha said. "She *was* paramount in saving the ship."

"You did well, too, Lieutenant." Grady nodded at her. "I'm fortunate to be surrounded by competent officers, especially considering how useless I felt until the very end." Grady patted his sword scabbard.

Ahn winced. Rysha didn't think the words had been meant as a slight against her or her piloting skills, but Ahn said, "I'll have to practice to get better at bringing the flier close enough for someone with a *chapaharii* sword to attack. I've been in the position you were in, sir, and I know it's frustrating not to be able to reach the target. In the battle with Morishtomaric a few years ago, I had to tie a rope to my ankle so I could run out on the wings."

Grady's mouth dangled open at this image. Rysha expected him to say that was ludicrous and that whoever had been in charge of that mission should have been punished for allowing Ahn to take such dangerous measures.

Instead, he called out, "Does anybody have any rope they can spare?"

Most of the crew were gazing at Shulina Arya with enraptured expressions and didn't seem to hear him.

"I'll go look for myself," Grady said. "And help with repairs. Or will Captain Trip be able to use his magic to do everything?" He looked dubiously toward the fliers.

Trip remained in his cockpit, slumped forward with his forehead resting on the dashboard. He looked so out of it that Rysha worried he'd been injured. If he had been, he hadn't said anything.

She took a step in that direction, intending to check on him, but paused when the captain jogged back out on deck, holding what looked like a sack of marbles. At first, it seemed he would keep going and thrust the bag out to offer to Shulina Arya, but her jaws parted in interest, and the motion happened to reveal even more of her fangs. The captain stuttered to a halt.

"I'll give them to her." Rysha walked toward him. "Are you offering the whole bag or just one?"

"She would eat the whole bag?"

"You should see what she does to a tray of tarts."

The captain looked inside and plucked out the largest jawbreaker Rysha had ever seen, its spherical surface covered in blue, yellow, and green swirls. Though she doubted the captain was lying about the contents of his stash, Rysha sniffed it to make sure it was indeed food. The ultra-sweet scent didn't appeal to her, but she also hadn't spent all day flapping her wings and carrying a rider.

She walked the jawbreaker to Shulina Arya as the crew watched.

"You suck on it," Rysha told the dragon. "They're too hard to chew. Well, they are for humans. I don't imagine anything could break a dragon's jaw."

Suck? Shulina Arya sounded puzzled. Maybe dragon anatomy didn't allow for sucking.

"You'll see." Rysha held the treat out in offering.

A giant pink tongue lolled out, coming to rest on the deck. As large as the jawbreaker was, it appeared small in comparison. Rysha rested it in the center of the dragon's tongue and stepped back.

Shulina Arya lifted her head, drawing her tongue in. *It tastes good. Not as good as tarts, but tangy.*

She shifted her jaw around, opening and closing it without actually crunching down. Maybe she was *trying* to suck. The jawbreaker slid sideways and fell out between two large teeth. It clattered on the deck and rolled away. The tongue shot out, startling the crew as it landed on the jawbreaker and flattened, keeping it from escaping. Next, the tongue tilted and flexed as Shulina Arya tried to pick up her lost prize.

Rysha gripped her chin, debating if her duty as a rider extended to picking up saliva-covered candy to deposit—re-deposit—in a dragon's mouth.

Shulina Arya gave up on recapturing it with her tongue and instead floated the candy back into her mouth with her magic. This time, she crunched down on it. It sounded like bone breaking. Apparently, the treat satisfied her, because she turned her head toward the captain and his bag, her expression most expectant.

Rysha patted her on the neck and walked toward Trip. She trusted Shulina Arya could handle the rest of the bag on her own if the captain was willing to share it.

Trip's forehead still rested on the dashboard, and his eyes were closed. Rysha didn't want to disturb him while he concentrated on his magic, so she climbed into the empty seat behind him.

I am healing his injury, Azarwrath informed her.

She frowned, almost reaching forward to touch Trip. He *had* been injured.

Will he be all right?

Something floated back to her, then clanked onto the floor of her seat well. A bloody bullet. She grimaced. That was even worse than a dragon-beslimed jawbreaker.

Yes, Azarwrath said.

That's good. Can I help with anything? Rysha couldn't imagine what, but she felt like she should be doing more than sitting down. The captain was shooing his crew back to work cleaning and repairing the ship. It was a mess, with broken boards and soot everywhere.

I believe Telryn would find it extremely helpful if you rested your hand on his shoulder in a loving and encouraging manner.

Rysha snorted, amused that Trip had his sword, knowingly or not, lobbying for him to get feminine attention. She leaned forward, careful not to touch the bloody bullet with her boot, and laid her hand on his shoulder. She also rested her head against his upper back, though she lifted it when something tarp-like floated by.

Something for repairing the envelope? She glanced up as it sailed past and laid itself against the framework for the balloon in a spot where a giant charred hole had burned. It acted like a patch, and as she watched, the edges seemed to glue themselves to the existing fabric. Or melt to them, maybe. The material appeared coarse and strange, not like the typical patch fabric that would have been stored below.

That's because they had very little patch fabric down there, Trip spoke into her mind. *I'm making my own.*

Out of what?

Remember what I thought was lemongrass?

I remember that you only vaguely know what lemongrass is.

True. The long sticks are sugarcane. I'm pulping some of them and creating a fabric that should work for the short term.

Better not let Shulina Arya know you're destroying future tart sugar.

Actually, I'm extracting the juice before using the fibrous pulp. I had a discussion with the first mate—once he got over the fear of me speaking to him in his mind—about how not to ruin his cargo. I would have had the discussion with the captain, but he was distracted by your dragon.

Shulina Arya is a distracting being.

Yes. I'm a little disappointed that you didn't bring me a jawbreaker.

Sorry. Rysha peered over the side of the flier, wondering if any were left. Shulina Arya was pushing the empty bag around on the deck with her tongue. Trying to fit it inside to lick any remaining sugar?

"Trip, I'm growing more and more convinced that we could turn all dragons into our allies if we could just get them to sample our candies and baked goods."

He chuckled. *Maybe so, but what would happen if we ran out and—*

He sat up, frowning out toward the ocean.

"What is it?" Rysha asked.

"I sense another dragon."

As do I, Storyteller, Shulina Arya said. *I was distracted, or I would have noticed him earlier.*

Distracted? Is that what you're calling it? Though she joked, Rysha worried they were about to have to go into battle again.

"I believe it's the elder dragon we're looking for," Trip said.

Rysha looked at the empty jawbreaker bag. "Maybe we should have saved a few of those."

Weariness weighed down Trip's limbs as he piloted his flier to the south, in the direction he sensed the elder dragon. Once again, Ahn and Grady flew beside him. Shulina Arya and Bhrava Saruth were sometimes ahead, sometimes behind, and the bronze dragon, Telmandaroo, trailed far behind. Trip wouldn't be surprised if he disappeared and flew back to his islands. He *ought* to be grateful, since Trip's team had extracted him from a servile position, but Trip didn't expect that from any dragons.

I don't think I'm up for another fight, Azarwrath, Trip said silently, saving the words for the soulblade rather than the communication crystal. He didn't want his comrades to worry that he wouldn't be reliable.

He was sure he could summon some energy if they ended up battling the elder dragon, but repairing the airship had taken as much out of him as the battle. More. He never would have guessed how painstaking it was to turn sugarcane into thread and then weave the thread into fabric. The fact that he'd had to make so much of it hadn't helped. The next time he bought clothing from someone, especially if that someone had been the one to make it, he would leave a large tip.

"How far away is the dragon now, Trip?" Ahn asked.

"Still about twenty miles."

"He's not flying toward us, I gather."

"No. He's heading south and we're trying to catch him. Fortunately, he's set a languid pace."

"I don't suppose you can talk to him and invite him to head this way?"

"Are you in a hurry to have tea with him?" Trip had no idea how this meeting would go, and he believed a battle was as likely as a successful negotiation.

"I'm in a hurry to have these fish out of my storage hold. The sun beating on the hull isn't helping with the aroma."

"At least they didn't fall out during the battle." Trip had forgotten all about their bribes. He suspected the baked goods in his storage hold had been smashed from side to side and battered beyond recognition when he'd piloted the flier in loops and barrel rolls.

"Yes, that *would* have been unfortunate."

"Captain Ahn, I suspect you of having more of a sense of humor than your reputation suggests."

"Then you won't mind if I laugh when you find out Colonel Grady stuck a couple of our fish in your storage hold?"

"Uh." That wasn't true, was it?

Trip sniffed to either side of his seat. He poked his senses into the storage hold and *did* detect a couple of overly ripe fish lying inside it. He suspected the smell would grow noticeable before long.

Snickers came over the crystal. From Colonel Grady?

"Sir, you're not what I expected from an elite troops veteran."

"Just be happy I'm more fun than Colonel Therrik."

"A brick wall is more fun than Colonel Therrik," Ahn said.

"And less likely to fall mercilessly on you," Grady said.

Drysaleskar has contacted me, Shulina Arya told them. *He wishes to know why we're stalking him.*

Why did he contact you before me? Bhrava Saruth wondered. *I am the elder dragon in our group and clearly the leader.*

Shulina Arya is much prettier than you, Telmandaroo replied. *I would have contacted her first too.*

Prettier? Bhrava Saruth said. *That is not what my human worshippers say. They make statues of me. One even baked a cake in my likeness.*

I have informed him that Captain Trip has baked goods for him and wishes to make an offer, Shulina Arya said, ignoring the males.

Trip was beginning to think she was the most mature Iskandian dragon ally they had, propensities for scooters and roller-skates notwithstanding.

"Thank you," Trip said, speaking out loud so everyone would be apprised. It sounded like the dragons were sharing their telepathic words with everyone, but he wasn't certain Ahn and Grady would appreciate having *him* speak into their minds.

What do you want, human? a deep sonorous voice boomed into Trip's mind.

He took a deep breath. This was it. His idea, his mission.

Drysaleskar, we have heard of your greatness, and we of the Iskandian military, officers sent by King Angulus himself, have come to offer you a place in our homeland.

What do I care of human kings and human offers? If I want a place in your homeland, I shall take it.

My king has also offered to have lobster, fish, and other delicacies delivered to you. You could have a territory all your own in our appealing southern steppes. I understand dragons like a warm climate. There are springs and palm trees.

Why had he said palm trees? What was a palm tree to a dragon? Trip wiped his palm on his trousers, feeling ridiculously nervous about this. He tried to tell himself that it wasn't that huge of a deal if the dragon rejected his offer. Iskandia would be no worse off than before. But he wanted his idea to bear fruit. He wanted to find a way to make his country safe, for his little siblings and for everyone else.

Are you trying to trick me, human? You should know better. You have the blood of a dragon in your veins. You know our kind are not stupid.

Trip sensed the dragon's claw-like touch on his mind, his attempt to find the truth.

It's not a trick. Instead of building his bank vault around his mind, Trip left himself open, letting the dragon see his thoughts—not that he could have stopped one as powerful as this from pulverizing his defenses. *It is true that we hope to gain something from this arrangement. We've seen that other dragons fear you—*

Lesser dragons, yes.

—and we are hoping that they'll be less likely to invade our country if you've set up your home there. We are open to inviting dragons into Iskandia if they don't eat humans or the livestock that humans have tamed.

Humans are completely unpalatable. Livestock—this means cows and chickens and horses?

Yes, animals that humans have domesticated and that live on property they have claimed. Trip didn't know if a dragon could be made to respect property boundaries. Should he mention fences?

Humans cannot claim anything. The dragon laughed, a deep rumble that again rang with power. *They are so puny. They are fortunate that our kind do not simply exterminate them. Since they do not taste good, they are worthless. Worse than worthless. They get in the way, and they kill far more than their share of prey animals—animals that taste good.*

"He's circling toward us," Ahn reported. "Should we be worried?"

"I'm negotiating with him now," Trip said.

Ahn paused, then repeated, "Should we be worried?"

"Likely so."

Humans have developed weapons that can slay dragons, so perhaps you shouldn't dismiss them. There has been talk among humankind about exterminating dragons. Humans lived a long time without them in their world, and they're finding your return less than palatable. Trip didn't know if threatening Drysaleskar was wise, but he tried to make it a subtle threat and frame his words in such a way that the dragon might see him as an impartial outsider rather than a representative of the enemy.

I have seen human weapons. They are not a concern to a dragon of my power.

As for humans having worth, they can bring you food, very tasty food. I have brought samples for you to try, samples of what the king's ships would bring to you every week if you took up residence in the Tlongan Steppes. Trip hoped the fish now nestled in the storage hold wouldn't dull the appeal of the baked goods. Maybe a dragon would like a fish-flavored tart.

No doubt they are poisoned. Do you think me a naive hatchling?

Even though Drysaleskar didn't seem to have any interest in anything Trip was offering, Ahn was right; he was definitely heading in their direction now.

The telepathic equivalent of a growl rumbled in Trip's mind. It wasn't the elder.

Shulina Arya? Trip asked.

You have a female with you, Drysaleskar purred. *A young and nubile female.*

Trip almost choked. *That* was what the dragon was interested in?

She will go into her breeding cycle soon, Drysaleskar added.

Seven gods, was that why all the males were after Shulina Arya?

Rysha, Trip thought, narrowing his focus to her, *why didn't you tell me your dragon was the equivalent of a mare in heat?*

Uh, I didn't know. We haven't discussed a lot of girl stuff yet. We mostly talk about nobly slaying things.

Drysaleskar banked to fly in close, and another mental growl emanated from Shulina Arya. Bhrava Saruth must have woken up to what was happening, because he veered abruptly toward her. If he spoke, it wasn't to Trip, but from his body language, it was clear he thought he was defending his female.

Trip dropped his face in his hand. This wasn't how he had imagined these negotiations going.

Bhrava Saruth must have drawn too close to Shulina Arya for her comfort, because her head darted sideways, and she snapped at him, almost shaving scales off his neck. Bhrava Saruth flew away, his tail tucking.

You can't want that old scale-rot-covered dinosaur, Shulina Arya, he protested, this time sharing the words with everyone.

The elder dragon laughed again.

Trip glanced back. Telmandaroo was flying closer now, too, watching the exchange intently.

Trip shifted uneasily, not because he cared about the dragons' mating interests, but because Rysha was on Shulina Arya's back. What if this grew violent?

Drysaleskar sailed closer to Shulina Arya. Bhrava Saruth tried to fly to intercept, but so much power smashed into him that he was hurled away like a cannonball.

GOLD DRAGON

Trip winced, feeling the very outer edge of that power. He shuddered at the glimpse of how strong the elder was.

Once again, Drysaleskar angled toward Shulina Arya. She kept flying straight ahead, as if she meant to ignore him, but when he got close, her head darted to the side again. She snapped at him, just as she had Bhrava Saruth, but this time, her jaws came close enough to sink into scale and flesh.

The elder dragon roared and backed away, erecting a defensive barrier. Shulina Arya followed and threw herself into a half roll to let Rysha get close.

Rysha swiped at Drysaleskar with her sword, and his barrier popped.

Trip clenched his fist around the flight stick, his shoulders so tense they hurt.

"I thought we wanted to make an ally of that dragon, not attack it," Ahn said. "What's going on?"

"He wants Shulina Arya to become his female," Rysha blurted. "And he's being very rude about it."

Fortunately, Drysaleskar backed off, and Shulina Arya didn't follow him. She straightened her path again, falling back to travel alongside the fliers. Bhrava Saruth and Telmandaroo came up behind her, but not too close. They seemed to be offering help if she needed it, but Trip doubted she needed or wanted it.

"Are we staying out of it?" Ahn glanced back at Grady, but he only lifted his hands.

Trip didn't know what to do, either. Maybe this was a sign that they should turn around and give up, but he hated to accept defeat so easily.

"I think it would be dangerous not to," Grady finally said. "More dangerous than battling dragon pirates over ships they're plundering."

"Agreed," Ahn said.

Then they both looked over at Trip. As if *he* had a clue what to do. Up until he'd met Rysha, he'd never even had a real grownup relationship of his own. Was he supposed to know something about dragon relationships just because he'd been sired by one?

Human, Drysaleskar said, and Trip realized the dragon was speaking to him alone. *This female doesn't see how magnificent I am, but she is clearly part of your flight.*

My what?

Your flight. A group of dragons is a flight. Do humans know nothing?

Ah. Forgive my ignorance.

Unlikely. Do you have influence over her or the human female that she allows to ride her?

Trip's first instinct was to say no, decidedly and vehemently, but he couldn't help but pause. If Drysaleskar thought Shulina Arya would become his mate, or if she even *did* become his mate, would he stay in Iskandia? Would he live in the Steppes and perhaps visit Shulina Arya in the capital, and give other dragons a reason to avoid the country at all costs?

King Angulus would surely praise Trip if he could arrange for that. And maybe the silver dragon stalking Rysha's family's lands would be one of the first to flee. And his siblings could be raised in peace, knowing the only dragons that flew overhead while they were in their yards playing would be friendly ones. Or at least ones who'd promised not to harm humans. Could Trip extract such a promise from Drysaleskar?

It was tempting to try, or to ask *Rysha* to try. Trip had no delusions that Shulina Arya would listen to his mating advice, but she and Rysha had bonded almost from the beginning.

He gazed over at them even as the elder dragon gazed at *him*.

And he said nothing to Rysha. Trip knew she would be disappointed in him if he asked, and Shulina Arya might be too. She clearly wanted nothing to do with the boorish male. Even if it might help Iskandia, he couldn't bring himself to ask.

I do not, he finally answered Drysaleskar. *As a dragon, you must understand how little influence we males have over females.*

He expected the dragon to issue some arrogant statement of denial, but the grunt-like noise that sounded in Trip's mind seemed more like agreement.

Then you have nothing to offer me that I cannot get for myself.

The gold dragon banked and flew off to the west, away from Trip's team and away from Iskandia.

For a long moment, nobody said anything. They merely watched the dragon fly away.

"Does this mean I've been carrying fish in my storage hold all day for no reason?" Ahn finally asked.

"Yes," Trip said. "It also means I'm a poor negotiator."

Grimacing, he turned his flier back to the northeast, toward home.

CHAPTER 14

*S*O YOU SEE, RYSHA SAID, wrapping up her latest story, *Dramon the Bold, who desired nothing more than to go down in history as the greatest warrior ever, is now remembered as the inventor of modern glue. All he wanted was to make it so the visor on his helmet stayed up when he was riding all day, but today's bookbinders and artists seeking sealants for their canvases have him to thank for discovering that rabbit skin—essentially refined rabbit collagen—makes an excellent adhesive.*

Hm, Shulina Arya responded.

Usually, the dragon asked questions when Rysha finished a story, and she'd previously proven intrigued by science-related tales, so Rysha was surprised by the subdued response.

Maybe she was tired. The Iskandian coast had come into view again, with the sun setting out over the sea, casting interesting shadows inland. Rysha found the mixture of sunny hilltops and shady valleys remarkable from above, but it had been a long day. Perhaps Shulina Arya needed a nap. And some tarts.

"You doing all right, my friend?" Rysha patted the dragon on the side.

Yes, Shulina Arya replied. *But...*

Yes? Rysha asked, surprised by the hesitation. Shulina Arya rarely hesitated to speak her mind.

Do you know any stories of dragons falling in love with humans?

Ah, I know of many fictional stories, and of course, there are many accountings of human women being compelled to have sex with male dragons. I don't imagine love, in the human sense of the word, was involved though. Rysha glanced toward Trip, feeling a twinge of sadness for his birth mother, whoever the woman had been. Given what a blatant ass Trip's sire had been, Rysha was positive the poor lady had been magically compelled to sleep with him. She at least hoped his mother hadn't been physically forced. With a dragon, that probably wasn't necessary. Rysha shuddered, remembering her own experience with the bronze in Lagresh.

No, being compelled is not being in love, Shulina Arya stated firmly. *Neither is mating for biological needs, because one's breeding cycle comes and one has urges.*

I'll agree with that. It dawned on Rysha what this was about.

Shulina Arya hadn't said anything about the elder dragon's unwelcome advances, but it had to have been on her mind during the flight home. Bhrava Saruth and that bronze dragon had been faithfully trailing her the whole time. She didn't appear to appreciate their proximity.

You don't believe you'll find love among your own kind? Rysha asked.

What sounded in her mind reminded her of kids thrusting their tongues out and making rude noises. Loudly.

Male dragons are like male horses, Shulina Arya said. *They just want to mount something young and robust to satisfy their urges. They don't know about love. There isn't even a dragon word for love, not like the human word. The* romantic *word. You and Captain Trip are romantic. He* makes *you things.*

He's a good man, Rysha said carefully, not wanting to circle back to the dragon offering to take him as a mate if Rysha grew tired of him. *Perhaps you could come with us to the officers' club one evening, and he could introduce you to some nice young pilots. A pilot seems like a good match for a dragon. You would have a love of flying in common.*

That sounds fun. I could wear my new roller-skates!

Indeed. Rysha wondered if she should try to find a college student for Shulina Arya instead of an officer. Or even a pre-college student? No, even if she acted young when she shape-shifted, she was hundreds of years old as a dragon. It would take someone more mature than a teenager to handle a near-immortal lover.

"There's smoke inland," Trip said over the communication crystal, the first words anyone had spoken aloud in an hour. "A *lot* of smoke."

"Let's check it out," Colonel Grady said.

Trip cursed. "I also sense another dragon over there."

Storyteller, Shulina Arya blurted, as Rysha noted that the terrain under that smoke appeared familiar. *It is that silver dragon I chased the other night!*

"And that's my family's valley," Rysha said grimly.

Shulina Arya pumped her wings and arrowed toward the smoke, pulling ahead of the fliers.

"It's the silver dragon, Trip," Rysha said. "We're going to deal with him."

"I'm coming right behind you."

Fear churned in Rysha's gut as they flew past the coast and over green farmlands, vineyards, and grassy grazing land on the way to the southern highway and her valley on the other side of it. What if those thick plumes of smoke were coming from the manor? Damn it, her family had already been targeted by dragons. This wasn't *fair*.

She blinked away tears and wrapped her hand around Dorfindral's hilt. If that silver dragon had done anything to her parents or her brothers, she would shove the sword down its gullet until it came out the other end.

They flew over the highway where a few people on horseback had stopped to gawk at the smoke. Rysha scowled down at them, wondering what useless neighbors or passersby weren't going to help, but she couldn't make out their features from this high up.

As she and Shulina Arya neared the lake, Rysha could make out the source of the smoke. The vineyards behind the house next to the orchards, the orchards that had already been ravaged by a gold dragon's flames. Indignation flared within her. That couldn't be an accident. Someone—or some *dragon*—had deliberately chosen valuable plants, not random flora. But was it the silver? Silvers couldn't even breathe fire.

It was the silver, Shulina Arya said. *I sense him. He senses me and is fleeing. The coward.*

How did he light the vineyards on fire?

He could have done it with his mind.

They flew over the manor, and Rysha glimpsed people outside, running to collect water from the lake to try and put out the flames. She doubted they would be able to save the vineyard. Her brother's passion, the source of the wine he made, was in danger of total destruction.

She shook her head, again wondering why her family was being picked on by dragons.

Rysha? Trip asked, though his flier had fallen far behind.

Yes?

One of the men gathered on the road is Lord Lockvale.

Rysha caught herself growling like an enraged tiger.

I find that suspicious, Trip added.

I find it more than suspicious. Can you go down there and... And what, she asked herself. Capture him? Interrogate him? Trip couldn't do any of those things to a nobleman—or anyone who wasn't a known Iskandian criminal. *Question him,* she finished, hoping he could get telepathic answers that would be more accurate than anything that came out of Lockvale's mouth.

Trip hesitated, but only for a second before saying, *Yes.*

We'll be there as soon as we can.

The laws were still such that Trip would get into extra trouble for punching a nobleman—not that she expected him to do that—but *Rysha* could likely get away with it.

The silver is leading us toward the foothills, Shulina Arya said. *Is that still part of your territory?*

Yes, Rysha said, not wanting to explain inheritances and that her father and her uncle were the owners of the land, not she.

There may be caves back there that he's been hiding in, dampening his aura so that other dragons would not sense him.

Below, the terrain grew rockier and full of small canyons and gullies as the Ice Blades loomed closer to the east. For the first time, Rysha glimpsed the silver dragon flying ahead of them, a dark winged shape weaving through the treetops. The sun had dipped below the horizon, leaving the land fully in shadow.

Rysha could feel Shulina Arya's powerful muscles putting forth more effort as she tried to catch up, and she appreciated it. The silver dragon dipped behind a copse of evergreens and didn't come into sight again.

He's flown into a gully, Shulina Arya said, veering toward that copse. *Could it be a trap?*

Shulina Arya's nostrils flared, as if the scent of her prey filled them, and she didn't answer. If anything, she flew faster.

Rysha drew Dorfindral.

The gully was thick with vegetation, and rabbits and birds scurried for safety as Shulina Arya flapped past. At the end, a black hole marked a cave entrance, and they glimpsed the silver tucking his wings close to fly inside.

Oh, it's definitely a trap, Shulina Arya said. *He's been trying to make me believe he's injured, attempting to fool me with illusions, and now I'm getting an image of him hunkering inside, ready to turn and fight with his back to the wall. But I also sense hairline cracks in the rocks. He's made it so they're poised to fall. As if a rockfall would trap a gold dragon. He's also created an exit in the back of the cave, a way that he can slip out. The hole is covered with foliage.*

Despite her analysis of the trap, Shulina Arya arrowed straight toward that front cave entrance. Rysha eyed it warily, knowing that Dorfindral couldn't protect her from physical attacks, such as rockfalls.

But Shulina Arya flew upward at the last second. Instead of going into the cave, she landed on the boulders above it. A great cracking and snapping came from below, and the ground quaked. Then it shifted as tons and tons of rocks collapsed downward.

Shulina Arya flapped her wings to hover above the cave instead of standing on it. Pulverized rock and dust flew up, the earthy scent tickling Rysha's nostrils. A roar of distress came from the cave—or what was left of it.

How do you like being the one smashed? Shulina Arya cried.

The rocks stopped shifting, and the dust settled. Rysha had no way of sensing what was below them, whether the silver was still alive, if any of the cave remained, or if the dragon had been squashed.

He's still alive, Shulina Arya said, the words quieter in Rysha's mind. *He's pretending to be injured and buried alive, perhaps dying, but I am not fooled. I grew up being taught by crafty bronzes. I know all the ways of dragon trickery. I believe he will realize we are not leaving, and then he'll throw off the rocks and try to flee. We'll be here, ready to pounce.*

Rysha was about to ask how long they would likely have to wait—she worried about Trip and the task she'd given him—but then the rocks shifted alarmingly. Numerous boulders flew into the air all at once.

Some would have struck Shulina Arya, but she had a barrier up, so they bounced off. Rysha glimpsed dusty silver scales as more boulders shifted.

Do not think you can take this land from me, a voice roared in Rysha's mind.

Ah, excellent, Shulina Arya thought. *He is going to fight.*

Chatter sounded over the communication crystal as Trip brought his flier down on the highway not far from the group of men staring at Rysha's smoking land. To his surprise, he heard General Zirkander's voice and those of several Wolf Squadron members.

"Don't shoot yet," Zirkander said. "Hold steady. Blazer, you need to get Therrik closer so he can swing that letter opener."

"I'd be happy to, sir, if his heavy ass wasn't weighing down the back of the flier and slowing us down."

"It's not my *ass* that's heavy, Major," Therrik growled.

"Sir? This is Captain Ahn. I'm with Trip twenty-five miles south of the capital. We're returning from our mission."

"Come on up to the city, Ahn. We've got some fun for you to join in on."

Trip winced at the confirmation that whatever battle they were fighting was happening in the sky over the capital. He thought of his little siblings in different houses throughout the city, of how their surrogate mothers weren't mages and had no way to protect them from magic.

"There's a silver dragon over some property down here, and something is on fire," Ahn said.

"It's Ry—Lieutenant Ravenwood's estate, sir," Trip added, hoping Zirkander would understand that meant something to him. He was worried about the capital, but he couldn't leave Rysha to battle the silver dragon—and whatever scheme this nobleman was enacting—alone.

"Must be nice to have an estate," someone said. Pimples?

"Not if a dragon is always lighting it on fire," Duck drawled. "Do we—awk, look out!"

Machine gun fire banged over the crystal.

"Come help us when you're able," Zirkander said. "We've got a mess up here."

"Yes, sir." Ahn was flying in circles above Trip, and she looked down at him. "Colonel Grady says we need to go join them, but you and Ravenwood can stay here and deal with the silver. And then come to help."

"Good," Trip said, relieved nobody was ordering him away. He had already landed, and the horseback riders were glancing his way. He wanted to reach them before they decided to run.

The bronze coward is skulking away, but I shall fly to the city to assist with the battle, Bhrava Saruth announced. Trip had almost forgotten about him and Telmandaroo. *Since Shulina Arya has unwisely refused my magnificent help.*

She seems to refuse a lot you offer her, Trip remarked, powering down his flier and unfastening his harness.

She does. It is extremely odd. I am a very handsome dragon, far superior to that crusty elder that wanted to rub her scales earlier.

Bhrava Saruth flew overhead on his way toward the capital, and Ahn's flier also sailed off in that direction. The buzz of her propeller soon faded.

Feeling alone and outnumbered, Trip took a deep breath as he strode toward the group of men. There were six of them. Normally, he wouldn't find that daunting, but if they were all nobles, dealing with them would be tricky. They wouldn't likely be intimidated by a soldier.

Trip had thought they might take off down the road when he approached, especially if they were engaged in something nefarious, but they continued talking and pointing and didn't seem concerned about him.

With a pistol on one hip and Azarwrath on the other, and in his full army uniform, Trip hoped he looked authoritative. He let a little of his *scylori* show as he approached the group, but then decided it might be better to let it all out, especially if he hoped to get the truth from Lockvale.

Several of the men looked down at him from atop their horses, but Lockvale did not. He made a point of yawning and looking toward the smoke.

"Do you think the fire will spread to the house?" he asked, the words for his comrades, not for Trip. "That would be unfortunate. Much trouble has befallen this family this spring, hasn't it?"

Nobody answered him. His five comrades were looking at Trip in the fading light, their mouths parted, as if stunned.

"What do you have to do with it, Lockvale?" Trip asked bluntly, not wanting to dawdle, not with Rysha chasing a dragon and a battle going on in the capital.

Finally, Lockvale turned to look down at him. His eyes narrowed, but he didn't seem as affected as the others by Trip's aura. "Commoner, I insist that you call me *Lord* Lockvale."

Trip hadn't made a fuss at the Ravenwood's family dinner, and he regretted it now. If he had been more straightforward and hadn't worried about offending people, he might have learned enough to keep this fire—and who knew what other damage had been done?—from occurring.

"Get off your horse, *Lord* Lockvale," Trip said, putting some of his power in his voice. "Let's talk."

Three of the men Trip wasn't looking at scrambled off their horses. Lockvale started to shift, as if to dismount, but caught himself and sneered. He glanced toward Azarwrath.

"I don't know what power you think that sword gives you, but if you use it on me, I'll report you for molesting a nobleman."

Trip willed Lockvale to float into the air, eliciting a startled cry from the man. The horse neighed with fear and ran off. Trip set Lockvale down on the road, facing him. Fury burned in the man's eyes. Trip scraped through his surface thoughts, but the nobleman was too busy being furious with him to think about what had caused the fire.

"Are you aligned with the silver dragon bothering the Ravenwoods?" Trip asked.

"You don't get to question me, you arrogant boy. You think because you wear an army uniform you have authority over the nobility?"

The men around him shifted backward, as if all they wanted was to avoid notice. And Trip did ignore them. He held Lockvale's gaze and tried to find the answers he wanted.

His question had prompted the man to think of an image, of him standing in front of a silver dragon, offering a plate of apples and speaking. Speaking of plans to force Lord Ravenwood, a school rival from years back who Lockvale had never liked, to sell his land for a fraction of its worth. Since Lockvale's father had lost most of his family's land, he felt it his duty to acquire an estate for his children and siblings, so they needn't join the growing legions of the noble poor who'd lost so much of their power and influence over recent generations. And if he could take Ravenwood's excellent estate, the land so fertile and so close to the city? That would certainly be ideal.

Lockvale raised a hand to his temple, and alarm flashed through his emotions for the first time.

"What did you offer the dragon to get him to comply?" Trip asked. "Surely, not just apples."

Lockvale's sense of alarm tripled at this proof of mind reading.

"Get out of my head," he shrieked, glancing at his buddies and waving at Trip, as if to order them to do something.

Trip looked coolly at them, and nobody moved. Some scurried farther back, not noticing that they stepped into thick mud beside the road.

"What did you offer the silver dragon?" Trip repeated, rummaging through Lockvale's thoughts again.

Unfortunately, the nobleman was aware of Trip's mental intrusion now and fought harder to block it, and his rage and fear clouded salient thoughts. Trip wished he hadn't felt rushed and had been subtler, as that might have had a better result. Now, he could feel discomfort—almost pain—from the man, so he lessened his pressure. Reluctantly. He was worried about Rysha and the city. If General Zirkander was up in the air, the squadrons weren't likely dealing with a simple, easily repelled attack by a single dragon.

Trip did his best to plant the image he'd already seen firmly in Lockvale's mind, of him and the dragon talking over apples. Lockvale flashed to another image, of the silver dragon attacking people and devouring apples from trees on another estate. His neighbor's land, Trip sensed. Men had gone out to fight the silver, but Lockvale had been clever and made an offer to it instead. He'd told the dragon that if it would work with him, together, they would acquire a great deal of land, land full of fruit and livestock that the silver could enjoy whenever it wanted. And nobody would attack it. The dragon would be allowed free rein of the land, as soon as Lockvale acquired it.

Trip grimaced, realizing it wasn't a dissimilar offer to the one he'd made to Drysaleskar. But the Tlongan Steppes were the king's land, and he had the right to use them in a negotiation. This land belonged to someone else, to Rysha and her family. Trip clenched a fist, angry at the man's scheme, angry at *him*.

Lockvale grabbed his temples, fell to his knees, and cried out. "He's attacking me!"

Startled, Trip drew back, removing his mental touch. But Lockvale started screaming.

"Stop him, stop him. He's a witch! *Shoot* him!"

He's feigning that pain, Azarwrath said with disgust.

Lockvale stole glances at his comrades, but none of them were moving against Trip. They were alarmed that Lockvale was being hurt, but they weren't willing to risk themselves. Further, they were being affected by Trip's aura, which made them want to stay on his good side, even though they had no idea who he was.

Lockvale snarled, stuck his hand under his jacket, and jumped to his feet, gripping a pistol.

Though startled, Trip raised his defenses instantly. Lockvale fired, but the bullet was deflected.

His eyes bulged in disbelief, and he ran toward Trip, firing again.

His chest bumped against the barrier, and he stumbled, falling backward. Trip used his power to tear the pistol from his grip.

"You're scheming against the wrong family, Lord Lockvale."

Trip lowered his barrier for long enough to float the pistol into his grip. As he held it in both hands, Azarwrath flared with red light, ensuring everyone could see. Trip channeled power into warping the metal, making it look as though he was breaking the firearm with his bare hands. He bent the barrel so it would never fire again and tossed it to the ground.

"If you or this dragon bother the Ravenwoods again, you'll have to deal with me." *Even scarier,* Trip added, switching to telepathy so the man would fully understand that he was a sorcerer, *you'll have to deal with Lieutenant Ravenwood and her dragon. And her dragon is larger than yours.*

Lockvale screamed and dropped to the ground again, grabbing his head with both hands. "He's attacking me, hurting me!"

Trip stepped back, sensing the silver dragon on the move. When he'd landed, it had been at the far eastern end of the property, with Shulina Arya chasing it. Now it was heading back toward the manor and the highway. Once again, Shulina Arya flew after it.

Lockvale staggered to his feet, backing toward his friends. "You all saw it."

He still gripped his head, as if he were staunching some flow of blood, though there was none. He wasn't even hurt, unless he'd bruised himself rolling around on the road. Lockvale looked around for his horse, but the creature had moved far down the road.

Fire lit up the sky behind the manor, and Trip shifted his attention, more worried about Rysha's family than the nobleman.

He spotted the silver dragon weaving and diving as it tried to evade the flames. Shulina Arya came right behind, with Rysha on her back, but they weren't gaining. The speedy silver dragon was pulling away, flying toward the highway. Maybe it thought it could fly out to sea and get away.

"We'll see about that," Trip muttered, drew Azarwrath, and ran down the long drive toward the manor—and the dragon chase.

As his legs churned, he kept his eyes on the silver. He sensed it was injured, but not enough to slow it down. He also sensed that its mental defenses were up, so neither flame nor magical attack was hurting it.

As it soared toward him, Trip planted himself in the road and lifted his hands, imagining wind channeling itself to create a wall of air in the middle of the silver's path.

The dragon smashed into it headfirst, its body jerking and neck bending as if it had struck a brick wall. It started to fall, but then flapped its wings and recovered, shaking its head as if to shake away the stars dancing in its vision.

Shulina Arya spewed fire as she drew near. The silver glanced down at Trip, and he braced himself for an attack, but it flew off to the side of the valley, again pumping its wings so fast that it started pulling away.

Stop, you coward! Shulina Arya cried.

Trip marshaled his strength and conjured another wall in the air ahead of the silver.

This time, the dragon must have sensed it. The creature banked hard, talons grazing the magical barrier, then pushing off. It flew east again, back toward Rysha's manor and the lake.

Shulina Arya angled, trying to cut it off. Trip created one more wall, though he struggled to make it as effective now that he stood at a greater distance.

Wishing he'd run for his flier instead of heading up the long drive on foot, he took off running again. Shulina Arya gained ground as the silver avoided Trip's new wall. It stuttered in the air as raw energy buffeted its wings. Trip sensed Shulina Arya being subtler now, attacking with her mind instead of with fang and flames.

As he reached the lake, where tall trees grew along the shoreline, he lost sight of the combatants, the foliage blocking the sky. But he monitored with his senses as he ran. Azarwrath sent streaks of red lightning over the treetops and toward the silver. Trip tried to attack the dragon's mind, hoping to further discombobulate it. He sensed Shulina Arya drawing close enough for strikes with fang and talon—and sword.

Shots rang out ahead of him, startling Trip.

He spotted people standing outside the manor, some with buckets and hoses, others with rifles. They fired, hopefully at the silver dragon, whenever they saw it.

Trip kept running, wanting to warn them to be careful. Dorfindral would protect Rysha from magical attacks, but a stray bullet could get through, especially if she and the sword were focused on the dragon.

As Trip raced up the last part of the driveway toward the people, the dragons came back into view. He almost jumped at how close they were. The silver plummeted toward the manor, with Shulina Arya racing behind it, breathing flames and charring its backside. Trip sensed that the silver's defenses were down. More than that, the creature seemed barely conscious.

The observers on the ground yelled and scrambled back toward the manor as it crashed headfirst into the grass beside the driveway.

Shulina Arya swooped upward at the last second to avoid also crashing. Rysha waved toward the people—her family members, Trip presumed, though he hadn't used his senses to identify individuals yet.

Shulina Arya rolled in a pleased victory gesture, then glided down to land on the other side of the drive from the unconscious—or dead?—silver dragon. The creature's scales were charred, and flames burned in the damp grass to either side of it.

"Is everyone all right?" Rysha slid off Shulina Arya's back and ran toward her family.

There were about twenty people—Trip recognized her uncle, father, brothers, and her aunt among them. They all gaped back and forth from the silver dragon to Shulina Arya to Rysha running toward them. The prim and proper Aunt Tadelay was one of the people with a rifle.

Rysha hugged her father, and that seemed to break the spell. Trip was pleased to see them gather around her and give her hugs and back pats. The other night at dinner, he hadn't witnessed a lot of warmth from the family, which seemed so different from what he was used to with his grandparents, but their tensions had also been high.

They should know that you helped them, Azarwrath said. *Then perhaps they will feel less tense about you and will be more accepting.*

I don't know about that. Unless I find out that my three-thousand-year-old mother happened to be from the era's nobility, and I have no idea how I'd figure that out. It seems unlikely.

Telryn Yert, you are half dragon. This is far superior to having some generations-removed ancestor that helped a past king and was granted land and a title as a thank you.

Is that how it works? Trip admitted he'd never paid any attention to the history of the nobility or how one became a noble. Maybe he'd been designing paper fliers whenever it had been covered in school. If so, he felt ashamed that Azarwrath, who hadn't been born in this country, knew more about it than he did.

Yes. If your king wished to, he could wave his hand—or fill out some paperwork—give you a few acres of land, and declare you a noble.

Trip wondered if that actually happened or if all the land available for such things had been assigned long ago. Wouldn't a great hero like General Zirkander have been given a title and land by now if such things were still done?

Thinking of the general reminded Trip of the battle going on in the capital.

Rysha? he asked silently, hating to interrupt the hugging and talking—half a dozen people were explaining what had happened from their point of view. *I have to get back to my flier and go to the capital. There's a battle going on up there.*

Rysha pulled away from the group hug and looked back at him.

Stay here until the fire is under control and you know everyone's safe, he told her, not wanting her to feel she had to leave her family to come along. There were numerous soldiers in the capital with *chapaharii* blades now.

Rysha's father said something, but she held up a hand and ran toward Trip. She hugged him and said, "Thank you for the help," louder than necessary.

Wanting to let her family know that he had assisted her? He hadn't done much.

Trip patted her on the back. "I learned that Lockvale was behind this." He waved at the inert silver dragon. "I'll tell you more later, but you'll want to watch for him. He might try something else. He…" Trip gazed toward the highway. The lake and the trees made it so he couldn't see all the way back to it, but he had no trouble checking the area with his senses. The nobleman and his buddies had departed. "He's gone, but he was responsible. I saw it in his mind. He instructed the silver to make a nuisance of himself, scare off the workers, and also to destroy some of the property so your parents would be more inclined to sell. Cheaply. Once he had the land for himself, he promised the dragon it could stay on it and would be well fed."

"I don't suppose you have any proof other than…?" Rysha waved at his temple.

"I don't," he said grimly, understanding the problem, that they lived in a world where a nobleman's word would be given more weight than his, especially since he had used magic to learn what he knew.

"He ought to be locked up if he's the reason our vineyards are burning."

"I agree." Trip looked up—Rysha's father was coming over. "I have to go." He bowed clumsily toward Lord Ravenwood and waved to Rysha, not wanting to deal with her family's dismissive comments now.

"I'll be along soon to help," Rysha called after him as he retreated, running back toward the highway and his flier.

CHAPTER 15

TRIP SPOTTED SMOKE IN THE air as he flew north to the capital, but he didn't sense any dragons up there other than Bhrava Saruth. Had Wolf Squadron driven them all off? The chatter over the communication crystal had died down too. Normally, he might feel disappointed about missing a battle, but it had been a long day, and he'd dealt with more than his share of dragons.

The darkness made it hard to tell how much damage had been done to the city, but he sensed pain and fear from the people below as he flew toward the army fort. In several places, buildings burned, mostly warehouses and canneries along the waterfront, but fires also lit up the night farther inland, in residential areas.

His gut tightened as he thought of the babies. He had the addresses for all the mothers taking care of them and would check on them as soon as he could.

The hangar was well-lit with the big sliding door still open, so Trip flew straight in. The scent of smoke met his nostrils. At first, he thought the building itself had been burned, but the smoke came from the engines and tails of some of the fliers. A few damaged craft had barely made it back to the hangar, and they were parked in the middle rather than in their slots to the sides. A makeshift medical area had been assembled with blankets on the floor and officers sitting or lying on them and others kneeling or standing around.

Trip sensed Leftie and Duck among the injured, and he landed as quickly as he could, praying to the seven gods that the wounds weren't mortal, that he could heal them. The idea of losing a friend in a battle he hadn't been there for horrified him.

As Trip vaulted from his cockpit, General Zirkander, his face smeared with soot and his sleeve torn and bloodied, jogged from the office in the back.

"I've sent our report to the king," Zirkander told Tranq, Blazer, and the colonel from Tiger Squadron, all of whom slumped with weariness. "Sardelle is coming to help with healing." He started toward the blankets, then paused, spotting Trip running over.

"Sorry I'm late, sir," Trip blurted, feeling awful for coming in *after* the fight.

Had he made the right choice in staying to help Rysha's family and dealing with that fop Lockvale? Or might he have been more help here if he'd arrived sooner? Maybe he could have stopped people from being hurt.

"Make way, please," he said to those gathering around the blankets. "I can heal people."

Therrik was one of the people kneeling in front of them, and he stepped back, turning with a glower for Trip, his hand reaching for the *chapaharii* sword at his waist. Trip tensed. This wasn't the time for this. Therrik stopped his fingers before they wrapped around the hilt.

"Help Kaika," he growled, shifting out of the way. "She's one of the worst."

Trip sucked in a worried breath as he spotted her lying on the blanket, burns covering one side of her face and body. She should have been unconscious from wounds like that, but her face was contorted in a rictus of pain.

"You sure took your time getting here, Trip," Leftie said, his voice strained. He lay next to Kaika, also burned, though not as badly, and a deep gash lay open on his arm.

"Sorry." Trip couldn't come up with a flippant remark, not when he felt so much guilt for having missed the battle.

Azarwrath, will you help me? Trip asked, focusing on Kaika. *I don't know how to… I mean, I know it's just important to ensure she lives, but can we keep her from being scarred?*

Very likely. Begin. I will assist. She is the worst of those left alive.

Left alive? Trip glanced at the others on the blankets and saw Duck sitting up and gripping talon gouges in his abdomen while Pimples knelt beside him, making jokes about him being a low priority. Another charred officer, his face unrecognizable due to the burns, lay completely still. Dead. Lieutenant Beeline.

Tears welled in Trip's eyes even though he didn't know the man well.

Kaika moaned softly and brought a shaking hand up to grip Trip's arm. He took a deep breath and focused on her. She was alive and in pain, and she needed him.

He closed his eyes and, with Azarwrath's guidance, healed burns for the first time in his life. He was aware of voices, soft discussions going on behind him, but he didn't participate in them. He needed his concentration for this.

"Is the king coming?" That was Therrik.

"He's on his way," Zirkander said.

"Does he know..."

"I said she was injured and that she threw her sword in order to drop a dragon's defenses for us. It may have saved the night, even if we'll have to get it off the bottom of the harbor. And even if we still lost Beeline and Snail."

"Snail too, sir?" Blazer asked.

"I saw the fire hit his flier point blank. By the time it disappeared into the harbor, it was nothing but a charred husk. Damn it, I wish more people had tried the parachutes." Zirkander's voice was thick with emotion. "Better to lose fliers than pilots."

"Better not to lose *anyone*," Therrik snarled, his voice also heavy with emotion. And frustration. "And better not to lose any more of the swords. They just got the one, right? We're sure Kaika's is on the bottom of the harbor?"

"I saw it hit the water. Nobody saw any dragons dive down for it—only two of them had those hook things. Graspers. Whatever you want to call them. Seven gods, I need to stop thinking of the dragons as animals without tactics beyond biting and clawing and breathing fire. We're fortunate Bhrava Saruth arrived to help drive them off. I shouldn't have sent both our warrior dragons along on Trip's mission."

"We would've driven them off without him. We had them on the run."

"On the run with one of our swords. And only because Phelistoth showed up to help. We have more swords than we used to, but not an unlimited supply, and it's clear they're targeting them now, trying to get them away from us."

"They won't get any more," Therrik said with determination.

"Let's hope not. We need to watch out for treachery as well as open attacks. Bhrava Saruth said these were some of the same dragons that dropped a building on your head."

"Fortunately, my head isn't my deadliest part."

Zirkander grunted. "Did you just insult yourself, Therrik? That's my job."

"I'm in the mood for self-flagellation."

"Now you're using vocabulary words. You're not trying to make me think you're smart, are you?"

"Not now, Zirkander." Therrik moved away from him and crouched next to Trip, the tip of his sword scabbard clunking on the cement floor.

Trip tensed, aware of the big man's presence, and especially aware of Kasandral. But all Therrik did was rest a hand on Kaika's shoulder, on the side that hadn't been burned.

"Shit," Kaika rasped. "Therrik is giving me sympathy. That means I'm going to die for sure."

"I think Dragon Man is fixing you," Therrik said, "but you look like the inside of a volcano. Fat chance you'll get Angulus to kiss you again."

"Looks don't matter when your tongue is as talented as mine."

"Uh huh, you and your tongue better keep the lights off."

"I always do. My tongue likes dark and mysterious environs."

"Was that an innuendo? If so, disgusting."

"I don't know what you're talking about."

Trip smiled slightly, glad Kaika had the strength to trade barbs with Therrik, but he kept his eyes closed, kept pouring his energy into mending her burned muscle. The skin was impossible to repair, so he and Azarwrath built new skin, accelerating the process by thousands of times. Trip let the more experienced soulblade take the lead and simply lent his power for the task.

"Sardelle," came Zirkander's voice from behind Trip. It stood out to him more than the murmurs of the other pilots and ground crew who were attending the wounded men and the damaged fliers. Trip sensed her and also that Angulus had arrived. He radiated distress and concern.

Someone touched Trip's shoulder. Sardelle.

You have her? she asked quietly into his mind.
Yes, ma'am.
I'll work on Duck and Leftie.
Thank you.

Trip kept his focus on Kaika, not wanting to fail her or Angulus or anyone else, especially when he could sense the unease lurking within everyone else here. Nobody thought this attack had been a fluke. The dragons would be back.

The light of the magical illumination globes Shulina Arya had created showed the charred, smoldering remains of the vineyard. At least the fires were out now. She had helped squelch them, moving large quantities of water from the lake to dump onto the flames as the family watched in open-mouthed awe.

Now, Shulina Arya lay off to one side while Rysha, her father, aunt, and Krey walked down the path that had once meandered past the vineyard to a pergola, benches, and a fountain. The stone fountain was blackened but still standing. Only ashes remained where the wood structures had been. Rysha blinked back tears, remembering roughhousing with her brothers under the pergola and playing cards with her grandfather before he'd passed.

Only a handful of vines in the back corner had escaped the fire. Aware of how many years her brother, and their grandfather before him, had spent creating unique and desirable cultivars, Rysha hoped some could be saved and replanted.

"It could have been worse," Father said, looking toward the manor and the lake.

Krey gave him an anguished look.

"At least we all survived this time," Father said.

"I know," Krey said, "but there'll be so much extra work to do to replant. And there won't be a harvest for *years,* not for the grapes or the apples and pears that the other dragon took out. It'll take a long time for the vines and trees to regrow and bear fruit again."

As Rysha listened to the growing argument, she looked toward Shulina Arya and also toward the sky. The valley was quiet, but she had no idea what was going on in the capital. Now that the fires were out and she'd verified that her family had survived, she needed to report in.

"Shulina Arya?" she asked, heading toward the dragon. She looked tired, her tail wrapped around her supine form. Rysha hated to ask her to take her on another flight.

Yes, Storyteller. I am ready to do battle again, if need be, but I believe it has ended.

"Oh? Can you sense the city from down here?"

I can sense other dragons. There were many in the city earlier. Now, I sense only Bhrava Saruth and Phelistoth.

"Does she talk back to you?" Aunt Tadelay asked from the shadows along the path.

Rysha jumped. She hadn't realized her aunt hadn't gone back to the manor. She noted with some bemusement that Tadelay still had a rifle. The butt rested on the ground, and she didn't look like she intended to fire on the dragon. Shulina Arya certainly didn't appear concerned. She rested her chin on her tail and gazed at Rysha and the valley behind her.

"Yes, telepathically."

Aunt Tadelay arched a skeptical eyebrow. Then the other eyebrow flew up and her gaze jerked toward Shulina Arya.

"What did she say to you?" Rysha asked dryly.

Tadelay hesitated, her lips turned down. "That rifles are ineffective weapons for defending young ladies from dragons."

"Is that what you came over here to do?"

"It crossed my mind, but it doesn't seem very…" Tadelay spread a hand toward the resting dragon. "It's not what I expected."

"Shulina Arya is a *she*, the only female I'm aware of that likes humans."

"To eat?"

"No, but she does like our food. Sardelle makes tarts for the dragons, and I understand there are regular orders from Donotono's Bakery in the capital. I just tell her stories. She seems to like those almost as much as food. Did you see the other gold dragon that flew past? He likes humans, too, though he believes they should worship him. And give him belly rubs. Sometimes, he turns into a ferret to encourage that." Rysha realized she was babbling, but she wanted her family to understand that not *all* dragons were a threat. And that Shulina Arya was the reason that the silver dragon wouldn't bother them again.

Aunt Tadelay scratched her head, not seeming to notice when she pushed her hat askew. "When your mother and I came to the capital, we truly believed you needed to be saved from…" She extended her hand toward Shulina Arya again, who flopped over on her side and either stretched her jaw or yawned. It might have been both. Fortunately, she didn't look threatening in that position, even with her fangs on display. Her tongue lolled out, and Rysha smiled, remembering the jawbreaker incident. "Dragons," Aunt Tadelay finished.

"Just *some* dragons. But with Shulina Arya's help, along with this sword, which has an affinity for slaying dragons—" Rysha touched the hilt but didn't draw Dorfindral, lest he get overly excited by Shulina Arya's proximity, "—I can defeat them. Granted, Shulina Arya does a lot more than I do, but together, we're a good team. And the country needs someone who can defeat enemy dragons right now."

Aunt Tadelay shifted her gaze toward the smoldering vineyard and then toward the front of the house, where the gas lamps illuminated the dead silver. Rysha wondered whose responsibility it would be to move the body. And where did one put a dead dragon, anyway? If her uncle Sabber had been here, he might have offered to taxidermy the head for his hunting lodge.

After a long moment of consideration, Aunt Tadelay looked back to Rysha, eyeing her up and down. Rysha felt rumpled after multiple battles and a full day of travel, but she stood up straight, hoping her uniform wasn't too mud-spattered and wrinkled.

"I'm beginning to see that," Aunt Tadelay allowed.

"Trip helped, too, though it would have been harder for you to tell he was doing something. Every time the silver dragon smashed into an invisible obstacle, that was Trip's work."

"He's… a sorcerer, then? It's true? I thought your brothers were gossiping."

"He's half dragon. It's a very long story, but I love him, and he's good to me. He made me a fancy display case to hold my elite troops initiation medallion and the awards he's sure I'm going to earn in the army."

"You're truly determined to have a career in the military?" Aunt Tadelay didn't seem that comfortable talking about Trip and latched onto that.

Rysha didn't push. This already seemed like progress, that her aunt had seen what Shulina Arya was capable of, and had also seen what *Rysha* was capable of.

"Yes, Aunt. And speaking of that, we need to get back to the city. Dragons are causing trouble up there too."

"It's a daily event anymore. I wish something could be done."

"We're working on it. We'll find a way to protect Iskandia's borders. Just give the king and the military time."

Aunt Tadelay took a deep breath. "I shall find it encouraging that your brain is helping with the problem."

Rysha didn't think her brain had been that useful of late, but she didn't object to the statement. Someone in her family seemed to finally be coming around to her side.

Since Father and Krey were still arguing about vines, Rysha decided to leave her parting words for Aunt Tadelay. "Be very careful if Lord Lockvale comes around again. Trip questioned him while we were chasing the silver. It was, uhm, telepathic questioning, so he doesn't have any evidence, but he found out that Lockvale conspired with that silver dragon, that they were plotting to get Father to sell the family estate cheaply."

Rysha watched her aunt warily, immediately wishing she hadn't said anything about telepathy. Even if the secret was out about Trip's magical powers, she doubted her family would find actual proof of those powers any less creepy than his Wolf Squadron comrades did.

"*Lockvale*," Aunt Tadelay snarled, not commenting on telepathy or creepiness. "I *knew* that's what he's been doing. We *all* knew. He's not the subtle genius he thinks he is. *Fool*. I even suspected he was aligned with that dragon. It was all too convenient otherwise."

Rysha nodded, glad she wouldn't have to convince her family Lockvale was trouble. She knew her parents were smart, despite their lack of support for her military career, and hadn't truly believed they would be taken in, but she appreciated this reassurance.

"Just keep an eye out. If you or Mother or Father or anyone needs anything, or sees anyone else suspicious, get word to me as soon as possible, and I'll come down and be a rabid guard dog for the property. *We'll* come down." Rysha pointed at Shulina Arya, even though the dragon's eyes had closed, and her breathing was deep and even, so she didn't have much of a guard dog mien. "We can get here quickly."

She worried her aunt might scoff, despite what she'd seen tonight, but instead, she nodded solemnly, stepped forward, and gave Rysha a hug. The muzzle of her rifle clunked the back of Rysha's head, and she was fairly sure Dorfindral's hilt poked her aunt in the ribs, but it was a hug, nonetheless. A hug between women who would do what was necessary to protect the family.

"Father, I need to go," Rysha called when they broke apart. "I'll be back as soon as possible."

He looked over, frowning, and opened his mouth as if he would protest, but Aunt Tadelay shook her head. Father closed his mouth. He hesitated, then lifted his hand in farewell.

"Shulina Arya?" Rysha rested a hand on the dragon's side, hoping she would rouse easily. She hadn't seen her sleeping before and didn't even know where the dragon bedded down for the night. All Rysha knew was that she objected to stables. "We need to go back to the city and see if they need help."

One violet eye opened. *Tarts?* Her voice sounded sleepy, and Rysha regretted that she couldn't leave the dragon snoozing. It had been a *long* day.

"Uhm, maybe afterward. We can check." Rysha doubted baking tarts had been Sardelle's priority today if dragons had been attacking the city.

Shulina Arya did the telepathic equivalent of mumbling something incoherent—or maybe it was coherent in dragon?—and rolled onto her stomach so Rysha could climb onto her back. The illumination spheres she had created faded, and Father and Krey headed for the house. The shadows hid the destroyed vineyard, but Rysha remembered the image all too well, the charred remains of the vines near the black skeletons of trees in what had once been a beautiful orchard.

She didn't know when she would find the time, but she vowed to ensure that Lord Lockvale couldn't harass her family or anyone else anymore. One way or another.

CHAPTER 16

"IT'S NOT GOING TO GLOW or vibrate or detect ghosts or anything now, is it?" Leftie asked.

"What? Your arm?" Trip was sitting on a blanket with him, the last of the people he'd healed. Sardelle had healed Duck and another injured pilot who'd arrived later, entering the hangar bleak-faced and devastated after admitting that he had crashed his flier into the harbor.

"Yes, my arm that you magicked up and left all tingly." Leftie rotated the limb, eyeing it suspiciously. The gash that had been there, a wound so deep the bone had been visible, was the faintest of scars now, and Trip thought even that would fade with time.

"You're supposed to thank a healer," Sardelle said. "Not complain."

She'd finished and now stood, watching General Zirkander, who had only stopped working for a few brief words here and there. Though night lay deep outside now, he was sawing, sewing, and replacing hull and wing material right alongside the ground crew and several other officers. Trip could tell he was worried the dragons would return again soon and without warning.

"Oh, it wasn't a complaint, ma'am." Leftie lowered his arm. "Just a concern. I'm not comfortable being magicked."

"I should think it preferable to the alternative."

"I guess. I'm just... It's still tingling, Trip."

Leftie extracted his lucky ball-on-a-chain charm and kissed it. This was the fifth time he'd felt the need to do so since Trip started healing him. Trip was positive Leftie didn't kiss it that often when he was flying into battle against impossible odds.

"That's because it's finishing growing new skin. It's supposed to tingle. I promise that ghost detection is not in your future." Trip patted him on the shoulder and stood up.

Blackness encroached on his vision, and he held his hands out to steady himself.

Easy, Azarwrath said. *You've done a lot today. Your body needs rest.*

I don't think anyone is getting any rest tonight. Trip looked toward Zirkander and the others and felt another wave of guilt for not having been here for the battle.

I missed it too if it makes you feel better, Jaxi spoke into his mind.

Trip didn't think he'd left his bank vault door open, but he was tired, so maybe he was easier to read. Or maybe Jaxi could simply guess from his face.

I was helping teach a twelve-year-old to catalog medicinal herbs when the dragons came, Jaxi added. *A scintillating task, let me tell you. By the time Sardelle and I reached the army fort, all the fliers were already up in the sky and engaged in battle. There was no way for us to join Ridge.* Jaxi sounded like she felt as bad about missing out as Trip. *If Bhrava Saruth had been here, Sardelle and I could have flown into battle on his back. Or at least gotten a ride to the fort so we could go up with Ridge. He likes having us with him.*

I'm sure it's a helpful advantage for him.

It absolutely is. If I had been up there, maybe he wouldn't have lost people.

She sounded distressed on Zirkander's behalf—or maybe she'd known the pilots who had been lost?—so Trip didn't point out that it was something of an arrogant thought. Besides, hadn't he thought something similar in regard to himself earlier?

"Trip," Zirkander said, walking up behind him. "Ahn and Grady gave me their reports, but I want to hear directly from you about the meeting with the elder dragon. Is it true that there's no chance that he'll take up residence here and act as a large golden scarecrow?"

Zirkander's uniform was rumpled and stained with soot and engine grease, and he looked wearier than a sled dog at the end of a five-hundred-mile trek. Trip wished he had better news.

"Sorry, sir." He seemed to be apologizing a lot tonight. "Unless Shulina Arya develops an interest in him, I don't think so."

"What?" Zirkander looked at Sardelle with a puzzled expression.

She lifted a single shoulder.

"Drysaleskar found her fetching, sir," Trip said, "but she rebuffed his attempts to woo her." *Woo* was hardly the word to describe the clumsy advance he had witnessed, but he lacked a better term.

"Is she even old enough to be wooed?" Another look at Sardelle. Maybe Zirkander considered her his guide to all things magical. And dragon-related. "I've seen her on wheels."

"If she is, I suspect she would be more drawn to a younger soul," Sardelle said, then yawned and rubbed her neck. "I want to check on our surrogate mothers to make sure nothing happened to them or the babies in the attack."

Zirkander nodded.

"Trip, do you want to come along?" she asked.

"I... want them to be all right, of course, but—" Trip extended his hand toward the fliers, "—I'm sure the general needs me here."

"We can always use your engineering knack, Trip, but you may want to be elsewhere for the rest of the night." Zirkander glanced toward the doorway. "You may have noticed Angulus came up here to check on us—and Major Kaika."

"Yes, sir. I sensed them leaving about ten minutes ago." Trip remembered Kaika refusing to be carried, saying she had recovered and was fine, and that she would walk out at Angulus's side, but what did that have to do with Trip being elsewhere?

"You may not have noticed a castle administrator who caught up with Angulus outside the hangar as he was coming in. He drew him aside and reported a complaint filed a little earlier."

Trip's stomach sank. Could the incident with Lockvale have caught up with him already?

"No, sir. I didn't notice."

"I wasn't eavesdropping, but Jaxi has a knack for it."

Pardon me, but it's called observing, not eavesdropping. It's not as if I hopped out of my scabbard, sneaked out there, and leaned myself against the wall where they were speaking.

"I suppose it was Lord Lockvale who made the complaint?" Trip sensed an indignant grumble from Azarwrath.

"Yes. What happened?" Zirkander regarded Trip gravely, his eyes troubled. Seven gods, what had the nobleman said?

"He's been teaming up with a silver dragon to try to drive Rys—Lieutenant Ravenwood's family from their land. I questioned him so I could get the truth."

"*How* did you question him?"

"Just with words and telepathy. I mean, I asked him questions about it so I could read his thoughts. That's not—" Trip glanced at Sardelle, not sure how much Zirkander truly knew about magic and what sorcerers were capable of, especially since he seemed to hide in his office or the duck blind whenever magic was happening in his house. "It's not that hard to do."

Sardelle nodded, as if to back him up, but her eyes were troubled too.

Because Lockvale reported a lot more than questioning, Jaxi said. *He wants you hanged.*

Trip almost fell over. *What?*

"He said you assaulted him in front of witnesses, used your magic to pin him down, and then you tried to kill him," Zirkander said.

"Sir, I never hurt him. I was just trying to get answers. He lunged at me with a pistol. I put a barrier up, and he bounced off it—after trying to shoot me—but that's it. I swear."

Trip lifted his hands and gulped in deep breaths, trying to stave off the panic rising, but memories popped into his mind of all the times he and his grandparents had been forced to move when he'd been a boy. Because he'd been accused of witchcraft, or of causing strange and otherworldly things to happen.

To have a nobleman do the accusing… How could he fight back? This could end his career. Or his life.

No, Trip would run before letting anyone kill him, but run where? His life and everything he loved and wanted to be was here. Only his grandparents were back east, but it wasn't as if he could go there—it would be the first place the army would look for him.

Zirkander rubbed a hand down his face. Even though he didn't say anything, Trip couldn't help but feel he'd disappointed the general. At the least, he'd made trouble for him.

"Was Lieutenant Ravenwood there, by chance?" Sardelle asked. "Another witness to contradict this man's claims—"

"They're sleeping together," Zirkander said. "Nobody is going to believe she's an unbiased third party."

Trip grimaced. He wasn't surprised Zirkander knew, but lamented that he hadn't been subtler with Rysha, that their relationship had become common knowledge among their superior officers.

"She wasn't there," Trip said. "I went down to deal with Lockvale while she and Shulina Arya chased down his dragon."

"Is the dragon still alive?" Sardelle asked. Did she think *it* would have testified?

"No."

"Ah."

Zirkander rubbed his face again. "All right. Like I said, I want you to disappear for the rest of the night. It sounded like the military police might be sent to collect you. Tonight, Angulus is going to be busy hugging Kaika and admonishing her for getting hurt again, but we'll go together to talk to him personally in the morning, before any overly eager subordinate can throw you in a cell. For now, go with Sardelle, and sleep at our place."

"Do you think Angulus will believe a civilian over one of his soldiers that he knows?" Sardelle asked him.

"He doesn't know Trip that well, and I honestly don't know how he feels about him. You know how hard he is to read—for those of us without telepathy. And he may very well know and have a long past with this nobleman. The nobles have gotten preferential treatment throughout history, and they certainly expect it. Even though Angulus is a modern man, he's always careful not to snub tradition. I would hate for Trip to be turned into some example."

"Hm."

Trip couldn't read Sardelle either. Unlike Lockvale and most others he encountered, she could protect her thoughts.

"We'll go then," Sardelle said, inviting Trip along with a hand wave. "And see you later." She patted Zirkander on the chest. "Don't stay out here all night."

"I'll try not to. Trip, we'll have your back."

Trip was tempted to ask Zirkander if he believed him but sensed that he did without asking. A feeling of relief washed over him. Even though Zirkander didn't have the power to belay orders from the king, at least he would argue on Trip's behalf.

"Thank you, sir."

As Trip and Sardelle, riding a pair of the army's mares, passed through the gate in the city wall and headed into the quieter suburbs outside, Trip scribbled another item on the list he'd started. None of the mothers had requested a self-rocking cradle, but it seemed like a good idea. A clockwork version that could be set to rock for a certain length of time.

"You know it's too dark for most people to see to write, don't you?" Sardelle sounded tired but also amused.

"Yes, ma'am. But I'm odd. Rysha tells me so."

"You don't mind being called odd?"

"No, she likes odd boys."

"I see."

"And it's not like the label was a surprise to me."

Trip had called Rysha odd, too. Or at least alluded to it. He thought that made them a good match. He just hoped none of the fallout that might come from Lockvale's accusations—gods, would the story be in a newspaper in the morning?—would damage her reputation or that of her family.

"In my time, my *original* time, you would have been called special or even remarkable, not odd."

"Would a nobleman have made up accusations about me to get me in trouble?" Trip asked glumly, caring little about labels and more about the possible avalanche rolling down the side of a mountain toward him.

"The *referatu* didn't place themselves above mundane humans, but we did have our own government and judiciary system, so if one did, we would have dealt with it in house." Sardelle sighed, gazing at the dark houses they rode past. "But it's unlikely a mundane, even a noble, would have dared falsely accuse a mage. Even a true accusation would have been unlikely to surface."

Trip looked at his list, then tucked it away, letting it remind him that there was at least some good news. They'd visited seven of his little siblings, and they and their surrogate mothers had all been doing fine. The women had been scared during the attack, naturally, but none of their homes had been damaged.

Still, seeing how much damage the rest of the city had undergone—and he knew it would look even worse when the sun rose—had left Trip more determined than ever to find a solution, to protect the babies and everybody here in Pinoth.

As they neared the turnoff for the Zirkander house, Trip sensed dragons there. They were shape-shifted, with their auras dampened, or he would have detected them from much farther away.

"Ma'am, were you expecting visitors? Dragon visitors?"

"You mean Phelistoth?" Sardelle must have stretched out with her senses, too, because she added, "Oh. I see you don't. Those are the bronze dragons from the king's meeting."

Trip nodded. "Shulina Arya's parents."

He nudged his mare into a gallop. Even though he wanted to believe any relative of Shulina Arya's would be a friend and ally, he didn't know much about these two dragons yet. So far, he'd had nothing but bad experiences with bronze dragons. Telmandaroo had been the best of the bunch, wherever he was now, and even he had wanted to make Trip a minion.

Sardelle's mare also picked up the pace, and they soon rounded the corner that led to her house. Moonlight gleamed silver on the surface of the pond at the end of the street, and Trip thought the clear sky and pleasant temperature a poor match for how the night had gone so far. Storms and torrential rain would have been more appropriate.

Lanterns burned in all the rooms in the house, the soft yellow light visible through the curtains. A brighter light streamed out through the living room window, a warm golden glow.

Trip raked the house with his senses. Tylie was inside, as were the babies, Sardelle's newborn and Zherie. Her toddler was also there, sleeping up in the children's room. The two younger students that lived here since their parents weren't local slept out in the small bunkhouse in the back.

"Nothing seems… amiss," Sardelle said, no doubt doing a similar check. "Other than those two unexpected guests."

Trip tied his horse to a railing and jogged for the door. Since Tylie sat in the living room with the dragons, he assumed—hoped—that meant she was monitoring whatever they were doing.

They're disassembling one of the stasis boxes, Jaxi said dryly. *You didn't notice that in your perusal?*

No, Trip replied. *And, uh, why?*

Don't ask me. I can't read dragon minds. Or Tylie's mind, either. Though I am chatting with Wreltad, and it seems like 'scientific curiosity' may be the answer.

Tylie's soulblade? Trip had sensed the magical sword on previous visits to the house, but didn't think he'd ever had a conversation with him.

Tylie's soulblade. He's another old soul from Cofah. I believe he and the stuffy Azzy chat when you come to the house for lessons. I'm sure they get along fabulously, though Taddy is more interested in nobly slaying enemies than consuming fine wine and food. I understand he's upset nobody took him along to do battle, but Tylie is becoming more of a healer and animal handler than dragon slayer. Also, someone had to stay and babysit.

As Trip and Sardelle entered the house, a familiar male voice said, "It *is* one of the same ones. Look, there's the maker's mark."

Trip spotted the speaker, Bhajera Liv, in the same oversized suit jacket and goggles that he'd worn in the king's meeting. The lenses of the goggles were down and in use as he peered at a panel. He sat cross-legged on the floor near his partner, Wyleenesh, who was examining a bronze plaque. Disassembled parts lay all around them.

Tylie sat on the end of the huge wrecked-flier-parts couch, reading a book and taking notes. She looked more like a supervisor—or babysitter—than someone involved in their project.

"Good evening," Sardelle said, sounding serene though she had to feel distressed by the mess on her floor.

Some of those tiny screws and pieces would be painful to step on when barefoot if they weren't all cleaned up. Trip knew this because he'd often disassembled things on his grandparents' living room floor—and heard the subsequent cursing when he hadn't picked up all of the pieces.

"Greetings, human female," Wyleenesh said, raising a hand in a vague greeting. "We heard about the half-dragon creatures from a past millennia and *had* to investigate."

Sardelle looked at Tylie, who merely lifted a hand, palm toward the ceiling. Trip took that to mean she hadn't invited them; they'd just shown up. And it wasn't as if one could say no to dragons coming into the house.

"We were among those who worked on the stasis technology back then," Wyleenesh said.

Trip leaned forward, suddenly much more interested. "You were alive thousands of years ago? When the babies that were in those chambers were originally born?"

"I should say so, yes. We were quite young and exuberant, much like Shulina Arya is now."

"I was never like Shulina Arya is now," his partner said dryly.

"I didn't know you then, but I do believe that. You're rather stodgy."

"I'm practical."

"Stodgily practical."

Bhajera Liv sniffed and went back to examining the plaque. Trip couldn't imagine why a dragon would need magnification goggles or whatever those were—Azarwrath had once shown him how to augment his vision with magic—and assumed they were an affectation.

"At the time, our kind were worried about changes to the climate we witnessed occurring," Wyleenesh said, nodding to Sardelle, whose interest also seemed to have perked up.

She came around to sit on the couch and face them. It was the first time Trip had seen her touch that couch.

"Dragons invented the stasis technology," Wyleenesh continued, "because we feared the world might grow inhospitable for our kind, but we believed if we could hibernate for a thousand or two thousand years, the climate might change and become more palatable again. As it does over time. But it turned out to be a brief trend toward cooler temperatures, and none of our kind felt compelled to enter the chambers. Until an illness came along that our kind did not know how to cure. It killed many dragons, and those afflicted started placing themselves in stasis, in the hope of coming out one day, in a time when a cure had been discovered."

"That's how Phel came to be here in our time." Tylie closed her book and leaned forward.

"Did you know Agarrenon Shivar?" Trip asked them. "Or—there was a bronze dragon who convinced the elders to force him to go into stasis and then sabotaged his chamber so that he eventually died. Did you know…"

The two dragons looked at each other, and Trip stopped talking, realizing he had no idea what the name of that bronze had been. What information he did know, he'd seen in a vision from the past. What if that deceitful dragon had been one of Shulina Arya's parents?

If it had been, Trip wouldn't feel any resentment toward them. Everything he'd learned about his sire suggested that his death had been a good thing for the world.

"We did know Agarrenon Shivar," Wyleenesh said, "though I cannot say it was an honor to have made his acquaintance."

"He was a buffalo's left ass cheek," Bhajera Liv said.

"Fortunately, you seem to be nothing like him," Wyleenesh said. "We were pleased to hear from Shulina Arya that you rejected Drysaleskar's suggestion that you talk her into accepting him as a mate."

Trip's breath caught. Sardelle and Tylie looked curiously at him. He hadn't realized Shulina Arya had been aware of that exchange. He felt guilty because, for however brief a time, he had contemplated Drysaleskar's suggestion. Was she aware of that? Or only that in the end, he hadn't done it?

"Drysaleskar is a buffalo's *right* ass cheek," Trip said.

Bhajera Liv threw his head back and laughed. "Most golds are some manner of ass cheek."

"Goodness," Wyleenesh told him, "I didn't know you could do that."

"What?"

"Laugh."

"I'm not *that* stodgy."

"Telryn," Wyleenesh said, looking at Trip again, "this was all long, long ago for us, but I did know Grenkolin, the bronze who built some of the large dragon-sized stasis chambers during that particular era. It seems he built smaller ones too. His mark is on that plaque, and likely on the insides of all the other chambers that those babies came out of. He was a bit of a—what is the term you humans use?—mad scientist. We also believe he was responsible, at least partially, for the building of the *Portal of Avintnaresi*, that which many of us were tricked into using to leave this world. I was actually consulted on the Agarrenon Shivar matter since it was a… delicate situation."

"Planning the murder of gold dragons often is," Bhajera Liv said.

"I believe I may have known your mother as well. There was a human woman who was a gifted engineer, especially given what a primitive time that was among humans, so she was known to many of us who considered ourselves scientists and engineers. I worked with her on a project once and saw her not long before Agarrenon Shivar was placed in stasis."

Trip found himself hanging on the dragon's words, his chest tight at the idea that someone might exist today who had known his mother, his birth mother, thousands of years ago.

"For a human, she was very bright," Wyleenesh said.

"Do you know—" Trip's voice was hoarse, and he cleared his throat before beginning again. "Is there any chance you know about her, uhm, relationship with Agarrenon Shivar? About how I came to be? I've worried that it wasn't…" He paused, not comfortable talking about those precise worries in front of dragons he barely knew.

"Hm, yes, Agarrenon Shivar had quite the harem, did he not?" Wyleenesh looked toward his partner.

Bhajera Liv, his attention back on studying the parts, waved a dismissive hand. "I paid no attention to his animal conquests."

Trip winced.

"The engineer—ah, what was her name?—Amilda of Songwater was likely too smart to be wooed by Agarrenon Shivar," Wyleenesh said. "Even if he poured magic into his request, she would have found a way to fight him off. Besides, she was a little older, I believe. I do have a difficult time telling human ages, but she was not like his usual full-bosomed young conquests, as Bhajera Liv called them."

On the chance the dragon had the name correct, Trip burned it into his memory. Amilda of Songwater. Maybe some history texts somewhere would mention her, and he could learn more.

"She probably wooed *him*," Bhajera Liv said, picking up another piece of the device to study.

"Hm, yes, that is quite possible," Wyleenesh said. "For a time, it was trendy for human women to seek out powerful male dragons for mating. The humans hoped they would have powerful offspring. I remember being a touch miffed that those women always seduced the *gold* dragons. They should have prioritized intelligence and sought out bronze dragons. Never is there love in the world for bronze dragons."

"You're not going to feel sorry for yourself again, are you?" Bhajera Liv asked.

"Is this not a suitable moment for it?"

"No."

"That's disappointing."

It is an interesting thought, Sardelle spoke privately into Trip's mind. *I know you've been concerned that you were born out of a forced union. These two don't know for sure it was otherwise, but perhaps it's true that your mother sought out a dragon because she hoped to have a remarkable baby who would grow into someone who could change the world.*

Trip knew she was trying to be encouraging and offer him hope, but since he'd done precious little to change the world, he mostly found this new idea daunting. If his mother had hoped for some super baby... he didn't think he was it. At least, he hadn't been yet. Perhaps there was still time to do something, to come up with some idea that could truly make a difference in the world.

I'd like to check on Zherie, Trip told Sardelle, wanting to make sure his little sister was all right, but also wanting an excuse to go off and find someplace quiet to think about these revelations.

Do you think she'll want to add something to your list?

Given that she's four months old, probably not. Trip smiled slightly. *You* could make a request.

You've already made us numerous things. Ridge is pleased with his coffee maker. Thus far, it's proven simple and durable, unlikely to be destroyed by even dragons.

That was the goal.

Come. Sardelle rose and headed for the stairs. *We'll check on them together. Olek is up there too. I've been gone a few hours, so they may be hungry.*

Trip had been trailing after her, leaving the bronze dragons to their studies, but he faltered.

I'll wait until you've left the room to start the buffet, Sardelle said dryly, glancing back. *I know witnessing breastfeeding makes you uncomfortable.*

Just when it's my commanding officer's wife doing it. Or women I don't know. Or women I do.

So, if men were doing it, you wouldn't be uncomfortable?

Disturbed maybe, but not uncomfortable.

I see.

As Trip followed her up the stairs, he started mulling over what he could do to help Iskandia with the dragon problem, and what he could do to be the man his biological mother may have dreamed he would be.

CHAPTER 17

A KNOCK INTERRUPTED RYSHA PUTTING ON her socks. After learning she'd been too late to help with the battle, she had let Shulina Arya head off to get some rest and had spent the night in her barracks room. Believing the knock might belong to Trip, she hurried to answer it. But Lieutenant Harper, the officer from next door, stood there, already in uniform and holding a newspaper.

"Rysha, did you see this? This is your boyfriend, isn't it?" Harper held up the newspaper.

It wasn't open to the front page—Rysha suspected the dragon attack had precedence there—but a few pages back, there was a picture of Trip. It was his military entrance photograph from his army record; he looked a few years younger and very stiff and uncomfortable in his uniform.

Rysha took the newspaper with a shaking hand, already guessing what this was about. She'd heard Trip had healed people and maybe even saved Major Kaika's life the night before, but she highly doubted the sensationalist-loving journalists would write him up for that.

Sorcerous Officer Wanted for Attempted Murder, the headline read.

She groaned. A large part of her wanted to thrust the newspaper back at Harper, not to read the lies and drivel the article would contain, but she made herself skim through it. Later, if she had to help Trip prepare a defense, she would need to know what that damn Lockvale had said.

...waylaid Lord Lockvale while the nobleman was riding innocently along the highway... witnesses observed an unwarranted and unprovoked attack... used heinous and vile magic to assault Lord Lockvale... barely survived the encounter... demanding the unstable and dangerous officer be hanged.

Hanged!

The paper crinkled as Rysha's hands tightened. She wanted to wad it into a ball and hurl it across the room.

"Is it true?" Harper whispered.

"Of course not," Rysha snapped, glaring at her. Harper had only met Trip once, and they had only exchanged a few words, so she couldn't expect the lieutenant to know better, but the fact that anyone would doubt Trip made her furious. "Lockvale has an agenda. He was trying to get my father to sell our family's land to him and—"

Rysha stopped as a realization smacked her in the side of the face like a wet towel. What if Lockvale was doing this because of *her*? Because she and Shulina Arya had killed his winged business partner and he now had no easy way to scare people and force them to sell their land? Lockvale would know he couldn't strike at her, since she was a fellow noble and he would need a lot of evidence to cause a judge to rule against her, but Trip wasn't a noble and he had dragon blood. Even if the return of dragons had changed a lot quickly for Iskandians, the average person still feared magic and those who could use it. A judge might rule against Trip out of fear or distaste. Rysha didn't know what Lockvale could gain from this, but if he was petty and wanted revenge... this could accomplish that.

King Angulus could overrule a judge, of course, but Rysha had not heard of many instances when he had done that. He liked to be seen as fair and impartial. Besides, Angulus didn't know Trip that well. He might believe there was some truth to these claims.

Rysha had to talk to him, to convince him otherwise, and to also convince him that it would be worth overruling any court's decision. Putting aside feelings and emotions, Iskandia *needed* Trip, now more than ever.

"It says the military police went to his barracks room but couldn't find him." Harper pointed to the last paragraph. "If he didn't do it, why did he run?"

"I'm sure he didn't run. He's probably at work and busy fixing fliers after the attack last night."

Rysha expected Harper to point out that the military police would have looked for him at work, but the lieutenant shook her head and whispered, "It was awful. There were at least eight dragons up there raining fire on the city. I heard they stole a bunch of our special dragon-slaying swords. Were you there? Lots of us were wondering where our dragon allies were."

Rysha winced. Even though they had been assigned a mission to look for the elder dragon, and couldn't have been expected back, she felt guilty because she and Shulina Arya had been dealing with her family's problems when the city had been in danger.

"The silver one finally showed up, but it was really our fliers that saved the day. They're written up on the first page of the paper." Harper made a flipping motion with her finger. "I've been on the night-watch duty, so I had time to read it all before the sun was even up."

Rysha closed the newspaper to read the front page where a photograph of the "brave, heroic, and fearless" General Zirkander shared space with one of Major Kaika, who'd been willing to sacrifice herself for the good of the city.

Rysha's heart nearly stopped at the word *sacrifice*. But she'd checked in at the flier hangar the night before, and she'd been told Kaika had been injured but not killed. The pilots had lost two of their own, but she'd heard all the blade wielders had survived, albeit not all of them had managed to keep their *chapaharii* swords.

Still, she skimmed the article to make sure someone hadn't lied to her to spare her feelings the night before. Whenever the journalist had penned it, Kaika had apparently been in critical condition. If Kaika didn't make it in to work that day, Rysha would track her down and make sure she was all right. Assuming she could get past all the fawning reporters who would be pushing through the gates and hoping to interview General Zirkander. She shook her head at all the accolades dumped on him when Trip was treated like a nobody who'd done nothing for the city.

"Thanks for showing me," Rysha said, managing a civil tone when she handed the newspaper back to Harper. "I better finish getting dressed and ready for work."

"It's a couple of hours until first formation. You're not going to look for him, are you?"

"If Trip doesn't want to be found, he won't be found. Don't worry about me." Rysha smiled and shut the door, though a part of her wanted to slam it.

She *was* going to find Trip and warn him, just in case he hadn't already heard. She didn't think he should run or would even consider leaving the city, but she did want to assure him that she would use all the connections she had to make sure he was treated fairly. And she definitely planned to request an audience with King Angulus. She didn't know him well, but she wasn't intimidated by him.

"Lots to do today," Rysha said, tossing her nightclothes aside and grabbing her socks. *Shulina Arya, is there any chance you're listening to my mind and want to come give me a ride?*

Unfortunately, only silence answered her. Shulina Arya was probably still sleeping somewhere. It didn't matter. Rysha would take one of the army's horses.

"I'm coming, Trip," she whispered as she jogged out of the barracks and toward the stables.

As the gelding trotted down the street toward Sardelle's house, Rysha spotted a very large gold dragon sleeping curled up on the lawn out front. An empty plate rested next to her snout.

"I guess that explains why there weren't any dragons available to give me a ride," Rysha said.

Clearly, she was going to have to figure out how to install an oven in her barracks room so she could bake tarts. Or maybe if she was careful with her lieutenant's pay, she could subscribe to a daily morning delivery from Donotono's. It did seem that she should reward Shulina Arya for all she did. And find a place for her to stay so she didn't have to sleep on Sardelle's lawn.

If Shulina Arya could sleep in a smaller shape-shifted form, maybe she could stay in the barracks, but Rysha had no idea if that could work. If a dragon fell asleep while shape-shifted, would she revert as soon as she dozed off? Rysha imagined the snapping of wood and breaking of walls and ceilings if something ferret-sized turned into something dragon-sized while in her room.

Shulina Arya opened an eyelid as Rysha dismounted, tied up her horse next to a couple of others, and strode for the door.

Good morning, Storyteller, she said in a muzzy voice, then dropped her eyelid shut again.

"Morning, Shulina Arya."

The door swung open before Rysha knocked. That was a little disconcerting, but at least it meant she wouldn't be waking up the household. The sun hadn't been up for long, and it was an early hour to call upon people.

She stepped inside to the smell of eggs frying and something cinnamon-scented baking in the oven. Her stomach grumbled, reminding her that she hadn't had breakfast yet.

"Perhaps we should test it with some local animal," a male voice said—it sounded familiar, but it wasn't Trip or General Zirkander.

"Don't even think of trying to put Scruffles in there," Tylie said. "I saw you looking at her earlier."

"I've worked with cats in the past," the male said, "and found they are not amenable to being placed into small spaces."

"Tell me about it."

Rysha walked farther inside, saying, "Hello?" as she looked over the back of the couch in the living room. She recognized Shulina Arya's parents in human form, sitting on the floor with a stasis chamber between them. One of the ones that had been broken?

Tylie sat on the couch watching them, a plate of eggs and frosted rolls in her lap. Through the kitchen door, Rysha glimpsed one of Sardelle's younger students manning the oven—the boy.

"We won't truly know if it's working again until we test it," one of the dragons said.

That was Bhajera Liv, Rysha remembered, the quieter of the two.

"Perhaps some squirrel or chipmunk or other woodland creature from the forest out back," the other one, Wyleenesh, said.

"Morning, Rysha," Tylie said with a wave.

"Hi, Tylie. Is Trip here?"

"With the babies." Tylie waved toward the stairs.

Rysha blew out a relieved breath. She'd been afraid he would have left town or that the military police would have caught up with him and arrested him.

"What's he doing up there?" Rysha had visited the stasis babies—his little siblings—with him before, but Trip always seemed a little awkward and uncertain about what to do with them. Good-hearted but clueless, as Sardelle had teasingly put it. Rysha couldn't imagine him up there rocking the baby girl to sleep or burping her over his shoulder. She *could* imagine Trip discussing engineering and flier technology with the baby, rather one-sidedly.

Tylie's eyes grew distant as she used her magic to check. "Mm, he's still working on something in their room. They're asleep. Well, no, Zherie is awake and watching him through the bars in the crib. Maybe he's entertaining." Her nose wrinkled, as if she couldn't imagine it.

Rysha had no problem imagining being entertained by Trip working on something—he was cute when his face scrunched up with concentration and he groped for a solution to a problem.

She left the dragons debating which woodland creature they should entice in to test the stasis chamber and went to look for Trip. She hadn't been upstairs in the house before and hoped she wouldn't stumble across General Zirkander walking around naked.

He's still at work, Jaxi spoke into her mind. *You're safe. Though Marinka was naked just a short while ago. She's at the age where she wishes to assert herself regarding whether or not clothing should be required.*

I think I can handle a nude toddler without being embarrassed.

But not a nude general? Embarrassment isn't the emotion most women feel when they imagine Ridge naked.

Uh, imagining things and being presented things in reality are slightly different.

I suppose. It's difficult to embarrass a soulblade, you know. I've seen everyone in the house nude.

Shulina Arya's parents too? Rysha asked.

No. Thus far, they've kept their tweed on.

There weren't that many rooms on the second floor, and Rysha soon found Trip, since the door was ajar. She pushed it open farther and started to step in, but paused. Large sheets of drawing-filled papers were strewn everywhere. Or were those schematics?

Trip leaned over a diaper-changing table that he was using as a desk. Rysha hoped he'd used his super sorcerer powers to sanitize it before starting.

She opened her mouth to ask but, since he hadn't turned around yet, spent a moment admiring him from behind. He was still in his fatigue trousers, but they fit well and gave a nice glimpse of his backside, especially since he was bent over. At some point during the night—had he been up all night?—he'd removed his jacket and draped it over a chair, so he stood in his short-sleeved undershirt, also nicely fitted. His dark hair stuck out in all directions, and she suspected he'd been shoving his hand through it all night, but he looked good tousled. She imagined it could be even more tousled if he engaged in something more vigorous than drawing.

She shook her head at her fantasies while wondering why journalists weren't writing about how wonderful and heroic—and handsome—he was instead of picking on him.

"I believe there's an office downstairs with a desk in it," she finally said, since he seemed too engrossed to realize she was there.

"There was a dragon sleeping in the chair in there when I peeked in." Trip turned and beamed a surprisingly warm and heartfelt smile at her, especially given that he should have been exhausted. "I was hoping you would come."

"Because you were bereaved without my companionship?"

"Because I need someone to check my math."

"Hm, math wasn't what I had in mind when I was looking at your ass." Remembering that there were babies in cribs in the room, she glanced over at them and corrected that to, "Your butt." She wasn't sure at what age babies started remembering things adults said, but it was probably a good idea not to use suspect language around them at any time.

Trip's smile widened. "Only because you haven't seen what I'm working on yet."

He waved for her to join him.

"Which dragon was in the office?" Rysha asked, knowing Shulina Arya seemed to prefer lawns, and it had looked like the bronzes had been up all night too.

"Phelistoth. He gave me a baleful look when I asked if I could use the office. Sardelle mentioned that he's cranky before he's had his coffee. And also after he's had it. And during all the times in between."

"He's not as amenable a soul as Shulina Arya." Rysha picked her way down the crooked aisle between the drawings strewn about, trying to guess what he was designing. A building? An airship? A combination of both?

"I don't think anybody is." Trip wrapped his arm around her shoulders and kissed her.

Before Rysha could get excited about that kiss and wrap her arms around him to lengthen it, he drew back and pointed at the drawing in progress. It seemed he was too excited about his project for extended smooching. That was what she got for falling in love with an aspiring engineer. Maybe it was for the best. Sooner or later, the military police would think to look here for him. If he was building something important, he had better do it before they came.

Although… as she looked at the schematic or blueprint or whatever this was shaping up to be, she couldn't imagine the actual structure being built in anything less than months. That would be a long time to evade the police.

"These are remarkably detailed." Rysha glanced at the pencil on the table and pen in his hand. "Are you doing it all freehand without any tools?"

"I have a tool." Trip leaned over and pulled something pink off the shelf next to a stack of diaper cloths. A six-inch ruler with a pink-spotted mushroom on the top.

"Ah, a staple for every architect. I'm impressed with how much you've done, but what is it exactly? It looks like a large building, but there's a runway, and an engine room and propellers… Those aren't balloons, are they? They look more like poofy pontoons."

"Poofy? That can't be an academic term."

"If you want me to check your math, you'll let me use whatever terms I wish."

"So long as you don't call my integers cute."

"Can they be handsome? I've always been inordinately attracted to the number seven. Primes are sexy in general, don't you think?"

Trip smirked. "You truly are as odd as I am. Are you sure you don't have any dragon ancestors?"

"You'd be the one to know. There is a portrait in my father's study of the original Lord Ravenwood, and people have compared him to an aardvark. It's a good thing he was granted land and a title, because I don't think he would have attracted the original Lady Ravenwood otherwise."

Rysha eyed the drawings on the floor more carefully, gradually getting a feel for what he was designing. As far as she could tell, he hadn't done a basic overview sketch, but... "Some kind of flying fortress?"

"More of a weapons platform, though I was thinking of a Cofah flying fortress that attacked the city three years ago. I remember seeing a sketch of it in the *Charkolt Reader* and then researching everything I could about it because I was fascinated. I was a little disappointed that it employed magic—dragon blood to be exact—and couldn't have flown without it. Though since I'm planning to use magic in this, I can't be an engineering elitist, I suppose."

"Magic? Like artifacts you create or dragon blood?"

"I will likely end up using a lot of my own power to create energy supplies for the engines, but I was actually planning to ask one of the dragons for some vials of blood, yes. And to see if I can pull in Dr. Targoson for this, as he has a lot more experience with making things from their blood than I do."

"Have our dragon allies proven willing to give blood before? I remember Kaika and Blazer taking vials from the silvers that attacked us in the Antarctic because there wasn't any left back here."

"I don't think they have, no, but it's possible the tart bribe wasn't high enough when they were asked previously. But if they're not so inclined, there's a relatively fresh dragon carcass in the yard beside your castle. My understanding is that the blood stays viable for weeks after a dragon's death, and months if it's bottled in something airtight. Actually, that's Jaxi's understanding. I'm quite ignorant on the matter. I just draw things." He waved the pink ruler. "So, the plan is to create this fortress that can hover indefinitely over the harbor or out at sea—it'll be fully mobile so it can be moved if necessary—and to mount weapons on it capable of tracking and shooting dragons."

"What about their barriers? Even the acid-bullets bounce off, right? Until the barriers are down? And what would keep the dragons from destroying your fortress?"

Trip grabbed a pad of paper with a bunch of arithmetic on the top page and a number circled at the bottom. "I'll need to do some testing—or maybe someone without dragon blood who wouldn't be bothered by it will need to do some testing—but that's about how many pounds of metal I believe we'll need from the banded iron quarry in Rakgorath.

I'm basing my guesses on what I saw in Bhodian's floating palace. He didn't actually have that much of the tainted iron mixed in with the building materials, but I think it would have repelled dragons as well as sorcerers. As you remember, it nullified my powers when I was completely surrounded by it."

Rysha well remembered unlocking the cage she'd found him trapped inside. "But how will you make magic-based power sources if the banded iron will be integrated into the weapons platform? Wouldn't they simply go out? The way your flier crystals did when we approached the quarry?"

"I've been thinking about that. Magic and the tainted iron were used together in creating the *chapaharii* blades, and I got a chance to study yours closely that night we altered the command words. I believe I can design the power sources to be immune to the influence of the iron. And I'll only be using a small amount of it. It won't be as deleterious to magic and magic users as that quarry itself was."

"This is an ambitious project, Trip."

"I know. And like I said, I'll need some help, but I think I can handle creating the majority of the weapons platform." Trip waved at the sketches. "And hopefully General Zirkander can put together a team to go collect some of the ore. As for the weapons themselves, I believe if we use the tainted iron for the casings of rockets that contain Dr. Targoson's acid, the weapons will pierce the dragons' magical barriers, allowing them to get through to break open on their scales."

"And they wouldn't be able to easily destroy the rockets because of the ore," Rysha said. "Much like our *chapaharii* swords."

"Yes."

The scale of the project daunted Rysha. Could it truly be made in anything less than years?

"The weapons I'm proposing could also be fired from the ground by a smart, sexy artillery officer—" Trip squeezed her shoulders, "—but by creating a mobile launch platform, they could be easily moved all over the country. I believe that with Dr. Targoson's help, I could also figure out how to instill commands in the dragon blood—apparently, the Cofah were doing that three years ago before they lost their source of it—that would cause the weapons to seek out and follow dragons, so the big creatures couldn't simply outmaneuver them. I'll refine my plans more. I have a lot of ideas. I'm positive I can make this work. And when it's successful, we can build more than one weapons platform and station the others around the country. If the dragons keep encountering them, they might realize it would be easier on them to simply leave Iskandia alone."

"I'm positive you can make it work too." Rysha smiled and patted him on the chest. She was less positive he could make it work in less than five years, but she was glad to see him using his passion for creating things for this. It made perfect sense to her. "May I ask what prompted you to start thinking of doing more than flying and shooting things and becoming a hero that way? Those were your words as I recall. I don't disapprove, mind you. I'm just curious."

He gazed down at the floor, then over at the cribs.

"Part of it was the attack last night and how bad I felt for not being there to help. I realized that I'm not immortal and I won't always be here for Iskandia and my relatives and descendants—should there one day be descendants." Trip smiled briefly at her. "Even when I am here, I'm only one man, and not nearly as powerful as an actual dragon, so the magic I can do at any one given time isn't the answer. Not to mention that I'll likely be fighting prejudices and outdated concepts all my life." He winced.

He must have heard about Lockvale's accusations.

"But if I create something that anyone can use, and that can protect a city—maybe even the whole country—without me having to be in the area... that seems like something I must do. Yes, it's taken me a long time to realize this. It's hard to give up those boyhood dreams. I still envy Zirkander his reputation and the adoration he gets from the newspaper journalists. And yes, I know that's immature and un-evolved." He smiled again. "It was actually a conversation last night with Shulina Arya's parents about my birth mother that changed something for me. One of them remembers her, you see. They thought she might have chosen to sleep with my sire of her own free will, not because she cared about him but because she wanted a half-dragon baby who would grow up to change the world. If there's any truth to that, it's daunting, I'll admit, to think someone conceived you thinking you'd be this great being, but it's also... I feel this expectation now. I don't want to fail. I know she's been gone for three thousand years, but I'd hate to disappoint her."

Rysha left her hand on Trip's chest as she listened to him. She thought it sounded awful, to choose a father—a sire—not out of love but to create more desirable offspring, but it did strike her as better than the likely alternative, that his mother had been forced against her wishes. Remembering that bronze dragon pawing over her in Lagresh still made her shudder.

"You couldn't disappoint anyone if you tried, Trip," she said.

"Lord Lockvale seems less than pleased with me."

"Only because you haven't made him a coffee maker."

Trip paused. "Do you think that would work?"

"Maybe you should keep gifts for the home in your cockpit. You could have tried wooing him with one on the highway. Though I wouldn't want you to make friends with the man who's been plotting against my family."

"I can assist people with their coffee woes without befriending them."

Rysha grinned, and was thinking of kissing him, but Trip stiffened and turned toward the wall. His eyes grew distant, and she knew he was investigating more than the paint.

"The military police are coming." He sighed, let go of her, and started stacking papers so he could roll them up. "I need to get out of here."

"Get out? Are you officially going AWOL?"

"I can't build this from a military prison."

"You can't build some huge half-mile-long flying weapons platform while you're out hiding in the woods, either. Trip, that's a job for fifty people. Plus, you need the banded iron ore from that quarry, right?"

"The woods aren't the place I have in mind. Have you seen Bhrava Saruth's temple? I was thinking of asking him for sanctuary there. There's a huge flat area out back. If I agree to worship him or rub his belly or make him tarts, I bet he would let me stay. Maybe he could even be convinced to help. Even better, only his human followers go out there, and there aren't many of them. No dragons would be caught there, so we could build the platform and spring it on our enemies before they knew anything about it."

"Make tarts? Trip, I've never even seen you make your own breakfast. Everything you eat comes out of the mess hall or a ration box."

"Yes, much to Azarwrath's lament." Trip rolled up his drawing-filled papers and grabbed the pen and pencils he'd been using. He reached for the pink ruler, but left it, perhaps afraid to borrow such a precious belonging without permission. "If I can't make tarts myself, I'll make a machine to make them. How hard can be it be?"

"Trip…"

He glanced at the door, then headed for the window and pushed it open. One of the babies woke up and gurgled a protest. Or maybe that was an incipient cry.

"Trip, wait." Rysha lunged after him and caught his arm.

"I can't stay, Rysha. They're almost to the front door."

"I don't care. Listen to reason for a minute. That being me, since I'm the only other one here over six months old."

She feared he would pull his arm away, dart out the window, and disappear into the woods, but he paused and looked at her.

"If you run and hide—if you go AWOL—you're only going to make things worse. *Much* worse. People will think you're guilty, that you have something to hide."

"General Zirkander told me to come out here."

"He told you to go AWOL?"

"No, he said to spend the night here and that we'd go see the king together in the morning. But then he never came home. And the military police did."

"Trip, don't make this way worse than it is. Just wait for the general. If you insist on being difficult, nobody can arrest you against your wishes, but that won't help your cause. If you let them take you, it would only be temporary. I'm sure Zirkander can find you right away. And if he forgets—which he won't—*I* will find you. Trip, I have a dragon, and I'm not afraid to use her."

He snorted, but he smiled too. Rysha found that encouraging.

"I'm positive that Shulina Arya would require no more than six tarts to be coaxed into perpetrating a prison break."

"I can imagine her riding in on her scooter with a key ring in hand."

"It could happen. And just in case you don't think my dragon and I will be enough to save you, remember that you do have a few powers of your own. I haven't heard anything about the prison in the fort being lined with iron from that quarry. You could turn the cell bars into a coffee maker if you get bored of waiting."

"This is true."

A pounding knock sounded at the front door.

Rysha watched Trip's eyes, still afraid he might panic and bolt. "I bet if you take your drawings along, you could work on them there."

"But will there be a ruler?"

"Sardelle's daughter would probably permit you to borrow hers for a few days."

"I'd feel bad if it was confiscated." Trip sighed and closed the window. "You say you're the voice of reason?"

"When compared to two babies and a dragonling man with a maniacal plan."

"Hm. All right. I shall attempt to be reasonable. While on my way to prison. And I *am* taking that ruler." Trip strode across the room to the changing table to pluck it up.

Rysha wagered he would ask Sardelle if he could borrow it on the way out.

Another gurgle came from a crib, and Trip paused to look in. "If I never see you again, Zherie, I want you to know that your brother thinks you have the potential to be a wonderful and brilliant person." He waved the pink ruler which elicited some giggles, then stepped toward the other crib. Rysha wasn't sure if Sardelle's newborn was awake yet. "If I never see you again, Olek, I want you to know that your mother's student thinks you have the potential to be a wonderful and brilliant person."

He saluted the baby with the ruler, then headed for the door.

"You think they'll remember that?" Rysha asked.

"Nah, but it makes me feel better about using their room all night and scribbling loudly in the dark."

"In the dark?" She followed him into the hall and toward the stairs.

"I didn't want to bother them by having lanterns lit."

Stern male voices drifted up from below, and Rysha didn't reply. Nervous energy coursed through her as she wondered if she'd done the right thing. She wanted to believe that a better result would come of Trip staying and dealing with this than running away—even if he only wanted to run away to build a weapon to protect the city from dragons—but she couldn't see the future and know for sure.

"There he is," a man said as Trip stepped off the stairs and into the living room.

Rysha glimpsed one of two uniformed men trying to stride through the door and into the house. But he bumped into an invisible barrier and stumbled back.

"Ma'am, we have orders to arrest Captain Telryn Yert. It's unlawful of you to stop us."

Sardelle stood inside the door, her shoulder to the wall and her arms folded across her chest as she looked at the men. "I'm not stopping you. But Captain Trip has several scaled friends who are here. It could be any one of them."

Trip paused with his hand on the back of the couch. The two shape-shifted bronze dragons wandered into the living room with coffee mugs and a plate of pastries in hand. Phelistoth followed them, also carrying a steaming mug, and he gazed blandly toward the front door.

Rysha leaned toward the window, wondering if Shulina Arya was still napping out there, but she only saw four more military police soldiers in the yard. Had they thought they would need the whole platoon to arrest Trip?

Then Shulina Arya hopped up onto the back of the couch next to Trip—as a golden ferret. For once, Rysha wished she'd stayed in her dragon form. She couldn't imagine anyone striding up to the front door to make an arrest—or do anything else—with a dragon in the yard.

The two soldiers at the door frowned at each other, frowned inside, and frowned even more darkly at Trip.

"Captain," the speaker said—he also held the rank of captain. "I insist that you come with us. We've been looking for you all night. First formation came and went, and you weren't at work. You're officially AWOL."

"That's not true," Rysha said. "General Zirkander told him to come here and wait for him. He's following orders."

"We have orders from the commandant." The MP captain held up a sheet of paper. "Judicial matters supersede all others. A civilian nobleman has made a serious charge against him. He is to be arrested and held until his case can be heard."

Shulina Arya hopped onto Rysha's shoulder, startling her. *What is happening, Storyteller? Is your mate to be punished?*

No, Rysha thought firmly, hoping she was right.

"Ridge will be home later today," Sardelle said. "I suggest you have a seat and wait for him. My houseguest isn't leaving until he's had a chance to talk to his battalion commander."

The soldiers looked at each other again, even the captain appearing uneasy. Rysha guessed that they would prefer to arrest Trip and get out of there before Zirkander arrived. The general was hardly known for being a tyrant, but he did have a big reputation to swing around.

"Later today, ma'am? We have orders to detain Captain Yert *now*."

"You'll find it difficult to get into the house, and unless he walks outside of his own accord, I don't see how you'll detain him."

"Captain Yert," the MP officer tried, addressing him to his face this time. "Won't you cooperate and come along? I'd hate to have to write down that you resisted arrest. It's going to look bad enough that you were difficult to find."

"Is that human attempting to take one of our own against his wishes?" Wyleenesh asked, a half-eaten dragon claw pastry in hand.

Trip's eyebrows lifted at the "one of our own" comment, and he looked heartened.

I can get rid of these interlopers, Storyteller. Simply let me know if it is acceptable to incinerate them.

No, they're on our side, Rysha replied. *Technically.*

"I'll come," Trip said. "I don't want to cause any more trouble. It wasn't my intent to cause any at all."

Sardelle shook her head. "Trip, a Cofah invasion is trouble. This is merely an interruption to breakfast. And not even that for everyone." She extended a hand toward the noshing dragons.

Trip smiled. "General Zirkander will know where to find me when he learns of this." He nodded to her. "Thank you for your hospitality, ma'am."

Rysha followed after him, intending to ride back with them until they reached the intersection that forked off and up to the castle. At that point, she would head up there and stand outside the king's door until she was granted an audience.

"You can stay if you want to," Sardelle told Trip quietly as he approached the door.

"I can get out if I need to," he said, equally quietly. "A nice cell will give me time to finish my drawings."

"I don't think the fort is known for *nice* cells."

Trip shrugged and walked out.

Even though Rysha had argued for him to cooperate, she flexed her hands in distress as she watched the big men turn him around and handcuff his wrists behind his back. She was the only reason Trip was in this situation. If not for her, he never would have crossed paths with Lockvale.

"I hardly think that's necessary," Sardelle said, then lowered her voice, "or going to be effective if he wants to escape."

Trip smiled sadly back at her, and then at Rysha, holding her gaze longer.

"Ow," one of the men yelped, yanking his hand back.

"What'd he do?" another asked, reaching for his pistol.

"It was the sword. It's baking hot. You can't touch it."

"Witch sword," one of the men in the yard whispered, making superstitious gestures.

"Remove it and hand it to us, Captain," the MP captain said.

"If a soulblade doesn't want you to hold it, you won't be able to hold it," Trip said.

"Well, you can't keep a weapon. It's against official arrest procedure."

"Even I can't make Azarwrath do anything against his will."

"Az-what?"

"The sword."

"Take it off and leave it here then."

Trip slumped at the order, his chin drooping to his chest. Would he comply?

Storyteller, are you sure these men don't need to be incinerated? They are having unpleasant thoughts toward your mate.

I know. And no. They're in the same army as we are.

Perhaps this army should be pruned of substandard soldiers.

By incineration?

Indeed!

After a long minute—and perhaps a conversation with Azarwrath—Trip magically unbuckled the scabbard and floated it to Sardelle. She accepted it gravely.

"How come *she* can touch it?" the soldier with the burned hand grumbled.

"Because she's Zirkander's witch," a man in the back muttered.

Sardelle's eyes tightened at the corners, but that was her only acknowledgment of the comment.

The MPs led Trip to a steam wagon, the back half designed to hold prisoners. Rysha curled her fingers into fists as he was put inside with a couple of soldiers to guard him, as if he were a criminal. The vehicle trundled away, belching black smoke from its stack, and rolled up the street until it disappeared from view.

Sardelle laid a hand on Rysha's shoulder. "Ridge will get him out as soon as he's able. Jaxi already told him what happened. He's swamped in the aftermath of the battle—he didn't get any sleep last night—but he promised he'll collect Trip as soon as the work day is over."

Rysha nodded. "Thank you, ma'am, but I intend to fix this even before then."

"Oh?" Sardelle asked, sounding a touch wary.

"I'm going to see the king."

The golden ferret on Rysha's shoulder rose up on her hind legs and chittered.

"And so is Shulina Arya."

Rysha thought Sardelle might consider this a rash action and try to dissuade her.

All she said was, "Perhaps if she were to take a more imposing form, it might help you gain an audience more quickly."

"We'll discuss it on the way over."

Shulina Arya hopped off Rysha's shoulder, ran out the door, and turned into a dragon on the walkway.

"Or we'll make a decision right now," Rysha amended.

One of the babies cried up in the nursery—hungry for breakfast, no doubt. Rysha was surprised they'd been quiet all through her conversation with Trip.

"I shall wish you luck then," Sardelle said. "And if you see Ridge today…" She eyed the empty plates and mugs around her living room. "Tell him we need more groceries, whenever he gets a chance."

"Yes, ma'am."

CHAPTER 18

THE DOOR CLANGED SHUT, AND the corporal who'd been left to stick Trip in his cell turned the key.

Trip wondered if the military police had any idea how easily he could unlock a lock with his mind. The bars were made of steel, not iron, and certainly not the tainted iron from the Rakgorath quarry, so they wouldn't be an impediment.

But, as Rysha had pointed out, sneaking out and disappearing would make him look guilty. He would stay for now and see what happened. He wanted to finish his drawings, regardless. Maybe Rysha would come by to check his math—too bad they hadn't gotten a chance for that earlier. Magic made manipulating metal and powering engines much easier, but he still had to have the physics right if he wanted his contraption to stay in the sky.

"May I have my drawings and pencils back?" Trip asked politely as the guard backed away.

They had removed his handcuffs, but failed to return the items he'd had in his pocket and, most importantly, his work. Had Azarwrath been there, he would have said something about the indignity of a sorcerer allowing such things to be done to him. But the soulblade was back with Sardelle for now. Even though he wasn't as chatty as Jaxi, Trip found he already missed Azarwrath's companionship. Or mentorship, as the soulblade would no doubt call it.

"Captain said to keep your stuff locked up in the evidence room."

"The drawings I'm working on, blueprints for a weapons platform prototype, may help with the defense of the country."

"Sure they will, Captain. Pilots are known to be genius scientists."

"I have some mechanical aptitude," Trip said, attempting to subtly influence the soldier with his power. He let his aura seep out as well, in case it helped. "Besides, there's nothing wrong with letting me have some paper in here, is there?"

The soldier met his eyes, his mouth drooping open. He seemed entranced, but mustered another argument. "It might be witchy paper."

"It's just paper. *I'm* the witch. Though the more correct term is sorcerer. Bring the papers, please."

"I'll bring the papers, please." The corporal disappeared around a corner and headed into the main building.

Trip kept a mental finger on the man's mind, not letting up on the influence, though he always found it disconcerting when people lost their autonomy and obeyed. Creepy, Major Kaika would have called it.

He wondered if it was selfish to hope that Kaika would feel fondly toward him after he'd healed her the night before, and that in her fondness, she would speak of him to the king. In a positive way. A simple, "You should probably let Captain Trip go," might be sufficient. Presumably, she had his ear, since she had his lips.

The guard returned, his expression still dazed, and slid the papers between the bars. Trip took them and the pens and pencils that followed.

"Is there anything else you need, Captain?" The guard bowed his head, his tone so deferential that Trip almost let go of all influence, his discomfort at manipulating someone returning in full. But he didn't want the man to remember himself and insist on taking the papers back.

"No, Corporal. Thank you for your assistance. Return to your duty."

"I'll return to my duty." The guard shuffled away.

Trip sat on the floor in the windowless cell, nothing but some faded charcoal marks on the back wall for decoration, and spread his papers out. The only light came from a single lantern at the end of the hall—Trip couldn't see it from his cell—but fortunately he didn't need it. What he needed was a few dozen ingots of tainted iron, thousands of tons of regular steel, and a legion of workers to help him build his structure. He wasn't sure how he would get any of that from jail.

Shulina Arya landed in the courtyard mere steps from the castle's front doors. The guards poised next to those doors, along with eight others on the walls, pointed their rifles at Rysha and the dragon.

Trusting that Shulina Arya would protect her, Rysha slid off and strode up the steps. The dragon extended her long neck, and her head followed her up the steps. They gazed together at the guards.

"I request an audience with the king," Rysha said. "I'm Lieutenant—Lady Ravenwood." She decided being from a noble family would be more likely to get her an audience than being a lowly officer. Even if she'd passed the elite troops training, she was still just a lieutenant, one of thousands in the service.

One guard looked flummoxed and like he didn't know what to do with his rifle. The other gazed back at her blandly, as if dragons landed in the courtyard on an hourly basis.

"Do you have an appointment?" he asked.

"No, this is an emergency."

"The whole city is in a state of emergency. The king doesn't have time for extra appointments. He's got military advisors, contractors, and officials scheduled all day."

"Will you at least tell him I'm here and let him decide? It's a matter of security and safety for the entire country." Rysha thought of the schematics Trip had been drawing, that he wanted to turn into a reality, and decided it wasn't *entirely* hyperbole to say that.

"I'm sorry, Lady Ravenwood, but we're just the door guards. We don't address the king directly. That's not our place."

"Can you find me someone who does?"

"No, ma'am. We don't address that person, either. We just keep people out unless we've been advised to let them in. And we haven't been advised to let you in."

"Only because the king doesn't know I want to come in," Rysha said, though she didn't truly know if he would receive her. There were thousands of nobles in the country. Who knew how many pestered him on a regular basis? Though that damn Lockvale had certainly caught his ear quickly enough... "If you don't let me in, I intend to wait here on your doorstep all day." She tilted her head toward Shulina Arya to imply they wouldn't have much luck moving her.

It occurred to her that with the dragon's help, she could likely walk straight through the castle to whatever office or conference room Angulus was seeing people in. Would he appreciate such boldness? According to Kaika, it had worked for her once. She'd blown up an urn rather than strolling in with a dragon, but the tactics seemed similar.

"If you want to do that, it's unlikely we can stop you," the guard said. "Just don't let your dragon trample the shrubbery, please."

I have located your king, Storyteller. He is in an office outside of a bed lair, meeting with a pair of male individuals.

Is a bed lair like a bedroom?

I do not know. Dragons do not build rooms for themselves.

"Is Major Kaika in the castle today?" Rysha wondered if she could get an audience with her and through her, see Angulus.

The guards glanced at each other.

"We don't know that information, ma'am."

Rysha guessed they did but had orders not to gossip. Great.

"Then I'm afraid I must invoke the Feudal Convocation Agreement of 698, Section 12, Paragraph 13, sub-paragraph 3 where it explicitly states that in times of war, any noble may bring advice and advantages directly to the king and shall not be delayed in meeting with him. Anyone who seeks to delay such an important meeting will be subject to punishment not to exceed nine hundred days in prison."

One of the guards scratched his head. "We're not at war."

"What do you call our relationship with the dragons who want to take over our country? I posit that we are most assuredly at war, at the least with the coalition that attacked yesterday, and perhaps with half of the entire dragon race." She lifted her chin, doing her best to look righteous and far too authoritative to question.

"Uhm, you better check with his steward," one guard told the other.

"*Me?* What's wrong with your legs?"

"Yours are younger and longer."

Shulina Arya, are you prepared to protect me and yourself from gunfire if I force my way inside? Rysha asked silently, worried this wasn't going anywhere.

You are protected now.

Thank you.

Rysha took a deep breath, intending to stride between them, using her unarmed combat skills if need be, but one finally huffed and said, "Come on, Lady Ravenwood. I'll check." He lowered his voice to a mutter. "Don't want to get stuck in jail."

Storyteller, this guard is thinking unkind thoughts toward noblewomen.

That's absolutely fine as long as he's leading us to the king.

Shulina Arya shifted into human form so she could fit through the doorway. Fortunately, she didn't appear with a scooter or roller-skates.

He's intending to take us to someone called Lord Millwood.

That's the head steward, I think. The king would be preferable. Rysha hated the idea of asking the dragon to manipulate someone, but this would all go quicker and be easier if she could. *Can you convince him that he truly wants to take us directly to the king?*

Certainly. He has a meager mind.

Rysha decided not to ask what Shulina Arya thought of *her* mind.

"This way," the guard repeated a few times as he took them through wide halls, past audience and banquet halls, and up a set of stairs to a series of personal suites.

Rysha had never been to this part of the castle and grew more nervous as they stepped into a carpeted hall lined with portraits of the former Masonwood kings. What would she do if Angulus truly resented this intrusion?

The guard stopped before a door and lifted a hand to knock, but paused, his face screwing up in confusion. Maybe he'd figured out someone—or some dragon—was manipulating him.

Rysha knocked before he could dwell on it.

It wasn't until the voices inside stopped that she realized people had been talking. She hoped it wasn't a truly important meeting. Maybe she would get lucky, and it would be Angulus and Kaika having tea together, and Kaika would make light of the interruption, ensuring Angulus did too.

"Enter," a voice ordered. That was definitely Angulus. And his tone wasn't inviting.

Do you want me to go first, Storyteller? Shulina Arya asked. *The ire of human kings does not concern me.*

No, thank you. This was my idea.

Mentally bracing herself, Rysha opened the door and strode into the spacious office.

Fire crackled in the hearth, and Angulus stood behind a desk and before one of two large windows. Two men in almost matching gray suits were in the middle of a presentation, complete with easel, pointer stick, and text and charts printed on large cards.

"I beg your pardon, King Angulus," Rysha said, clicking her heels together and saluting sharply. "I don't have an appointment, but I must talk with you about an important matter." She kept herself from saying it was of country-wide security, since he would likely see through that.

"There aren't any appointments available because he's booked," one of the men at the easel whispered to her, frowning. "*We* had to wait three *months* to present our concerns. Given the destruction dragons have been doing to crops…" He glanced at Angulus. "Well, it's not my place to object."

Rysha looked at the top card on the easel, prepared to feel bad—or at least rude—if their concerns were important and time-sensitive. It showed a picture of a pond next to equations dealing with volume and drainage rates, followed by a summary of the equipment and manpower needed to turn a wetlands area into agricultural land.

"Did you check your math?" Rysha asked, spotting an error in one of the equations. They would need a few tons more fill dirt than they were requesting to fill in the wetlands for farming.

"Of *course* we did." Both men whirled toward the equation she pointed at.

"Seven gods, is that—someone didn't carry the—Sire!" One man blurted while the other positioned himself to block the view of the card. "Please forgive us, but the gentleman who prepared our data should have been double-checked. We, uh, aren't as ready as we thought. Many pardons."

They hurried to fold the easel, grab the cards, and rush out, nearly knocking over the guard in the doorway. The guard still looked puzzled and was frowning at Shulina Arya.

"Jasfer," Angulus said, meeting his eyes and pointing at Rysha. "Explain."

"She invoked the, uh, Feudal Convocation Agreement of 697—no 8, sir. Section 12, Paragraph 13, sub-paragraph, uhm, something."

"There's no such document," Angulus said.

"What?" The guard gawked at Rysha.

She shrugged, almost feeling bad for him, but she was on a mission, damn it.

"Go." Angulus flicked his fingers toward the guard. "We'll talk later."

The man fled, his expression promising he did not look forward to that discussion.

"Lieutenant Ravenwood," Angulus said, facing her as the door closed. "Explain. No, wait." He strode from the window to the open back door that led into a private suite. "There's a wayward lieutenant out here with a dragon."

Rysha arched her eyebrows and thought about protesting that she was *wayward*, but Angulus didn't sound angry, and she didn't want to provoke him. Shulina Arya was poking around the room, peering at books on shelves and picking up and fiddling with what were likely priceless objets d'art.

"Sounds like a vast improvement over the stuffy people you've been talking to all morning," came Kaika's voice from the next room over.

"That remains to be seen," Angulus said.

Kaika walked out in a lush brown robe and fluffy tiger-striped slippers. She carried a steaming mug of something and smiled, but she didn't look like herself. First off, Rysha had never seen Kaika out of uniform, even when they'd been traveling together, so that was startling, but more alarming was that most of the hair on the left side of her head was gone or cut extremely short. Rysha had heard she'd been burned, but she didn't see evidence of wounds, other than the missing hair. The robe might hide a lot, though. Rysha glanced at Kaika's hands and bare shins.

"I don't suppose dragons can grow hair back?" Kaika looked at Shulina Arya, who was spinning the wheel on a gold-and-silver ancient fidget ball from the Dumeriun civilization. Rysha was positive only a few of those devices remained in existence.

Shulina Arya looked up. "You wish to be hairy?"

Angulus held up a finger. "Be careful how you phrase your request."

"What, you couldn't love an ape?"

"It depends what the ape's propensity for injuring itself is. Apes probably don't fling themselves in front of fire-breathing dragons."

"Ah, so now you're thinking of replacing me with a zoo specimen."

She smirked and elbowed him. Angulus gave her a tender smile, and Rysha looked away, not sure she was supposed to witness their intimate moments. Though a part of her was glad to know Angulus had tender inclinations, at least somewhere in there. He always appeared so stern at speeches and in his photographs. Rysha had met him a few times over the years at the semi-annual social gatherings among the nobility, but he'd always seemed distant at those, like a man who either didn't want to be there or who was, despite his job, uncomfortable in crowds.

"What's wrong, Rysha?" Kaika asked, glancing at Shulina Arya. "Other than gullible guards and math-challenged agri…thingies. I forgot who those people were."

Kaika's eyes crinkled, and Rysha sensed that she at least approved of her tactics.

"The MPs came and arrested Trip," Rysha blurted, then winced, realizing she shouldn't have led with something that sounded like it was a personal problem for her. She had to make the king understand how important Trip was to the country.

Surprisingly, Kaika slapped Angulus on the chest with the back of her hand.

"What? *I* didn't arrest him."

"You can wave your hand and have him un-arrested."

"Mm," Angulus said, very neutrally.

"He was in the middle of working on a solution for our dragon problem, and they dragged him away from his drawings," Rysha said, already sensing that this wouldn't be as easy as asking for hand-waving. She'd been afraid of that. "And if dragons come again, and he's locked up, the city will be at a disadvantage. I know you drove them off yesterday without us here, but we can certainly help with the next attack. And if Trip can get his hands on some of the banded iron from Rakgorath, he has an idea that may solve our problem forever. At the least, it would make the dragons hesitate to attack us."

Angulus's lips pressed together, and Rysha sensed she was pushing too hard.

"Also," she said, to wrap things up, "he didn't do what that idiot, Lockvale, is accusing him of. All he did was ask Lockvale questions, which I *asked* him to do. That bastard has been plotting against my family, trying to bring down the value of our land and scare all our workers away so he could buy our estate cheaply. He even talked a silver dragon into colluding with him."

Angulus's eyebrows drew together. Was this the first he'd heard of the dragon? She knew her parents were proud and that her father wouldn't whine to the king for solutions to his problems, but they should have reported a silver dragon lurking around the countryside.

"I know the MPs picked him up," Angulus said, focusing on that first. "*Lord* Lockvale—" his voice held mild reproof at Rysha's failure to use the honorific, "—has made an accusation of attempted murder and has four witnesses who came forward, willing to back up his claim. There's a fifth that the police are trying to locate. Captain Trip needs to be held until a formal inquest can be put together and both sides can be heard. Trip will be invited to bring in character witnesses. Lord Lockvale's witnesses will also be questioned separately to see if their stories match. They are known acquaintances of his, so that may raise a judge's eyebrows, but at the same time, they are all from respected noble families, and none have criminal records."

"Because it's not a crime to bring down somebody's property value and attempt to get their land, apparently," Rysha said, unable to hide her frustration. She'd promised Trip that rational heads would win the day, but what if that proved wrong?

"Captain Trip, on the other hand, is—"

"An honorable man who has risked his life repeatedly to help Iskandia against pirates and dragons, and who flew across the world to destroy their portal. Sire, all he wants is to be a hero and help people. He's not a murderer. He doesn't like to use his power for the greater good if there's any bit of moral ambiguity in doing so." Rysha looked at Kaika, hoping for support.

Kaika did open her mouth, but Angulus spoke first.

"Captain Trip is now widely known to have dragon blood and be a sorcerer," Angulus said, "which does raise questions about his character and motivations for those who believe all magic is evil."

"But he's up in his flier fighting dragons every chance he gets," Rysha said. "How can—"

"I know," Angulus said, raising his hand again. "*I* know we owe him our gratitude. But if I simply have him released and tell Lord Lockvale that the captain won't be charged with any crimes, I will be seen as ignoring a judiciary system that has existed for centuries. When kings have done that in the past, there have often been political repercussions. Occasionally *beheading* repercussions. Though people may believe differently, I'm not a tyrant with absolute authority, nor would the country support me if I wished to be."

"I understand that, Sire, but—"

"Just give it time, Ravenwood. If Lord Lockvale is lying, a clever military defender should be able to ferret that out."

"I haven't noticed that people try hard to be clever when defending witches," a familiar male voice drawled from the hallway.

General Zirkander walked in, wearing his dress uniform with his cap in hand. Major Blazer, also in dress uniform, stepped inside after him.

"We'll make sure to find someone who will be impartial," Angulus said without missing a beat.

"How did you get in, sir?" Rysha whispered when Zirkander stopped next to her. She didn't see any guards loitering in the hallway.

"Told them I needed to see the king," he whispered back.

"And that worked?"

He winked.

No wonder Trip wanted to be a beloved national hero.

"In all honesty, Sire," Zirkander said, the amusement dropping from his face, "I'd prefer he be defended by someone who's *partial* to him. What happens if the military judge decides he's guilty and should be hanged? That's what this fluffed-up noble is asking for, in case you didn't see the paper."

"I saw it," Angulus said, his tone cooling.

Rysha wondered if the king would correct Zirkander for the lack of an honorific. Or even a name.

"He made his complaint during the middle of the dragon attack," Angulus said. "I was not pleased."

"He's the one who should be thrown in jail. For interrupting you when the city was in danger, when you were doing important things."

"You're interrupting me now. Unfortunately, that's not a crime."

"I can't possibly be interrupting important things though." Zirkander looked at Rysha, then at Kaika, seeming to notice her robe and slippers for the first time. "Well, I guess I could be. But really, Sire, it's almost noon."

Angulus issued an audible sigh and looked skyward.

"Sir," Rysha whispered to Zirkander, "I'm not sure you're helping."

Major Blazer, who'd taken up a position near Rysha, grinned at her. "More people should dare tell him that."

Should I be doing something to assist you, Storyteller? Shulina Arya had left the fidget device on a shelf and was looking back and forth between the various people in the room. *I can gaze into your king's eyes and make him more amenable to your suggestions.*

Tempting, but Rysha shook her head. *Just be prepared in case we need to break Trip out of jail.*

Perhaps we should find this Lord Lockvale and incinerate him. Would that not solve your problem?

Rysha couldn't keep from making a choking sound. Fortunately—or unfortunately—Angulus was too busy glaring at Zirkander to notice.

"Look, Sire," Zirkander said, lifting his hands. "I understand that you need to appear impartial and be fair to everyone, but Trip in a cell is useless to us. Sardelle said he's designing something to fight the dragons, some kind of..." He looked at Rysha.

"He called it a flying weapons platform. He said if he can get Dr. Targoson's help, they can make a large structure that launches dragon-seeking rockets full of acid that can eat through their scales, and he wants to use some of the ore that the *chapaharii* blades are made from to make the platform impervious to magic. Physical attacks would still be a concern, but if people were stationed there around the clock and could fire the weapons..."

Rysha trailed off because Angulus was staring at her. She couldn't tell if it was in exasperation or not.

"Is this actually a thing?" Angulus looked at Zirkander and at Kaika, too, though she only shrugged. "How long has he been working on this?"

Zirkander opened his mouth, but Rysha spoke first. "The drawings are almost complete. He said he's ready to start construction soon."

No need to mention that he'd started the drawings the night before.

"Did you check his math?" Angulus twitched an eyebrow toward the spot where the easel had been.

"I didn't get time, Sire. The MPs came and took him away."

Angulus grunted. Acknowledging that the arrest was inconvenient?

Rysha hoped so. "The main thing he needs is the tainted ore, as he calls it, and someone who can handle it without getting headaches and passing out."

"Someone?" Angulus asked. "Just one person? To help him build a flying weapons platform?"

"He did construct a locomotive in the desert almost by himself," Kaika said.

"What?" Blazer said. "We helped. We carried scrap metal out of the dragon's lair for him."

"I believe he was also going to ask Bhrava Saruth for help," Rysha said. "He was thinking of doing it out at the dragon's temple since no other dragons go out there, so it would be easy to make it a secret project. Perhaps Shulina Arya's parents would consider helping too. They seem to like science and engineering. Also, they might not require Trip to worship them in exchange for their assistance."

Angulus blinked slowly, though nobody in the room truly appeared surprised by the comment.

They would certainly not do such a thing, Shulina Arya said. *Believing yourself a god is the sign of a delusional mind. All sane dragons know this.*

"I'd like to learn more about this project," Angulus said, "and would approve it going forward if it looks as promising as you've made it out to be."

"Excellent, Sire." Zirkander snapped his fingers. "We'll just have to get the project leader out of jail, and we can get started right away."

Angulus gave him a flat look, but Blazer and Kaika both nodded. Even though Rysha wasn't sure Zirkander was the best advocate—Angulus didn't seem to adore him as much as the newspapers did—it did please her that Trip had this many people fighting for him.

"The impartiality problem we discussed still exists," Angulus said. "You have my word that I won't let anyone rule in favor of hanging him—not that we truly have the power to harm him, regardless—but I need it to appear that I'm not dismissing Lord Lockvale out of hand. His father may have been a drunk and a gambler, but his grandfather was one of *my* grandfather's right-hand men and instrumental in keeping the peace with the Cofah in their time."

"Can't Trip be punished somewhere besides a jail cell in the fort?" Zirkander asked. "Oh, I know. What better punishment for a man than being forced to serve the delusional dragon who thinks he's a god out at his temple?"

"I approve of that idea," Kaika said.

"I like it too," Rysha said.

Angulus still wore that flat look. Rysha couldn't imagine Kaika falling for a man without a sense of humor, so she decided to assume that Angulus had one but that it disappeared when Zirkander walked in the room.

"Stay," Angulus said, then walked past Zirkander and Rysha and out the office door.

For a few seconds, nobody spoke; they only looked at each other in puzzlement. Kaika didn't seem to have any insight into where Angulus was going.

Then Shulina Arya groaned into Rysha's mind. *I will not stay.*

She turned into a parrot, used her magic to open the window, and flew outside.

Rysha gaped after her. *Shulina Arya?*

I will return when he is done handling his bars.

"What just happened?" Major Blazer asked.

"I don't know," Rysha said. "I—"

Angulus walked back in, carrying an iron case. He thunked it down onto his desk, opened the lid, and stepped back so they could see inside. A plain-looking iron bar rested inside.

Rysha guessed what it was immediately, though nobody in the room would be able to sense it the way Trip did. And the way Shulina Arya had.

"You had the sudden urge to fetch a paperweight, Sire?" Zirkander asked.

"Zirkander." Angulus sighed. "When was the last time someone told you it's a good thing that you're so competent at flying and shooting things because your mouth would have gotten you kicked out of the army years ago, otherwise?"

"Yesterday, Sire."

"Consider it said today, as well."

"Yes, Sire."

"As soon as I got Major Blazer's report back with information about that quarry, I had Colonel Anchor from Cougar Squadron send a team over to retrieve some of the ore. I debated on whether I needed to open trade negotiations with Rakgorath's leaders, but as far as our intel department believes, nobody claims that part of the continent, and it was easier not to have to deal with the various city-states. The pilots took a few miners along, and they extracted the ore without incident. I have ten bars like this in an iron vault, and we can get more if necessary. My intent was to save them and perhaps see if Sardelle or Captain Trip could figure out how to make more of the *chapaharii* swords, but I have to admit, this talk of a weapons platform appeals far more to my modern mind than pigstickers. Or dragon stickers."

"So Trip can start working on the structure?" Zirkander asked.

Angulus narrowed his eyes. "I want to see his blueprints first and have one of my engineers look over them. If this weapons platform seems feasible, he can get to work. We'll work on the cover story. I'm not sure worshipping a dragon sounds enough like punishment. The newspapers better report that he's out there under guard and scrubbing latrines with a toothbrush."

"Do dragon temples *have* latrines?" Kaika asked.

"Two up front, one in the back," Zirkander said, "for the comfort of his worshippers that travel to seek out his blessings."

"And you know this, why?"

"I helped with the initial construction, remember."

"I thought you just finagled the land for it from Angulus."

"If only it had ended there." Zirkander pointed toward the door. "Can I go get him out now, Sire? Assuming I arrive with a toothbrush in hand?"

"Yes, and don't forget to bring the blueprints." Angulus closed the lid on the box.

"I better go find Shulina Arya," Rysha said. "Uhm, may I be dismissed, Sire?"

She felt odd asking for his permission to leave since she'd barged in without any permission, but that was expected.

He grunted and waved at the door.

"Actually, wait a minute, will you, Lieutenant?" Kaika crooked a finger and nodded toward the suite behind the office.

Angulus looked up. Kaika made a shooing motion at him, as if to indicate he should follow Zirkander and Blazer out.

"I'm being kicked out of my own suite?" Angulus asked.

"Just for a little while. We need to talk about woman stuff."

Angulus mouthed the words but did not repeat them aloud.

Rysha paused before obeying Kaika's wriggling fingers to make sure this would be allowed. Even though Kaika was her superior officer, Angulus was her superior… everything.

"Fine," he said, heading for the door. "I'll see if the math has been corrected yet or if my noon appointment simply fled in shame."

CHAPTER 19

A DOOR CLANGED, THE NOISE PIERCING Trip's groggy consciousness. After he'd finished his sketches, the lack of sleep during the night had caught up with him, and he'd lain down to rest on the floor.

He sensed General Zirkander and Major Blazer as they arrived in front of his cell, and he lifted his head. Had they come to extricate him? Or just to visit? The smoke from one of Blazer's cigars tickled his nose. Neither officer seemed stressed or concerned, so Trip took that as a good sign.

He pushed himself to his feet to salute. Then he wiped his chin, hoping he hadn't been drooling.

"The history books and legends rarely mention sorcerers snoring," Blazer observed.

"No, there have been many things I've learned from being married to a sorceress that would have otherwise remained unknown to me."

"Can you share them?"

"I believe drooling habits are the kind of thing a husband isn't supposed to reveal about his wife."

"Unfortunate."

"So, Trip." Zirkander eyed the papers spread out over the floor. "I hear—and now see—that you've been doing some drawing."

"Yes, sir."

How much did he know about Trip's project? Had Rysha spoken to him? Or Sardelle? She'd come in a few times during the night, and Trip had mentioned his goals.

"It's a tradition in the fort's jail. I believe this was the very cell I spent a night in once." Zirkander looked toward the back wall. "Yes, I can even see the remains of the map I sketched in charcoal. Hm, you'd think someone would come through with water and a sponge once in a while."

"You were in jail, sir?" Trip asked.

Blazer smirked, not appearing surprised at all by this revelation.

"Indeed, I was. I've been AWOL before too. For the good of the country, naturally."

Blazer's smirk deepened. "That's not what Colonel Therrik said."

Zirkander waved away the comment and pointed to the drawings. "Do you have something you can show the king? Something decipherable?"

"Yes, sir. The drawings are ready to be put into production. I just need to be released..." Trip spread his hand toward the locked gate.

Zirkander poked it with a finger. "Am I correct that you could have left at any time?"

"Yes, sir, but Rysha told me it would be better if I didn't run, that I'd look guilty if I did."

"She's a smart lady." Zirkander fished in his pocket and pulled out the key ring for the various cell locks. "You're not *free*, Trip. Not until there's an inquest and we figure out a way to prove that Lord Lockvale and his cronies were lying. But, providing Angulus approves these drawings—you need to convince him you can actually make this thing—the place where you spend your days will be shifted from this prison to Bhrava Saruth's temple. I understand you've the urge to become one of his worshippers and clean his latrines."

Trip had been nodding, but he paused at the addendum. "Latrines, sir?"

"That's the story we'll be circulating to the press. While you're working on this weapons platform. Angulus has some fancy ore for you, though you'll probably want someone who doesn't have dragon blood to work with it, right?"

"Ideally, sir."

"We'll find you some people. Lieutenant Ravenwood mentioned you also wanted Tolemek. We'll get him. If there's anyone else you think can help make this a reality, make a list. You'll be the project leader and get whomever you need."

"That means he can get someone else to clean the latrines, right?" Blazer asked.

"Are you volunteering?"

"To work for Trip? No, he's odd."

"We all are, Major." Zirkander patted her on the shoulder. "We all are."

Rysha sat on the edge of a purple upholstered chair with a combination button and tuft poking her in the butt while wondering what Major Kaika had brought her into the king's suite to discuss.

Woman stuff. That could mean anything from an injury to a reproductive organ to an unplanned pregnancy to some kind of problem with her cycle. But seven gods, why would she bring some lowly lieutenant in to discuss *that*? True, Rysha believed they'd bonded and gotten closer on their various missions, but Sardelle would be the more appropriate person to consult for all those things.

"I've been in Cofah prison cells with more comfortable furnishings." Kaika waved at the button-tuft chair, then chose a leather lounger for herself, though she sat on the end rather than sprawling across it. "His wife chose them for aesthetic purposes. Or to torture him. I'm not sure which. Apparently, redecorating the castle is the job of the queen—it's an age-old tradition for new queens to change everything as soon as they're officially appointed. It would almost be worth taking the job just for that. Replace all the pink, pastel blue, and purple with some good old army green and black." She winked.

"The *job*?" Rysha gaped at her. "Of being *queen*? Did he *ask*?"

Maybe she shouldn't have been so shocked, but she hadn't realized their relationship had been going on that long or was that serious. She *did* remember that the two had shared a rather passionate reunion at Sardelle's house when Kaika, Rysha, and Trip returned from Rakgorath. And for Kaika to be monogamous, when she seemed so inclined to experiment often and with numerous partners, maybe it meant they were truly in love.

"Oh, he's asked dozens of times. I've always scoffed and declined because really, can you see me as a queen? He acts like it wouldn't be a huge scandal and says he'd deal with the fallout, but I'm not a noble, and I'm definitely not what Iskandians look for in royalty. I'm positive I'm not what *anyone* looks for in royalty." Kaika pushed her hand through her hair, then grimaced at the unexpected shortness.

"Well," Rysha said slowly, formulating her thoughts as she went, "I would happily call you queen, but you're everything I've always wanted to be, so I may be biased." She blushed after the words came out, realizing how cheesy they sounded.

"That *can't* be true, or you would have jumped at the chance to go to the Sensual Sage with me."

"*Career*-wise, you're everything I want to be."

Kaika's face screwed up as if she were working on one of Shulina Arya's jawbreakers. "I'm trying to get better at accepting praise, but it's not easy. Anyway, listen, this is what I want to ask you about. Angulus asked again last night, no doubt prompted by the distress of me nearly being burned alive by dragon fire. He's just lucky he got there after Trip had wriggled his fingers and fixed what should have been horrific scars." She touched the left side of her face and shuddered visibly. "But the crazy thing is, I think he would have offered even if he had seen me like that. I don't understand it, but he *likes* me. He even likes it when I talk straight to him and refuse to be intimidated by his status. It drives him crazy when Zirkander does the same thing."

"Well, we can admire things in the opposite sex that irritate us in the competition. I think that's pretty typical." Rysha realized her words might be misconstrued and held up a hand. "I don't mean that Zirkander is competition to him for *you*—I assume not—but just in general. I don't know them well, but I get the notion that there's some jealousy there. Which doesn't seem to make sense from the most powerful man in the country…"

"No, you're right. Being born into power is a lot different than coming from nothing and earning a place of honor in the world. And if I'd met Zirkander before he snuggled up to Sardelle, don't think I wouldn't have tried to get his trousers off." Kaika grinned at her.

"Er. You don't say things like that to the king, do you?"

"Nah, but I don't hide my randy nature, either. He's been the recipient of much of that randiness of late and seems to like it. Judging by the growling and shouting."

"*Ma'am*, this isn't the kind of *woman stuff* I thought you wanted to talk about." Rysha gripped the chair's arm, wondering if it was too late to flee.

"It's not. I mean, it's loosely related, but…" Kaika's humor faded, and she looked down at her lap and plucked at the sleeve of her robe.

Everything about the uncertain gesture was so unlike the Kaika she knew that Rysha didn't know how to react.

"Last night, I said yes," Kaika said.

"To a marriage proposal?"

Kaika nodded. "I'm sure part of it was that I was so relieved to be alive, and he was so relieved I was alive, but… I'm worried it wasn't the right decision. I mean, I love him, and I'd like to be with him. Even though I've often told him it would make more sense if he went off and found some queenly noblewoman to marry, I've known it would hurt to watch him do that. If he did. His advisors and friends tell him to do that, of course. To take another shot with a woman he can have heirs with, but that's not *his* priority. He doesn't even think he can father children." Kaika pushed her hand through her hair again. "Sorry, I got off the topic."

"I think it's allowed. A proposal is a big deal."

"Yes. I'm just not sure I did the right thing. We haven't told anyone yet. You're the first I've talked to, and he hasn't had time for talking about things unrelated to ruling a nation. I could back out…"

"Do you want to?" Rysha was surprised Kaika had chosen her as her confidante for this, and hoped she could be helpful.

Kaika studied her sleeve again. "It's hard to say. I want to be with him, but the idea of dealing with all the crap that would come with the position is enough to give a person nightmares."

"Would you have to quit the army? The elite troops?" Rysha couldn't imagine Kaika folding up her uniforms, locking them in a trunk, and sitting on some throne crafting doilies. Wasn't that what the last queen had done?

"No. We've had that discussion numerous times. After three years, he knows I'm a bird that can't be caged. A very tall gangly bird."

"Like an ostrich."

"I do have a long neck." Kaika stroked it thoughtfully. Or dubiously. "The reason I asked you in is that I'm concerned about dealing with the nobility. You're normal, but not many of them are that I've noticed."

"Did you just call me normal, ma'am? Nobody has ever said that about me."

Kaika snorted. "You're not a pretentious snob is perhaps what I should have said. I'm not good at handling obnoxious people if I can't resort to fists. Possibly explosives. Angulus says queens aren't allowed to blow up their own people. Only enemies."

"That sounds restrictive."

"I thought so."

"If you're asking my opinion on whether you should do it…" Rysha lifted her eyebrows, not positive if Kaika truly wanted some lieutenant's opinion or merely a sounding board.

But Kaika nodded firmly. "Yes, your opinion. As someone who's dealt with the nobility and as a fellow officer who likes to blow things up. Or at least stab them with her sword."

"I think that the nobility won't know what to make of you. They'll talk about you behind your back—never to your face and absolutely never to Angulus's face. They'll frustrate you if you let them, but my suggestion for a strategy would be to find a few quirky but influential souls you can befriend who can be your guides and who will also report gossip to you. I know, we should be above gossip, and I can't see you reveling in it, but it's good to be aware of the machinations that are currently in play out there. And there are *always* machinations." Rysha thought of Lockvale and curled her fingers around the edge of the seat. "But in the end, this is about more than fitting in—or not—with the nobility. I know this isn't how you think, but it's truly an opportunity for you to change our country for the better. The last few queens have been wallflowers, frankly, and if not for Queen Thasadonia eighty years ago, women wouldn't be allowed in the military or to vote or to participate in politics or anything. As a historian and a woman, I feel it's important for there always to be some influential women in power—influential people of any group that's historically been downtrodden or taken advantage of. It's easy to take rights for granted and forget how hard people had to fight to get them in the first place, and the first time you're not paying attention, someone can take them away. I think—I *know*—you could be someone who makes Iskandia a better place for women, a place where it's not weird to want to become a pilot or an elite soldier. It's just a normal thing that some people like to do, regardless of their sex."

"Rysha, if you're looking for someone to enact massive political changes, that's not me. I wouldn't know the first thing about getting laws passed."

"You don't have to be political. Just by being you, you'd be a role model for other women, as you were for me. But I only heard about you because I was army-mad and wanted to make a name for myself, and I found you as someone who had done exactly that. If you were queen, *everybody* would know about you."

Judging by the kink to Kaika's lips, she didn't think that was a great thing.

"You could just be you," Rysha repeated. "Also, at the wedding, you should wear your dress uniform instead of some frilly gold or red velvet dress or whatever the style is this year."

"Won't the nobility find that scandalous?"

"Oh absolutely."

Kaika snorted. "This isn't the advice I was expecting to get."

"What were you hoping for? For me to say no, you shouldn't do it?"

"No. I'm not certain it's not a mistake, but I want to do it. I guess I just wanted some advice on dealing with the nobility. I don't care what they say about me, but I don't want Angulus to be hurt, emotionally *or* physically. Is it possible they'll be so upset with me as his wife that they might plot against him?"

"By hiring an assassin, you mean?"

Kaika winced. "I understand Ahn's father is still in the business. And there are others."

"Angulus is considered fair by the populace and the nobility. I think it's more likely someone would assassinate you." After the words came out, Rysha regretted them—what a thing to tell someone.

But Kaika's eyes flared with a familiar inner fire. "They could *try*."

"You're not supposed to look excited when I suggest someone might try to assassinate you."

"I like a challenge. I'm a little concerned that things may turn drab. I won't be able to go on covert missions anymore if my picture is in newspapers around the world and I'm known globally as the queen of Iskandia."

"You could go on diplomatic missions and pretend you're there to be decorative and sign things on the king's behalf, then go snooping around in people's castles and palaces."

Kaika tapped her chin thoughtfully. "I do like snooping. All right, good. This has given me some hope that a marriage could work out."

Rysha smirked.

"What?" Kaika asked.

"I'm amused that you were concerned until I suggested diplomatic snooping and assassins coming after you."

"I don't want to be bored or surrounded by insufferable people I have to pretend I like. I've never been good at that."

"Talk to my Aunt Tadelay sometime," Rysha said. "She's a firm fixture in the nobility, and she never pretends to like anyone. She'll let you know exactly what she thinks. Unless she walks in on you naked and having sex. That has a tendency to fluster her."

Kaika arched her eyebrows. "Is this something that happened to you? Recently?"

"Possibly."

"You do know one of the first rules of sex is to lock the door, don't you?"

"We weren't planning to—I mean, we were going out on a date, not staying and—er, things just happened."

Maybe Aunt Tadelay wasn't the only one who got flustered when discussing such things.

"I suppose it's good that Zirkander is going to let your randy captain out of jail, though less good that you'll have to go to a dragon temple to visit him. Do temples have doors that lock?"

"I don't know, ma'am, but he'll be so busy building his project, he'll probably be immune to the suggestion of being dragged off behind locked doors."

"You just have to be assertive. And know how to distract a man. I can give you some tips."

"That's not necessary, ma'am."

"No? You've given me helpful advice. It only seems fair."

Rysha looked toward a window, hoping Shulina Arya would be back to collect her—or rescue her—soon.

CHAPTER 20

TRIP HAD NEVER BEEN SO tired in his life. An atypical heat wave had come in, drying up the spring rains, and hot sun beat on his back as he manipulated metal with his mind. Over and over and over. He felt like an athlete training for competition. Would all this practice at manipulating elements turn him into a more efficient mage? Or would it simply melt his brain into mush?

Clangs and bangs came from elsewhere on the flat rocky lot behind Bhrava Saruth's temple. It hadn't been flat enough to work on when Trip had arrived four days earlier, so his first effort had gone into leveling it. Now, the base of his massive structure stretched over it, lightweight despite its substantial length and width. In the end, an airship would be able to land on the platform, if necessary, or an entire company of soldiers could be taken up to fight from it. The weapons that would perch atop towers along the outside perimeter were being constructed elsewhere in the temple. Trip would soon start to work on the engines and the massive propellers and housings that would keep the platform aloft.

"I need more dragon blood," came a call from the temple.

That sounded like Dr. Targoson.

Since Trip was the project manager, he assumed all orders, questions, and complaints were meant for him. He left the seam he was smoothing and trotted inside, glad for a chance to escape the heat.

A few of the men working on the structure glanced his way, but none of them objected to him leaving. So far, his team was working out well. They were mostly army engineers, men with experience building bridges, military fortifications, and all manner of related structures. He also had a few civilian smiths and metalworkers from the capital.

Everyone was sleeping at the temple and had strict orders not to speak with anyone outside about the project. The king worried that some of their enemy dragons, especially the group that had stolen one of the *chapaharii* blades and proved willing to use trickery to gain what they wanted, would find out about the platform and sabotage it before it was built. Until the weapons were installed, the structure would be vulnerable. Trip hoped his belief that other dragons would avoid Bhrava Saruth's temple because they found him annoying proved true. The island it was built on lay a few miles north of the city in an inlet in the cliffs. A dragon flying directly overhead would be able to see down to the yard where they worked, but a dragon simply flying down the coast wouldn't notice the area.

It is highly inappropriate for a dragon god's worshippers to wish samples of his blood, Trip caught Bhrava Saruth saying as he stepped into the cool shade under the high arches and stone ceiling of the main temple. *Did we not agree that samples from those bronze dragons that have been loitering around would be sufficient?*

"They're not here," Dr. Targoson said, frowning back at Bhrava Saruth.

Targoson had a number of tables set up in a back corner of the temple with laboratory equipment stretched across them. The rocket housings and the beginnings of a rocket launcher rested on the floor nearby, but he was working on creating more acid now. A compact burner heated a ceramic pot of the stuff, and sulfurous steam arose, making Trip wrinkle his nose.

"I may be able to find them and ask them to come," Trip said, walking up to the table. "I've noticed our dragon helpers have been scarce since the tainted ore arrived."

"*I'd* like to be scarce." Targoson pushed back the tangled locks of dark hair that tended to fall into his eyes.

"Because you don't approve of the project? Or because the ore is bothering you?" Trip had it locked in iron boxes currently. He could sense it, but it wasn't giving him the constant headache that came with more direct exposure. He would have to oversee the part of the project where it was woven into the structure of the platform and the rocket housings, and he dreaded that.

"Because that dragon seems to believe that everyone who's here working is officially one of his worshippers now. Earlier, he was wandering around asking what offerings people had brought today."

"I'll have to order some baked goods to be delivered for him and our other helpers." Trip hoped he could get the army to pay for that. He'd learned that his own pay had been put on hold pending the outcome of the inquest.

"I understand sheep are acceptable too."

"They don't come in tidy bags with paper napkins."

"I've yet to see a dragon use a napkin. I imagine they just magically clean themselves off."

Trip remembered his attempt at mud removal. "Do you not?"

He knew that Targoson had dragon blood in his veins and sensed him drawing upon his power while he worked on the acid.

"Use magic for bathing? No. I don't use it for much of anything. Sardelle taught me to levitate a pencil and light a lantern with my mind, but I haven't had time to learn much else. This—" he waved at the bubbling pot over the burner, "—I do intuitively. Much like you manipulate metal, I imagine."

Trip nodded.

"It comes easier than the other stuff for me," Targoson added.

"Doctor," Trip said, eyeing the steaming pot, "have you found acceptance here? You're Cofah *and* have power. It seems like people here would be mistrustful."

"Call me Tolemek, and the people here are mistrustful of me. Less so now that it's been three years and I've helped them repel a number of attacks, but I rarely have strangers walk up to introduce themselves and ask if I want to be friends."

"Does that happen to anybody?" Trip couldn't recall a time, but then, he lacked Leftie's looks and charisma.

"To Zirkander, I'm sure. Men ask him out for drinks. Women ask him if he's monogamous. Older women ask him to speak to their children's classrooms."

Trip quirked an eyebrow. That sounded like something Targoson had witnessed directly.

"So, you stay for Captain Ahn?" he asked.

"For her and because I have found a place here. Even if I'm not warmly welcomed by many, some do include me in their lives and seem to appreciate my presence. And King Angulus gave me a state-of-the-art lab and lets me order anything I like in terms of tools and ingredients."

Targoson—Tolemek smiled. Trip hadn't seen him do that before. He supposed he would also be excited if someone gave him a workshop full of modern tools and an unlimited budget.

"A lot of what I do is fulfill orders from the army," Tolemek continued, "but I'm paid fairly for my creations, and they aren't all weapons anymore." He glanced at the pot of acid. "Usually. I also have time for my side business. I just purchased a house in a very nice area of town. It's high up on a hill and overlooks Cas's father's estate." His smile turned a bit smug, as if this was some coup. "We enjoy spending time there."

"I was thinking of buying the lot across from General Zirkander's house," Trip offered, more because Tolemek had brought up houses than because it was relevant. "Someone put a for-sale sign up on it a couple of weeks ago."

His questions about being accepted were mostly prompted by his upcoming inquest and the ease with which someone's spurious claims had resulted in him being held. Even now, though he was out here working on his project, two military police were stationed in front of the temple and escorted him to and from the premises. Most nights, he stayed out here with the other dedicated workers so he could avoid the indignity of being walked to the barracks like a criminal.

Trip believed that King Angulus thought him valuable and wouldn't let this inquest end in a death sentence, but it stung him to the core that it could even be possible. If he hadn't been a strange-looking sorcerer with skin too dark for a typical Iskandian, would these charges ever have stuck? Did Lockvale's word—and that of his comrades—get that much more weight simply because he was a noble?

"Most young officers would be horrified by the idea of building a house across the street from their battalion commander's."

"I'd like to help out with my little siblings whenever possible, and since everyone who needs training goes to Sardelle's house, it seems logical."

"Yes, I was there last summer when Zirkander talked Wreltad and Jaxi into helping him build that bunkhouse in the back for students. *Most* high-ranking military officers would hire a contractor for such work."

"Were the swords that helpful?" Trip could imagine dragons allowing themselves to be bribed for food and other pleasures of the bodies, but what could convince a soulblade to move boards and hammer nails?

"Wreltad is Zirkander's buddy. I'm sure he was helpful. I understand Jaxi helped cut down a few trees and shape the lumber. Via incineration."

"I suppose if you don't have a circular saw, fire is a valid method of—" Trip frowned as something plucked at his senses.

He walked toward the open back of the temple, the stone roof supported by columns far enough apart that a dragon could easily fly between them. The surf roared, waves crashing against the rocks nearby, and the men continued to work in the lot. All appeared calm, but Trip sensed a dragon. It wasn't Bhrava Saruth. He was chatting up—or maybe blessing—a couple of women in the front of the temple. It also wasn't one of the other Iskandian ally dragons. Trip had grown accustomed to dragons being around lately, so he wasn't surprised he hadn't felt another one slip in until it had gotten close.

The newcomer seemed large and powerful. A gold?

Trip peered toward the tops of the cliffs framing the inlet, and his breath caught when he spotted the dragon perched atop the rocks in the distance. Yes, it was a gold. A male. And he was looking down on the yard and the goings on below.

Trip hoped the dragon would think little of the structures humans built, and simply fly off, but even if he did, his presence here couldn't signify anything good. It suggested the dragon coalition was spying on the city, perhaps preparing for another attack. Even worse, it could mean that they'd heard about Trip's project and planned to destroy it before it was done.

An alien presence brushed Trip's mind, and he buried his thoughts deep inside his mental bank vault. He looked out toward the workers and did his best to camouflage them, to hide them and their thoughts, though he doubted he could fool a dragon, especially a gold dragon.

"Trouble?" Tolemek asked, walking up behind him. He looked in the direction Trip was looking. "Ah. I don't suppose he heard me request dragon blood and wants to help out."

"That seems unlikely."

As they considered the gold dragon, it sprang into the air and lazily flew out of sight to the north.

"Hm," Tolemek said.

"I wonder if we can get some of the other dragons to spend a few days out here, ready to defend my project if it gets attacked."

"They've been scarce since the iron was brought in."

"True."

Trip doubted he could count on the tainted iron by itself keeping dragons away, but maybe he would leave a few of the bars out around the project site.

"Only Bhrava Saruth refuses to leave his temple for long," Tolemek added, "lest he miss the arrival of adoring worshippers."

Trip sensed unfamiliar people entering the temple from the front—soldiers. More military police. They had to have come for him. He grimaced at the idea of being taken away from the project when there was so much work to do in what he assumed would be a short time.

"Captain Trip," one of the two uniformed men approaching said.

"Sir." Trip spotted the pins of a major on his collar. The younger man walking at his side was a lieutenant. Trip realized they were likely from the judicial department, not the police.

"I've come to inform you that your inquest will be in three days, early in the morning," the major said. "Lieutenant Foxlin has been assigned to be your defender."

Trip had no idea who that was but worried a lieutenant wouldn't have a lot of experience. Had nobody higher ranking been willing to sign on to defend him? But maybe a younger officer would be more open-minded and less likely to dismiss him as something less than human because of his blood.

"At the king's request, you've been granted surprising latitude…" The major looked around the temple, including to where Bhrava Saruth sat in human form on what could only be considered a throne with a woman in his lap and another kneeling on the dais, his hand on her head.

Trip wondered exactly what kinds of "blessings" the dragon was giving.

"I knew he wasn't cleaning latrines," the lieutenant muttered.

Trip had the urge to take them out back and show them what he was working on, but there were a lot of reasons to keep that a secret for now.

Further, even though he trusted himself—and Rysha had come over one evening to check his math—he couldn't be certain the weapons platform would do all that he'd promised until they got it in the air and a dragon attacked.

"So, make sure you're there on time," the major finished, pulling his gaze back from Bhrava Saruth.

"Yes, sir," Trip said, though he wished he could push it back a couple more weeks until he'd finished everything here. Or push it back until half past never.

What did Lockvale stand to gain from this, anyway? Was it all out of spite? Because Trip had embarrassed him in front of his friends? But those same friends were testifying to an attempt at murder, so they were clearly willing to stand with him.

With their news delivered, the major and lieutenant hurried back the way they had come. Hunches to their shoulders and the quickness of their pace suggested they couldn't wait to leave the temple. Because a dragon god lived there? Or because they suspected it oozed magic?

Trip rubbed the back of his neck, wondering if the average person would ever accept that magic and sorcerers could be useful.

CHAPTER 21

THE EVENING BEFORE TRIP'S INQUEST, Shulina Arya dropped Rysha off at her family's manor. Rysha faced the double-doored entrance, squared her shoulders, took a deep breath... and didn't move.

"Do you want to join us for dinner?" Rysha asked the dragon, looking for a reason to stall.

Also, she wouldn't mind someone who would support her as she argued with her mother and father. She'd come down to ask one or both of them to travel to the city—she would happily provide winged transportation to get them there quickly—and act as character witnesses for Trip. At the least, it would be nice if they talked about how Lockvale had been pressuring them to sell their property. That ought to make the noble's presence there the night of the fire appear more suspicious.

The eating would be done with forks and knives and spools? Shulina Arya asked.

Spoons, yes.

I find human eating implements confusing. Why do you simply not use your teeth and tongues?

Some foods are difficult to eat with teeth and tongue alone. Rysha remembered the dragon's difficulty with the jawbreakers and thought she could understand.

Though sweets are enjoyable, I prefer simple food I can eat with my fangs and talons. Also the pleasure of the hunt. While you dine, I believe I shall seek a sheep.

"All right." Rysha thought about suggesting that a wild ram would be a better choice than one of her family's woolly livestock, but after killing that silver dragon, Shulina Arya deserved a sheep if she desired one. "I'll see you later."

Let me know when you wish to leave.

"Thank you. I will. And thank you for toting me all over the place. I have to admit it's very convenient to travel so quickly."

Indeed so. Human legs are so stubby and slow. Everybody should be a rider, so they can have access to a dragon.

"A shame there are more humans in the world than dragons, as your parents pointed out."

Shulina Arya flew off, and Rysha had no reason to dawdle further. She opened the door, traveling the hallway and several rooms before finding her mother in the library. She sat at a desk, books stacked to either side of her and one open under her hands. The university term had just ended for the summer. Maybe she intended to catch up on personal reading.

"Rysha," Mother said, looking up and smiling. "It's good to see you again so soon."

"Thanks, Mother, but I came on business." Rysha walked into the library. "Personal business, admittedly. I was hoping to talk to you and Father."

Mother's smile faded. "Is this about that military inquest starting tomorrow? Centered around your... friend?"

Her gaze shifted to a newspaper on one of the stacks of books.

For the last three days, Trip had been on the front page. He wasn't doing anything except hiding out and working on his project, so she assumed Lord Lockvale had a friend at the press he'd asked to stir things up. So far, the articles had been outcries against the sudden influx of those with dragon blood into the capital and the surrounding countryside. The journalists hadn't mentioned Trip's little siblings, but Rysha had read between the lines that Lockvale had heard about and was counting them, as well as supposing that more dragon-blooded children would be born soon. Rules had to be established and precedents established, he argued in one interview, or soon mundane human beings would find themselves enslaved to sorcerers once again.

As if that had ever happened in the first place. Rysha shook her head in disgust.

Her mother lifted her eyebrows, and Rysha remembered the question.

"It is about that," she admitted. "I'm hoping that either you or Father will come to the capital and testify. You don't have to say anything about Trip, just that Lord Lockvale has been up to dastardly practices and can't be trusted."

A faint clink sounded behind her, Aunt Tadelay standing in the doorway and stirring a mug of tea with a spoon.

"Rysha," Mother said, "I understand you wanting to defend your friend, but we've only met him once, and we don't truly know anything about him."

"Other than that he has admirable assets." Aunt Tadelay smirked and brought her mug to her lips.

Mother blinked. "Tadelay, you're not referring to that—that *night*, are you? I thought that mortified you."

"I was extremely mortified. But neither that nor his strategically placed pillow kept me from noticing assets. And understanding why young Rysha might be smitten with him."

Rysha's cheeks warmed at this uncertain defense.

"Smitten," Mother said. "That's the word the newspaper used."

"They're mentioning me?" Rysha had seen most of the articles but must have missed that one.

"The journalist said it's likely he's using his power to influence you so that he can marry you and gain a place for himself in the nobility."

"Mother, surely you don't believe such nonsense. Or you, Aunt Tadelay. You know what the silver dragon was up to and how Lockvale was trying to take advantage. He came here openly, trying to buy our land."

"I'm aware of that," Mother said, "but we don't have any proof he was working with that dragon."

"Trip said he was."

"The Trip who is being accused of attempted murder."

"Lockvale's doing that to save his own reputation. *He* should be on trial here, but because he started this hubbub, nobody seems to remember that he was up to sleazy practices, even my own family, the one targeted by said practices." Rysha realized she was yelling, and she took a deep breath, struggling for control. She had planned to be measured and rational, not bellow at her mother.

A throat cleared in the hallway. Her father had joined Aunt Tadelay in the doorway.

"We haven't forgotten, honey. I certainly haven't." He shared a nod with Tadelay. "But like your accused officer, we lack evidence. It would be our word against his if we attempted to press charges. And since nobody ever saw him with this silver dragon, nobody who has come forward about it, there's nothing to link him to it in the eyes of the law. Further, as you know, all the noble landowners in the region know each other and interact with each other regularly. Starting feuds never went well in the past, and it's not something I wish to do now, not over this. He was stopped, it seems, and with the dragon gone, we can get our workers back."

"He was stopped because of *Trip*," Rysha said, turning to look into all three sets of eyes.

"Actually, he was stopped because of you and your dragon, was he not?" Aunt Tadelay asked.

"We never would have caught that silver without Trip's help. He was creating magical walls so the silver had to turn. You were outside, Father. You saw that, right? The silver was too fast otherwise."

"Hm," her father said neutrally.

"Listen," Rysha said, "you don't have to love him or think he's the right person for me." Though she wished they would. "I'm just asking for someone to come to the city tomorrow and testify, to talk about the pressure Lockvale has been putting on the family to sell."

Father sighed. Mother fiddled with one of the books on the desk.

Rysha's shoulders slumped. It was such a small favor to ask, but maybe she'd been foolish to think her family would come through for her. It wasn't as if she'd received any approval from them these last few years. Why did she even bother coming home? It was a waste of time.

She pushed past her father, not caring that her shoulder rammed against his, and hurried into the hallway.

She had almost reached the front door when Aunt Tadelay stopped her by calling her name. Rysha looked warily back at her, her hands in her pockets and her shoulders hunched. If anything, her aunt probably wanted to chastise her for stomping out without asking permission to leave or saying goodbye. A proper lady didn't do such rude things.

"I'll be there tomorrow," Aunt Tadelay said.

For several seconds, Rysha stared at her, not understanding. "You'll come to the city? To the army fort? For Trip?"

"For *you*." Aunt Tadelay pursed her lips. "If your Trip is a sorcerer, I don't think he needs *my* help."

"He won't use his powers for his own personal gain. He has morals and ethics."

"No wonder he's being picked on by Lockvale. I will be there to say exactly what I think of him and what slimy scandalous things he's been involved with, not just in regard to attempting to acquire our land, but in his relationships with other nobles as well." Aunt Tadelay's eyes narrowed.

Rysha suddenly wondered how much dirt she had on Lockvale. And on everyone in the nobility for that matter.

"As for your virile sorcerer… Dear, I feel like you have the power to make this problem go away and you're not using it."

"What do you mean?"

"Did you not just complete elite army training that allows you to pulverize men with your fists?"

"Yes, but—"

"And do you not have some kind of magical sword? And a great golden dragon that breathes fire and rips lesser beings into tiny pieces indistinguishable from the blood meal our gardener sprinkles on the lilac bushes?"

"Technically, yes, but—"

"No, no buts. You are a grown woman with more resources than any woman has likely ever had in the history of women. Go and deal with Lockvale yourself."

"By turning him into blood meal? If I do that, you'll end up testifying at *my* inquest."

"Just *tell* him you'll do that. That your dragon will incinerate him if he doesn't drop the charges against your captain."

"You think I should threaten him?" Rysha wasn't horrified by the suggestion so much as she was startled that her aunt was the one making it.

"Of course not, dear. The nobility aren't so crass. You *pressure* him. Imply that if he doesn't tell the truth, your dragon will breathe fire all over him."

"How is that different from a threat?"

"Because you're a noble lady. Ladies don't make threats."

"I…"

Aunt Tadelay shooed her toward the door. "Run along. Deal with him before it gets late. It's terribly rude to visit after dark, you know."

"Right, a threat should be made before sundown. To be polite."

"Pressure, dear. Pressure."

Trip yawned and sat down on the temple steps, looking out over his project as dusk deepened.

He'd completed and installed the four engines that would spin the massive propellers that would keep the platform in the air, along with eight crystalline energy sources he'd created. The design had been inspired by the *referatu* light devices that powered the fliers, but intended from the beginning to provide power for an engine. Trip had also imbued them with *chapaharii*-sword-like magic to allow them to work alongside the tainted iron. He hoped they would be effective and that they would last, but he had to admit he'd created them intuitively, without much reliance on math or engineering, and time would be the ultimate test. As would their first attempt to lift the platform into the air.

A lot of finishing touches remained such as places for soldiers to be protected from the weather—and dragon fire—when manning the weapons, and the rocket launchers themselves needed to be mounted and tested. But the bare bones were there. And he was exhausted. His brain hurt and even his body hurt from bending over and working. On top of all the mental and physical labor, his inquest was tomorrow.

He groaned and flopped back onto the marble floor of the temple.

Someone in uniform was walking toward him with a lantern in one hand and a jug in the other. General Zirkander.

Trip was surprised to see him. He had let everyone else go for the night, since they were almost done except for the fine work that required good lighting and rested minds. Even Bhrava Saruth had gone off somewhere, perhaps to be worshipped by one of his nubile female devotees. Trip had been alone for the last hour, trying not to think about what he would do in the morning. He had to go to the inquest—there was no doubt about that—but should he use his power to attempt to influence people? Or would that backfire on him and provide support for the opposition's arguments about how vile sorcerers were?

Maybe General Zirkander would have some advice.

"Sardelle said you were still out here," Zirkander said, ambling toward Trip.

"Here and my barracks room are the only places I'm legally allowed to be, sir." Trip's weary brain kicked into gear, and he realized he needed to salute. He scrambled to his feet to do so.

Zirkander waved for him to sit back down. "I would have guessed a bunk in a barracks room would be a more appealing place to sleep, but then, I haven't been out here at night. Is that marble floor more comfortable than it looks?"

"No, sir." Trip sat on the steps again. "The sound of the ocean is nice, and it is peaceful. Damp, but not too cold this time of year."

Zirkander sat next to him, setting the lantern to one side, then offering Trip the large stoppered brown jug.

"Beer, sir?" Trip asked.

"Beer."

"I thought you might be coming to give me advice about tomorrow."

"Beer is *much* better than advice." Zirkander removed the stopper and took a swig to demonstrate.

The second time he offered the jug, Trip accepted it and drank. The rich stout flowed down his throat easily. Apparently, generals could afford better beer than captains.

"Though if you want advice, mine would be to get hammered tonight and let tomorrow take care of itself."

"Tempting, sir, but I'm not convinced tomorrow will take care of anything without my influence. I'm afraid… uhm, Rysha brought me one of the newspapers, so I wouldn't be surprised when extra accusations came up in the inquest."

"I'm not sure a *newspaper* is what I would want my girlfriend to bring me if I was incarcerated in a dragon temple."

"She also brought cookies."

"Ah, that's an improvement."

"Except that there were only three by the time she got here. I guess Shulina Arya ate the rest. Still, they were good. Cinnamon raisin."

"If it makes you feel better, the oven is constantly running at my house, and I hardly ever get anything but scraps."

Zirkander took the jug back and drank again. Maybe he planned to get hammered too. Trip hoped that wasn't a reflection on how he believed the inquest would turn out.

"I'm not convinced that weapons are the best way to deal with dragons," Zirkander said. "I'm disappointed that Angulus didn't take me up on my suggestion of lobbing baked goods onto Cofah shores every week, thus to ensure all dragons would feel compelled to live over there. Sort of like installing a bird feeder."

"Does he take you up on any of your suggestions, sir?" Trip smiled.

Rysha had described how her meeting with Angulus had gone before and after Zirkander showed up. Trip had been surprised to learn that Angulus didn't seem to love Zirkander—or his suggestions. The general *did* have a mouthy streak that not everyone appreciated.

"More often when we're having private meetings than in front of other people. But this was my suggestion, that you be sent out here for your punishment." Zirkander thumped him on the arm. "You're welcome."

"I can't be upset since I've gotten to work on my project. I am somewhat distressed by how many of Bhrava Saruth's trysts I've had to witness."

"He trysts out in the open?"

"Often in that throne in the main room. Sometimes in the back—there's a large bed in his private room, which is full of non-edible things that people have brought him. I have to confess, I didn't truly think he had worshippers, that anyone fell for that."

Too late to take back the words, Trip remembered that Zirkander had admitted to following the dragon once. Trip had assumed it was a joke or something done to appease Bhrava Saruth, but who knew?

Zirkander smirked. "I suspect most of them are using him, pretending to worship him in order to get what they need. And I don't think he cares if his followers' worship is heartfelt and real or a bit of a sham. He just likes the attention."

"Multiple times a day, from what I've seen."

"I would have thought you were too busy working outside to notice the attention he gets. Multiple times a day."

"I was, but I can sense, uhm, strong feelings or emotions. And sometimes, everybody out here can *hear* the strong feelings of emotion." Trip took a drink, a long one this time, to wash away the memories.

"I'm sure he's using his dragonly, uh, what's it called?"

"*Scylori.*"

"Right. I'm sure his allure pulls people to him, but he *does* genuinely heal them and bless them. I'd assumed his blessings would be a joke, but he gave me one three years ago, and I still heal a lot faster than normal. I can nick myself shaving in the morning, and it's completely healed by the time I get dressed. For you, that's probably normal, but my blood is plain and boring."

Trip was glad the people who came to Bhrava Saruth got something out of it and weren't only being used to satisfy the dragon's urges. The whole setup with the temple and the fake religion reminded him uncomfortably of Agarrenon Shivar and his cult. Bhrava Saruth seemed much more benign, but Trip still hated the idea of anyone using power to influence other people for their own gain.

As he wondered if he needed to do that very thing tomorrow.

He groaned and dropped his face between his knees.

"I know the beer and the company are good, so I'm going to assume something else is disturbing you," Zirkander said.

"I'm just conflicted. Tomorrow, do I just sit there like a lump and let my fate be decided by a heartless military judge and some young lieutenant law defender who never even came out to speak to me? Or do I use my power to influence people—the judge, I suppose is the most important one—and make sure things come out in my favor? I know I can walk away at any time, no matter what happens, but then what? I would be an outcast, and I could never come back to my unit, never visit my grandparents in Charkolt, never spend time with Rysha again unless it was in secret... She deserves better than that, than some criminal she has to skulk around to see."

Tears stung Trip's eyes, and he looked out at the night and away from Zirkander, embarrassed. He hadn't wanted to break down in front of his commanding officer.

Zirkander patted him on the back. "I don't think it'll come to that. Look, the king is on your side, even if he's trying to appear like he's not. He's got an announcement tomorrow that's going to give the newspapers something scintillating to talk about, and they're going to forget all about you and your inquest. I doubt any journalists will even show up. I gather he's delighted that he got a yes and gets to make the announcement regardless of your situation, but he was pleased to hold off a couple of days and strategically make it tomorrow morning, to take some of the attention off you."

Trip wiped his eyes and looked at Zirkander, trying to puzzle through what he was talking about. He didn't mean to read his commanding officer's mind, but Zirkander was smirking and thinking about Kaika and Angulus holding hands, then kissing in front of a crowd.

"He got a yes... to a proposal?" Trip hadn't known Angulus and Kaika were that committed. Though he'd seen one of their reunion kisses and heard rumors that they'd been seeing each other for years, so maybe he shouldn't have been surprised.

"He did."

"She's not noble, right?"

Zirkander laughed. "About as far from it as you can get. A lot like me. Though I don't think her family tree has as much dead wood on it as mine."

"Huh." Trip wondered if it was selfish of him to promptly think of himself. If the non-noble Major Kaika could marry the *king*, wasn't it possible that the non-noble Captain Trip could marry a certain Lieutenant-Lady Ravenwood?

"Don't worry too much about tomorrow, Trip," Zirkander said. "It's sure to be interesting, but if you're lucky, it will not be because of you."

"I would love for my life to be un-interesting, sir. Aside from slaying dragons and defending Iskandia."

"A good goal to strive for." Zirkander placed the jug on the stairs at Trip's feet, then stood up. "I better get home to Sardelle and the children. Just wanted to make sure you had the means to get hammered if you so wish. And that you'll be all right. *Will* you be?"

Trip also rose to his feet, feeling he shouldn't sit while a general stood. "I think so, sir. Thanks for coming out here."

"I'll be at the inquest tomorrow too. Several of us will be. Just in case someone needs to glare daggers at this Lord Lockvale. You know Wolf Squadron isn't afraid of any nobles."

"Yes, sir. Thank you, sir."

Zirkander gave him another pat on the shoulder and turned to leave.

"Sir?" Trip asked, glad for the support but also wondering if… Was Wolf Squadron protecting their own just because the pilots always would? Or did they believe he was innocent? "You know I didn't do it, right? Hurt him or even threaten him?"

"Of course," Zirkander said simply, tilting his head.

Trip brushed his mind, checking to see if he was telling the truth. And… he was. Trip had to blink away tears again. He hadn't been here in the capital, working with Wolf Squadron and under General Zirkander for that long, so it touched him that his commander believed him and knew he wasn't the kind of person who would use his power in a vile way.

"Thank you, sir."

Zirkander gave him a lazy salute and headed off into the night.

CHAPTER 22

FULL DARKNESS FELL AS SHULINA Arya sailed farther south, away from the city and toward the oceanfront property Aunt Tadelay had described as the Lockvale estate. Rysha had known vaguely where it was, but she'd never had a reason to visit it since the Lockvales hadn't had any children her age when she'd been growing up. If not for the dragon's keen eyes, she never would have located the castle-like manor perched on and blending into a rocky bluff overlooking the ocean. Few gas lamps burned in or around the structure, and smoke only wafted from one of the many chimneys.

Rysha imagined the view was magnificent during the day and was surprised the Lockvales were dealing with financial difficulties.

There are no sheep, no cows, no chickens, and no farmlands down there, Shulina Arya observed. *Nothing but rocks.*

I'm sorry I was ready to go before you found a succulent sheep to sink fang and talon into, Rysha thought, believing the dragon was upset that she hadn't gotten her dinner.

No, Storyteller, I am merely observing that the land where this castle exists has few of the things humans covet to sustain them. Dragons would also find it unappealing.

Ah, I see now. Yes, if the Lockvales weren't able to derive much income from their land, that could explain some of the financial problems. *Let's go to the front door, please.*

Shall I remain in my dragon form? I very much like your aunt's idea of intimidating this man, and perhaps incinerating him, thus protecting your mate.

We should try to avoid incinerating Iskandian subjects. Not that the thought didn't have a slight appeal to Rysha. If a dragon incinerated a man when nobody was around to see it, who would even know who had been responsible? Evidence would be at a minimum. *Also, it looks like you're too large to fit through the front door in your current form.*

Yes, this is true. Human doors are so miniscule.

Actually, the large carved-oak doors at the front of the manor towered impressively to Rysha's eye, and perhaps Shulina Arya could make it through them, but she imagined the rooms inside would prove a tight fit.

They landed on the front walkway, and Rysha slid off the dragon's back. *Can you tell if he's inside, by chance?*

She didn't know if Shulina Arya had taken note of Lockvale the night they'd flown over the highway where he and his cronies had been watching the fire. *Rysha* hadn't noticed them until Trip said something.

There are two men inside, Shulina Arya said.

Rysha tapped her fingers on her thigh. It would be more convenient if nobody but Lockvale was home to witness her *pressuring* him. Admittedly, she didn't know if he was one of the two men inside. It was possible she was too late, that Lockvale had gone up to the city a day early to avoid having to get up early to travel for the inquest.

One man is up a set of stairs in a small room reading a book. The second is downstairs, not far from this door, in a much larger room with many seats. He is eating and has many newspapers spread around him.

Does he seem smug as he gloats over articles about Trip?

Rysha didn't truly expect the dragon to be able to discover that, but Shulina Arya said, *He does seem smug. And most contented. The way Bhrava Saruth acts when he's getting belly rubs.*

Let's hope that's him. Rysha strode toward the door. *And that the other man is far enough away that he doesn't hear us talking to Lockvale. It's probably a butler or other servant who's retired for the night.*

Except Rysha expected to have to do more than talk. She touched the hilt of Dorfindral, glad she had the sword along. When soldiers weren't on missions, their weapons were usually checked into the armory, as Rysha's pistols and rifle currently were, but she'd argued that the *chapaharii* blades were too valuable to keep in there. It had helped that the armory sergeant had possessed a smidgen of dragon blood, and Dorfindral had flared threateningly at him at the suggestion of being placed inside.

Rysha tried to open the front door, deciding that sneaking up on the man so he didn't have time to think, would be preferable to knocking and waiting. Lockvale might not even answer the door at night, assuming that nothing but trouble came visiting after dark, especially these days.

"He would be right," she murmured and stepped back. The door hadn't budged. "Shulina Arya?"

Rysha didn't hear the click of the lock over the rumble of waves crashing below, but she did detect the faint thump of a bar being set aside. This time, she succeeded at pulling open the heavy door.

She stepped into a grand foyer with stone walls, a stone floor, and a timber ceiling high above. All manner of portraits of deceased Lockvales were on display.

Shulina Arya came in and stood beside her. She had switched to her human form with two pigtails sticking out to either side of her head and a mischievous ready-for-action gleam in her violet eyes.

"Ah." Rysha didn't want to be fussy when the dragon was helping her for no reason other than friendship, but... "Could you perhaps choose a more intimidating form?"

Shulina Arya looked down at herself, her pigtails flopping forward as she did so.

"How about a tiger?" Rysha suggested.

That is a feline, yes? I do not believe I've seen a tiger before. We must take a trip all around this new world, so I can observe all the mighty predators.

"I'll take you to the zoo in the capital as soon as there's time." Rysha liked traveling as much as the next person, but her superiors might object to her taking months off to show the dragon the animals of the world.

Shulina Arya looked at her, perhaps getting an image of a tiger out of her mind. Then the dragon blurred and shifted before Rysha's eyes, turning into an orange-and-black-striped cat with a long tail. A *small* cat.

"Larger, please." Rysha re-formed her tiger image in her mind—it probably didn't help that she'd only seen them at the zoo as a child—and placed it next to a human for comparison.

Oh, yes. A truly magnificent predator! Shulina Arya shifted again, then stood on all fours beside Rysha, their heads at the same height.

That was larger than Rysha had imagined, but she didn't complain. An oversized tiger should be even more intimidating. The fangs were certainly long and visible.

"Good, let's find him." Rysha nodded for Shulina Arya, with her magical senses, to lead her to the man with the newspapers.

The dragon padded toward one of multiple halls that opened off the foyer, soundless on those cat's feet. She soon stopped in front of an open door.

Rysha peered into a large sitting room with multiple fireplaces and a stone floor decorated with bearskin rugs. Antique swords, axes, and firearms hung on the walls, along with dozens of stuffed animal heads. Several old suits of armor towered about the room on pedestals.

She spotted Lockvale sitting at a table near one fireplace with a bowl of soup and a wine glass, papers strewn around him as Shulina Arya had described. The man was still dressed for the day, which Rysha was thankful for. She would have felt like a bully threatening someone in pajamas. She felt like a bully, as it was, and reminded herself this was for Trip, Trip who had only come into this man's sights because he'd been helping her.

Chin firm, Rysha strode into the room with Shulina Arya. She was halfway to Lockvale before he noticed them.

He leaped up, knocking his chair over. "What is this? You dare intrude in Lockvale Manor?"

He gaped at the tiger in disbelief.

"I dare, yes." Rysha stopped a few feet away from him. He'd moved around the table to put it between himself and them. "Because you dare make up ridiculous charges to slander someone honorable and with a great deal of integrity. More than that, you're trying to have him *hanged*."

"Because he's a *witch*, you fool of a girl. All those people should be hanged."

"All those people who have been helping defend the country from dragons, Cofah, and pirates?"

"So they tell us. But it's only a matter of time before they take over again, as they once tried to do. That—that *man* used his evil power to read my *mind*. I was completely incapable of fighting back. When I tried to defend myself, he didn't even have to lift a finger to send me hurling backward."

"As I understand it, he was defending himself from you."

"I didn't try to read *his* mind."

"You just tried to shoot him."

"Because he's a *witch*."

Rysha wished she had a way to record his words like music on a phonograph so they could be played back at the inquest in the morning.

"Just like that one who's been manipulating Angulus for the last three years," Lockvale snarled.

"Sardelle?" Rysha couldn't imagine who else he might mean. It had to either be she or Dr. Targoson.

"She controls him, and she controls the pilot Zirkander. Why more people don't see that, I can't imagine. She's got them all under her thumb. Angulus used to be different. It used to be that if I or one of the other nobles went to him with a problem, he promptly did something to help. *Now*, he's siding with witches."

Lockvale eyed the tiger warily. "That's not a real animal. It's some illusion. Some *witch* magic." He squinted at Rysha. "Are you experimenting with magic? I never would have thought a Ravenwood would turn to sorcerous ways." He glanced toward the fireplace mantle. Both a sword and a rifle hung above it.

Rysha dropped a hand to Dorfindral. "I'm not a witch, and neither is the tiger. This is the gold dragon Shulina Arya, shape-shifted into a form suitable for walking into your castle. And eating you if need be."

Shulina Arya put in a timely roar, and Lockvale's eyes bulged as he stumbled back from the table.

"That had better be a joke, girl," he said, edging closer to the fireplace.

"Lord Lockvale." Rysha stalked down the table opposite him, intending to head him off if he went for a weapon. "I am here because you falsely accused Captain Yert of attempted murder, and his efforts to build a weapon to defend the city from dragons are being interrupted because of your ridiculous inquest. I insist that you drop the charges, that you say you were mistaken and have realized the truth, that Trip was only defending himself."

"Ridiculous. He attacked me."

He actually seems to believe that, Storyteller. However, I can see into his thoughts and see that events unfolded as Captain Trip described. This man believes mind-reading is a heinous crime and that when your mate created a protective barrier around himself, it was the same as attacking. This man is most foolish.

"You weren't there," Lockvale added. "You don't know what happened."

"Actually, the dragon here is reading your mind and knows exactly what happened. It's a shame you don't. Perhaps you should learn about magic instead of insisting it's pure evil and wetting yourself whenever it's mentioned."

Lockvale's eyes flared with indignation. Aunt Tadelay possibly wouldn't have approved of Rysha bringing latrine talk into the discussion.

"He's manipulating you." Lockvale thrust a finger toward Rysha. "The same way that witch manipulates the king. Get out of my home now, or I'll add your name to my official complaint against your captain. I have friends in the city." He waved toward the newspapers with his other hand. "Don't think I can't make this happen."

May I incinerate him now, Storyteller? I am tired of listening to his ignorance and arrogance.

Lockvale must have heard the telepathic comment because his eyes grew even rounder. He lunged for the weapons above the fireplace.

Rysha ran to cut him off, but her boot hit a newspaper that had fallen to the floor, and she skidded. It only took her a second to catch her balance, but it was long enough for Lockvale to yank the sword off the wall. He spun toward her, gripping the weapon in both hands.

Rysha slowed before reaching him, seeing from his grip and his stance that he had experience.

"You will get out of my home *now*," Lockvale growled.

"Not until you promise to revoke the charges against Trip."

Rysha drew Dorfindral. *She* had experience too.

The blade glowed green, and she saw the alarm in Lockvale's eyes, this proof that more magic was in effect. But he didn't back down.

Seeing the glow made Rysha think that Lockvale might have some dragon blood in his veins, but Dorfindral urged her to attack the tiger behind her rather than the man, so she suspected it was only glowing because of Shulina Arya's proximity. That meant that if she fought Lockvale, she would have only her own skills to draw upon. The blade wouldn't help. So be it.

"Not only will I not revoke them, but I'll add your name. I don't care whose daughter you are. You broke into my *home*." Lockvale snarled and leaped at her.

Do you wish me to flatten him to the ground, Storyteller? Shulina Arya asked as Rysha whipped Dorfindral up to parry.

Not unless I'm losing.

Rysha blocked a barrage of blows, sensing Lockvale's frustration and anger. He hammered at her without finesse, though she did recognize a dueler's classic thrusts and attacks.

She backed up as she parried, keeping an eye on the furnishings as she further studied his technique. He wasn't as fast and clean with his blade work as the elite troops she'd been practicing with, and she kept him at bay without much trouble, ensuring her body remained relaxed, her arms fluid. She picked out four combinations of thrusts and slashes that he favored, repeating them over and over.

Rysha waited until he launched into one of the familiar routines, anticipated him, and burst into motion. She batted the flat of her sword against his knuckles as he swung into his second attack in the combination. He cried out, dropping the weapon. Before it hit the ground, she kneed him in the groin, then employed a leg sweep to knock him off his feet.

He fell to the stone floor, and she stepped on his chest before he could roll away. She pressed Dorfindral's tip to his throat.

Lockvale opened his hands and looked at her face. He seemed more wary than truly afraid, and she didn't think he believed she would kill him. Which was true. She had to figure out how to extract a promise from him in such a way that he wouldn't feel justified in later ignoring it.

"Shulina Arya, can you show him what truly happened? And make him understand it?"

The other man is here. I am preventing him from entering the room.

Without moving her sword tip from Lockvale's throat, Rysha looked toward the doorway.

"I understand what happened," the newcomer said, presumably the man who had been reading upstairs. "I was there. Gemmon wanted me to join the others in testifying against the officer, but I would not."

"He's not an officer; he's a *witch*," Lockvale snarled.

"I suspect he's both."

"Go back to your books and puzzles, Jhag. This has nothing to do with you."

Jhag—that was Lockvale's younger brother, wasn't it? Not the butler Rysha had guessed would be in the house with him.

"What will you do to him, Lady Ravenwood?" Jhag asked.

"I cannot let his ignorance and prejudice put my friend's life at risk," Rysha said, trying to sound grim and determined, like she might truly kill Lockvale. She glared down at him, making her eyes as hard as she could. "I will do whatever I need to do to protect him. Just as he would do anything to protect me."

If my rider does not slay him, I will incinerate him myself, for he has proven himself an enemy and a hater of those born of dragons, Shulina Arya said, wood creaking under her large feline form. She'd hopped onto the table and sat on her haunches, her tail swishing about, knocking newspapers onto the floor. *Though perhaps in this form, I should simply devour him? Tigers devour humans, do they not?*

She shared a graphic image with all of them of a tiger chasing down a man, springing onto his back and bearing him to the ground, then ripping his head off and beginning its meal.

"Seven gods." Jhag gripped the doorjamb.

Rysha had to fight to maintain her position, not to back away and lower her sword. That vision was so vivid that it would have been intensely disturbing even if it hadn't reminded her of the bear that had nearly eaten her back on that barge in Lagresh.

"I'll do it," Lockvale said, his voice so squeaky Rysha could barely hear him.

That inspired an idea for her, that and the fact that she didn't quite believe Lockvale.

Shulina Arya? she asked silently.

Yes?

Can you do something to his vocal cords to keep him from speaking? A temporary injury or some damage that could later be healed?

Yes, I can do this.

Good, do it please.

"Excellent," Rysha said in response to Lockvale. "To ensure that's the case, my magical blade here has left a stamp on your throat." She stepped back, drawing Dorfindral from Lockvale's neck, and waving the sword so he would take note of the green glow.

But Lockvale was busy taking note of something else. He winced, touching a hand to his throat, then opened his mouth to speak. His lips and tongue moved, but no words came out.

"You'll tell no more lies," Rysha said. "But if you visit the king and take back the one you told about Trip, I'll return to your home and heal the damage to your vocal cords. If you don't, then you'll never speak again."

She didn't need magic to sense his rage and indignation.

Does this mean I don't get to devour him? Shulina Arya asked, the words for everyone in the room. She oozed disappointment. *In this feline form, the idea seems oddly appealing.*

Lockvale pushed himself to his feet, looking for a moment like he might snatch up the sword and attack Rysha again, but Shulina Arya also stood, her violet eyes exuding power as she looked at him.

Lockvale unclenched his fists, then turned his back to them and stalked to a window overlooking the sea.

I guess that means the meeting is adjourned, Rysha thought.

Shulina Arya hopped off the table, and they walked toward the door where Jhag still stood, his face ashen. He hurried to step aside.

Rysha hadn't intended to evoke any promises from him—especially if he had been the one man in that group on the highway who'd been unwilling to throw Trip to the wolves—but after pausing to let them pass, he hurried to catch up and walk at her side.

"I'll make sure he does what you asked," Jhag said quietly. "I think the threat of never speaking again will be enough to convince him, but if it's not…" He spread his hand. "I was there that night. I saw what happened. I didn't want to speak against my own brother, but everything he's been doing lately, including trying to get your family's estate—not to mention the Orehills' and the Tenderwoods' estates—has been against my wishes. It isn't what Grandfather would have wanted, and it's not honorable."

"Good," Rysha said as they reached the door, surprised at this unexpected support. "Thank you."

He nodded and showed her—and her tiger—out with a deferential manner. But Rysha wouldn't know until tomorrow if anything she had done here would truly have an effect. Maybe Lockvale simply wouldn't show up and the charges would stand. Maybe the man wasn't that attached to his voice anyway. Or maybe he would come in with a list of accusations that now included Rysha's nighttime visit. Noble blood or not, she could end up in a cell right next to Trip's for this.

"We'll see in the morning," she murmured.

Whatever happened, at least she had done everything she could.

CHAPTER 23

THE MILITARY POLICE ESCORTED TRIP up the walkway toward the one-story Army Justice Headquarters, a humorless brick building at the back of the fort, standing in the shadow of the bluff that held the flier hangars. Trip gazed up wistfully, feeling homesick for his cockpit and the chatter of Wolf Squadron as the pilots went off on training exercises.

That feeling intensified as he watched six fliers taking off. For training? Or because some threat approached?

Trip stretched out with his senses, checking for unfamiliar dragons. He sensed Bhrava Saruth, miles to the north and still at his temple, then Phelistoth near Sardelle's house. He hadn't sensed the bronze dragon Telmandaroo for several days and assumed he'd gone back to his pirate islands. Shulina Arya's parents weren't within range. He had no idea where they went when they weren't here reporting to the king or tinkering with ancient technology. Shulina Arya herself was closer than Trip expected, a few miles away and flying toward the city.

Currently, he didn't sense any other dragons, which was a relief. He'd been checking often for the gold that had spied on him three days earlier.

That morning, Trip had left Tolemek mounting the rocket launchers. The platform was almost ready for a trial run, but as long as it was on the ground without those weapons installed, it would be vulnerable to sabotage.

One of the police escorting Trip cleared his throat and jerked his thumb toward the front door. He didn't say, "Quit dawdling," because he was a sergeant and Trip was an officer, but Trip sensed the words among his surface thoughts.

Informing the man that he was searching for signs of enemy dragons probably wouldn't win him any lenience. Trip quickened his pace, telling himself the sooner he got this over with, the sooner he could return to his project. And once that was done, he could return to the squadron and his flier.

Assuming this inquest didn't go poorly.

The police marched him inside and down a drab hallway. They entered a room with two rows of chairs in the back behind a railing, chairs and tables in the middle, and a raised dais and throne-like seat in the front with a stool on either side. Nobody was up there yet, but the chairs in the back were surprisingly full given the early hour. General Zirkander sat next to Sardelle, Blazer, Duck, Pimples, and Leftie—Trip had barely spoken to Leftie because he'd been so busy of late—along with a few Tiger Squadron pilots that Trip had worked with a few times.

Seeing the group there—to support him or even testify?—warmed his heart. Of course, they were so busy reading newspapers that they didn't seem to notice him come in. Only Leftie, who was twirling his lucky ball on its chain, spotted him. He grinned and ambled over, bumping one of the guards in the shoulder, perhaps not by accident.

"Want to kiss my balls, Trip?"

The guard's eyebrows flew up.

"Balls?" Trip asked. "Is there more than one now?"

"There always was." Leftie winked and stuck a hand in his pocket. "But if you're referring to the metal ones, I've added a lovely tungsten luck ball to my collection. You see, the melting point of tungsten is almost twice that of gold, which my other ball is mostly made from. After my near miss with that flame-happy dragon last week, I was concerned about my lucky ball melting, so I had a backup made."

"The lucky ball you keep in your pocket?"

"Yes. Now I keep two."

"Don't you think *you'll* melt before the gold does?" Trip was pleased that he didn't see any signs of the burns Leftie had suffered the week before. He'd been certain that he and Azarwrath could heal the injuries, but he had been less certain they could prevent scar tissue. He hadn't seen Major Kaika in the last week and hoped she, too, was free of scars.

"If I do, I hope you'll be around to un-melt me." Leftie thumped him on the shoulder, then held up his new ball on its chain.

"I'm not kissing that," Trip said, though Leftie's offer made him happy—as did the fact that Leftie seemed perfectly willing to be healed by him these days. How far they had come.

"It's lucky. You might need luck today."

Do not do it, Telryn. No self-respecting mighty sorcerer should be seen leaving lip moistness on a metal ball.

Azarwrath? Trip checked with his senses and realized both Jaxi and Azarwrath were in their scabbards and tucked between the chairs that Sardelle and General Zirkander occupied.

Naturally. I came to ensure that you wouldn't do something foolish like letting yourself be hanged because you were afraid to use your powers in a morally questionable way.

And also to make sure you don't kiss Leftie's balls, Jaxi added. *I know Azzy was concerned about that.*

Trip smiled for the first time in… he didn't know how long. He'd missed Azarwrath's company—and Jaxi's, too, though he'd never expected *her* to be a permanent part of his life. A couple of times, he'd thought about slipping over to Sardelle's house at night to pick up the soulblade, but the military police had come to the temple at least twice a day to check on him. If they had come and he hadn't been there or in his barracks, he would have been relegated to a jail cell again. Also, they would have objected if their prisoner had been wandering around with a sword.

"How about you just kiss it for me?" Trip said. "And then rub some of your luck on me."

"You want me to rub you? That's disgusting."

"But kissing balls isn't?"

"Of course not."

A throat cleared behind Trip, and he sensed Rysha walking up. He turned to face her, his smile widening.

"That's not the discussion I expected to walk in on." She stepped forward and hugged him.

The two military police looked like they wanted to object to all these people coming close, but Trip didn't give them a chance to. He wrapped his arms around Rysha and kissed her.

"Oh dear, not this again," another woman's voice came from down the hall.

He broke the kiss, his smile faltering when he saw Aunt Tadelay approaching. She wore a prim black and blue dress and a matching blue hat with an ostrich plume stuck in the band, and her lips were pressed together in a thin line of disapproval.

"I promise we won't get naked and have sex here, Aunt," Rysha said, clasping Trip's hands.

Trip hadn't expected such bluntness from her, at least not with her aunt, and watched the woman's face warily.

"I certainly hope not," Aunt Tadelay said. "Public displays of affection make those around you uncomfortable and are completely unseemly, especially for proper noble women."

"There's a woman who's unlikely to kiss my balls," Leftie muttered from behind Trip.

"It's good to see you." Trip squeezed Rysha's hands and did his best to ignore Leftie. And the aunt.

"I came to offer support. And…" Rysha leaned around him to peer into the room. "Have you seen Lord Lockvale yet?"

Something about her tone made Trip believe she didn't expect to see the man. Had something happened? He was debating on poking into her surface thoughts when General Zirkander spoke.

"Haven't seen much of anyone yet. No judge, no witnesses for the opposition, no opposition. Could it have to do with King Angulus's recent announcement?"

Rysha grinned, as if she knew exactly what he meant. Trip hadn't paid attention to the newspapers this morning, but he looked now since Zirkander waved the front page in his direction.

"The engagement?" Trip asked, remembering Zirkander's words from the night before. "Is that truly something that would affect this?" He waved toward the room.

Even though Zirkander had suggested it would, Trip hadn't truly believed it.

That's because you're an unworldly youth who has no idea what the ramifications of a royal marriage are in the city where the king lives, Jaxi informed him. *In the entire* country. *All of Iskandia will be abuzz about this today. Even if he weren't marrying a commoner and a female soldier—that is entirely unprecedented, you understand—it would be huge news. But this addendum makes it absolutely scintillating to the masses.*

"Trip?" Rysha nudged him. Had she said his name more than once?

"Sorry, Jaxi is educating me."

"Ah. Have you missed her mentorship since she's gone back to Sardelle?" Sardelle, who was paying attention to Trip, now too, quirked her eyebrows.

"That's perhaps not a question I should answer when she's in the room."

"Oh?" Rysha asked. "Afraid she'll fry your balls?"

"Yes. And mine have a much lower melting point than Leftie's."

Aunt Tadelay, who was pushing her way into the room, threw him a startled look. Leftie grinned at Trip and winked at her.

"Heathens," she muttered and stepped inside. She looked at the empty dais and the empty seats behind the railing. "I came here to publicly shame Lord Lockvale for his heinous attempt to acquire our property, and he's not here. Nor are any of his cronies."

Trip looked at Rysha, surprised. She must have been responsible for her aunt showing up, but how had she ever talked the woman into coming to speak against Trip's accuser?

Rysha was looking at her aunt instead of at him. "Not here? That's so odd. Perhaps someone took your advice last night, Aunt."

Tadelay adjusted her hat as she turned to regard her niece. "Did someone? I hope my advice was followed in a dignified manner appropriate for a noble woman."

"Mostly dignified, yes. Pressure was used rather than threats. Though there was a sword fight..."

Trip started to grasp what they were talking about since distinct imagery drifted to the surface of their minds as they spoke. He shouldn't have been telepathically eavesdropping, but with the women standing so close, and with his curiosity brimming over, it was hard not to.

"So long as it was a dignified sword fight," Aunt Tadelay said. "Did your dragon assist you?"

"She did come along, but incineration wasn't required, so she mostly sat on the table and looked fierce."

Aunt Tadelay curled a lip. "On the table, dear? Where people eat?"

"She changed into a tiger first."

"I'm not sure that's any less unsanitary."

Rysha turned her smile toward Trip again. "I can explain later," she said, though he sensed a hesitancy from her, as if she didn't want to explain. Or didn't want him to know that she'd stepped in on his behalf to solve his problem for him? That did not bother him whatsoever.

I think I got the gist, he whispered into her mind and hugged her again. He refrained from kissing her since so many eyes were upon them, but he did rest his forehead against hers.

Aunt Tadelay issued a distressed sound. "So *much* public affection."

Thank you, Trip told Rysha, ignoring everyone else.

It was the least I could do after you stepped in to help my family. I'm not positive they deserved your help, but I do appreciate it. One day, I hope they'll come around and realize that you're a wonderful man.

I was thinking of building them a coffee maker.

She grinned and swatted his chest. *That could do it.*

"If Major Kaika can get a king, I don't see why a captain couldn't get a princess," Pimples said from the end of the row of seats.

"You're not still pining after that Cofah princess, are you?" Duck asked him.

"We write letters to each other. And I sent her a fancy design for a bookcase that frames her reading nook in the palace. She invited me to come to Cofahre, but I told her I'd be shot on sight there and invited her to come here instead. I told her I'd build us a treehouse full of bookcases."

"You think she's going to leave a palace for a treehouse? Did an otter fall on your head?"

"She likes treehouses. She told me so."

"Uh huh."

"Clear the way," the military police said, abruptly pushing people away from the doorway, then snapping to attention as a colonel in a dress uniform strode in. His name tag read: *Srandark*.

Trip didn't recognize the name. Hadn't a lieutenant been assigned to him? Or maybe this was the judge?

Srandark pinned Trip with a cool gaze, and Trip's hope that the rest of the world would forget about his inquest disappeared. Not only had someone remembered, but that *someone* looked dyspeptic. Before the officer said a word, he reminded Trip of his old squadron commander, Colonel Anchor.

"Don't witches salute when a superior officer walks into the room?" the colonel demanded.

Trip whipped up a salute, feeling foolish for the lapse in courtesy—it ought to have been automatic after all these years in the army—but he'd been distracted. And distressed.

Trip felt someone's presence behind him, Zirkander coming over to stand by his shoulder.

"He's a sorcerer, Colonel," Zirkander drawled, his voice as casual as typical, but his eyes uncharacteristically hard. "They've got different rules than witches. Different genders, too, I understand."

The colonel, who clearly hadn't seen Zirkander when he walked in, cursed under his breath and snapped up a salute of his own. Trip sensed that he hadn't expected to run into anyone who outranked him in his own inquest room.

Sardelle came to stand on Trip's other side, somehow not looking out of place, though she was one of the few people not in a military uniform. "Technically, there can be male witches, but we have only sorcerers and sorceresses in Iskandia, those trained in the *referatu* way."

The colonel's eyes grew round, and he stepped back, radiating discomfort at this open talk of magic. Then his belt unbuckled, and his trousers dropped to his ankles.

"Is that the *referatu* way?" Zirkander murmured, his eyes much friendlier as he considered Sardelle.

Sardelle raised an innocent hand.

Jaxi snickered into Trip's mind.

Extremely immature, Azarwrath remarked.

Tell me you didn't laugh, Jaxi said.

I did not.

Liar.

Aunt Tadelay, the recipient of a full-on view of pale underwear as Srandark bent to yank up his trousers, gasped and whirled away, raising a hand to shield her eyes.

Trip might have laughed, but something in the distance tickled his senses. He turned toward the north wall, as if he could see through it, and stretched out with his mind.

"I thought Colonel Tlen was presiding over this inquest," Zirkander said, not commenting on the clothing mishap.

Srandark shot him a dark look as he refastened his buckle. "She was pulled away by a political officer to be consulted on the king's upcoming nuptials."

"Hm." Zirkander looked at Sardelle. "We may have made a miscalculation."

"There's trouble coming," Trip said.

"Not necessarily," Zirkander said. "Jaxi can keep dropping his drawers all day."

"*Ridge*," Sardelle admonished.

Technically, I can, Jaxi told them. *That hardly required a strenuous amount of effort.*

Trip shook his head. "I mean dragons. I sense them coming in. A lot of them."

"The same group as before?" Zirkander's tone lost all its amusement.

Trip nodded. "There are at least eight, and a powerful gold is leading them."

"How far out?"

"Forty miles, but it won't take them long to cover that."

"Is your platform ready to fly?"

Trip hesitated. "It'll fly, but we're still in the middle of mounting the rocket launchers. Nothing's been tested."

"Eight dragons sound like a good way to test."

Trip wanted to protest—no dragons, no wind, and a beautiful sunny day sounded like a good way to test his project—but what was the alternative? Go up in fliers with nothing greater than the *chapaharii* swords and some acid-filled bullets, and risk losing more people?

"It was six dragons last time," Zirkander said softly, perhaps thinking the same thing, that it would only be worse if they didn't have a way to change the odds.

Trip nodded firmly. "I'll do my best to get it in the air, sir."

"Good. Take Ravenwood and her dragon. If you can't get it in the air right away, get a ride up to the hangar, and get your butt in a flier."

"Yes, sir."

If Rysha minded being given orders by a different battalion commander from her own, she didn't show it. She squeezed Trip's hand, then ran to her aunt for a quick hug and to issue a warning to lie low.

Zirkander turned to his officers, all of whom had rushed to gather around him. "Leftie and Blazer, get up to the hangar and prep the fliers. Pimples, go round up our elite sword wielders. Duck, sound the alarm, warn the city. Sardelle—" As Zirkander turned toward her, Trip wondered if he would presume to give her orders, "—I'd love to have you up there with me if you feel you're able." He glanced toward her stomach, though her figure had mostly returned to normal proportions since she had delivered the baby.

"I'm ready." Sardelle reached between the chairs to pull out the two soulblades. "And Jaxi is chomping at the bit." She tossed Azarwrath to Trip as Rysha rejoined him.

"Good," Zirkander said. "You know I pine when you're not in the air with me."

"And Jaxi?"

"Yes, I pine without her fireballs incinerating enemies."

With Azarwrath in hand, Trip was ready to take on the dragons, so he didn't wait to hear more. He started toward the door, but found the colonel blocking the way.

"I don't know why you think there are dragons coming when the city alarms aren't sounding," he said, "but I have an inquest to start in—"

His trousers descended.

"Cursed badgers' teats," the colonel hollered.

Zirkander grabbed the officer and pulled him out of the way, so Trip didn't have to. "Get in the way again, and she'll incinerate your pants."

"*Who?*"

"My wife's sword."

Trip, already racing into the hall, didn't hear the colonel's response, but he was starting to understand why someone would pine for Jaxi in her absence.

Rysha ran at his side. "You think your platform is ready?"

"Seven gods, I hope so."

CHAPTER 24

*T*HE DRAGONS ARE VERY CLOSE, Storyteller, Shulina Arya said as they flew over the city toward Bhrava Saruth's temple.

Rysha and Trip rode on her back, and Rysha could feel the tension in his stiff body. He had to not only be worried about the attack—never before had this many dragons assaulted the capital all at once—but also about the performance of his weapons platform. Would it do everything he wished? And everything he had promised the king? Not getting a chance to test it first was asking for trouble.

They'll be visible on the horizon at any moment, Trip said. *I sense that they're flying toward the city, but the temple is on that same heading. Shulina Arya, we need to get there first just in case...*

You think they'll attack your platform while it's still on the ground? Rysha asked.

I don't know, but I'm sure they know it exists. I had a gold dragon spy on it one day. It's possible they don't know exactly what it is, but they're smart enough to make some guesses. The spy would have sensed the tainted ore.

I am very fast, Shulina Arya said. *We will arrive first. And then we will go into valiant battle.*

Rysha hoped she wasn't thinking about confronting all eight at once. She would prefer to let those dragons sail overhead, become focused on the city and the fliers, and then come in from behind to attack one at a time.

The temple came into sight, its rocky island tucked inside the protective inlet. The gray and black weapons platform in the back was as large as the temple itself with railings to keep anyone from falling over the side once it was airborne and twelve towers positioned around the edges with weapons on them. At least Rysha hoped the rocket launchers had been mounted. She spotted someone in a white jacket with dark hair kneeling atop one of the towers.

Tolemek doesn't have all the rocket launchers installed yet, Trip told her grimly. *Only four of the twelve are mounted. I should have been here to help him this morning.*

Rysha reached back and patted his leg.

Bhrava Saruth is not here to defend his temple. Shulina Arya sounded surprised. *He is at the butte in the city where the fliers are taking off.*

The city needs dragons to help, Rysha thought. *Is there any chance Phelistoth or your parents are on the way?*

My parents are not on this continent. They are doing more research on population problems and have been discussing breeding prey animals, the way humans breed livestock, to increase the availability of desirable food for dragons.

A noble pursuit, but not one that would help the city today. *What about Phelistoth?*

He is outside of the city at the house of magic, picking up the sorceress Tylie.

Good. At least, Rysha thought it was good. She hoped Sardelle's children would be fine with all the adults in the house gone. Would the younger students watch over them?

She'd been a little surprised Sardelle had volunteered to go up with Zirkander, and that he'd seemed to expect that she would. What would happen to their children if they both died in battle? Maybe the odds were against that, but they had to have considered it. Were they so dedicated to the city and the country that they were willing to risk themselves? Maybe they believed it necessary, that to lose their sovereignty to the dragons would be unacceptable, for them and for their children.

As Shulina Arya dove toward the back of the temple, the first dragons came into view, two large, powerful golds leading the flight.

Rysha worried about what would happen if all eight descended to deal with Trip and the weapons platform—and her and Shulina Arya—before continuing on to the city. She pulled her spectacles strap out of her pocket and affixed it, having a feeling she would need that extra security before the day was over.

They landed in the center of the steel platform, with Trip leaping off before Shulina Arya folded her wings in. Rysha thought he would run up to talk to Tolemek, but maybe they were already in telepathic communication because he ran instead toward a ladder that led down into the platform itself, toward the area housing the engines.

Before he reached them, the deck thrummed, a sign of them starting up.

I feel the magic of this place, Shulina Arya said. *Your mate has made powerful artifacts.*

Will those dragons sense them? Rysha said.

Of course. But I also sense... There is something most unpleasant embedded in this structure. Shulina Arya lifted her taloned foot and peered at it, as if something distasteful might be sticking to the bottom.

The banded iron, Rysha said. *We're hoping dragons won't like it.*

I certainly do not. Shulina set down her foot but soon lifted the other one to peer at it.

I'm going to attempt to camouflage the platform now, Trip spoke into their minds. *I'm not sure how effective it will be—the tainted ore will fight me. If Shulina Arya can help, I would appreciate it. Even under ideal circumstances, my meager talents wouldn't fool dragons.*

I will do so, Shulina Arya replied, *though it is unfortunate that we don't have a trap to spring. We could have lured them all down here.*

The two gold dragons came into view again, flying over the cliffs above the island. They were much closer now, their powerful muscles rippling under their gleaming scales as they pumped their wings.

Rysha held her breath, feeling vulnerable and out in the open. Dorfindral hummed on her hip, seeming to cry, "Fight!" into her mind.

"Soon," she whispered.

Four silver dragons came into view, following the golds, and two bronze dragons came after them. Trip had been right. Eight total.

One of the bronze dragons dipped a wing and peered down toward them. Had he seen through the camouflage? Since Rysha couldn't sense magic, she had to trust that it was there.

The bronze straightened his path and continued after the others. The dragons disappeared over the cliffs, still heading toward the capital. Alarm gongs sounded in the distance. The city was alert. Rysha hoped it was ready.

The thrumming under Shulina Arya's feet increased, and Rysha felt the reverberations through her body. One end of the platform tilted upward, then dropped back down. It wobbled like a top for a few seconds, and Rysha worried that meant it wouldn't lift off. But then all sides rose at once. As incredible as it seemed without the help of balloons of any kind, the platform inched upward.

The enemy dragons have engaged your people, Shulina Arya said.

Tolemek ran down the ladder from the tower he'd been on and, without glancing her way, raced to a pile of materials, grabbed what he needed, and ran to the next tower. Trip climbed out of the engine area and also sprinted for the materials pile.

Rysha realized there was little she could do since she hadn't seen the most recent blueprints and didn't have any experience assembling rocket launchers. A part of her wanted to stay and protect Trip while he finished working, but she could check back on him later. The city needed her sword and Shulina Arya's fangs and magic.

"Trip," Rysha yelled, "if you don't need us, we're going to join the battle."

Good, he told her. He was running toward a tower with heavy-looking materials floating in the air behind him, but he paused to look at her, to meet her eyes. *Be careful. I love you.*

Rysha's heart lifted. He'd implied before that he felt that way, but he had never said the words.

I love you too, Trip. Rysha patted Shulina Arya's scales to let her know she was ready to take off. *You be careful too,* she added. *I'd be most distraught if you died before I convinced my family that they like you and approve of you.*

You're going to convince them of that? Trip climbed the ladder to the bare tower, nothing but the base of a rocket launcher installed there so far. *I thought I had to make them a coffee maker.*

That will certainly help, especially right now, since I don't think they've yet hired back any of the servants.

They had servants to make the coffee?

Of course, Trip. Noblemen and women don't make their own beverages.

He snorted. *Major Kaika as queen is going to be downright scandalous, isn't it?*

I have no doubt of that. Rysha imagined Kaika getting up from some function at the castle and heading into the kitchen to refill her own beverage as the servants gaped in flustered distress.

As Shulina Arya flew over the cliffs and toward the harbor, Rysha wondered if Kaika would be in one of the fliers, taking her *chapaharii* sword into the air for battle again. It was hard to imagine her not wanting to fight, but with her hair not grown back from her last encounter with a dragon, she might not be as eager as usual.

Ah, excellent, Shulina Arya said, beating her wings hard as the battle came into view. *There are plenty of dragons still left for us.*

They were *all* left. The fight had barely begun. Fliers were still taking off from the bluff.

It looks like you can take your pick of worthy opponents. Rysha took a deep breath and drew Dorfindral. *I'm ready.*

The weapons platform rose ponderously, and Trip grimaced, watching the engines and propellers with his senses as his hands worked to ratchet down the base of one of the rocket launchers. A small stack of rockets gleamed in the sun, resting in the cradle he'd built into the top of the tower for them. He could sense the dragon-blood-derived acid inside, along with an explosive charge, but barely. His head throbbed from the proximity to the tainted ore, which was incorporated all throughout the platform, and most heavily concentrated in the rocket casings.

"In theory, you should pop magical barriers," he muttered to the weapons. "We're about to find out if that's true."

Are you steering this platform, Captain? Tolemek asked into his mind.

Not yet.

The weapons platform had to clear the cliffs before it could head south toward the city. Trip hoped it would move laterally faster than it was lifting, or the battle would be over by the time they reached the harbor.

There's a wheel and levers in the wheelhouse that will let a mundane person steer it, Trip added.

As strange as it seemed, this whole structure would ideally be controlled by those without dragon blood, those who wouldn't be repulsed by the tainted ore. With that in mind, he had designed it for mundane hands.

That wasn't my question. I want to know if you're going to keep us from running into that cliff over there.

I'll handle it. Trip didn't think they were close enough to worry about it yet. *Just keep installing weapons, please.*

Tolemek grunted. *You sound like Zirkander. Except he doesn't say please. I'm low enough ranking that I'm used to asking politely for things.*

It's a good policy to maintain. Are we testing these rockets before we sail into the middle of the battle and start firing them? I know you said they would be drawn to dragons, but have you figured out how to make sure they go after the right *dragons?*

By asking our allies to make sure they're farther away from us than the enemy dragons.

That's it?

I couldn't think of any other way to select targets based on their alliances or temperament. In the future, if the weapons platform proves effective, we won't need our allies in the air.

Good luck telling Ravenwood's female that. She seems bloodthirsty.

She just enjoys pitting herself against others in noble battle. Something that Trip could understand. He lamented that he would be stuck on the platform during the fight instead of in his flier.

Uh huh. Looks like company is coming.

Trip lifted his head. They had cleared the cliffs and could turn south toward the city now, but a dragon was heading their way. One of the silvers. Had it been sent to investigate the platform? Or destroy it? The dragons must have guessed it represented a threat.

I guess we'll get a chance to test the weapons, Trip replied. *But not this one. The launcher isn't operational yet.*

He envisioned himself grabbing one of the rockets and throwing it like a spear.

Towers Two, Five, Nine, Ten, and Twelve should have working launchers, Tolemek said from his spot on Tower Six. *I made sure one on each side of the weapons platform was operational.*

Good idea.

Trip jumped up, thinking he would have to run to the closest working launcher, but he saw that Tower Two already had a rocket loaded in it. He could detonate it remotely with his power.

He eyed the dragon's approach, its silver form growing larger as it flew over the suburbs along the coast north of the city. When Trip had been making his calculations, he'd decided the ideal range for the weapons would be less than eight hundred yards so the dragons wouldn't have much time to react. The rockets would launch like bullets, but he could still envision the magical creatures twisting quickly enough to grab them out of the air with their talons, then throwing them away before they could explode.

"Three... two... one... now," he whispered and pulled the launch lever with his mind.

He sensed a click, as the ignition system activated, but the rocket didn't fire.

Cursing, Trip leaped from his tower and ran across the deck. He magically elevated himself to Tower Two as the dragon swooped in close. The silver came right at him, talons extended, and Trip sensed it drawing upon its power.

Azarwrath? he asked as he wrapped a barrier around himself. He knelt behind the malfunctioning launcher, in part for cover but mostly because he had to fix it.

He realized right away that his barrier was thin and weak, barely extending beyond his body. He groaned—it was because he knelt on the tainted iron. Even the small bit threaded through the top of the tower was enough to disrupt his abilities.

Lending my power, the soulblade said as the silver hurled a mental attack.

Something like a hurricane battered Trip's mental defenses as the dragon came in. Fortunately, its attack was weaker than Trip expected. Maybe the tainted iron affected it, even though the dragon wasn't touching the platform.

It screeched, and its talons slashed as it neared Trip, trying to snatch him up like a falcon snatching a mouse from a field. Those talons clashed against his barrier and bumped off, but the blow sent a jolt through him.

Trip snatched one of the rockets from the cradle as the dragon flew away, banking to come around and attack him again. He hefted the weapon to his shoulder and hurled it toward the creature's chest with all of his physical and mental power.

The dragon tried to dodge, but it was too close. Trip sensed its barrier popping and the rocket continuing through. Even though he hadn't thrown it with the power of one of the launchers, it was designed to explode on impact, and it did.

Trip funneled more power into his barrier as it blew, yellow fire engulfing the dragon, and a wave of energy flowing in all directions. It hammered Trip's defenses, and he dropped to one knee, gritting his teeth and struggling to keep up his magical protection. He imagined the tainted ore under his knee mocking him, and for a second, he was back in Bhodian's barge, defenseless as his powers flagged.

The dragon thumped to the deck, screeching in pain. A gunshot fired, and Trip shook his head, thrusting the memories from his mind. He jumped to his feet in time to see the silver also recovering, running and flapping its wings as it headed for the side.

Tolemek fired again, using a pistol loaded with his acid bullets. The dragon's defenses were down after the beating it had taken, and acid already coated its scales, oozing between them and biting into flesh. The bullet smacked it in the backside. The dragon didn't stick around to take more abuse. It leaped over the railing and flew away.

Trip jumped down from the tower and ran to the side of the platform to see where it went. Had they hurt it badly enough to put it out of commission? Or was it merely inconvenienced and on its way to attack someone else?

The dragon flew toward the harbor, then dove abruptly. At first, Trip thought it was after a flier or ship down in the water, but it plunged below the surface. He sensed its pain, its attempt to get rid of the acid burning through its scales. They might not have killed it, but Trip hoped its discomfort meant it wouldn't be able to return to the battle.

"If I'd known you were simply going to throw the rockets like hook balls," Tolemek said, coming up beside him, "I wouldn't have bothered installing the launchers."

"The launcher didn't work." Trip jerked his thumb toward the tower.

"Ah, this is why I wanted time to test everything."

"Me too."

Trip ran back to the tower, hoping he could quickly find and fix the problem. The weapons platform was almost to the harbor now, and he could hear the pounding of machine guns, the cries of men and dragons, and the thrum of propeller blades. Again, he wished he was in his flier, but he had to accept that he'd chosen this fate for himself and that once he got his platform fully operational, it had the potential to be far more helpful to his country than Trip alone.

He just hoped he could train others to operate it, because between the dragon's attack and the power-sucking attribute of the ore, his head ached so badly he thought he would throw up. And the battle had just begun.

Some of the fliers are heading this way, Tolemek told him. He'd climbed one of the other towers and had a good view of the battle. *With a gold dragon chasing them.*

This way? Why?

Maybe they think we have a working rocket launcher to use.

Trip groaned. Would any of the others work or did they all have the same problem?

He peeked up from his work. He was about to find out.

CHAPTER 25

"THEY'RE AIMING FOR OUR SWORD wielders again," came Zirkander's voice over the communication crystal. "Fly crazy. Keep them confused."

Rysha listened as she and Shulina Arya chased after a gold dragon pursuing several of the fliers. It was pure luck that she wore the uniform that still had the crystal buttoned in the pocket.

"Don't we always fly crazy, sir?" Captain Duck drawled. "That's in the rules, isn't it?"

"Get crazier. You're the one with a gold dragon trying to polish your butt with her breath."

"Her? Do we know it's a her?"

"Don't get excited, Duck," Leftie said. "She doesn't look like she's into big ears."

Rysha couldn't believe the pilots could trade jokes when they were being chased by a dragon. A few of the fliers looped away, flying upside down and twisting to come back in and fire at the big gold. But their bullets bounced uselessly off the dragon's shields.

Rysha silently urged Shulina Arya to fly faster, to get her there so she and Dorfindral could do something about those shields. She already crouched, ready to lash out as soon as she could.

The fliers that didn't loop back to attack flew straight to the north, toward the hulking weapons platform that had come into view, the noises of its engines and propellers audible for miles around. Whoever was leading that squadron—Zirkander? Tranq?—was heading for it. Rysha hoped Trip had something waiting if they succeeded in leading the dragon within the platform's range.

Surrender your foul blades, the gold chasing the fliers commanded. *We will let you live if you do not threaten us further, but know that we have claimed this land for our own.*

We've almost caught up to her, Shulina Arya told Rysha. *Be ready.*

Rysha was ready, but all she could see so far was dragon butt and dragon tail. Shulina Arya shifted slightly, beating her wings furiously to try to draw even with the enemy. But the gold wasn't even paying attention to them. It flew at top speed, attempting to catch one of the fliers—was that Colonel Grady in the back?

The gold breathed fire at it as the pilot corkscrewed away, dipping low and out of the fire's path.

Another gold dragon flew in from the side, almost ramming into the enemy. For a moment, Rysha was confused as gold dragons seemed to be everywhere.

It is I, the god Bhrava Saruth, cried the newcomer.

He snapped at the enemy, only to have his fangs deflected by magic, but two riders were astride his back, and one leaped up. Major Kaika. She rode behind Sardelle, who sat with her soulblade raised aloft. A fireball leaped from Jaxi's tip and slammed into the dragon's barrier. But it wasn't until Bhrava Saruth twisted in the air, tilting his back toward the enemy so Kaika could slash with her *chapaharii* blade that her defenses dropped.

The female shrieked a protest and whipped her head toward them, snapping at Bhrava Saruth. Shulina Arya ducked as the tail lashed through the air toward *her* head. Rysha jumped up, slashing as the tip streaked past.

It had to be the least fatal place to strike a dragon, but she felt faint satisfaction as Dorfindral slashed through the tip of the tail, lopping off six inches. A screech of pain assaulted her ear drums.

Brace yourself, Shulina Arya warned as she rolled sideways.

Something slammed into them with the weight of a tree trunk toppled in a storm. Even though Shulina Arya's defenses had to have been up, a jolt of pain rattled every bone in Rysha's body. She dropped to her belly on Shulina Arya's back, barely keeping her grip on Dorfindral.

You dare maim my mate? A furious cry thundered in her head, making her gasp with pain.

It was only then that Rysha realized the second enemy gold dragon had joined in.

She forced herself to sit up as Shulina Arya turned to face him. The gold female was injured but still in the fight, battling Bhrava Saruth and also giving chase to the fliers. They were flying over Trip's platform now. Rysha hoped he could help, because Shulina Arya had decided to face this new threat.

I dare defend my new homeland, Shulina Arya cried, flying straight toward his head. *You are not welcome here.*

The male tilted and dipped, evading her blunt attack. *You think you are truly welcome? These humans only wish to use you, as they used our kind a thousand years ago. They know they are weak and defenseless without us, so they befriend any dragon weak-minded enough to allow it.*

Shulina Arya growled and banked, flying toward him again. Rysha crouched, hoping she would get close enough for her to use Dorfindral.

A half-dozen voices came out of the communication crystal in her pocket, shouting words like, "...got me" and "...too damaged to fly."

"Land on the platform if you have to." That was Zirkander.

Shulina Arya flew close, this time anticipating when the male dove away from her. She followed, opening her maw and spraying fire at him. His shielding deflected the flames, as expected. He banked sharply, evading her again.

Why are you running, coward? Shulina Arya demanded.

Rysha feared it was because he was buying time, keeping Shulina Arya busy so his allies could attack the city at will.

She peered down and around, looking for the rest of the dragons. Her heart sank because she saw she was right. Two silvers and a bronze were attacking the castle and destroying the artillery weapons on the army fort's walls. The other two silvers had joined the gold female and battled against Bhrava Saruth and the fliers.

The female hurled fire at those fliers every chance she got. Rysha feared none of the aircraft were getting close enough for the sword wielders in the back seats to do any damage.

Or so she thought. Abruptly, one of the men with a *chapaharii* blade sprang from his seat behind the pilot. Was that Colonel Grady again? He leaped into the air and slashed at one of the silver dragons. He was close enough for his blade to strike its barrier, and judging by the distressed shriek that came from that direction, he was successful.

But Rysha's stomach sank when Grady's momentum shifted and he started to fall. He wasn't over the platform. He would fall all the way to the city below and die for sure.

But he halted abruptly, swinging thirty feet below his flier. On a rope, she realized. He'd tied a rope around his ankle.

His pilot headed toward the platform as the other fliers up there turned on the silver dragon, firing from several sides to take advantage of their enemy's defenses being down.

Stand still and fight, Shulina Arya growled at the gold male. *You are too big and too gold to act like a scared antelope.*

The male chuckled into their minds. *When you have expended all of your energy, I will swoop in and attack, and knock that odious sword from your human's hands.*

Rysha might have responded with a snort, but she realized the chase had taken them past the breakwater and out over the open ocean. Had the gold intentionally led them out here? She could still see the battle and the weapons platform, but if she were to drop Dorfindral out here, the water would be deep, and retrieving it would be more of a challenge than in the harbor.

Not that she intended to drop it.

Shulina Arya, what if we play a game of our own? Let's lead him to the army fort and make it easy for the artillery officers to shoot at him. Rysha would have suggested taking him to Trip's platform, but she hadn't seen it fire any weapons yet. Unfortunately, launching the structure may have been premature. She hoped it wouldn't be damaged with all the fighting going on around it.

I do not think he will give chase. He is a coward. He—

A whistling sound reached Rysha's ears, and she twisted to look back. The male spun in the air to face something streaking toward it at blistering speed. The dragon flapped his wings, trying to twist away, but the object struck his defenses.

Rysha thought that would be the end, that it would bounce off, but somehow, it went *through* his invisible barrier.

"Trip's rockets," she blurted.

The projectile clipped the leg of the moving dragon instead of hitting him in the side, and she feared that it wouldn't do much damage. Then it exploded, a ball of fire erupting with ferocity that would have impressed even Jaxi.

Shulina Arya wasn't content to watch. Seeing her foe distracted, she streaked toward the flames.

As they died out, she reached the male and poured flames of her own onto him. His defenses were still down, and he writhed and jerked in the sky.

Shulina Arya dodged a wing, and her long neck darted in. She sank her fangs into his flank.

The male screeched, and his tail whipped about. Once again, it came toward Rysha. She ducked and slashed upward as the tail passed over her head, almost laughing because she took the tip off again.

"Guess that's going to be my signature move," she muttered.

The male shook off Shulina Arya, but not without losing large chunks of flesh and scale from his side. As he dove away, Rysha noticed something viscous on his scales, the liquid—the acid—burning between the cracks.

He's ours now, Shulina Arya cried, flying straight downward after the dragon and toward the ocean.

Rysha's stomach grew queasy, but she held on, ready to hack at more than a tail.

The wind tore at her eyeballs as they descended, tearing her eyes even behind her spectacles. She almost missed the moment when the male drew up, talons dragging in the water as he attempted to evade Shulina Arya one more time.

No, more than that. He was hoping she would plummet into the water and that he could take advantage.

She pulled up, as he had, but sank slightly into the water, and that slowed her down.

The male spun and used his magic to defy gravity. A huge wave of power crashed against Shulina Arya, seeming to slam into the side of her head—or maybe tear into her mind—just ahead of his physical attack. Shulina Arya moaned in pain, the woeful sound echoing in Rysha's mind, and flopped into the water.

Rysha didn't realize exactly what had happened until his great maw snapped straight toward her.

She dropped to her stomach, the jaws barely missing her as they clacked together inches from her head. Shulina Arya's mental defenses were down.

Rysha rolled onto her back, afraid she would roll right off Shulina Arya, and slashed upward with Dorfindral. The male yanked his head back, already preparing for another bite, and she only skimmed his chin.

"Damn it." Rysha sprang to her feet.

Shulina Arya shifted her wings, trying to pull herself out of the water. The male's head came in again, crimson eyes ablaze as they focused on Dorfindral. He meant to destroy that sword, those eyes said, or at least knock it halfway to Cofahre.

He lunged in, fangs glinting in the sun. Rysha waited until the last second, then sprang aside as she twisted enough to whip the sword backward. The dragon, jerking his head around to snap at her again, turned right into her attack. Dorfindral bit into his scaled snout.

He yelped and drew back, but not before the blade sank three inches in and drew blood.

Rysha came down on Shulina Arya's back, the dragon's scales slick with water. She slipped and slid off and into the ocean. She came up quickly, keeping an arm up with Dorfindral held aloft.

Though the male's snout bled, his eyes remained aflame with intensity. He lunged in for another attack.

But Shulina Arya twisted abruptly and seemed to spring from the water, as if she'd leaped off a diving board. Her head intercepted the male's, fangs flashing as she bit the side of his face.

A huge wave of water washed over Rysha, and something under the surface clawed her. She screamed in pain and backpedaled in the water, realizing it must have been one of their talons. Her thigh burned, but she kept Dorfindral ready and above the surface in case the male escaped Shulina Arya and came at her again.

Not that it would be easy to *see* that. The dragons splashed and created huge waves as they wrestled, half in the water and half in the air. Rivulets ran down Rysha's spectacles, and the waves tugged at the strap holding them on.

Roars and screeches came from the writhing dragons, and she struggled to follow what was happening. The male had been injured—that acid ought to be eating into his scales even in the water—but he was also huge, one of the biggest she'd seen. Would he win by sheer weight and strength of limb?

A huge roar sounded over the surf, and a splash soaked Rysha's face. A wave carried her upward, and she gaped at the empty ocean all around her. The dragons had both disappeared under the surface.

We are fully operational, Trip thought, projecting the words out for Tolemek and also Zirkander and Sardelle.

He'd been keeping track of Bhrava Saruth and Wolf Squadron as the dragon and the fliers battled near his weapons platform. Trip knew Zirkander hoped he would launch rockets into the enemy dragons and had intentionally led them in this direction. Trip had cringed since he had malfunctioning rocket launchers, and the dragons had stayed too far away for him to simply hurl the weapons with his hands and power. He hadn't been able to get the first launcher working—it seemed to be missing a crucial part—but he'd run over to the next tower and, with a few tweaks, had gotten *that* one working.

He'd launched their first test rocket out to sea where Shulina Arya had been battling another gold. Though it had made his head pound, he'd used his power to guide that rocket, ensuring it would strike the enemy and not Shulina Arya and Rysha or another of their allies.

He'd hoped the explosion and the acid would combine to bring the dragon down immediately. It hadn't, but it had weakened the gold and knocked down its mental defenses. He was tempted to send another rocket out, but Shulina Arya was wrestling with the other dragon, and they had both disappeared below the surface. He hoped Rysha was all right.

Bhrava Saruth, Trip said, sharing the words with the dragon and also Sardelle, *go out over the city and join Phelistoth in defending the castle, please. I'm going to fire more rockets, and their natural tendency is to hit the dragon closest to the platform.*

His aching head made him wince at the idea of trying to control another one manually.

Sardelle was the one to respond. *It's a tight battle here. Are you sure you want to be without any ally dragons whatsoever? It would be just you and the fliers.*

I know, but that means any dragons I aim at are enemies.

I'm letting Ridge know.

"Incoming," Tolemek yelled from a tower where he was trying to finesse another of the launchers into working.

Trip spun, expecting a dragon, but a flier headed straight for the platform, black plumes of smoke coming from the engine. A soldier gripping a sword hung from a rope swaying back and forth in the air behind the craft. They were coming in too fast. The soldier would be battered senseless if the pilot landed with him dangling back there.

Trip did his best to push aside the throbbing in his head and focus on the soldier—he recognized Colonel Grady's aura.

When you're over the platform, cut the rope and let go of your sword, he told the colonel as the flier approached, coming in too quickly for a landing with the thrusters. The pilot—was that Duck?—wasn't going to attempt a wheeled landing, was he? The platform was large, but not as long as a runway. He would never make it. *Trust me,* Trip added when Grady didn't reply. *I'll bring you down easy.*

When Grady was over the platform, he slashed the rope attached to his ankle, let go of the sword, and twisted in the air to drop feet-first toward the deck.

Stop the flier, please, Azarwrath, Trip thought as he gathered air under Grady and slowed his fall.

My power is weakened by all this tainted iron, but I'm trying.

Thank you.

As soon as Grady's feet touched lightly down, Trip turned his attention to the flier. It came bumping and tottering to a stop in front of his tower.

Duck flopped back in the seat, blood running from a gash in his temple. He barely appeared conscious.

Trip jumped to the deck and ran toward him, also checking Grady for injuries. He was limping, his leg throbbing with pain, but he hurried to pick up his *chapaharii* sword again. He held the blade aloft, his face determined.

"Can you get us back in the air, Trip?" Duck asked, rolling out of the cockpit. His legs almost buckled when he landed.

Plumes of smoke came from the engine. It looked like a mess. Trip had faith that he could fix it, but...

"I don't have time. Someone has to fire rockets at those dragons." He waved toward the fliers buzzing past, diving and weaving, trying to simultaneously avoid attacks and bring their sword wielders close enough to cut down their enemies' shields. "You'll have to..."

Trip trailed off because one of the gold dragons was heading straight toward him, its maw wide open, flames roiling in the back of its throat.

"Take cover," he barked to the others.

Trip strode toward the dragon, pulling out Azarwrath.

"Allow me." Grady lifted a hand and stepped in front of him.

Trip didn't want to hide behind anyone else, *chapaharii* blade or not, but he reluctantly acknowledged that he could more easily concentrate on his magic if Grady took the brunt of the attack. He raised a barrier to protect himself and as much of Duck's flier as he could. Drawing upon his magic again made his headache shift from pounding pain to fierce stabbing pain, and Trip dropped to one knee, panting. Blackness crept into his vision.

Grady glanced over his shoulder at him, but the gold was almost upon them, so Trip waved him forward.

"What's wrong?" Grady yelled as he crouched, fearless in the face of the flames.

Fire poured from the great creature's maw as it flew at them, looking like it wanted to incinerate them *and* the flier. Duck scrambled under the craft to get out of the way. Trip's barrier wavered under the dragon's attack, and it felt as if a mallet slammed into the side of his head, but the fire didn't get through, not to him and not to the flier.

Grady leaped, trying to slash through a dragon toe, or maybe just bring down its defenses, but the creature didn't get close enough.

As it soared past over their heads, banking to come around for another attack, darkness flirted with Trip's vision again. He pressed his knuckles to the deck. He couldn't pass out, not now. His comrades—his *friends*—needed him. *Rysha* might need him.

This rocket launcher also needs work, Tolemek sighed into Trip's mind.
Of course it does. Use the one I was just at. It's working.

With the dragon out of reach for the moment, Grady spun and touched Trip's shoulder. "Captain?"

"It's the ore I infused into the weapons platform. It resists magic and makes it very unpleasant for those with dragon blood to be around."

Trip winced. "Painfully so."

He pushed himself to his feet, his hand on the flier for support, and faced the opposite direction. The dragon had turned and was picking up speed, coming in for another attack.

Nearby, Tolemek raced up the ladder to the working tower, the one Trip had used earlier. He loaded a rocket, but it wouldn't be ready to fire in time. The dragon arrowed toward Trip again, its maw gaping open.

Once again, Grady ran in front of him, to the nose of the flier. Duck still crouched under it, his eyes glassy—he looked like he could collapse at any moment. Trip wished he could spare a moment to heal him, but he put all his power into shielding them again, fearing Azarwrath's weakened help would not be enough.

This time, as the dragon unleashed its fire, Grady drew back his arm and threw his *chapaharii* sword. Startled, Trip envisioned him being incinerated and hurried to extend his barrier around him. But Grady hurled himself to the side, rolling under the flier for protection as flames bathed the deck and struck Trip's defenses.

He sensed the tiny pop as the blade pierced the dragon's barrier, and the magic disappeared.

Knowing he had to take advantage, Trip summoned all the power he could muster and flung it, targeting the dragon's mind. He imagined talons raking through the creature's brain, doing damage, making it want to flee out to the ocean and never return.

A screech of anger and pain slammed into his mind so hard that it threw Trip from his feet. The deck quaked under his back, and for a confused moment, he thought something had happened to the platform, that it was in danger of crashing.

But the dragon had slammed into the base of one of the towers.

Grady snatched his fallen sword from the deck and raced toward their enemy. The dragon struggled to rise, to get its defenses up. Trip blasted it with what little energy he had left. The creature shook its head, as if the attack didn't bother it, but it still didn't rise. Couldn't rise. Trip realized the tainted ore was affecting it, just as it affected him, making the dragon weaker.

Grady ran right up to its side and plunged the sword between its scales.

A shadow fell across the platform, a silver dragon streaking in. Two fliers fired at its tail, but the creature had its barrier up. Icy gray eyes focused on Grady as it flew down to help its comrade.

Trip rolled to his knees, trying to think of something to do, but he couldn't stand much less fight.

Then a soft *thwack* came from the side. Tolemek firing a rocket.

It blasted straight toward the incoming silver, sliced through its barrier, and struck it in the side. An explosion ripped through the air, smoke and flames filling the sky, and the deck quaked again.

Trip lifted an arm, shielding his eyes. Something spattered against the deck. Blood?

"Ugh," he groaned and climbed slowly to his feet, still using the flier for support, still fighting to remain conscious.

Scratches like nails on a chalkboard sounded. The injured gold dragon lumbered out of the smoke. Trip lifted Azarwrath as it came toward him. Fortunately, the soulblade had more strength left than he had. Red lightning streaked out, slamming into the dragon's scales. The creature's barrier was still down, and another screech hammered Trip's ears.

Belatedly, he realized the dragon wasn't coming for him. It charged past him, blood streaming from a dozen gashes on its side. Grady pounded after it, taking a chunk out of its tail before the dragon stretched the lead and leaped over the railing and off the end of the platform.

Grady skidded to a halt, gripping the railing with his free hand. The gold dragon flapped away, but its wingbeats seemed feeble, its body bobbing and wobbling like a drunken bumblebee. It flew north along the coast and away from the city.

Trip hoped that meant it was out of the fight. He turned to find the corpse of the silver dragon sprawled on the deck and grimaced at the mess his rocket had made. At least it had worked. With luck, the other dragons would see this and realize it was far better to avoid the weapons platform now. *And* the city and people it protected.

We are fully operational, he told Zirkander again, looking to the sky where the fliers swooped about, dancing with the remaining two dragons.

I saw, Zirkander replied. *Thank you, Trip. Also, feel free to shoot these last two. If you can get their defenses down, we'll handle the rest.*

Working on it, sir.

Trip started toward the tower, staggering as he left the support of the flier, but then remembered Duck and paused. He needed help.

Tolemek, can you handle firing rockets at the remaining dragons?

"Stay," Grady said, jogging up, then passing him on the way to the tower. "I'll help him."

"Yes, sir," Trip said.

He knelt beside Duck, but Duck waved him away. "Get the flier working and in the air. My ouchies can wait until after the fighting's done."

"Ouchies, Captain? That's not a very manly word."

Despite Duck's attempt to push him away, Trip checked his wounds.

"I'm done being manly. Think I'm going to take a nap." Duck slumped backward onto the deck.

He had a concussion in addition to the bloody gash, so Trip didn't blame him. Though his head throbbed, and he wanted to follow that dragon's example of running and jumping off the platform with its tainted iron framework, he made sure Duck was stable before going to work on the flier.

CHAPTER 26

R YSHA TREADED WATER WITH ONE hand, her cut thigh burning. She waited, turning in circles in case one of the dragons came up behind her. What if the one to come up was the male? Or what if *neither* of them came back up?

She blinked away tears at the thought of Shulina Arya dying. She was the most wonderful dragon Rysha had met, and Rysha had only been her rider for a few weeks. To lose her so soon wouldn't be fair. And what would she tell Shulina Arya's parents? Children were supposed to outlive their parents, not the other way around.

Spitting out some of the water that kept washing into her face, Rysha kicked harder, trying to lift herself to see over the waves and to the coastline. They hadn't flown *that* far out, had they?

She groaned when she spotted the black rocks of the breakwater and the butte that held the flier hangars. They had to be a mile away. An easy run but a long swim, especially while carrying a sword, wearing boots and clothing, and dealing with an injury. But she would do it if she had to.

She decided to head toward shore now. It wasn't as if Shulina Arya couldn't find her and pick her up if she came up. And if the male was the one to survive the fight, Rysha didn't want to stick around. She would be an easy target in the water.

Something brushed against her leg, and she gasped and whipped the sword in that direction the best she could underwater. To her surprise, she hit something.

A gray fin broke the surface nearby, and she sucked in a startled breath. With her water-spattered spectacles, she must have missed the shark's approach.

The fin turned, heading toward her again.

Seven gods, was she going to survive a dragon battle only to die to an oversized fish?

A shadow fell over her, and she jerked the sword up, fearing an attack from the sky as well.

Gold scales flashed, and a dragon dove into the water right in front of her. The wave hurled Rysha ten feet, and fresh fire burned in her leg.

Rysha? Trip asked in her mind from wherever he was.

Busy right now.

She flailed her arms, almost dropping Dorfindral. Damn it, she was *not* losing that sword again.

The gold dragon came up—Rysha still couldn't tell which one it was and whether that had been a missed attack or an interception. It shot out of the water like a dolphin while shaking its head like a dog putting a rat out of its misery. Something flew free of its maw, bloody and mangled. The shark.

It flopped limply into the water.

The dragon's head lowered and violet eyes gazed into Rysha's own.

"What took you so long?" Rysha croaked.

For a cowardly male with many injuries and missing scales, he proved magnificent when we finally engaged in battle! Shulina Arya turned so her back was to Rysha and she could climb on.

"Magnificent?" That was not the word Rysha would have used, not for any of these enemy dragons.

Yes, we engaged in a most valiant skirmish. We were still fighting when we went into the ocean.

Rysha was surprised a shark or anything else would have come close with that going on nearby. But maybe it had been an opportunist shark, hoping to munch on the loser.

She clambered onto Shulina Arya's back, holding on tighter than necessary. She was tempted to bring up the notion of harnesses or saddles, but she wouldn't have wanted to have been underwater for five minutes while dragons thrashed right on top of her.

Rysha, Trip spoke into her mind again. He sounded exhausted. *We're finishing off the last two dragons with the rockets. Stay well away from the harbor and the platform with Shulina Arya. The rockets automatically go for the closest dragon unless I'm there to steer them elsewhere, but the tainted ore and the battle have drained me, so I don't have the strength for that. I may have to leave the platform and put the weapons in another's hands.*

All right. We're a mile or more out at sea for now. We should be fine.

Good.

They had no sooner finished the conversation than a silver dragon came into view, flying straight out to sea at top speed. Straight at *them.*

Another contender for us to battle against, Shulina Arya cried and took off toward the silver.

"Wait, did you hear Trip's warning?" Rysha could see the massive gray platform floating over the coastline and didn't want to go anywhere near it now.

Yes, we will not go as far as the harbor. We will not need to. This dragon is coming to us.

"Convenient," Rysha muttered.

Soaking and sore, she'd lost all interest in battle. But Shulina Arya sped eagerly toward the silver as the silver sped toward her.

Despite the blood running down her leg and the water running down her spectacles, Rysha gripped Dorfindral tightly and readied herself for another fight. But as she did so, she wondered why a silver would sprint toward a larger, stronger gold dragon.

It was less than a hundred yards away when Rysha saw something like a black bird arrowing out to sea after it.

"Not a bird," she whispered. "Trip!"

That had to be one of his rockets.

I see it, Shulina Arya cried. *I will knock it aside.*

"You can't. It has that special iron in it. It—"

Rysha broke off as Shulina Arya swerved abruptly. Because the *silver* swerved. It was trying to go under her. So the rocket would hit Shulina Arya instead of it?

"Careful," Rysha blurted, realizing Shulina Arya meant to engage with the other dragon. "We could both get—"

The silver screeched and whirled, not trying to fly past Shulina Arya, but slashing with its talons. It moved so quickly Rysha couldn't follow it.

Shulina Arya twisted to defend herself, but the smaller dragon's maw came in and clamped onto her shoulder, silver eyes glaring at Rysha as its fangs sank in. At the same time, Shulina Arya bit into her foe's neck and raked its underside with her talons.

The dragons contorted in the air. Rysha scooted up Shulina Arya's back and slashed Dorfindral toward the silver's face. But before her blade sliced in, something slammed into the dragons, hurtling Rysha off Shulina Arya and into the water again.

A boom sounded, hammering her ears, and white light flashed. Screeches of pain erupted from both dragons as a shockwave knocked Rysha back and under the surface.

Icy, dark water smothered her and almost knocked her spectacles off, despite the strap. She clutched at them with one hand as she kicked to the surface. Her head broke free, and through the water running down her lenses, she saw both dragons splash down.

The silver's side was charred, scales torn free and revealing blood, but Shulina Arya must have been hit too. She moaned and lay limply in the water.

Fear swelled in Rysha's throat as she swam over, lugging Dorfindral behind her.

Trip! she cried. *Are you listening now? One of the rockets got us. Trip!*

Rysha reached Shulina Arya's side, touching her cold, wet scales. Blood leaked from between some of them and into the water. Others had scorch marks on them, and was that acid from the rocket?

"Damn it." Rysha stroked the dragon. "Shulina Arya, you're going to be all right, right? You can't die out here, because... because..." Rysha struggled to get more words out through her constricted throat. Moisture blurred her vision, and she couldn't wipe her eyes with her spectacles on. Of all the dragons, surely, she least deserved death. She was too young and exuberant about life. About everything. "I need a ride back to shore," she finished, her words a croak.

A moan emanated from Shulina Arya, and her wings fluttered weakly, then went limp. The silver wasn't moving at all. Rysha glowered over at him, hoping he'd taken the brunt of the rocket's explosion. It had been meant for him. It wasn't fair that the dragon helping her people defend Iskandia had been hurt.

While she was looking toward the silver, the waves lifting and lowering her and the dragons, she spotted a gray fin again. Two others followed it. This time, she spat a string of curses, more enraged than terrified.

If they went after Shulina Arya while she was too injured to defend herself...

"Eat the silver one," she shouted at them, as if they could understand.

She gripped Dorfindral's hilt tightly. The sharks would understand being bashed in the head with a sword.

We're coming, Trip spoke into her mind.

Hurry! Shulina Arya is hurt.

I saw, he said grimly.

Grimly because he felt bad that one of his rockets had wounded her? Or grimly because he didn't think she would make it?

One of the gray fins veered toward the silver dragon, but the other two headed toward Rysha and Shulina Arya.

Growling, Rysha swam out to intercept them. Dorfindral felt like a dead weight in her hand, but she aimed the point toward the closest fin, hoping to get lucky. Unfortunately, the sword wouldn't assist her against a non-magical enemy.

The fin veered, and she twisted as she treaded water, and stabbed. She clipped something, but the sword slipped off the slick flesh. She sensed more than saw the shark turning toward her, racks of razor teeth snapping at her.

Rysha kicked away and thrust again with the sword, lamenting that the water slowed her movements. But the shark had been headed straight toward her and almost impaled itself. She hit resistance, shoved harder, and the blade sank in. The shark thrashed and spun away, clubbing her with its tail. She slashed after it, determined to deter it from attacking Shulina Arya.

She missed, but the shark sped away. Now, where was the other one?

Rysha rotated in a slow circle, squinting through her spattered lenses for a gray fin. But the sharks seemed to have disappeared, all three of them. The water had grown calm. Rysha swam back to Shulina Arya's side and touched her scales, but didn't get a response this time, not even a moan.

Trip? Rysha thought, afraid to ask, afraid she wouldn't like the answer.

Above you.

Rysha looked up as a gold dragon soared overhead, flying low above the water. Bhrava Saruth. Sardelle and Trip rode on his back.

Trip slid off the side and splashed into the water a few feet away.

The silver dragon has fallen to a deserved death, Bhrava Saruth announced, banking to fly circles over them as Trip paddled to Rysha's side. *Shulina Arya is barely alive. But she is not so far gone that a god can't heal her. Yes, I will do this, and she will be most grateful to me. Perhaps she will wish to engage in the mating flight.*

Seven gods, Trip, Jaxi spoke into their minds, *heal that dragon before she's indebted to horned and horny here.*

I'll do my best. Trip patted Rysha briefly, the water making his movements awkward, then swam close enough to Shulina Arya that he could place his hands on her side. He closed his eyes, treading water with his legs as he rested his forehead against her scales.

Rysha wanted to hug him and thank him for coming, but that would interrupt him. Instead, she put her back to them, watching the waves for shark fins.

They will not come back, Bhrava Saruth said. *They sense that a mighty predator has arrived.*

Trip? Rysha asked.

The god Bhrava Saruth!

He's been like this the whole battle, Jaxi told her. *He took down a puny bronze that was half his size, and now he's extra full of himself.*

I wouldn't have guessed he could get… fuller.

No, it's true.

Shulina Arya's head rotated to the side. She'd been on her back with her wings and tail stretched out, floating in the water.

Captain Trip, Shulina Arya thought. She sounded pained, but Rysha took hope from hearing her telepathic communications. *I was foolish.*

It happens to all of us, Trip replied.

They both kept Rysha in the conversation, which she appreciated. She swam close to Shulina Arya and rested a hand on her scales again.

I did not fully understand your weapon and that the silver meant to hide behind me. That coward. I only wished to engage in another battle. My blood was cold with the desire to slay my enemies.

Have you already healed her? Bhrava Saruth asked. *I meant to do that myself. I was merely trying to figure out how to do so without landing in that loathsome water. There is kelp all over the place. Disgusting.*

Such a persnickety god, Jaxi observed.

It is good that you have healed this female and ensured she will not feel indebted to that dragon, Azarwrath added.

I'm glad I had the strength left to do so, Trip thought. *I'm tired after the battle, though I feel better now that I'm away from the platform. Is it ironic that I built something that was as harmful and unappealing to me as it is to dragons?*

Not since you're half-dragon, no, Rysha thought.

Trip opened his eyes and paddled back, giving Shulina Arya room to stir her wings. He looked at Rysha as she did the same, then offered her a crooked smile and plucked a long strand of kelp off her shoulder.

He must have sensed her pain from her injured thigh, because he let his hand linger, coming to rest on her sleeve. Warmth flared in her leg, tingling intensely then itching, making her want to scratch the spot. But the sensation soon faded, along with the pain.

"You're getting more efficient at that," Rysha said. "Thank you."

Trip bobbed his head in acknowledgment.

"Do you have the strength to fly back, Shulina Arya?" Rysha looked up at Bhrava Saruth, who still circled, probably glad nobody had told him to come down for a dip. She might have to ask him for a ride back, but wanted to make sure Shulina Arya was fit enough to escape the waves and fly back.

Yes, Storyteller, and you and your mate must fly with me. I would be most distraught to return home without my rider on my back.

We wouldn't want that, Trip thought and floated out of the water as Shulina Arya rolled over onto her stomach.

Rysha couldn't believe either of them had the strength for magic or flying, but at least it wasn't far to shore. She sheathed Dorfindral and climbed up Shulina Arya's wing to her back.

It appears that all of our enemies are vanquished, Bhrava Saruth announced.

No more little bronzes for you to pick on? Jaxi asked.

I was heroically defeating an enemy of Iskandoth, not picking on anyone.

I noticed you let Shulina Arya handle the gold dragons.

I have battled and defeated many gold dragons.

The words faded from Rysha's awareness as Bhrava Saruth stopped circling and headed toward shore. Sardelle lifted a parting hand, though Rysha trusted she would see them both again soon.

Shulina Arya hadn't responded to the comments. Maybe she was further healing herself or marshaling her strength for the flight.

Rysha found a spot in front of Trip, twisting to pat his leg. "Thank you for coming."

He rested his hand on hers, gazing at her with his dark green eyes. His short hair was plastered to his head, and his uniform sodden, but he was still appealing. Perhaps because he'd just finished drawing upon his magic to heal Shulina Arya, he was radiating his *scylori*, and she had a hard time looking away.

"You're a heroic and sexy rescuer," she added, smiling.

"Am I?" With his free hand, he plucked seaweed off his shoulder and tossed it into the water. He left his other hand on hers, warmth and a tingle of magic coming from it.

"Definitely."

"Good." He leaned forward and kissed her, his touch caring and tender. *Don't let your dragon fly in front of any of my rockets again, please. I was terribly worried. Sardelle nearly fell off Bhrava Saruth when I screamed into their minds that I needed a ride.*

You should learn how to turn into an eagle or seagull so you can fly on your own when a flier isn't available.

What would a seagull have done against those sharks? Viciously pecked their fins?

The history books say that shape-shifted sorcerers retained their powers.

Hm? Did the history books say how the sorcerers shape-shifted in the first place? Because this hasn't been covered in my lessons with Sardelle.

Probably because she doesn't know how to do it. Few ever did. I think it took someone who was a fairly recent descendant of a dragon.

So, I'd need to ask an actual dragon?

Maybe. Or you could wait for one of your little siblings to grow up and figure it out. Maybe one will be smarter than you.

I feel I should be offended by that comment.

And yet, you're still kissing me.

Trip wrapped his arms around her and pulled her close. *Yes.*

CHAPTER 27

THE CASTLE GARDENS WERE IMPRESSIVELY green, lush, fragrant, and flower-filled, especially given that less than a week had passed since the dragon attack. The *last* dragon attack, Trip hoped.

The finishing touches for the weapons platform were still in progress, but it hovered in the sky over the city around the clock, at least for the time being. There had been discussion as to whether a proper landing and storage area should be built for it, but Trip had assured his commanders and the king that it was like a sailing ship and built to withstand existing in its element year round. Also, that the power sources he had created wouldn't burn out for a long time.

"You're looking dapper and dashing today, Trip," came Rysha's voice from behind him.

Trip had sensed her coming, but she'd been walking and talking with Major Kaika as she strode into the garden, so he hadn't wanted to interrupt. Now, he turned to smile warmly at her. Rysha and Kaika wore their dress uniforms, both appearing sharp and professional. Kaika continued on, but Rysha stopped in front of Trip.

"Thank you," he said aloud, though he was tempted to use telepathy. He hadn't expected the gardens to be so crowded, with dozens of conversations going on all around and a man playing a woodwind instrument in front of a hedgerow. "You look good too."

Rysha smiled and tucked a deep pink lilac flower into the pocket of Trip's uniform jacket. The bushes were in bloom all over the garden, an array of purple, blue, white, and pink, and their sweet scent filled the area.

"Did you cut that from one of the king's lilac bushes?" Trip asked.

Rysha patted Dorfindral's scabbard, which hung in its usual place on the left side of her belt. The medal recipients weren't technically supposed to be armed, but when Trip had asked Zirkander about it, he'd said to bring Azarwrath. Rysha must have received the same advice from Kaika about her blade. Trip smirked at the idea of using a sword to cut flowers.

"Is that allowed? It seems like taking the king's flowers might be deemed a heinous crime, punishable by public flogging or life in prison." Trip kept waiting to hear whether or not he was going to spend *his* life in prison. The dragon attack had interrupted his inquest before it could start, but when he'd left that Colonel Srandark glowering, he'd expected he would have to see him again. However, when Trip had reported in for work the next morning, none of his superiors had said anything about it. The whole week had been like that, and now, he was getting a medal. Did they give medals to people before throwing them in jail?

"I was merely pruning the bush," Rysha said. "Its flower production was overzealous, completely dwarfing that of the neighboring lilacs."

"So, you're saying that bushes that outshine the others and don't fit in should be trimmed back to match the herd?" Trip arched an eyebrow.

"The herd? Trip, do they not garden in Charkolt? Bushes don't grow in herds."

"I see you avoided my question."

"Only because your metaphor distracted me by tripping and falling on its nose." She stepped closer and patted him on the chest. "You know I'm partial to bushes that stand out."

"Hm." He knew they weren't supposed to display affection while in uniform, but he slipped his arm around her waist, just for a moment.

"On that note, I see you're not radiating your *scylori* today."

"No. I tried letting a little show one day, and everyone kept asking me if I'd gotten my hair cut."

She snorted. "It's possible you weren't doing it right. Dragons just let it all hang out."

"If I did that in the king's garden, I'd be in even more trouble than a flower bandit."

Her next pat was more of a swat. "I mean that I don't think they try to modulate their auras. It does seem to be naturally diminished when they shape-shift—perhaps that's part of why they evolved to change into other creatures, as a defense mechanism to hide from other dragons. But even when Shulina Arya is human, you still feel her otherness. And want to gaze at her in an enraptured state. And bring her baked goods."

"I mostly want to tug on her pigtails and ask how much she would charge to babysit some of my siblings."

"It's possible you have some inborn immunity to the effects of dragon auras."

"Possible."

She gazed thoughtfully at him, and he could tell she expected a response to her observation.

"I have decided that I don't want my *scylori* to affect my friends or family or comrades, so I'll keep it in check during my day-to-day life, but if there are opportunities when it may prove useful, I won't hesitate to let it shine through. And I won't try to hide what I am anymore. I suppose now that I've been written up in the newspapers, there isn't much point of that anyway, but… I've spent too much time hiding what I can do out of a fear of rejection, and it shouldn't have taken me nearly as long as it did to realize that I could build something like that." He waved toward the weapons platform. Most days, it had been positioned a little north of the city, but today, the corner was in view from the gardens. "I love flying and will happily continue to be a member of Wolf Squadron for as long as they'll have me, but if I can do more by stepping out of the cockpit, I have to be ready to do so."

"I do believe you may be maturing, Trip."

"I have to. Otherwise, this older lady I know might get tired of my youthful antics."

"She would be more likely to get tired of having sex in a tiny barracks bunk. Perhaps we should pool our resources and rent a small apartment with a large bed."

"I *was* going to build a place on the lot across from General Zirkander's house, but I saw that the for-sale sign disappeared. I hope whoever bought it doesn't mind dragons sleeping in the yard across the street."

"Huh. I wonder what crazy person has been real estate shopping in the capital when dragon attacks have been a weekly event of late." Rysha smiled as she spoke the words.

"What do you know that I don't know?" Trip was tempted to skim through her surface thoughts, but he tried to respect her privacy. Most of the time.

Someone clapped his hands, and the woodwind player increased his volume for a few seconds before winding down.

"I know that the ceremony is starting." Rysha winked and walked over to stand with the elite troops sword wielders who were also being given medals.

Trip? Rysha thought, glancing back at him. *Are you listening?*

I'm always attentive to your needs.

Exactly what a woman wants to hear. Rysha looked skyward, toward the weapons platform. *When you get a chance, use your dragonly powers to paint a mural on the bottom of that, will you? It's all beams and girders and conduits and who knows what. It's hideous. There have already been newspaper articles complaining that it'll bring down property values in the city.*

So does having dragons light your neighborhood on fire.

Or your orchard or vineyard.

Trip grimaced. He hadn't meant to remind her of that. *Sorry.*

It's all right. I'm merely suggesting that if it's possible...

My dragonly powers didn't grant me the ability to do artwork, but I'll see if I can find an interested party who would like to work on it for little-to-no pay.

Excellent.

I think Tylie likes art, Trip said, inspiration striking. *I've seen her wandering around the house with brushes.*

She already babysits for little-to-no pay, doesn't she? Rysha asked. *She may be looking to move up the financial ladder.*

I'll ask. Maybe I can find someone to babysit for her while she paints.

That... actually could be easier than you think soon. She gave him that knowing smile again.

Once again, he was tempted to pry, but someone thumped him on the back.

"Nice flower, Trip," Leftie said. "Very manly."

"Not everybody can afford to adorn himself with gold balls." Trip allowed himself to be drawn over to join the other pilots.

"Just *one* of my balls is gold. The other is tungsten."

Duck, Pimples, and General Zirkander all turned toward Leftie, their faces taking on expressions ranging from puzzled to deeply concerned.

The musician played the final notes as the king walked in flanked by his bodyguards. Even though more than two dozen soldiers were receiving medals, Trip suddenly felt nervous and worried he would do something wrong. There had to be close to two hundred people in the garden, including two journalists with pads and pens and a photographer with a large box camera set up near the king's small dais. What if Trip tripped on his way up to get his medal? The two previous times he'd been awarded medals, they had simply been given at the front of the end-of-day company formation back in Charkolt. Not in front of royalty. Or photographers.

Two assistants trailed the king and the bodyguards, one carrying a velvet-lined box with the medals inside and the other carrying a tray with its contents hidden by a silver dome. As the king turned to face the gathering, the medal recipients lined up in tidy squads. The rest of the people, a mixture of soldiers and civilian relatives, found seats.

As soon as everyone was quiet, King Angulus started a speech about bravery and selfless sacrifice and protecting the country. Trip would have paid more attention, but he was distracted by sensing a dragon approaching. Not an enemy this time, fortunately. Shulina Arya.

Did she plan to come watch her rider get a medal? If she flew over the garden in her dragon form, that might alarm those audience members who weren't yet accustomed to seeing dragons up close. Trip looked toward the garden entrances, also envisioning her arriving in human form and on a scooter.

While he was looking back there, his gaze snagged on two familiar faces, faces he hadn't expected to see here. His grandmother and grandfather stood behind the seating area with Sardelle.

Trip lifted a hand and almost spoke to them telepathically before catching himself. They might have gotten the newspapers and learned more about him than they had ever suspected—he'd written a couple of letters since coming out west and had mentioned embracing his talents and studying with Sardelle—but he still hadn't broken the dragon-sire news to them, and he'd been intentionally vague when explaining where his little siblings came from. He doubted they were ready for telepathic greetings.

They saw his wave, smiled, and waved back, appearing supportive rather than judgmental. Not that he'd expected anything less from them. After all, they had sacrificed much over the years, moving often to keep him safe.

Not far from them stood Rysha's aunt Tadelay. Trip was glad she wasn't looking at him, because he would have blushed horribly—he still hadn't gotten over the circumstances, and lack of clothing, of their first meeting.

To his surprise, Rysha's mother and father stood next to her aunt. Trip hoped their presence here meant they were coming to accept Rysha's enlistment in the army. Though they were nudging each other and pointing at Major *Kaika*, not at their daughter. Quite a few people in the audience were doing that. And the box camera seemed to be pointed in her direction. Were some—or many—of these people here to see the future queen? Maybe they had little interest in the soldiers receiving medals.

Oddly, Trip found that a relief. Maybe nobody would even look at him.

Leftie cleared his throat and poked Trip with an elbow. "He said your name," Leftie whispered.

"Oh!" Trip blurted, turning back to the front and catching King Angulus looking at him as Duck strode back from the dais, having just been pinned with his medal.

Trip's first instinct was to sprint up there so he didn't cause a hold up, but that would be a good way to draw attention, and he'd just been delighted that the attention was focused elsewhere.

He lifted his chin, let a tiny bit of his *scylori* show, and strode forward, attempting to look dignified. Angulus's eyebrows twitched. Trip hoped he wouldn't ask if he'd had a haircut recently.

While Trip was in the middle of saluting, Angulus's gaze flicked to his chest—no, to his *lilac*—but he didn't comment on it. Maybe Trip should have tucked that fully inside the pocket.

"We thank you for your service to Our country, Captain Telryn Yert," Angulus said solemnly and held his hand out toward one of the assistants.

The blank-faced man placed a gold medal in Angulus's grip. Trip hoped Leftie wouldn't ask that he receive tungsten instead of gold.

"I suspect you'll be pleased to know," Angulus said in a low voice, stepping forward to pin the medal on the flap of Trip's jacket pocket, the one opposite the pocket holding the non-regulation lilac, "that Lord

Lockvale, once he recovered his voice, came to see me with his brother. He said that he believed he made an error that night outside of the Ravenwood property and that you did not attack him."

Once he got his voice back? What did *that* mean?

Trip resisted the urge to glance back at Rysha, though Angulus *did* look in her direction, smiling slightly.

"I'm glad to hear that, Sire. Does that mean there won't be an inquest?"

"It does. I would suggest you go out of your way not to irk any nobles in the coming years, but they are an easily irkable bunch."

Trip sensed he was referring to the rigmarole he was dealing with in the wake of announcing his engagement.

"I'll try, Sire, but it may be hard if Lieutenant Ravenwood invites me to another family dinner. Her kin haven't yet accepted how handy it can be to have a sorcerer around."

"Oh? It was my understanding that Lady Tadelay finds your assets appealing."

If the king hadn't been holding his pocket flap, Trip might have fallen over. Was he referencing the night of… nakedness? How could he have heard about that? Surely, he didn't have tea regularly with Tadelay. Did he?

Trip's cheeks grew so warm, they felt like someone was painting the insides with a blowtorch.

"Yes, my assets," Trip managed to respond, since Angulus was looking at him, eyebrows raised. "I try to make them useful."

"I'm sure Lieutenant Ravenwood is pleased."

"I…" Seven gods, what did he say to that?

"On an unrelated note, you might be curious to know that an elder gold dragon has appeared in the Tlongan Steppes and is apparently waiting for lobsters to be delivered to him."

"Drysaleskar?"

Angulus nodded. "It seems he reconsidered your offer."

"Oh, uhm." Though Trip was relieved to be discussing something other than his assets now, he didn't know how the king would take this. Now that they had a working weapons platform capable of driving off dragon attacks, would he be willing to pay tribute to an old grump simply for taking up residence in their country?" "Will you be sending the lobsters?"

"Yes. It won't hurt to have him down there, so long as he behaves himself, especially since it'll take a while to make more of those platforms to station around the country."

"Yes, Sire."

Trip was glad the king planned to go through with the offer they'd made to the dragon. It would be better to have too many allies than too few, and who knew what the future would bring? He remembered Shulina Arya's parents' presentation about population difficulties and assumed there would continue to be clashes between humans and dragons.

Angulus finished with the medal and rested a hand on Trip's shoulder. "I don't know if your commanders and fellow pilots tell you this—knowing Zirkander's people, I doubt it—but We are deeply appreciative that you have joined the Iskandian army and are using your powers to help protect Our people."

"Thank you, Sire," Trip said.

"While I must appear fair and impartial to the populace, know that you can come to the castle any time if you want to see me about dragons or your siblings or anything else. The guards have instructions to let you in, though I suspect you could get in on your own."

"Er, yes, Sire, but an invitation is nice." Trip was stunned by the offer. He wouldn't have expected the king to want a lowly captain to pester him any day, much less any *time* of the day.

You're a powerful sorcerer, Telryn, Azarwrath put in. *Your military rank is immaterial.*

"Just avoid times when I'm making *my* assets useful," Angulus said. "Unless it's an emergency."

"Yes, Sire." Damn, there went that blowtorch again.

Angulus patted him on the shoulder and nodded for him to return to the queue. As Trip strode back, the first of the elite troops sword wielders, Colonel Grady, headed up. Rysha, Captain Brex, and Captain Onkali were also receiving medals—Trip had seen those two officers during the battle, flying behind Pimples and Ahn, and he'd healed Onkali for burns afterward.

Major Kaika, Colonel Therrik, and General Zirkander stood off to the side, watching the proceedings. It seemed they weren't being awarded medals this time, though the awards and ribbons on their dress uniforms indicated they had received many in the past. Maybe the king and the army had decided to highlight the newer generation of soldiers. Or maybe Angulus would have simply felt odd pinning an award on his fiancée's chest.

"What was he talking to you about up there?" Leftie whispered.

Angulus had said a few words when each of the other pilots had gone up, but as Grady soon returned, Trip realized the king had spoken to him longer.

"My assets," Trip said, not wanting to fuel any envy, not that Leftie would necessarily want an invitation to the castle. An invitation to a brothel, more likely.

"Seems like that would have been a short conversation, not a long one."

Trip elbowed him, which prompted General Zirkander to look over and raise a finger to his lips.

After the male officers received their awards, Angulus crooked a finger for Rysha to come up. Trip sensed Shulina Arya on the move. Earlier, she'd landed on a rooftop down the hill from the castle. Now, she flew swiftly toward the gardens.

Trip debated whether he should warn the king, but Angulus hadn't included an invitation to make telepathic contact in his offer.

Your dragon is coming, he said silently to Rysha as she walked toward the dais.

I know. She's very excited for the ceremony.

Because you're being honored with a medal?

Because we're *being honored.*

A shadow fell across the gardens, and the spectators looked up, many gasping in surprise and alarm. Some of them looked to the king for a cue, saw that he didn't bat an eye, and settled quickly. Others looked uneasily toward the exits. Trip sensed Sardelle spreading a feeling of unconcern and contentment, trying to influence the spectators. It seemed to work. They settled further, turning their attention back to the king.

Shulina Arya glided into the gardens and found just enough room to land and sit on her haunches between the dais and the first row of medal recipients. The soldiers scooted back to give her more room.

As Trip checked the king for a reaction, he realized Angulus had expected this. Had he *invited* the dragon to come?

Like he could have stopped her. Jaxi snickered into Trip's mind. *You've seen his guards ineffectively chase her in human form.*

She is difficult to catch when she's wheeled.

Angulus started talking to Rysha—and to Shulina Arya, as well, Trip realized when he glanced up at the dragon's head. Trip hadn't paid attention to what he was saying to the other medal recipients, since he'd been speaking in a low, private voice, but curiosity drove him to magically augment his hearing so he could listen in.

"As I recall," Angulus was saying, "I had some reservations about permanently assigning a magical sword to such a young officer and also allowing her to become the first dragon rider Iskandia has seen in over a thousand years."

"I do remember that, Sire."

Angulus started to speak again, but Shulina Arya bent her long neck so that her large head was level with his and Rysha's. Her violet eyes regarded them from only a few feet away. Murmurs went through the crowd, and the king's bodyguards fingered their weapons.

Trip caught Colonel Therrik's mutter of, "It's not worth being king if you have to let dragons breathe on you."

Zirkander elbowed him, much as Leftie had done to Trip earlier.

"Don't tell me you and your sarcastic mouth weren't thinking the same thing, Zirkander."

"Actually," Zirkander whispered, "I was thinking that Angulus better finish pinning on that medal quickly and give the dragon whatever he's got under that cloche."

"Do you get used to that and stop finding it alarming?" Angulus asked Rysha, tilting his head toward Shulina Arya.

Shulina Arya appeared curious, unthreatening, and maybe even eager, but she still exuded typical dragon *scylori,* and it couldn't be easy to ignore her. Most of the spectators had grown silent and wore the enraptured looks Trip had come to recognize as they gazed at her. His grandparents looked as much stunned as enraptured, and he assumed this was their first dragon sighting. Certainly, their first up-close dragon sighting.

"It depends on how early in the morning it is when she pokes her head in, Sire," Rysha said calmly, appearing unflappable speaking to the king, as always. "And whether I'm wearing my spectacles or not. If I'm not, the large gold blur can be a tad alarming."

A mental throat clearing sounded in Trip's mind. Judging by how wry Angulus's expression became, he heard it too.

"I believe that's our signal to get on with things." Angulus accepted one of the last medals from the assistant with the velvet-lined box, then stepped forward to pin it to Rysha's pocket flap. He raised his voice so the spectators could hear him. "We are grateful for your assistance and your bravery in dealing with Iskandia's enemies and trust that you will have a long and fruitful career in Our military, since it is clear to Us that you were destined to be an officer and a dragon rider."

Angulus looked over at Rysha's parents before continuing on, and Trip was tickled when they squirmed under his gaze.

"We hope that there will be fewer attacks on Our fine country in the future," Angulus went on, "but We are relieved that you and the noble dragon Shulina Arya are here to defend Us."

Rysha grinned over at Shulina Arya, and Trip sensed the dragon had said something to her. She radiated pleasure at being called noble, and the tip of her tail lifted and waved about, the gesture somewhere between a dog wagging and a cat swishing its tail. Trip hadn't seen it before. Maybe excitement that she couldn't quite contain? There wasn't room for her to twirl here.

Zirkander, Therrik, and Kaika, who were standing behind the tail, scooted back lest they be whipped by the scaled appendage.

Angulus finished pinning on Rysha's medal, then waved to his assistant with the box. The man lifted a velvet tray and withdrew another medal from underneath it, this one larger, with a very long ribbon.

Angulus looked at Shulina Arya and seemed to be considering how to get it around her neck when the medal was lifted from his hands. The audience murmured as it floated through the air by itself. The ribbon unraveled and slipped over the dragon's head. It settled around her neck, the gold medal coming to rest against the gleaming scales of her chest.

"We also thank you for your help in defeating Our enemies, Shulina Arya," Angulus said formally, lowering his hands.

Nobly, Shulina Arya replied, the word going out to everyone.

"Nobly," Angulus agreed, then gestured to the second assistant.

The man watched the dragon warily as he approached with the covered tray. Shulina Arya's head shifted, her violet eyes locking onto the silver cloche with more intensity than she had considered the medal. The man halted, perhaps thinking those eyes were locked onto him. He looked like he might flee.

"Over here, Adlei," Angulus said firmly, pointing beside him.

But it was Sardelle, once again sending out a sensation of soothing, that affected the man. He managed to get to the king's side with the tray. Angulus accepted it, then held it toward the dragon.

"A small token of our appreciation, Shulina Arya." Angulus lifted the cloche with dramatic flair.

A gorgeous array of colorful miniature tarts of different varieties lay on the tray. Lemon, blueberry, apple, and ones made with exotic fruits that Trip couldn't identify.

A surge of delight emanated from Shulina Arya, one he suspected the entire audience experienced. Then her great tongue slid out to lick the various tarts. Trip, remembering the jawbreaker incident, imagined them falling onto the ground and the tongue following them, having difficulty picking them up. But Shulina Arya knew how to handle tarts. After this first taste, which Angulus watched with an unalarmed and bland expression he must have spent his entire reign mastering, the tongue withdrew, and the tarts floated one by one into Shulina Arya's mouth.

I wonder if Bhrava Saruth is going to be upset that he wasn't invited, Trip thought so the soulblades could hear him.

A second dragon would not have fit in the gardens, Azarwrath remarked.

I understand a similar assortment of tarts was delivered to his temple, Jaxi replied.

But no medal? Trip asked. *No adulation from a crowd of potential worshippers? Is a tart delivery enough? He seems like a rather needy dragon, and he* did *help with the battle.*

He did, Jaxi agreed. *And that's why the king invited him to come. But he declined. Due to extreme busyness. You see, there was a write-up recently in the newspaper about the bravery of Iskandia's dragon allies, and he and his temple were mentioned. Somehow, a line got in about his godliness and how he is available at his temple to give blessings, and especially enjoys blessing young, beautiful women.*

Uh, Trip thought. *Did he write that article?*

Sardelle and I suspect that he visited the journalist late one night and exerted his dragonly influence.

Is the journalist female?

It seems she is.

GOLD DRAGON

That dragon is shameless, Azarwrath said. *Though from what I remember of my era when dragons had more of a presence in the world, shame isn't a word in their language.*

Unsurprising, Jaxi said.

What of Phelistoth? Trip asked. *Was he recognized? He also arrived in time to help.*

He was not interested in being recognized. He dislikes crowds, especially crowds of Iskandians. He is, after all, a Cofah dragon, even if Tylie has chosen to live here. Angulus wasn't quite correct in naming Rysha as the first rider. Tylie has been riding Phelistoth around for years. She simply isn't a warrior at heart—and Phelistoth considers himself a scholar rather than a fighter—so they never stepped forward to proclaim themselves here to defend the country. That said, Phelistoth certainly ends up in a lot of fights for a dragon who doesn't like battles. It may have something to do with his aloof personality.

It does seem a shame if he wasn't recognized. No tart delivery?

Not tarts, but there was a large delivery of coffee beans to the house with a thank-you note from Angulus with wishes that Phelistoth would enjoy the variety of exotic blends from other continents. You know that you and your lieutenant are the main reason that coffee made it to Iskandian shores. Given how many people drink the stuff, you probably should have received a second medal for that deed.

Once Shulina Arya had finished the tarts and sufficiently licked the tray, she sprang into the air with her medal around her neck and twirled and twisted impressively. Trip didn't know if she was intentionally putting on a show for those below or merely expressing her pleasure and appreciation of her treats, but ooohs and ahhhhs came from the crowd as she gyrated in the air, defying gravity. He sensed a palpable wave of disappointment when she disappeared from view, flying back to that rooftop to wait for Rysha to finish.

The king thanked everyone for coming and invited them to enjoy snacks and drinks that would be brought out shortly—presumably, it had been deemed wise to wait for the dragon to leave before serving the refreshments intended for human guests.

"Is she as pleased as she seemed?" Trip asked when Rysha came to stand next to him.

The formal rows had broken up as soon as the king left the dais, his bodyguards surrounding him to keep him from being flocked by onlookers. Trip doubted anyone aside from the sword wielders had weapons or presented a danger to him, but the bodyguards were likely also there to keep people from pestering him about wedding details. He *did* walk straight over to join Major Kaika. After head nods and polite murmurs of "Sire," Therrik and Zirkander stepped away from her side.

"Very pleased," Rysha said. "She kept me up late last night asking how the ceremony would go. I had no experience receiving awards—unless one counts the medals I won in sports, math, and spelling competitions as a youth—so I couldn't tell her. I did relay stories of historical medal ceremonies for prominent heroes throughout the ages, though I couldn't remember any tales of kings giving awards to dragons."

"I imagine it happened occasionally in the First Dragon Era."

"You would think so. I find it hard to believe that Shulina Arya is the first dragon delighted by such things. I believe it's now a proven fact that sweets are the way to their hearts. But if Shulina Arya wants to believe she's the first dragon to have been so honored by a human king, I see nothing wrong with that."

Trip nodded. "Seems reasonable to me. Do you think his comment about the army being your destiny will change your parents' opinions of your career? I noticed he looked their way."

"We'll see. I'm more concerned about changing their opinions of you." Rysha clasped his hand. "Why don't we go to them and see if they're affected by how dapper and dashing you are? And flower-adorned."

"I'm willing. And my grandparents are here too. They'll be pleased to see you again, I'm sure."

"That's them at the buffet table, isn't it?"

"Yes, they've never been to the castle. I'm sure they're eager to enjoy the offerings. Though my grandmother is probably already commenting on the food and remarking how her recipes are superior."

"Perhaps you can distract her by asking her about the empty lot they recently purchased." Rysha's eyes twinkled.

It took Trip a moment to understand what she was implying—and to realize why she'd been acting like she knew something that he didn't earlier.

"I understand your grandmother has already had a long chat with Sardelle—she's interested in helping out with your siblings—and that your grandfather has ordered lumber to start building soon."

"How did you know all this before I did?" Trip wondered if his grandparents had sent a letter and he had missed it. He couldn't remember the last time he had checked the mail room at the barracks.

Her eyes twinkled even more. "I haven't been spending all my time at Bhrava Saruth's temple, building weapons and cleaning latrines."

"Huh."

Telryn, Azarwrath said as Trip and Rysha walked hand-in-hand toward the crowd, *I do believe you should visit your grandparents first. They're far more pleasant than Rysha's parents, and it's been longer since you've seen them.*

You just want me to go to the buffet table and try the king's food, don't you?

I have been observing the offerings as they've been brought out. The lobster is dripping with butter, there's chilled caviar, and oh goodness, what are those slender steaks with some kind of jam on them? You must try everything, Telryn.

"Are you all right?" Rysha asked, watching his face.

"Yes, it's just that my sword wants to fatten me up."

"Perhaps if you learn to shape-shift and fly, you'll have the metabolism of a dragon and be able to eat whatever you want."

"Is it the flying that allows that or their size?"

"I don't know. That would be an interesting scientific study. I wonder if Shulina Arya would lend herself to it."

"Her parents would be interested, I imagine."

"It's too bad they didn't come to the ceremony," Rysha said, "though I imagine there's a limit to how many dragons can fit in the king's gardens."

"Not really." Trip pointed to a couple of familiar men at the buffet table dressed in professorial attire.

Rysha laughed. "Oh good. I didn't see them before."

Hurry, Telryn, or those shape-shifted dragons will eat all the food.

EPILOGUE

R YSHA STROLLED ARM-IN-ARM WITH TRIP through the castle hallway toward the gardens, this time for a wedding rather than an awards ceremony. She would stand next to Kaika as one of her two chosen kin watchers, Major Blazer being the second. As kin watchers, they were responsible for ensuring the groom was sufficiently healthy and able to care for his bride. The duty amused Rysha vastly, given that Kaika was the last person who needed anyone to care for her... and Angulus surely qualified in any regard. But it was tradition. Fortunately, until the ceremony began, she was free to mingle and grope Trip's arm.

He looked particularly handsome today, having chosen his dress uniform rather than the fancy suits and sashes that many of the male guests favored. She knew it was because he didn't want to spend money on clothing—he was carefully hoarding his nucros to help support his siblings—and that was fine with her. He looked good in a uniform. And whether intentionally or by accident, he seemed to be exuding a little of his dragon *scylori* today, which meant she would think he looked good in a threadbare bathrobe. Or nothing at all. Her thoughts drifted to the latter, and she smirked at him when their eyes met before they stepped out into the gardens.

They had both been busy with their duties the last few weeks, but the evening before, the weather had cooperated, and they had *finally* strolled along the beach together. She'd picked up sand dollars. He'd picked up rusted tins and warped springs for whatever toy he planned to build for the children next. After that, they'd had a romantic dinner and she'd taken him back to her room, where they'd spent a lovely and uninterrupted night together.

Trip blinked. "You're imagining me naked."

"And *you're* reading my mind."

"I didn't try. I... it was near the surface."

"It often is."

His eyebrows rose. "Truly?"

"Yes, and if you don't often think of me naked, too, I'm going to be disappointed."

Another couple walked past then, an older husband and wife Rysha recognized from some of the social gatherings the nobles attended, and they gave her a scandalized look. She assumed they would fall over when they saw that Kaika and *both* of her kin watchers were active-duty military and attending the wedding in uniforms instead of fluffy, frilly dresses.

I do think of you naked often, Trip said, switching to telepathy, for others were strolling past them and into the gardens. *But I'm male. I believe such fantasizing is part of our nature. I always thought—your Aunt Tadelay has been reinforcing this notion, by the way—that women were less lustful and controlled by their, uhm, reproductive urges.*

You ought to know that's not true. I'm usually the one to drag you off to bed because you're distracted making toys and puzzles for babies, and gifts for Sardelle and me. Besides, you've met Kaika. You know she's plenty lustful.

This is true. It's hard to imagine her and Angulus... I mean, he's so serious and unflappable. He barely reacts to anything outwardly, at least when he's around us.

I'm sure he lets loose in bed and howls like a wolf.

Trip looked horrified and braced himself on the wall. *I didn't need that image in my head.*

You brought it up.

Are you sure? That doesn't sound right.

Positive. Rysha swatted him on the butt and nodded toward the doorway.

GOLD DRAGON

They stepped outside onto the elaborate brick-paver pathway that meandered through the gardens, leading to the same open area where the awards ceremony had been. Most of the lilacs had faded, but roses, hydrangeas, snapdragons, peonies, and winged dragons were all in bloom, filling the area with sweet and spicy scents.

Rysha had been surprised when such an early wedding date had been announced—had foreign dignitaries even had time to travel here for it?—but she'd read between the lines that Angulus was concerned Kaika would get tired of the snide comments from the newspapers and the nobility and change her mind. He must have figured that once he got his promise necklace on her, she was most definitely his.

"Are you nervous about standing next to Kaika?" Trip asked, switching to the spoken word, presumably since nudity was no longer being discussed.

"A little bit. I'm surprised she asked me. We've been through a lot, but I've really only known her for a few months. I'm honored, of course, but she's known Blazer for years."

"Maybe you're the only other woman she knows." He smirked at her.

She gave him another swat, though she admitted it *was* possible. Kaika had all manner of men that she worked with and likely considered friends, but in the almost-all-male elite troops, it wasn't as if she interacted with other female officers that often. And because she was busy and traveled so frequently for her missions, she might not have that much time to pursue local friendships, especially since she'd been seeing Angulus for the last three years. *He* was the local friendship she no doubt preferred to invest most of her time in.

Trip nudged Rysha and drew her off the path so they wouldn't be in the way. "I was joking. She sees you as her protégé. I think she was joking when she first used that term when we all met in General Zirkander's office, but it's not a joke to her anymore. She trusts you and sees you as her successor. She's quite pleased that you've managed to survive all we've been through without getting killed or kicked out of the army."

Rysha snorted. "Have you been reading her mind too?"

"Only the surface thoughts."

"Totally acceptable then."

"Sometimes, they ooze out of people, and I can't help but notice."

"That sounds like something Jaxi would say."

"Yes, I believe it was her excuse originally and that I'm stealing it from her."

Rysha withdrew a handkerchief and removed her spectacles to wipe a smudge. Her optometrist was bemused—and beriched—that she'd gone through five pairs since starting her elite troops training. She wasn't sure dragon riders were meant to wear spectacles. But oh well, she'd worn them since she was ten. And she felt proud to have passed the training and to have survived all the tests with her crummy vision. Still, sometimes she wished...

She shook her head and started to lift her spectacles back to her face, there being no point in such wishes.

But Trip caught her wrist before she could. "I almost asked you last night," he said, nodding toward her spectacles.

"What? Have you come up with some superior form of vision correction?" Rysha had heard of experiments regarding miniature lenses that could be applied directly to the eye, but she couldn't imagine them staying in place.

"That's exactly it, actually. If you're interested. It's something I've been thinking about ever since I was an ass and broke your spectacles."

"Are you talking about the time I lost control of my sword and attacked you? That wasn't your fault."

"I know, but it bothered me to do it. And I know it bothered you that I... knew to do it. That you had that weakness, and I exploited it."

Rysha swallowed, memories of her feelings returning along with memories of the event.

"Yeah," she admitted. It wasn't as if she could lie to him.

"I've done some reading and talked to Sardelle about it. I believe I can do something."

Rysha placed her spectacles in his hands. "I'll gladly accept any improvements you can make." She wasn't sure about the eyeball lenses, but perhaps he could do something so her spectacles would never break or fall off in battle.

Trip nodded, lifted a hand to the side of her face, and gazed into her eyes. She gazed back at him, deciding she shouldn't think of nudity while he was concentrating on her spectacles. Or was he? He was simply holding them with his other hand. He seemed to be concentrating on *her*.

A little tingle warmed her eyeballs, almost an itch. It was deep inside of them, an itch she couldn't scratch.

A trickle of fear flowed into her, and she was tempted to pull away. Seven gods, what if he messed up, and she lost her eyesight *completely*? But she trusted Trip. He wouldn't mess this up. Even if something went wrong, he would fix it. He fixed everything.

Trip blinked a few times, and she noticed moisture in his eyes. His fingers moved on her face, stroking her cheek. She hoped his touch and his emotion were because he was reading her thoughts and was moved by her trust, not that he feared he'd messed up and she would surely go blind.

One corner of his mouth quirked up. *Do you* feel *blind?*

No, but—

His eyebrows lifted, and she realized the itching and tingling had stopped. She turned to look toward the front of the gathering, and her mouth dangled open. She could *see*. Everyone and everything in the gardens was so crisp and clear, she couldn't believe it. Even with her spectacles, she hadn't seen things in the distance this well.

"You did it," she whispered. "Will it last?"

"It's possible it won't last your whole life, but I think I can correct it again if necessary. And it would be a gradual diminishment, nothing that would happen overnight."

She wanted to hug him, but she wanted to stare at everything and everyone around her too. And the flowers. She could see the individual petals on the roses from twenty feet away.

"Trip," she blurted, whirling back to him and grabbing his arm. "You—I—" She gave up on words and kissed him.

"Is that allowed?" came a whisper from behind her. "I thought only the king got to kiss people today."

"If a woman wants to kiss you, it's always allowed."

Rysha drew back, recognizing the second voice as belonging to General Zirkander, and remembering she and Trip were in the middle of a garden filled with dozens if not hundreds of people. True, they had stepped off the main walkway, but it wasn't as if she had pulled him behind a bush for private smooching.

"Good afternoon, sir," Trip said, saluting him and nodding to the officer with him. Captain Pimples.

Rysha hurried to salute as well.

Zirkander also wore his dress uniform, appearing far more ironed and polished than was typical for him. She'd heard he would be one of Angulus's two kin watchers, along with a seventy-year-old nobleman—Lord Talidraw—who'd been friends with Angulus's father and had known him since he'd been in diapers. Historically, a king would have had two kin watchers from the nobility, thus to ensure that a suitably healthy—and noble—woman would be chosen and that no sneaky commoners would slide their way into the nobility. A couple of generations ago, King Orlenis, seeking to appease the common man and acknowledge their growing power, had started the trend of including a military man, so Rysha wasn't surprised that Angulus had chosen an officer. She *was* surprised he'd chosen Zirkander, since he seemed to find the pilot hero a tad… overly irreverent.

Zirkander returned the salute, but was then pulled off to talk to a general Rysha didn't know, leaving Captain Pimples behind. Pimples, who wasn't looking at them.

"Come in, come in," he said, waving to someone lingering outside the gardens. "I'll introduce you to all my— No, they're obnoxious. Never mind. I'll show you the gardens. And there's always great food here. Do you want some Iskandian wine? We've got all different kinds. Like red. And, uhm, white."

Rysha might have listed some grapes for him, but Pimples was focused on the bronze-skinned, dark-haired woman in spectacles who poked her head through the doorway leading out to the gardens.

"My brother said to wait for him and his entourage," she whispered, eyeing her surroundings. "Is this it? It's so quaint." She wore a yellow and azure silk dress in a flowing style favored in Cofahre, and appeared to be in her early twenties.

"How big are the gardens at your palace?"

"You can get lost in them. But it's not *my* palace." She crinkled her nose. In distaste?

The words clicked together before Rysha recognized the woman—it had been some time since a photograph of Princess Zilandria had been in an Iskandian newspaper.

"Well, dragons or sorceresses or, ahem, foreign invaders seem to blow up half the castle every few years," Pimples said, "so I don't think the king has been motivated to expand and make it more of a target."

"We're having similar problems with dragons."

Trip stirred beside Rysha.

That's Princess Zilandria? he asked silently. *If so, her brother would be...*

Trip turned toward the doorway, his eyes getting that distant aspect that meant he was utilizing his power.

Prince Varlok, Rysha thought, though Trip must have already figured it out. *It makes diplomatic sense that some of the Cofah would have come for the wedding of a ruler in another country. Admittedly, I wouldn't have expected their ruler to come—the princess makes more sense. But... Ah, I bet they heard about your weapons platform and came to have a look. Perhaps barter for the schematics.*

I suppose that would be up to Angulus, but I'm more concerned about my chance to honor my word to Grekka. This is good. I thought I'd have to take a trip to Cofahre to give the prince that dagger, so he'd have proof of how his father died. But I can just give it to him here. Of course, I don't have it at the moment. I think the king may have it. I gave it to him to look at when the babies were being removed from the stasis chambers, and then I was distracted, and I didn't think to ask for it back. I wasn't sure if I could.

Rysha patted Trip's arm as Pimples led the princess into the gardens. He looked like he meant to guide her through the crowd to the servants walking around with trays of food, but he noticed Rysha and paused.

"Zia, this is Lady Ravenwood. She's a scholar. She knows all about dragons and relics and things."

"Oh?" Zilandria—Zia?—looked Rysha up and down.

She was several inches shorter than Rysha and seemed dubious about Pimples' introduction, perhaps because of the uniform and sword. Maybe Rysha should take her spectacles back from Trip, so she would look more scholarly.

"It's an honor to meet you, Your Highness." Rysha curtseyed, though she wasn't sure that was the proper etiquette when in an army uniform.

"Do you enjoy academic studies?" Zia asked.

"I do. Mathematics, history, and archaeology. My mother is a professor, and my sister is following in her footsteps. I... wanted to ride dragons and poke things with swords."

"In Cofahre, only men poke things with swords. I don't think anybody is riding dragons. Are you?"

"Yes. Her name is Shulina Arya."

"Really? I would love to meet her. And talk mathematics with you."

Rysha bowed her head. "I would be honored, Your Highness."

"You can call me Zia. I'm going to visit the university while I'm here. I'm trying to talk my brother into letting me finish out my studies here. For a more eclectic education. The professors are rumored to be quite good."

She smiled shyly at Pimples, and Rysha suspected her interest in Iskandian studies had little to do with the university's professors.

"I'm sure you would enjoy it," Rysha said.

Pimples captured Zia's hand and led her into the gardens.

"Was that young woman making moon-eyes at Pimples?" Trip sounded dumbfounded.

"Why not? He's a good-looking young man. And he's smart, isn't he? Perhaps not about wine, but didn't one of your comrades say he's good at math and has architectural aspirations?"

"Good-looking? Is he? Huh."

"He's quite comely. I don't know why he has that name. His skin is lovely."

"I heard a rumor that Tolemek had something to do with that. A cream he sells. Supposedly, Pimples was a test subject and gets free formulas for life."

Trip looked toward the entrance again as several shaven-headed men in flowing blue garments that didn't quite hide their sheathed scimitars and daggers strode in and fanned out. They scowled at Trip and Rysha, waving their hands, to try and back them away.

Rysha, suspecting this was the equivalent of King Angulus's cadre of bodyguards, was inclined to do as requested, but Trip narrowed his eyes, lifted his chin, and exuded his *scylori*. It had its usual effect on Rysha, making her want to slip in close and start rubbing things of his. The bodyguards blinked and backed away. One almost stumbled into the person walking through the doorway, a man Rysha also recognized from photographs—he was mentioned far more frequently in Iskandian newspapers.

"Prince Varlok." Trip stepped forward and bowed to him. "I am sorry for the loss of Dreyak."

Varlok wore flowing silks not dissimilar to those of his sister, so the bow was likely more correct than a salute. As Rysha recalled, some of

Varlok's younger brothers had served in their military, but he hadn't, being more of an academic.

"Captain Yert," Varlok said without looking at his name tag—he seemed to know exactly who he was dealing with. He didn't so much as glance at Rysha, but women rarely had prominent roles in Cofah society, so she wasn't surprised. "I spoke to your king when I arrived yesterday, and he showed me a certain dagger."

"Did you touch it and see what happened to your father, Your Majesty?"

"I did."

Varlok's tone was neutral, his face difficult to read. If he had mourned his father's death, he showed no sign of it here, not in public. Perhaps not in private, either. Nothing Rysha had read or heard about Emperor Salatak suggested he had been a lovable man.

At least it looked like Trip wouldn't have to do anything to see his promise through. Rysha suspected he was relieved. She knew he hadn't been excited about the idea of piloting into the heart of Cofah territory, not when their snipers and watch tower artillerymen so enjoyed shooting at Iskandian fliers.

"Lieutenant Ravenwood?" Kaika asked from behind. "Do you have a minute?"

Since Varlok didn't look like he would miss her, Rysha stepped away without hesitation. She wondered if Trip would get a thank you from him. Not that Trip had been the bearer of good news, but at least he'd borne it.

There weren't any quiet places in the gardens, as more and more guests kept coming in, but Kaika drew her to a patch of lavender against a wall, the flowers getting ready to bloom. Summer had finally come to Iskandia, and there weren't any clouds on the horizon promising rain. Angulus and Kaika had lucked out.

Though Kaika appeared more nervous than lucky. She kept patting down her uniform, or maybe wiping her damp palms on it, and reached for her hair, as if to comb it, but since they were outdoors, she wore her uniform cap. Maybe that was a good thing, or she would be raking her fingers through it. She'd cut it all short for the wedding, to match the side still growing back after being bathed in dragon fire, and even though it would bewilder Kaika to hear it, Rysha suspected shorter locks would soon come into fashion because of her.

"You're not thinking of backing out, are you?" Rysha asked. "Dozens of foreign dignitaries traveled far to use this wedding as an excuse to spy on Trip's weapons platform."

Kaika snorted. "That's the truth. No, I just wanted to thank you for coming to stand by my side." She grinned. "In uniform. I've been getting an earful from a clothing designer who creates custom dresses for many of the noblewomen when they get married, and she's appalled and flummoxed that her services weren't needed for this."

"Madame Vovary, and yes, I can imagine. She's in high demand. Even noble ladies have to book her a year out."

"I assume the king gets to jump the line. She keeps telling me it's not too late, that we could at least spruce up the dress uniform." Kaika looked down at the blue and gray. "She suggested a frill around the hem. She also pulled out a poofy light blue ball. I have no idea where she thought that would go."

"Maybe you could ask Leftie," Rysha said. "He likes balls."

"Something that should alarm any women he's seeing."

"Yes. And you're welcome. For standing by your side. I'm honored you asked. The other lieutenants in the barracks are terribly jealous. This and the ball afterward are being considered the social events of the year, I understand. There are private parties going on among those who weren't invited."

Kaika nodded. "I heard there's going to be a lavish shindig tonight at the Sensual Sage."

Rysha wrinkled her nose, not wanting to think about what a lavish shindig at a brothel would be like. She imagined drunken orgies and a proliferation of adult toys. "Should the king be concerned that you stay apprised of the goings on there?"

"It's hardly my fault that I'm on their mailing list. I suspect that once I officially move into the castle, they'll stop sending me their brochure."

Rysha's mind boggled even more at the idea of a brothel mailing out seasonal brochures.

"Though I *have* been wondering if I should keep my little house in the army fort," Kaika said.

"In case things don't work out with the king?" Rysha hoped Kaika didn't have that in mind. Even though she didn't know Angulus well, she knew this was his third marriage, and she hoped it would be the final one, that this would bring him—them—happiness for the rest of their lives.

"In case a dragon or sorceress burns down the castle. Again. I'd hate to lose my souvenir beer steins, the way Zirkander did when someone blew up *his* house."

"Ah, I see. The king might actually prefer it if the souvenir beer steins were stored somewhere else."

"Nah, he wouldn't mind more junk around the castle. He has dusty musical instruments all over the place that he collects. It seems that if they're more than a hundred years old, they're valuable. Do you know he can play the lute and sing? It's moderately entertaining. He's serenaded me a couple of times."

"Perhaps he and Colonel Grady could get together to perform for… someone." Rysha didn't know who. She couldn't imagine a king showing up with a lute at a tavern. Maybe when he'd been just a prince, such things wouldn't have been seen as odd.

"Careful. Don't volunteer to be his audience. He sings a lot about nature and symbolism—or so he claims. All I remember is flowers weeping with the morning dew glistening on their petals. But he sits patiently while I talk nostalgically about the old 37-A dragon bombs, so I guess I can listen to flower songs."

"Clearly, you two are a perfect match."

"You're the first person who's said that, however sarcastically." Kaika thumped her on the shoulder. "That's why you're standing beside me."

"Oh, is being supportive required?" Blazer asked, strolling up beside Kaika, her cigar leaking smoke into the air.

"Do you mind?" Kaika plucked the cigar out of her mouth. "This is a non-smoking wedding."

"What? The invitations didn't mention that. And you said we didn't have to get girlie and mannered and such for this, that we're making a statement."

"Yes, but it's a non-smoking statement." Kaika held the cigar away when Blazer reached for it.

"Are you even allowed to be out here?" Blazer asked. "I thought the bride was supposed to hide among her ladies attending and make a dramatic appearance right before the music starts."

"I shooed away the people who showed up wanting to attend me. I can put on a uniform by myself after almost twenty years in the army.

I even bathed myself and trimmed my own fingernails. It's appalling what noble people pay others to do for them."

"You're going to put people out of business if you don't use their services, ma'am," Rysha observed.

"I hardly think that's true. Besides, Angulus said I was saving the taxpayers a lot of money by singlehandedly being responsible for this being the least expensive of his three weddings, and likely the least expensive of *any* wedding. They should love me. I also said no to the florists, the jugglers, and the person who makes decorative pamphlets for all the guests. A thousand nucros? For a stack of calligraphy cards? Who would pay that?"

"Well," Rysha said, "at least you said yes to him."

"You may be the first queen in history to *save* the country money," Blazer said.

"Maybe so. I helped him do his own bathing and nail trimming this morning too." Kaika grinned a tad wickedly. "I admit, it was half bribe. I'm trying to get him to say his part of the oath without using my loathed first name."

"Your parents are here, aren't they?" Blazer asked. "Won't they be confused if he just confesses his love to a Kaika?"

"I make them call me Kaika too."

"Don't they find that weird, ma'am?" Rysha asked.

"They shouldn't have given me such a dreadful first name if they wanted—"

The musician changed his tune, playing the refrain of the Royal Ceremony, a cue for the guests to find seats and for everyone involved in the wedding to take their places.

Kaika clapped Blazer and Rysha on the back, then strode out of the gardens so she could come back in on Angulus's arm.

With nerves tickling her stomach, Rysha headed to the front of the gardens, to the same area where the king had stood to deliver their medals. Now, his assistants carried velvet trays with promise necklaces on them, and a royal officiator waited to perform the ceremony, with a priest from the Order of Nendear looking on. It was no longer the most dominant religion in the country, with devotion divided between the seven gods, along with a smattering of agnosticism mixed in, but the Order had backed the throne for centuries and continued to do so, so the priest would bless the union. Bhrava Saruth, when he'd heard about the preparations, had offered to take the priest's place and give a far more meaningful blessing. Angulus had sadly informed him that some nods toward tradition had to be given.

As Rysha took her spot with Blazer behind the officiator, she caught herself patting and smoothing her uniform, the same way Kaika had been doing. She snorted at herself. She didn't have to do anything except step forward on cue, give Angulus a look over, and say, "Yes," to the question of whether he looked healthy and fit and like a good provider for his wife-to-be. But it seemed terribly presumptuous for a lieutenant to make such a judgment over a king.

She wondered if General Zirkander, who had a similar responsibility when it came to Kaika, would follow the script or make some irreverent joke. Even now, the corners of his mouth kept twitching, as if he was having all manner of amusing thoughts about the proceedings.

Rysha smoothed her uniform again, then caught herself. She was sure she looked fine. Besides, who would be looking at her?

You look beautiful, Trip spoke into her mind. He'd finished speaking with Prince Varlok and now stood with Leftie, Duck, and a few other Wolf Squadron pilots. *Almost as beautiful as last night.*

I was naked last night.

Exactly.

I'm afraid it would be scandalous if I got naked here.

I thought this wedding was already scandalous. Three out of four newspapers said so in their headlines.

It would be four out of four if nudity broke out in the castle gardens.

It's possible our people are terribly repressed.

That sounds like something Major Kaika would say, Rysha observed as the music swelled, promising the bride and groom would soon appear. *You aren't getting brochures from the Sensual Sage, are you?*

No, but Leftie recommended that place. He went and had a good time.

I'm sure he did. Did the ladies there like his balls?

I believe they're paid to like men's balls.

No wonder he enjoyed himself. Rysha looked around the crowd, most of the people now sitting, and marveled again at how crisply she saw everything. She spotted Varlok in the front, surrounded by an entourage of people in the currently fashionable flowing silk attire. The princess sat at the end of the retinue with Captain Pimples next to her, his Iskandian uniform in stark contrast with their dress. He and the princess stole shy smiles at each other.

Maybe this won't be the only wedding this summer, Trip observed, following Rysha's gaze.

Oh? Rysha pretended to misunderstand him. *Should I brace my parents for something more dramatic than you appearing at the dinner table with me?*

I'd be amenable to making long-term plans with you, though I think I should get some more money saved up first, so we can buy or build a place of our own.

Married officers are offered free fort housing, you know. Maybe we could get Kaika's old place. I hear it comes with beer steins. Though I'm sure you're right. There's no hurry. Rysha smiled across the gardens at him, not wanting to pressure him. She wasn't sure marriage was something she was ready for, anyway, since that seemed to lead to children, and she couldn't imagine that right now. She'd only just been accepted into the elite troops. She looked forward to missions and countless adventures before settling down. Would Trip understand and wait? Surely, he had adventures of his own in mind.

No hurry, he agreed, gently returning her smile. *Though I don't think children are a requirement of marriage. I assume Major Kaika doesn't have any planned.*

Not that I've heard about, but you never know. Angulus may want an heir, and tradition dictates that the queen's womb is the ideal place for one to originate.

I suspect nothing about this marriage will be traditional.

True.

The music rose to a crescendo, and the bride and groom appeared at the entrance to the gardens. They walked arm-in-arm slowly, stately, and to the pace of the now more subdued music. It morphed from *The Royal Ceremony* to *Heralding of the Wedding,* each of the songs at least five centuries old. It was too bad Kaika hadn't bucked tradition there, too, and invited Colonel Grady to play something. Maybe Angulus could have joined in, though songs about weeping flowers might not be on point for a wedding.

I'm not sure if I should warn you or not, Trip said, *but Bhrava Saruth and Shulina Arya are on the roof of the west wing. They just arrived.*

Uh, maybe you should warn Angulus.
He hasn't invited me to speak to him telepathically.
I don't think I ever invited you to, either, Rysha pointed out.
You're fortunate that I'm perceptive and could tell you'd been missing out on this your whole life and would love it.
Uh huh. And you don't get that feeling from Angulus?
Oddly, no.

Kaika and Angulus reached the dais, stepping up to join the priest, officiator, and kin watchers. They clasped hands and faced each other. Angulus had worn his typical hard-to-read expression during the walk up, but his eyes glinted as they met Kaika's. She quirked an eyebrow at him, and they both broke into smiles.

Rysha had never seen the king smile and decided he should do it more often. But maybe Kaika was the only one who could twitch an eyebrow and elicit such an expression from him. If so, Rysha definitely thought they should stay together.

The officiator cleared his throat, and the murmurs of the crowd quieted as he spoke about the bride's and groom's duties to each other, present and future, and the long life they would spend together. Angulus and Kaika gazed at each other, not looking like either was paying much attention as they took turns making playful facial gestures. The officiator first called the male kin watchers forward to scrutinize Kaika.

"Do you, being faithful and loyal friends of King Angulus Masonwood, affirm that you have researched the vitality and emotional stability of Astuawilda Kaika and found her a suitable mate?"

Kaika propped a fist on her hip and looked like she would punch either man if they responded with anything but an emphatic yes. Of course, that surly gesture might also be in response to the use of her first name.

The nobleman's lips thinned, and Rysha had the sense he'd been pressured into accepting that this match was good for the country, but he nodded and said, "Yes."

The officiator's gaze shifted to Zirkander. Angulus's eyes narrowed.

"I can't *personally* attest to her vitality," Zirkander said, eyes twinkling, "but my research does indeed suggest that she is well endowed in that area."

Rysha watched Angulus warily—maybe *he* would be the one to punch someone. But he actually appeared faintly smug. Or pleased?

He's suspected that Kaika and Zirkander have explored each other's vitality in the past, Jaxi said, surprising Rysha by speaking into her mind. *Since that was something of a promise to the contrary, he's happy to hear it.*

Rysha spotted Sardelle in the crowd, wondering if she knew her sword was chatting up the wedding participants, but she was lifting her eyes skyward. It might have been in response to Zirkander's typical irreverence, or she might have been looking toward the west wing and the dragons perched on the rooftop.

The officiator cleared his throat. "It's a yes or no question, General."

"Ah, then yes." Zirkander bowed to Angulus and Kaika, then stepped back into his spot.

The officiator offered a similar question to Rysha and Blazer, asking them to attest to Angulus's suitability. Rysha, her cheeks warm simply from being included and having everyone looking at her, simply stepped out, glanced at Angulus without seeing him, and said yes. She stepped quickly back into her spot.

Blazer strolled out and considered Angulus more thoughtfully. "I'm not terribly well equipped to comment on a man's suitability, but he seems sturdy and stout enough to handle Kaika's vitality."

Off to the side, journalists were clucking their tongues with disapproval while hurrying to scribble down direct quotes.

The officiator sighed. "Again, it's a yes or no question."

"No room for creativity? Disappointing. Then I shall say yes." Blazer bowed, as Zirkander had done, and stepped back.

Rysha shook her head, unable to imagine being irreverent at someone's wedding, *especially* a royal wedding.

Fortunately, Angulus didn't appear distressed. He was quick to meet Kaika's eyes again and smile.

"Pilots," the officiator muttered under his breath, followed by what sounded like a string of curses. But he recovered, raised his voice, and said, "The wisdom of the kin watchers prevails, as we trust it always will." He looked to the priest.

"This union is blessed by the holiest and oldest of the gods, Nendear," the man said.

Rysha wondered how much he got paid to say that handful of words. Or rather, how much would be donated to his Order.

"Then, King Angulus Masonwood and Major Astuawilda Kaika, I invite you to touch lips to make official this union of souls."

They came together so quickly it was as if someone had been physically restraining them up until that moment. Rysha would have expected a chaste public kiss from Angulus, but wasn't surprised when Kaika wrapped her arms around him and gave him a passionate lip plant. He returned the kiss with equal intensity, and Rysha doubted either of them was aware of, or cared about, the onlookers.

"It's going to be more than their souls that are *unioning* tonight," Zirkander said.

The old nobleman at his side frowned darkly at him, frowned at the length of the kiss, and also frowned over at the journalists, who were all scribbling furiously.

I usually yawn at newspapers, Jaxi said, *but I do expect tomorrow's edition to be interesting.*

I just hope Kaika doesn't regret this one day, Rysha replied. *I know she won't regret Angulus, but he does come with a whole locomotive full of freight cars.*

Indeed, and you encouraged the wedding!

I know. Rysha hoped Kaika wouldn't one day be cursing her.

If it makes you feel better, Sardelle also encouraged it. Two years ago. A year ago. Six months ago. Did you know that there have been many proposals?

So Kaika said. I'm going to find the fact that they're still kissing promising for their future happiness.

Their future horniness, at least.

A shadow fell over the gardens, and a hundred people gasped. Rysha looked up, hoping Shulina Arya wasn't the dragon about to cause a stir.

Bhrava Saruth landed in front of the dais, where Shulina Arya had landed to receive her medal at the ceremony. His wings stretched out, and he looked quite magnificent. Or terrifying. Depending on one's point of view and how well one knew him.

Angulus and Kaika broke their kiss, if not their embrace, to look over at him.

I, the god Bhrava Saruth, have come to bless this union, and unlike with the human gods, my blessings are useful.

He's not at all cocky, is he? Trip asked into Rysha's mind.

He's been waiting for just the right moment to make a dramatic appearance, Jaxi said.

Rysha imagined all the soulblades and sorcerers present having had long telepathic conversations with each other while the ceremony was going on.

A golden glow emanated from Bhrava Saruth, and more gasps came from the crowd. It spread and gathered around Angulus and Kaika. Zirkander pointedly took a step back. The nobleman, the priest, and the officiator could only stand and gape.

"Should we be alarmed?" Angulus asked, looking at Zirkander and then Rysha.

"I don't think so, Sire," Zirkander said. "But if you don't want children, you may need to be extra careful in the future. Bhrava Saruth's blessings *do* seem to improve fertility."

Kaika made a face that was hard to read. Angulus actually looked a touch heartened. He looked over to Rysha, as if for a second opinion.

"I only know about one dragon, Sire. My understanding is that she's still on the rooftop."

I would not presume to interrupt a human mating ceremony, Storyteller. I merely came to watch. It's very romantic. Like in the stories. Someday, perhaps I will have a romantic mate, rather than a horny dragon overly obsessed with breeding cycles.

Rysha rubbed her face, not certain whether that comment applied to Bhrava Saruth or Trip's new elder dragon contact. She did hope the telepathic comment had only gone to her.

The gold light faded, and Bhrava Saruth shifted positions, lowering himself to all fours and folding his wings in. *Climb aboard my back, newly mated humans, and I will take you for a ride to a private place where you can consummate your relationship.*

Angulus eyed Bhrava Saruth dubiously, his mouth open and a likely rejection on his lips. But Kaika grabbed his hand and pulled him toward the dragon. Rysha didn't know if she was excited by the offer of privately consummating their relationship or if she simply wanted to escape all the watching eyes.

Though Angulus still appeared dubious, he allowed himself to be tugged off the dais and climbed onto Bhrava Saruth's back.

"There's a nice arch in Crazy Canyon that looks out over the sea," Zirkander called to them. "I recommend taking a blanket and a picnic basket though."

Sardelle's eyes narrowed, and Rysha imagined her silently admonishing him. Whatever she said, he winked at her.

Such preferential treatment is available to all those who give up their inferior gods and come to worship the god Bhrava Saruth. With that announcement—judging by the startled exclamations, it had gone out to all gathered in the gardens—he sprang into the air, flapping his wings and carrying Angulus and Kaika out of sight.

"*Inferior* gods?" the priest asked in the most indignant tone of voice.

"I knew I should have charged more than usual for presiding over this wedding," the officiator mumbled.

Storyteller, are you done with your duties? Shulina Arya asked.

Rysha glanced at Blazer and the others around her. They all looked uncertain except for Zirkander, who was strolling toward Sardelle. He seemed to assume the king and Kaika wouldn't be back and that the wedding had adjourned.

I think so, Rysha replied.

I wish to instruct your mate.

Rysha met Trip's eyes across the gathering. *I'm sure he would be amenable to learning new things. Is this something to do with magic?*

Indeed it is.

After Bhrava Saruth disappeared with his riders, the murmurs of the crowd died down. Until Shulina Arya appeared overhead, gliding into the garden to land in the same spot Bhrava Saruth had vacated.

Trip walked toward her, his expression curious. She must have shared her words with him.

Rysha joined him at Shulina Arya's side as her head swung on her long neck, lowering to look into Trip's eyes.

It is not an easy thing to learn to shape-shift, she spoke into their minds. *I did not learn until I was well out of my nest. But if someone helps you to do it a few times, you learn what it feels like, how to call upon the magic that allows you to defy the laws of nature.*

Trip stood listening, his eyes riveted to hers.

You have helped my rider to see better. This is excellent. I know little of how human eyes work, so it would have been difficult for me. I am appreciative. I will show you how to change shapes.

Trip nodded, though he looked stunned. And speechless.

Shulina Arya shifted in front of their eyes, turning into her human form with a flowing white dress covered with sparkling gold glitter and her blonde hair in a high ponytail. She spun a pirouette. Trip's brow furrowed slightly. She reached out and touched his arm, some telepathic communication going on between them.

Trip studied the grass, his face intense with concentration. He seemed oblivious to how many people had been watching this since Shulina Arya landed. Numerous jaws had dropped when she shape-shifted. In a world where magic hadn't existed, or had barely existed, for centuries, Rysha could understand the reaction. At least nobody had come running in with firearms.

Trip's outline wavered before Rysha's eyes, and she stared. Was he doing that or was Shulina Arya? He blurred and solidified a few times, then between one eye blink and the next turned into a miniature form of Bhrava Saruth. A human-sized gold dragon.

Shulina Arya stepped back and giggled. *That is not the form I would have chosen, but it is suitable enough for a first attempt. And the dragon form is most amenable to flying, mate of my rider.*

Flying? Trip whispered telepathically, his voice full of awe. He lifted one golden wing and then the other in self-inspection.

Yes, follow me. I will show you. Shulina Arya shifted back to her natural form, then sprang into the air, wings flapping.

Trip imitated her, though his wing flapping was more wobbly and uncertain. Still, he managed to gain altitude. Rysha watched as he curled his legs in and flew over the garden wall, disappearing from sight.

She looked over at the journalists. They were gaping—more than one had dropped his pencil completely—but a couple recovered and bent to their notepads, writing so fast their hands would cramp up.

This is fantastic, Trip told her a few minutes later, from wherever he'd flown.

I believe it. Are you going to let me ride you? Rysha didn't know if he was large enough for that, but maybe his magic could compensate.

A naughty image flashed into her mind, and he said, *You can ride me anytime. Now you've got me imagining you naked again.*

Excellent.

THE END

AUTHOR'S NOTES

THANK YOU FOR FOLLOWING ALONG with the adventures of Trip, Rysha, and their many, many friends.

As you know if you read the original series of Dragon Blood books (if you started with *Dragon Storm* and haven't yet tried the earlier stories, *Balanced on the Blade's Edge* is free everywhere, so go snag a copy, please!), this world has existed for many years for me. There are thirteen novels in it to date, and there will be at least one more (I know this because I'm about to start writing it, a new installment in the original series).

I guess it's obvious that I enjoy spending time here, but it's a little amusing to me because I originally wrote *Balanced on the Blade's Edge* (what later became Dragon Blood, Book 1) as a stand-alone novel. I had no intention of turning it into a series. It was a fun little fantasy adventure and romance that I worked on when I needed a break from another project. It wasn't meant to inspire one series, much less two.

But this is how things often work for writers. A side character who was meant to die early on turns into a hero with his own series (or at least his own novel—yes, I'm looking at you Therrik), and a book turns into an entire world.

You may find it interesting to know that when I wrote the first couple of Dragon Blood books, I had no intention of bringing any actual dragons into the world. They had been dead and gone for a thousand years, and that was a good place for them. You see, I was never a huge dragon fan growing up. Oh, I thought they were pretty, and I may have had a couple of 5,000-piece dragon puzzles glued to my wall as a kid, but mostly, I saw them as the hulking creatures that got your adventuring party killed in a D&D game. Nothing good ever came from sneaking into a dragon's lair and having its eye slowly open...

But then this dragon blood showed up in Book 3 (*Blood Charged*), and it seemed there had to be at least one dragon somewhere in the world. In Book 4, we found Phelistoth. And he was arrogant and not terribly fun. Clearly, I needed to introduce more dragons, some with better personalities. So, a couple of books later, Bhrava Saruth came into existence. The first dragon god (ahem) in the story.

He had more personality than any other dragon in the series, and he was a lot of fun to write. I didn't think I'd top him with a dragon that was even *more* fun to write. But then I started the Heritage of Power series, the portal opened, and suddenly, there were a lot more dragons in the world. Most of them still weren't as fun as Bhrava Saruth, but I knew the first time that Shulina Arya twirled that I would enjoy writing her.

Here, in this last novel, she kept trying to steal the show. The title of *Gold Dragon*... does it refer to her? To Bhrava Saruth? Or to Trip shifting into his little dragon form at the end? Hm. You'll have to decide. (Bhrava Saruth assures me the book was named after him. He did defeat that half-sized bronze dragon, after all.)

So, what's next, you might wonder. I mentioned that I'm going back in time, at least as far as the chronology of the world is concerned, and writing *Oaths*, an eighth Dragon Blood novel, but will there be anything after *Gold Dragon*?

I honestly haven't decided yet. Heritage of Power started out as a trilogy that morphed into five books, and I never envisioned it as being a super long series. I feel like the story is ending in a good spot. Trip has more or less come to terms with what he is, he and Rysha are happy with their relationship, and she's attained her goal of following in Kaika's footsteps. I believe all of the major plot threads have been wrapped up.

I *am* curious what will happen when Trip's little siblings grow up, but I'm not sure I'm ready to jump ahead twenty years in the timeline to find out. Shulina Arya tells me she wants a romance of her own (complete with chivalry, a considerate hero, and many, many valiant battles), so I'm kicking that idea around.

If there's something *you* would like to see, feel free to write and let me know. LB@lindsayburoker.com.

Also, if you have time to post reviews for *Gold Dragon* and the other books in the series, I would appreciate it. It helps folks decide to try the books, especially those who don't yet know they've *always* wanted to read about dragons that turn into ferrets and like belly rubs.

That's it from me for now. Thanks again for following along with the whole series!

Reading Order for all the stories in the Dragon Blood/Heritage of Power world:

Dragon Blood

Book 1: Balanced on the Blade's Edge
Book 2: Deathmaker
Book 3: Blood Charged
Book 4: Patterns in the Dark
Book 5: The Blade's Memory
Novella 5.5: Under the Ice Blades (Kaika and Angulus's story)
Book 6: Raptor
Book 7: Soulblade
The Fowl Proposal bonus scenes
Shattered Past (Therrik's story didn't get a number, but it takes place between 7 and 8)
Book 8: Oaths (April, 2018)

Heritage of Power

Book 1: Dragon Storm
Book 2: Revelations
Book 3: Origins
Book 4: Unraveled
Book 5: Gold Dragon

Made in the USA
Monee, IL
28 December 2020